Paging Dr. Turov

Gibby Campbell

ISBN 978-1-912768-48-6

Published 2019
Published by Black Velvet Seductions Publishing

Paging Dr. Turov Copyright 2019 Gibby Campbell
Cover design Copyright 2019 Jessica Greeley

Visit us at:
www.blackvelvetseductions.com

For Jim

Chapter One

Abby was rushing. She had been taking a nap when the hospice call came in. The patient was not expected to make it through the night, and they needed her to sit vigil with the dying man. This would be her first to take place in a hospital. Most vigils occurred in nursing homes with older patients that had no family. This man was younger, and his family was not going to make it in time.

Abby hurriedly secured her dark blond hair in two long pigtail braids. It would have to do on such short notice. She did not have time for makeup, but she swiped some concealer under her eyes in a half-assed effort to perk them up. She stared at her reflection in the mirror. At twenty-nine she looked more like a nineteen-year-old. Her green eyes were too big in her narrow, heart-shaped face. Her figure was slight, and even though she was five feet nine, people often assumed she was much shorter.

Abby grabbed an apple and some crackers from the kitchen. She debated if she had time to swing through Starbucks, but then she realized the ICU probably had coffee. The information from hospice was on her printer. She grabbed that and the book she was currently reading. The patient would likely be unconscious, and the book would give her something to do.

Abby hopped in her car and plugged in the address on her GPS. The Cleveland Clinic was massive. Even though she volunteered there every Wednesday afternoon, she had no idea how to find the heart center. As she pulled into traffic, she called out the number for Rachel on her Bluetooth. Her friend would not be pleased she was canceling their craft get-together, but at least she had a good reason this time.

Rachel picked up on the first ring. "You had better not be canceling on me! I already bought the supplies."

Abby sighed and tried to explain. "I'm sorry, Rach. Hospice just called, and they need someone to sit with a dying man. They can't find anyone else to do it."

She could sense Rachel's disapproval through the silence. Then her friend's lecturing voice came over the phone.

"Abby Shea, patients die all the time. He won't be alone. There will be nurses around him. You have to quit doing this. It's not healthy."

She could hear the concern in her friend's voice. Of course, Rachel would say that. She was a nurse practitioner at Fairview Hospital and saw more than her fair share of death. She was also a good friend and had been protective of Abby ever since the accident. She knew Rachel thought she was reliving her own experiences with Nate. But it was more than that. Abby wanted to help others, and she wanted to stay busy as much as possible. She could not explain it to her friend, but somehow she found stillness in her volunteer work.

She tried a peace offering. "How about I come over tomorrow night. I'll buy us pizza, we can do the pumpkin craft, and we can drink wine. Joel can do his stargazing, and if it gets late I'll just crash there."

Rachel reluctantly agreed. "That's fine. But if you cancel on me again, I am officially disowning you as a friend! Where is your vigil?"

Abby grinned. "The clinic. And yes, I will be safe. Love you."

"Love you too."

They hung up, and Abby concentrated on the road. It was getting dark out, and Cleveland rush hour was in full force. The clinic was not in the safest neighborhood, but she trusted her car would get her there with no problem. She barely paid attention to the landmarks whizzing by. Her sense of direction was awful in the daylight, but at night it became so much worse. Her trusty GPS never let her down, though, and twenty minutes later Abby pulled to a stop in front of the clinic's heart center. She had been lucky to obtain a parking spot right on the street. She hurried out of the car, pulled her hospice badge from her purse, and headed inside.

Chapter Two

Victor scowled at the latest lab reports. The patient wasn't as stable as he would like him to be, but they had no choice. His aortic valve was a mess, and if they didn't replace it now the man would surely die. Victor slugged down the remains of his coffee and looked at his watch. The anesthesia team should be about ready for him. He punched in Yuri's phone number on the cell and impatiently waited for him to pick up. The asshole waited until the fourth ring.

"What the hell took you so long?"

Yuri responded calmly over the phone. "Dr. Turov. It's always good to hear your friendly voice. To what do I owe the pleasure?"

"Listen, you sarcastic bastard. I have to cancel our dinner plans tonight. I have a patient I need to open up." He glanced at his watch and stood to go.

Yuri tutted on the phone. "Victor. You need to slow down. You are the chief of cardiothoracic surgery now. Surely you can find someone else to do this procedure."

"Not this one. It's too risky, and the man is only forty-four."

Yuri was unfazed. "You can't save them all, my friend. And you need a life for yourself. I was going to tell you about a new woman I met at the club. I think she would be good for you."

Victor paused halfway out the door. He thought about what his friend had said. Yuri understood his tastes when it came to women. It had been three years since his last real relationship. Lord knew he needed to get laid. But he had tired of the old lifestyle. The women he had dated were just in it for his money or his control. The older he got, the less alluring that became. Hell, he was thirty-seven now. It wasn't worth it anymore, especially considering how busy his career had gotten.

"I'm not interested."

He could hear the humor over the phone. "Don't tell me you've gotten all soft and want a regular relationship? That would mean I'm a better psychiatrist than I thought."

For the first time all day Victor laughed. Dr. Yuri Kopyev was an esteemed and excellent psychiatrist at the University Hospital. He spent his days helping bipolar and schizophrenic patients navigate their frightening worlds. He was also Victor's best friend, and the two had traversed medical school in Moscow before moving to the States. Yuri had lectured him for years about the perils of his chosen lifestyle, but he had also accepted it as part of who Victor was.

Victor set the record straight. "No, you suck as a doctor. And I have no interest in some boring, nagging relationship. I still like my women soft, compliant, and wet. But I don't have the time or the energy for any of that right now."

There was silence over the line. Finally, Yuri spoke, but only to say, "Okay, my friend. Good luck with your surgery. We'll reschedule when things are less hectic."

The two hung up, and Victor headed to the prep room. He knew this wouldn't be the end of it. Yuri had been bugging him more frequently about his lack of social life. This was hypocritical considering his friend hadn't been on a date in over a year. But the esteemed psychiatrist made it his business to annoy Victor whenever possible. Two could play at that game, and Victor made a mental note to point out Yuri's growing waistline the next time he saw him. It was, after all, a sign of future heart disease. As he walked into the surgery, he looked at his team and started barking out orders. It was going to be a long night.

Chapter Three

It had been four hours since Abby had arrived at the clinic, and the patient showed no signs of slipping away. The nurse had been kind in getting her settled in the room. Normally the patient would have been transferred to the hospice floor, but they had no beds available, so he remained in the critical care unit. They had disconnected all of his equipment except for one oxygen tube and an IV for pain medication. Abby knew this had been the patient's wish, and she watched as he continued to labor with his breathing.

The sound was awful, but she had gotten used to it and only tuned in when it stopped. Then he would draw in another shaky breath and continue on with his struggles. She marveled at the will of the human body to live. It had been so different with Nate. He had lain still in the bed, a ghost of the man she had known before the accident, and when he had died there had been no sound at all. The thought had always brought her peace. Nate had been a fighter in life, so she knew her decision had been the right one.

But Abby wasn't going to think about that now. She stood up to stretch and walked around the room. In her hospice training, she had been told to follow her instincts when interacting with vigil patients. This man's chart said he was Catholic, so she had said some prayers over him early on. She had also requested a visit from the hospice priest to anoint the man, but Father Thomas had yet to show up. Abby had tried talking to the patient and singing, but she got the sense he couldn't hear. So instead she had been reading her book and holding the man's hand. For the umpteenth time, she wondered if a vigil was necessary. But the patient had requested it, so she continued on.

Abby could have left at any time. A volunteer vigil was only meant to be a few hours. But there was no one to replace her, and she couldn't leave the poor guy alone. She was an introvert at heart, but somehow the buzz of the hospital staff all around her that evening was comforting. It made her want to stay.

Abby peeked out and realized they were busy. There were twelve rooms total in the unit, and they all circled around the nursing station. Each room had a large glass window that spotlighted the bed inside. She could see all but one of the rooms were occupied.

The nurse assigned to her room was Mary. She had the look and smell of a heavy smoker, and Abby guessed her to be around fifty years old. Mary had confessed she was thrilled to have an easy patient for a change, and she had promised to stop in as much as possible to chat.

Sure enough, Mary poked her head in the room when she saw Abby up and about. "How are you doing, hon?"

Abby smiled and stretched. "Good. His breathing is starting to slow down a bit, but he's still hanging in there."

Mary nodded. "They go when the good lord is ready to take them, and not a moment sooner. I've got an admit coming in soon. Why don't you take a break before he gets here, and I'll stay and keep an eye on Mr. Jones?"

Abby gratefully accepted. She could use the toilet in the patient's room, but she always felt guilty doing that. Instead, she grabbed her purse and headed to the public restrooms. On the way back she would grab a coffee from the kitchen Mary had shown her earlier. That should get her through the night.

Five minutes later Abby rounded the corner, balancing her coffee and a magazine she had found to read. She noticed a gurney being pushed down the hallway, and she realized Mary's admit was on its way. She ducked back into her patient's room and warned the nurse.

Mary grimaced. "Don't worry, hon. I knew he was coming. I'd best get out there before Dr. Dictator has a stroke."

"Dr. Dictator?"

Mary laughed. "Our lovely chief of cardiothoracic surgery. I was warned he would be escorting his patient to the floor."

Abby grinned. Rachel had often told her tales about testy doctors and the egos they sometimes carried with them. She had cringed at the stories and secretly marveled at her friend's ability to put up with it. But Rachel didn't take shit from anyone. Now she looked at Mary curiously.

"That bad, eh?"

Mary nodded and made a face. "Dr. Turov is an excellent surgeon, and his patients usually survive. But he can be a prick on wheels to work with. I've been doing this for years, and he is the most controlling doctor I have ever met. He only uses specific meds and procedures, and if you disagree with him he will tear your head off. Not to mention he expects the labs and monitor set up immediately."

Mary sighed.

"And here I thought I was going to have an easy night." She gave Abby a wave and quickly ducked out of the room.

Abby watched her rush into the room next door. The gurney was being wheeled in, and she caught a brief glimpse of a tall man in scrubs following it. She presumed him to be the surgeon. Then she turned back to her patient. His breathing was definitely slowing down.

Chapter Four

Victor watched as Mary rushed into the room. He was relieved because she was one of the better nurses, but he didn't stop to say hello. Instead, he started barking out orders as she began checking the monitor. He wanted labs and an x-ray as soon as possible, and he ordered his standard medications for sedation and antihypertension.

When things were set up to his satisfaction, Victor settled down into the chair by the bed.

Mary looked at him nervously. "Are you spending the night with this one, Dr. Turov?"

Victor gave her a curt nod. "I have a bad feeling, Mary. I'm staying until he is more stable."

She was surprised and pleased he knew her name. "Very good, then. Can I bring you some blankets and a pillow?"

Victor nodded again but kept his eyes on the monitor next to the bed. "Thank you, yes. Can you also bring me some black coffee?"

She bit her tongue. It was not a nurse's job to bring a doctor coffee but then again not many doctors spent the night in the room of a patient they were concerned about. "Yes, doctor," was all she said as she scurried out of the room.

She was only gone a few minutes, but when she returned she saw Dr. Turov in the nurse's station looking pissed.

She silently handed him the coffee as he barked out, "Mr. Smegel's blood pressure is rising. Get him on a nitro drip STAT!"

Mary rushed to comply, dropping the blankets and pillow on the chair as she went. She noted from the monitor the pressure had barely budged, but Dr. Dictator would be all over it of course.

When Mary returned to the nurse's station, she saw Dr. Turov reviewing the monitor. He slugged down some coffee. "Thank you," was all he said, but then he flashed her a rare and gorgeous smile.

Not for the first time, Mary pondered how such an intense man could be so damn hot. And how the hell did someone so young get to be so successful? But then her thoughts were interrupted when he started barking out orders again. Oh yeah. The good doctor had a success rate unrivaled by any other hospital in the world. Of course, the clinic used that to their advantage, and they rewarded the man handsomely for his efforts.

As Mary got ready to send off the labs, she noticed Dr. Turov frowning as he looked at the monitors.

He pointed to Mr. Jones' blank screen and then nodded in the direction of the hospice client's room. "Why is that patient not online?"

Leave it to the dictator to notice.

Mary quickly explained. "He just became a hospice client this afternoon. They don't have any beds, so he's here until they can move him."

Victor nodded. Sadly, their hospice unit ran a booming business.

As Mary went to check on his patient, Dr. Turov peered into the adjoining hospice room. He saw a young woman sitting by the bed. The wall light was set on low, and it cast a soft glow over her blond hair. He guessed her to be in her late teens. The girl's head was bent, and she was holding the patient's hand while turning the pages of a magazine with her other hand. There was something vulnerable about the way she held herself, and he found he couldn't look away. Victor shook the thought off and headed back into his patient's room.

"Mary, why is there a teenager sitting with the hospice client? I thought we didn't allow kids in the ICU."

Mary looked up from the IV line and smiled. "That's not a teenager, Dr. Turov. She's a volunteer with hospice. The patient did not want to die alone, so they sent her in to sit with him. I would guess Abby is in her twenties."

Victor did not look convinced. "Well, she looks young. And she's reading in that dim lighting and is going to ruin her eyes."

Mary mentally shook her head at the doctor but said nothing. She finished her task and was about to close the door as she left the room.

"Leave it open."

She nodded and left the door ajar. As she did so, she noticed him reach to dim the lights in the room. It was easier on patients, and he should know that was why the volunteer had done the same.

Victor leaned the recliner back and tried to get comfortable. His six-foot, five-inch frame did not fit well in any hospital setting, but it was especially obvious in the tiny chairs. He stared at the monitor and prayed for Mr. Smegel. He had never been a patient man, and he wanted either something to happen or for the man to stabilize so he could go home.

As he tapped his foot, he noticed a male in his forties walk into the unit. He was dressed casually in jeans and a sweater and had the build of a football player. Victor watched as the man spoke to Mary and then headed into the hospice room.

Abby looked up from her book and saw Father Thomas smiling at her. It was ten thirty at night, and she was shocked to see him there so late.

"I didn't think I would see you!" she exclaimed.

Father Thomas smiled and gave her left hand a squeeze. "Hi, Abby. I was held up at a meeting. I got here as soon as I could."

Abby stood up and stretched. She saw the priest had the patient bio printed off and in his hand. She quietly told him how the man's breathing had slowed down.

"We'd best get the anointing done, then" he responded.

As the priest set up, Abby excused herself and slipped out of the room to use the bathroom. She walked past Victor's room and peeked in. She could see two long legs sticking out from a recliner in the dark . Victor looked up as she passed and noted the blond braids swinging. He went back to watching the monitor.

When Abby returned, Father Thomas was ready. He grasped her hand and the patient's hand and started the prayer. Abby joined in on the Hail Mary and Our Father. She always got a bit teary-eyed during these prayers, but she had learned to hide it well. When he was finished, Father Thomas got ready to leave.

"How late are you going to stay here?"

She shrugged as she walked him out the door. "I'll probably stay until he passes."

Father Thomas gave her a piercing look but said nothing. As they walked past Victor's door he stopped, leaned down, and gave her a hug. "Be careful when you head out. The weather is turning. Make sure you get plenty of rest tomorrow too."

Victor looked up and noticed the embrace. The man was holding the volunteer longer than was appropriate. As the girl turned away, he saw the guy give her tits an appreciative gaze. For some reason, it irritated the hell out of him.

Chapter Five

Another hour went by uneventfully. Victor was considering leaving and heading home, but then all hell broke loose. Mr. Smegel's heart rate spiked rapidly, and his blood pressure dropped. Victor jumped up to take a closer look and swore softly. He hit the alarm and started donning the protective gear before the nurses had even entered the room. When they arrived, he calmly issued orders and got ready. He was going to have to open Mr. Smegel up again and relieve the pressure. Otherwise, his patient would die.

It took less than fifteen minutes. When they were done, Mr. Smegel's numbers had dropped back down into the safety zone. The staff all looked at each other in relief. Victor thanked them and gave high praise before heading out of the room. It was a mess in there, and he needed to find a place to clean up. He glanced around the ICU and realized all of the rooms were taken. He hesitated but then headed into the hospice room. He could clean up in there without disturbing a family member. He knew the patient would be unconscious, and hopefully, the volunteer had gone home.

Abby had known something was going on next door when the alarm went off. The call had woken her from a light sleep. She got up and watched as staff members and equipment were rushed into the room. She said a silent prayer for the patient and turned her attention back to Mr. Jones. His breathing was less labored, but the gaps where he stopped breathing altogether were much longer now. She absently walked around the room and tried to relieve the kinks from her tight muscles. She was still standing and looking out the back window when she heard the door open. Abby turned around with a smile thinking it was Mary. The smile froze on her face when she saw the blood-splattered doctor standing in the doorway.

They looked at each other, and the tension in the room was palpable. Abby glanced down at the bloody gown before raising her glance to his eyes. Victor was watching her with an impassive expression on his face. His dark brown eyes were piercing, though, and she got lost in them before tearing her gaze away.

He was the first to speak. "I'm sorry for the intrusion. I needed a place to clean up, and I didn't want to disturb a patient that cared."

Abby raised one eyebrow and took in his appearance. She whispered, "Um, that doesn't look good."

He looked down at the blood and smiled. She noticed how the expression spread across his face and lit up those beautiful brown eyes.

"It looks a lot worse than it is," he assured her. Then he looked concerned, "The sight of blood doesn't bother you, does it?"

Abby pressed her lips together to keep from saying something stupid. She had no idea why she was so nervous. "No. I'm fine." Then she added with concern, "Is your patient going to be okay?"

He rewarded her with another breathtaking smile. "I think so. Time will tell, but his numbers have finally stabilized. He had a pericardial effusion with tamponade."

Abby nodded sarcastically. "Sure, those can be tricky."

Victor laughed as he turned the tap on and started washing. He peeled off his gloves and gown and threw them in the hazardous waste bag next to the door. As he did so she noticed the strong arm and back muscles under his scrubs.

He talked over his shoulder as he washed. "Sorry. I'm used to talking to medical people." As he turned to her to dry his hands he explained, "The patient had a build-up of fluid around his heart." Then he teasingly added, "That's not a good thing."

The volunteer grinned at him, and he noticed her huge green eyes, dark lashes, and the pink running across her cheeks. He was startled to realize how beautiful she was. He took a more assessing look and also noticed she was older than he had assumed…maybe early twenties? The thought gave him pause until he realized she was talking.

"…I don't imagine it would be. But, heh, at least he's better than my guy," she finished as she waved her arm toward the bed.

Victor looked past her at Mr. Jones' still figure. "How's he doing? You want me to take a look?" he asked.

She quietly nodded, and he walked past her to the bed. He pulled his stethoscope out, and she noticed his long fingers. They looked capable, and she felt a slight tremor run through her.

Victor listened to the patient's lungs and took in his halted breathing. He turned to the volunteer. "I would guess less than an hour." He looked at the dark circles under her eyes and added, "You must be exhausted."

Abby unconsciously yawned and stretched. "I'm fine. But it will be good to get home."

Victor gave her another appraising look but said nothing. She fidgeted uncomfortably under his stare and then nervously broke the silence.

"I'm Abby, by the way." She reached out to shake his hand.

Victor smiled softly and clasped her tiny hand in his. An electric shock hit them both with a surprising force, and Abby pulled her hand away quickly. Victor frowned as he stared down at her hand. It took him a moment to recover, but then he looked up at her nametag and read out loud.

"Abigail Shea. You're Irish, then?"

She shook her head and took a short step back.

"No, my husband is—was—Irish."

As she corrected herself, she turned away. Then she looked up and met the doctor's gaze. "I'm actually English."

Victor caught the slip and her discomfort but didn't comment. Instead, he said, "Well, Mrs. Shea, it is nice to meet you. I am Dr. Turov, and I am Russian."

He was teasing her, and she stifled a giggle. He smiled as he walked toward the door.

"I'll probably be here for another hour. If you need anything, don't hesitate to ask."

As he left, she blew out her breath and tried to shake off the encounter. It had left her unsettled but in a good way.

On the outside of the doorway, Victor paused. He was thinking just how pleasant their encounter had been.

Chapter Six

It was a little after two in the morning when Victor finally felt comfortable enough to leave his patient. He headed out to the nurse's station to give his final orders. As he talked to Mary, he kept glancing over at the hospice room. He could see Mrs. Shea standing near the bed, and he considered joining her, but then he mentally kicked himself. Victor found her very attractive, but she was way too young and undoubtedly lacked experience. Still, he couldn't get that shy and angelic demeanor out of his head or the way their fingers had sparked when they shook hands. He was debating what to do when Abby quietly walked up to the nurse's station.

She hesitated to interrupt them but then realized they were both looking at her expectantly. "Um, I think Mr. Jones passed away."

Mary jumped up, and Victor asked if she wanted him to confirm. They both headed into the room while Abby waited outside. When they returned, Mary got on the phone to notify the attending physician. Abby pulled out her cell phone, but she didn't have any reception. Victor noticed and asked if she wanted to use the one on the desk.

"Yes, please. I have to call and notify hospice."

He waved her over and asked for the number. Then he punched it into the phone all the while watching her face. As he handed her the receiver he softly asked, "Are you okay, Mrs. Shea?"

She nodded and turned away from him. He could hear her quietly reporting the death. She seemed fine, but he knew death could hit people in funny ways. He continued to watch her closely.

When the call was done, Abby smiled at both of them. "Well, thank you so much for all your help. I'm going to head home now."

"Where are you parked, hon?" Mary asked with concern. They both looked at her and waited for a response.

Abby thought about it. "Um, I'm parked right on the street." She had no idea which street her car was on, but there was no way she was telling them that."

Victor took up the cause. "Which street would that be, Mrs. Shea?"

She sighed and half-heartedly pointed to the left. "That one?" It came out as a question rather than a statement, and Abby could kick herself. She explained, "I was in a hurry to get here. But I'll know the entrance when I see it."

Mary replied, "Oh, sweetie. All our entrances are locked up at night with an alarm system. You won't be able to get out the way you came in. You'll have to take a walkway over to a parking garage, and then walk out of the garage to the street to get to your car." She gently added, "The direction you pointed to doesn't have a street, just more buildings. The clinic is huge, and everyone gets a little lost here."

Before she could comment Mary continued, "Let me call one of our security guards. They can escort you to your car."

Victor piped in, "It will take forever for them to get here, and Mrs. Shea is exhausted. I can drive her to her car. I'm leaving now too."

Abby looked alarmed. "Oh, thanks. But that's really not necessary —"

Mary cut her off. "That's a good idea. Do you know how to get home from here?"

Abby hesitated and then gave an honest reply. "Well, no. But I have a GPS. I'll just hit home and it will get me there with no problem."

Mary and Victor gave each other horrified looks. Victor was the first to speak. "That's not going to work, Mrs. Shea. Your GPS will take you the shortest route down Carnegie, or whichever road you are parked on. Those streets are unsafe this time of night. Stopping at any light would be dangerous for you."

Mary added, "Hon, you have to take MLK Drive at this time of night. We know that because we work here."

Abby looked lost but replied, "Oh, okay. Sure."

Victor sized up her look and took control. "Where do you live, Mrs. Shea?"

She hesitated but then responded, "Tremont."

"Good. That's very close to where I live. When I drop you off at your car, you will follow me to the freeway."

Abby tried to argue. "I really don't think—"

But he cut her off. "It's settled then." He put his hand out to take hers and smiled at the nurse. "Goodnight, Mary. Please call me if anything changes with Mr. Smegel's status."

Abby reluctantly took his hand. She knew before it hit she would feel a shock. When it did they both looked at each other, and Victor smiled. Abby pulled her hand away quickly. Mary called out goodnight as they walked toward the elevator.

Once inside Victor stared up at the numbers. Abby fidgeted nervously and stared at her feet.

When the elevator opened, he confidently turned left and strolled down the corridor. He was walking at a brisk pace and explained, "I have to get my keys from my office."

She nodded and hurried to follow. They rounded a corner and passed the entrance she had come in. When she pointed this out to him, Victor stopped to show her the alarm system on the doors.

Abby looked annoyed. "Why would they do that?"

"This is a dangerous neighborhood. Especially at night." He continued to walk at a fast pace, and she realized it was because his legs were so long. The doctor was quite tall!

When they arrived at the heart center, Victor pulled a key from his pocket and opened the door. He motioned for her to follow, and suddenly Abby was scared. Sure he was a surgeon, but she didn't know him. They were in an abandoned and dark hallway, and he wanted her to follow him into a dark office. She walked through the doorway but then held the door open and stood there. "I'll just wait here," was all she said.

Victor looked at her and assessed her face. He could tell she was scared, and the thought thrilled him. He knew he needed to tread lightly and so said, "Okay. My office is down the hall. I'll grab my things and be right back."

When he returned, he purposefully walked more slowly by her side and tried to make conversation.

"The physician parking lot is just down the hallway," he pointed.

When they reached the door, he opened it for her. She could see a few fancy cars parked in the gated lot. It was pouring rain out, and the air had gotten cold. Abby silently cursed. She hated driving in the rain. It was so hard to see the lines on the road, plus she tended to get lost. She realized she was grateful for Dr. Turov's assistance. He actually had been kind to her all evening.

Victor hesitated under the overhang and noticed for the first time she did not have a coat. "Where's your jacket?" he asked, and he couldn't stop his voice from sounding angry.

"Sorry. I didn't bring one." She wasn't sure why she was apologizing.

Victor took off his jacket and put it around her. "You'll get sick without a coat this time of year."

Abby couldn't resist. "You get sick from viruses, doctor, not the weather." She emphasized the word doctor to make her point. She was trying for funny, but it came out more as a challenge.

His eyes narrowed as he looked at her. To her, he simply said, "Wait here and I'll pull the truck up."

She watched as he walked over to a black Tundra. It was parked in the marked spot closest to the door. Apparently, Dr. Dictator ranked high at the clinic.

He intended to get out and open her door, but she had run to the vehicle and let herself in before he could move.

"Wow, did the weather get cold. A few more degrees and this could be snow!" she exclaimed.

Victor nodded and turned on the seat warmers. They would heat up before the vents did. The scent of her hit him full force—lavender and vanilla—and he breathed deeply. There was light jazz music playing in the truck, and he noted she automatically fastened her seatbelt. That made him happy.

As he punched in the code to open the gate, he looked at her. "Mrs. Shea, it is really nasty out. Why don't you let me drive you home? You can pick up your car in the morning. I can bring you, or I have a driver that can bring you. When she said nothing, he added, "Please. I have issues with control, and I will worry about you all night if you drive yourself."

Abby hesitated but then said, "I really want to take my car now." She could sense this was important to him, but there was no way she was letting him drive her to her house. The thought made her very uncomfortable. "I'm sure I'll be fine once I'm on the freeway. I grew up in Cleveland. I'm used to driving in bad weather."

Victor stopped just outside of the gate. As it closed behind them he put his truck into park. Then he asked for her cell phone.

"Um, what do you need my cell for?"

He smiled, but his eyes were serious. "I'm going to plug my number into your contacts. If you insist on driving yourself home, I at least ask you text me when you get there so I don't worry."

"Oh," was all she said as she handed over the phone. He noticed she'd entered a security pin to unlock it first.

After typing in the number, Victor handed back the phone. Then he headed in the direction he thought her car would be. As he drove he continued to draw in the scent of her. To make conversation he asked about her volunteer work.

"How long have you been working at hospice?"

She thought about it. "A little over a year."

"What made you choose it? I would think someone your age would go for a different type of volunteer work."

Abby looked at him puzzled. "Why would you think that?"

"Well, they deal with death on a regular basis. Most young people don't even think about death. I would guess a soup kitchen or meals-on-wheels would be more your speed."

Abby laughed. "Well, I do volunteer at a soup kitchen as well. And you're right, I'm one of their youngest volunteers. But I like it. I feel like I'm really helping." She couldn't explain it any better than that, but she added, "Besides. I'm not that young. I'm almost thirty."

He raised his brows at her age but didn't comment. She was more than old enough, and he realized that changed things considerably. He could sense she was uncomfortable and moved on.

"So you sit with patients when they're dying?"

She nodded. Abby explained what a vigil was and how they usually occurred. "I also volunteer at their front desk on Wednesday afternoons. I direct the family members to the patient rooms, the flower deliveries, and things like that. It's a lighter way to help out."

"So you don't mind seeing all that death?"

She thought about it. "I guess not. Do you? I would assume you see a lot in your line of work."

Victor nodded as he turned onto Carnegie. "I do mind. My goal with every patient is to keep them alive and living a good quality of life. When they die, it pisses me off. It's like I've lost control, and I really dislike losing control." He gave her a stern look when he finished his sentence.

Abby got lost in the look but then turned away and pointed at her little silver Focus. "That's me," was all she said.

Victor pulled up next to it. As she started to get out he reminded her, "Follow me all the way to the freeway, and text me when you get home."

She nodded and gave him a brilliant smile. "Okay. Thank you!"

Abby rushed to her car but still got soaked. When she was safely in the vehicle she breathed a sigh of relief. She only then realized how tense she had been in his truck. She quickly started up her car and noticed his Tundra waiting in front of her. Abby pulled out behind him and followed.

They had to circle around and make several turns to get on MLK. Victor drove at a reasonable pace, and she easily followed him. Once on MLK, the road was dark. She was grateful for his taillights in front of her to lead the way. They finally made it to I-90, and Abby merged behind him. The freeway was empty, but she continued to follow behind him. At dead man's curve, he went straight, and she was finally on her own.

When Abby pulled into her garage ten minutes later, it was three a.m. She sighed in relief and realized just how tired she was. She headed into her townhouse and kicked off her shoes. She went to take off Dr. Turov's coat, and only then did she realize she would have to get it back to him. She pressed her nose against the collar and breathed in deeply. It smelled faintly of cologne and strongly of him. She sighed. He was quite the man, and she realized it was the first time she had noticed one since Nate died.

As Abby was getting ready for bed, she realized she still hadn't texted the doctor. It took her a while to find his name. He had entered it as Victor Turov. She quickly sent a text.

Sorry. Almost forgot to text. Home safely. Thanks again!! Still have your coat.

His response was immediate.

Glad you are home safely. I was beginning to pace. Don't worry about the coat.

Seriously? He was pacing? What an odd man. Abby pulled on flannel jammies and curled up in the bed. As she fell asleep, her mind was still on the doctor—his piercing eyes, the shock of touching his hand, and the way he smelled. She drifted off into a very peaceful sleep.

Chapter Seven

The next morning Victor woke at his usual time. Because of the emergency surgery the previous evening, he had diverted his easier procedures today to some of the attending physicians. The more complicated ones had been moved to the afternoon. It was rare for him to have a morning free during the week. He stretched and then flipped back the covers. Even with free time, Victor could not make himself stay in bed.

As he was brushing his teeth, he thought back to last evening and Mrs. Shea. The woman had gotten under his skin. He couldn't remember the last time he had thought about any female this way, and the thought was disturbing. She was beautiful, to be sure, and had an innocence about her that was enchanting. But that still didn't explain his attraction. And what the fuck was that electrical current about?

Victor headed into the kitchen and flipped on the coffee maker. As he waited, he opened the back blinds and stared out at Lake Erie. He had bought the condo three years ago. It was in the heart of the newly renovated Flats, and he loved it. The location was convenient for work and offered numerous amenities including basement parking, a full-sized gym and pool, and plenty of restaurants. His condo had three bedrooms, two and a half baths, a vaulted ceiling with wooden beams, a gas fireplace, and a state-of-the-art kitchen. It even had an enclosed balcony that was heated for the winter but could be opened up in the summer.

Victor absent-mindedly stirred cinnamon into his coffee. He popped a sandwich in the microwave and opened his iPad. He was old fashioned and still preferred to get his news from the Plain Dealer. His only concession to modern technology was to read it electronically instead of having a paper delivered to his door. He quickly perused the headlines and then focused on the sports page. The Browns were doing better than they had in previous years, but they still had a long way to go.

Twenty minutes later Victor had exhausted his interest in the news. He had procrastinated as long as he could. The problem of Mrs. Shea had to be dealt with. Should he do the right thing and leave her be? Or was that sweet exterior of hers just a front? Clearly, she had been married, so she wasn't innocent. He didn't know if she was divorced or widowed, but it wasn't like she was a virgin. He was sure Mr. Shea had hit that on a regular basis, as any man would. Hell, the girl was almost thirty. So why did she throw off such an innocent vibe?

And how was it she could volunteer on nights and Wednesday afternoons? Didn't she have a job? Maybe she worked odd hours. Or had she divorced a wealthy husband and taken him to the cleaners? The thought made him frown. He had seen his fair share of money-grubbing women. It sometimes had to be tolerated to get what he wanted, but it was still irritating.

Then again, the woman had spent hours sitting with a dying man. That showed a level of caring he rarely saw in people, let alone someone he bedded. The woman was a damn enigma, and Victor was tired of thinking about it. He liked to tackle his problems head-on. It was clear he was not going to get her out of his mind anytime soon. The only sane thing to do was move forward.

Victor reached for his cell and flipped through his contacts until he found Jack's number. It had been years since he had used his services. He hoped the man could still provide what he needed.

Jack picked up on the first ring. "Dr. Turov. How long has it been?"

"At least three years," Victor said.

"That sounds about right. So what can I do for you? The usual?"

Victor thought about it. The normal report was good when it came to a typical female interest, but he was going to need more information on Mrs. Shea to make a decision.

"No. I want you to give me everything you can find out about this woman. Start with where she was born, raised, went to school, where she works, etc. I want to know who her family and friends are and how she spends her days and nights. I want medical records and financials if you can get them, and anything remotely of interest you can dig up. If this woman sneezes, I want to know about it. Is that clear?"

"Crystal clear. You want photos?"

"Yes. I want to see the people she's interacting with and where she lives. Her name is Abigail Shea, she's either divorced or widowed, she lives in Tremont, she volunteers for the clinic hospice, she drives a silver Focus, and she's in her late twenties. I also have her license plate and cell numbers if you need them. That should be enough for you to go on."

Jack laughed. "That's more than enough. Give me both numbers, and how soon do you want it?"

Victor didn't hesitate. "Tuesday at the latest. Is that doable?" He planned to visit Mrs. Shea on Wednesday, and he wanted the information before that visit. He gave the numbers and then added, "Oh, and I would like to know exactly when she is scheduled to volunteer at the hospice on Wednesday afternoon."

Jack confirmed. "It's going to cost you, but I can get it done. I'll be in touch."

They hung up, and Victor poured himself another cup of coffee. It felt good to get that taken care of. Now he had time to get in a workout. He could feel the usual anticipatory excitement of waiting on a report from the private investigator. Victor needed control, but he also loved the thrill of the hunt.

***

It was Friday afternoon, and Abby was driving out to Bay Village to do the promised craft night with Rachel. She had spent a productive day cranking out chapters on her current mystery. The work had calmed her mind, and she had all but forgotten about Dr. Turov. Abby was looking forward to a fun night of wine and crafts.

True to form, Rachel was waiting for her with the craft supplies spread out on the big high-top table. As Abby walked in, their four-year-old dog greeted her at the door. Charlie was a feisty ball of fur that had her wrapped around his little paw. She picked him up and gave him a hug before throwing his ball. He shot after it, and Abby dropped her overnight bag in the hall.

Joel walked up from the basement and gave her a hug. "Hi, Abs. How's it going?"

She smiled at him. Joel was an interesting guy. By day he worked as an accountant at a high-powered manufacturing company in Cleveland, but at night he threw himself completely into various hobbies. They included beer making, gardening, astronomy, and fishing. The latter was actually how they had all met. Nate had worked at the same company as Joel in the finance department. The two couldn't be more opposite. Whereas Joel was laid back and quiet, Nate had been high strung, outgoing, and aggressive. They had discovered a shared love of fishing and started heading out on Lake Erie to catch walleye and perch.

Eventually, that led to the wives meeting. Again, on the surface, it appeared the two females had nothing in common. Rachel was a nurse practitioner with an outgoing and ballsy personality similar to Nate's.

She was a clothes horse and had more designer bags, shoes, and clothing than a runway model. She was also extremely organized and ran her house like a tight ship.

Abby, on the other hand, was much shyer and more introverted. She would rather spend her time reading a book than talking to people. She was also a tad disorganized, especially when she was writing, and lacked any sense of fashion whatsoever. Abby opted for cotton t-shirts, jeans, and tennis shoes. Her only indulgence was her sexy underwear, but that was purchased through a website and only because Nate had encouraged it. Abby often felt like she was wearing a potato sack when in Rachel's presence.

And yet the women had soon formed a bond. They both loved dogs, crafting, and the theatre, and the two couples had quickly started spending time together. When the accident occurred, Joel and Rachel had been invaluable to Abby. She didn't know what she would have done without them. They had helped her to make the decision to end life support, and Rachel had taken over and organized the entire funeral afterward. Joel had driven Abby out on his boat to pour Nate's ashes into the lake. She had even moved in with them for a month because she couldn't stand being in her house alone. Eventually, she had bought the townhouse in Tremont and moved.

Now Abby approached the table and looked at the craft supplies. She grinned and asked, "What are we making?"

Rachel always picked out their projects and bought the supplies. She also followed instructions well, and her final projects were beautiful. Abby was more about the process than the final product, which meant sometimes her work was great and sometimes it was a disaster. Rachel never criticized her, though, and the two worked well together.

"We're making designer pumpkins and ghost cutout cards," said Rachel. She pulled up the photos on her cell phone to show Abby.

"Oh, those are adorable!"

"I knew you'd like them," said Rachel. "We ordered pizza, and it should be here in twenty minutes. That will give us time to paint the pumpkins."

She led Abby out to the open garage. A drop cloth was down on the cement, and their pumpkins were waiting. Rachel pulled out packets of pantyhose with designs on them. She explained they would pull those over the pumpkins and then spray paint the entire thing. Then they would pull the pantyhose off, and hopefully, the design would remain on the pumpkin.

They got started and chatted as they worked. Not surprisingly Rachel worked in a tight and neat area, and her paint went evenly on the pumpkins. Abby struggled with her spray can, and paint shot out in a garbled mess. Her pumpkins had drips from the excess paint, and she even tracked some of it in the garage. Rachel noticed and made her leave her shoes at the door. Some things never changed.

When the pizza arrived, Abby rushed out to pay. She could hear Charlie barking in the house, and Joel was yelling at him. Rachel walked over to help carry in the food and caught the delivery guy shamelessly flirting with Abby. After he left, she teased her friend.

"That little boy has the hots for you!"

Abby rolled her eyes. "He's like sixteen years old. I could get arrested for that."

"Yes. But think what you could teach him!"

They both laughed as they carried in the food. Joel quickly grabbed a slice and slopped cheese and sauce all over the table. Rachel yelled at him and told him to use a plate. He ignored her. Abby poured out some wine, and the three started eating.

"Seriously, Abs. You need to get back in the dating game soon," said Rachel.

Abby looked up from her food cautiously. Lately, her friends had been gently pressing her to date. She had a fear they were lining up a blind date, and she looked at them suspiciously.

Joel piped in. "You know if you don't start using it soon, you're going to lose it and go back to virgin status."

"Joel!" screamed Rachel. "That is so gross, and so not true. Ignore him, Abs."

Abby gave them both a wicked smile. "Not to worry. I use my little rabbit vibrator on a regular basis."

The two girls started laughing, and Joel muttered, "Rachel gives hers quite the workout too."

Now they were all howling with laughter, and Abby had to wipe the tears from her eyes. God, they were good for her soul!

While they were distracted, Charlie tried to sneak some food from the table. Joel grabbed the dog and then handed him a bit of cheese with sauce from his pizza.

"Joel! Dogs can't eat tomatoes," said Rachel.

"Sure they can," countered her husband.

"No. Tomatoes can cause tremors and heart arrhythmias."

Joel argued with her. "You're thinking of garlic. Tomatoes are fine."

The two continued to argue back and forth while Abby kept eating. She knew when the two started bickering it could take a while. They loved to argue, and neither liked to back down. Rachel once admitted she would disagree with him even when she knew he was right. She said she liked the thrill of the argument. Abby couldn't understand it. She avoided confrontations like the plague. She started clearing the dishes and had them done before the two finished their discussion. Joel had eventually searched online and determined Rachel was the winner. He should have known better. Rachel was in the medical field, after all.

When dinner was over he headed outside with his telescope. The girls moved on to their ghost cards, and Rachel put on the Hallmark channel. The movies were sappy and predictable, but they both loved them. They sipped wine and chatted as they worked. After one glass Abby was feeling the effects. She had always been a lightweight, and Rachel usually teased her about it. Tonight she didn't even bat an eye when Abby turned down a second glass. She could see her friend was getting tired.

Joel called them out to the front yard, and they took turns looking at the moon through the telescope. Eventually, Abby excused herself and went to bed. Charlie happily tagged along, and he ended up curling up by her side. They both were asleep within minutes.

***

The next few days flew by, and on Tuesday Victor was seeing patients in his office. They were the usual types of cases, and his waiting room was packed. As the top cardiothoracic surgeon in Cleveland, and quite possibly the world, he had a waiting list of people trying to see him. The hectic schedule suited him just fine, especially today when he was waiting for the report from Jack. It irritated him how much he wanted to see that report. This simply would not do. He was hoping the results would make her less appealing.

At four fifteen Jack sauntered into the office. Rebekeh, Victor's office manager, met him at the window and asked him to sign in. He explained he was personally dropping off a package for the doctor. Rebekeh looked at him suspiciously.

"You can leave that with me, sir. I'll be sure Dr. Turov gets it."

Jack would not back down. "This is sensitive material, ma'am. I need to hand deliver it to the doctor."

Now he had her attention. He could tell the middle-aged woman thought he was serving the good doctor legal papers. He tried to ease her concern.

"Please tell Victor his friend, Jack, is here. He'll know who I am."

She continued to look at him dubiously, but then she tried Victor's line. Burt, the nurse, breezed past and told her the doctor was in with a patient. She told Jack as much and asked him to grab a seat. He gave her a broad smile and carried the thick envelope into the waiting room. The man didn't sit down, though, and that worried Rebekeh. She was happy when the doctor came around the corner with a patient. He gave her instructions for the man's prescriptions, and she quickly wrote them down. Then she hesitantly told him about Jack.

Victor's face lit up with a smile, and he thanked her. Then he walked out into the waiting room and shook the man's hand. They exchanged a few pleasantries, and Rebekeh distinctly heard the man say he would "send the bill." Then he was gone, and the doctor headed back to his office with the envelope in hand.

Rebekeh had long since given up trying to figure out her boss. He was a private man, and his interactions with staff were limited to the job. He was a perfectionist and expected them to be as well, but he paid them generously and truly seemed to appreciate their work. She forgot about the incident and went back to her billing.

Victor took the envelope to his office and locked it in his desk. Jack had said it was "not your typical report." He wasn't sure what that meant, but he felt a thrill run through him. He still had a good six patients to see, but then he could head home and open up the envelope. He smiled as he headed to the examining room.

At six thirty that night Victor was finally home. He had changed into a pair of faded jeans and a Cavaliers t-shirt. He had eaten his dinner of steak, salad, and vegetables from a local restaurant. It was amazing what one could get delivered these days. Now he was settling down at the kitchen table with a small glass of bourbon and the eight by twelve envelope. It was thick, and he knew he had been given his money's worth. Victor tore it open and started reading.

Jack had been thorough to an extreme. The report was separated into eight sections with photos dispersed throughout.

The first section was titled History. It included Mrs. Shea's birthdate, and Victor noted it was coming up soon. He read about her parents, who had both died in the past ten years, where she had grown up, the fact she had two brothers living in the area, and where she had gone to school. Jack had even included her grades in high school and college and the extra-curricular activities she had participated in. It would appear Mrs. Shea was smart, with a 3.9 GPA, and she had gone for more nerdy activities such as the school paper and the yearbook club. The end of this section included her criminal report which was short and sweet. Mrs. Shea apparently had a lead foot, with three speeding tickets to her name. She had also been arrested in college for swimming naked in a fountain with some of her friends. The latter made Victor grin.

The next section was titled Relationships. He read about her brothers. One was a manager and the other a plumber. The manager was married with kids, but the plumber was single and appeared to have a drinking problem. She also had college friends scattered throughout Ohio and the Midwest, with one noteworthy male friend living in Chicago. Victor frowned. He was not a fan of opposite-sex friendships. Mrs. Shea also had several friends living in the Cleveland area, including three married couples she spent a lot of time with. There were no known boyfriends to report. Good.

Jack had included photos of both brothers and her friends in the area. On the back, he had labeled who was in each photo. Victor grinned as he saw Mrs. Shea in various poses. She looked as beautiful as he had remembered.

Nathan Shea took up most of the relationship section. She had married him at the age of twenty-two, and they had been married six years. He had been a financial officer at a large company in Cleveland, and he had made an excellent salary. Mr. Shea had no criminal record and not even a traffic offense to his name. Ironically the man had been killed in a car accident. A semi had t-boned his SUV. He had been on life support at Metro Hospital for three days before he had passed away. Victor thought about that. It could explain why she did the hospice gig now. He realized she had gone through quite a few losses in her young life. Jack had clipped the obituary at the end of that section along with a few photos of the couple. The doctor looked carefully at these and noted Mr. Shea had been a tall but thin man.

Employment was the next section in the packet. Jack had started with the ice cream shop job she held in high school, followed by the recreation center job she did throughout college. After she graduated she had worked as a social worker. This did not surprise Victor in the least. That had ended five years ago, and now Mrs. Shea worked as a writer. The estimated royalties from her books were not high, and he frowned. How the hell was she living off of that? A list of the books she had published was included, and Victor was impressed with the number. Jack had noted Mrs. Shea liked to work in public, and she would haul her laptop to the library or a coffee shop and spend hours typing. There were photos showing her working in a library.

The Financials section was next, and Victor's mind was put at ease when he saw her income. Mrs. Shea was wealthy. Her parents had left her some money, and her late husband had taken care of the rest. His life insurance policy had been worth one million. His employer had also kicked in a tidy sum, and the trucking company responsible for the accident had paid out a ridiculous amount in their settlement. Jack had noted she had not sued them; they had simply written her a check. Finally, the car insurance company had also paid handsomely for the poor man's death.

Included in this section was a list of Mrs. Shea's credit cards and numbers, her ATM card and pin, her bank account and brokerage account numbers, and her annuities. Victor was impressed with Jack's ability to obtain this information. He was also pleased to see how safe but diversified her money was. She did not have as much money as him, but she was certainly wealthy in her own right. The section concluded with the charitable donations Mrs. Shea made each year, and he noted the largest amounts went to the Catholic church and various animal shelters.

The Medical section was next. Jack, that son-of-a-bitch, had managed to pull her complete dental and gynecological records. Victor noted her teeth were healthy and cleaned twice a year. He was also pleased to see her gynecologist was a woman. That file was thick, and it took him awhile to read through the information. Mrs. Shea had suffered an ectopic pregnancy five years ago, and she had undergone an emergency hysterectomy at the young age of twenty-four. They had fortunately been able to save her ovaries, and she was currently still within normal hormonal ranges. The primary doctor's name and address were also listed. Victor noted she was not only a woman but also a Russian. That made him smile. Jack concluded by noting Mrs. Shea was not currently taking any medications.

The next section was titled Living Arrangements. It showed photos of her childhood home, college apartment, and house she had lived in with Nathan. It ended with the townhouse she currently owned in Tremont on West 10th. Victor read that the house was paid in full, noted its value, and the fact it had an attached garage and ADT security. Jack had even included a crime report for the neighborhood. The private investigator knew his customer well, thought Victor, and he was happy with the information.

Hobbies was the next tab in the report. She had quite a few. There was her charity work at the hospice and also a food shelter at a local church. This was located close to her house. Mrs. Shea also enjoyed crafts, reading, swimming, and lifting weights. Jack had included photos of her participating in each activity listed. He noted she had season tickets to the Cleveland Broadway and Great Lakes series, and she was a member of the Cleveland Art Museum. The private investigator had noted she had not gone to any bars, clubs, or participated in any "questionable" behaviors during the short investigation. She appeared to not drink, smoke, or do drugs. Good.

The final section was simply labeled Miscellaneous. Here, Jack had noted all of the little things about Mrs. Shea's life that might be of interest to the doctor. She shopped at the Westside Market and had been seen eating pizza, Taco Bell, and Panera Bread. Jack had noted that all of her food selections did not include meat, and she was possibly a vegetarian. He also pointed out she got up early and liked to walk in the neighborhood with a cup of coffee in her hand and her iPod blasting. She also tended to go to bed early, and her favorite flowers were daffodils. Victor wondered how he had found that out. Finally, he mentioned she tended to misplace items such as sunglasses, jacket, sweater, pens, etc. The photos here showed her walking and also looking under a table for something.

Victor finished reading and thumbed back through to look at all of the photos again. He thought about what he had learned. Aside from having money and losing her parents and husband at such a young age, her life was pretty normal. Victor had hoped for something off-putting to end this now. Had she smoked or done drugs he could have easily walked away. But no, Mrs. Shea led a clean and sweet life, and he wanted her even more now than he did before.

Victor drained his bourbon and put the glass in the sink. The decision had been made. There were things she would need to change. Surely her eating habits needed an overhaul, and he would need to assess the townhouse and soup kitchen more closely. The speeding and walking in the neighborhood would have to go. Safety was going to be a top priority with this one, and the thought gave him pause. He had never cared before, and he wasn't sure he liked the feeling.

He continued to think about her life. The male friend in Chicago might also be a problem, but he would cross that bridge when he came to it. Victor didn't share, and he didn't like worrying about other men. As for the hysterectomy, that made the whole birth control issue a whole lot easier. He grinned as he realized he wouldn't have to use condoms. Yes, the decision had definitely been made. Now he just needed to convince the girl.

While he was getting ready for bed, the phone rang. A quick glance showed him it was Jack.

He answered. "You've outdone yourself. The report was extremely thorough. I don't even want to know how you got some of this information."

Jack laughed. "You would be amazed at how lax security is in some situations." He went on, "I'm glad you liked it. I forgot to get you her hospice hours, and that's why I'm calling."

"Good. What did you find out?"

"She is there every Wednesday afternoon from one to four. She sits at the front desk when you walk in. She's also subbing for someone this Friday at the same time."

"Excellent. How did you get that information?"

Jack laughed again. "That one was easy. I just called them up and asked."

"And here I thought investigative work was challenging. I believe I am paying you too much."

"My reports are worth it. Take care, Dr. Turov." He hung up before Victor could thank him.

The doctor pulled one photo of Mrs. Shea from the stack. It showed her picking out lettuce at the Westside Market with a thoughtful look on her face. "Until tomorrow," he softly whispered.

Chapter Eight

Abby was sitting at the front desk of the hospice with her writing notes spread out around her. She was struggling over how to kill her latest victim, and it was starting to annoy her. It was hot in the lobby, and she was sweating a bit. She blew her bangs to unstick them from her forehead and took a slug of water. Hospice required their volunteers to dress professionally, and she was wearing a pretty dark gray dress that tied at the waist. It was sleeveless, and she wore a white jersey knit shirt underneath. Burgundy suede booties finished off the look, and even Rachel would have been proud of the ensemble. Abby's hair was piled in a sloppy bun on top of her head, and she absent-mindedly tucked a stray strand behind her ear. She frowned down at her notes in concentration, but then she realized there was someone at the desk.

Abby looked up to see Dr. Turov standing in front of her. She jumped slightly in the chair but recovered quickly.

"Dr. Turov. How nice to see you again. What are you doing here?" She couldn't keep the hint of an accusation out of her voice.

He smiled down at her. "Mrs. Shea. I was hoping you would be here. Our conversation got me thinking about my patients. I thought I would tour hospice so I can tell them about it if I ever need to make a referral."

She relaxed slightly. That made sense. "Oh. That's great. We do get a lot of patients in here with heart failure and COPD."

He nodded as she continued.

"Let me get someone to cover the desk, and then I can show you around." As she picked up the phone to call someone, she noticed that her hands were shaking. The man made her nervous!

While they waited, she asked him about his patient. "So how is the guy from ICU doing?"

"He's doing great. He's already transferred down to a regular floor, and I'm hoping to send him home sometime next week." It pleased him she had asked, although she might have just been making conversation.

Abby's face lit up. "That's awesome. Wow. You saved a life." Then she realized, "I bet you save lives all the time, don't you?" He noticed she had a look of awe on her face, and he was even more pleased. Being a surgeon had certainly helped his cause many times in the past.

They were interrupted by a formidable elderly woman, impeccably dressed in a stern black suit. "Okay, Mrs. Shea. Here I am," was all she said. The woman made to sit down in the chair Abby vacated, but then she took in Victor's presence. "Oh, my goodness. Is that Dr. Turov?" she asked, as she thrust out her hand.

He shook her hand and politely replied, "Yes. And you are?"

"I'm Mrs. Turner, the volunteer coordinator at the hospice. It is a pleasure to meet you, doctor. You have quite the reputation, and the clinic is lucky to have you." She turned to Abby. "Mrs. Shea, I had better take this tour. Dr. Turov is a celebrity."

Abby looked surprised. It took a lot to rile up Mrs. Turner, but she appeared to be star-struck by the doctor's presence. Before anyone could protest, the old woman had taken Victor's arm and led him down a wing.

Victor raised his eyebrows and looked back at the desk in frustration. He saw Mrs. Shea smiling at their retreat and realized the old lady had cock-blocked him! He politely listened as Mrs. Turner droned on and on about the services offered to grieving families. He had to admit they offered quite a bit, and he would keep them in mind with his terminal cases. But he really wanted to get back to the delectable female sitting up front.

They finally circled back to the front, and he could see Mrs. Shea talking to a visitor. They stopped at the kitchen adjacent to the lobby, but the old woman would not shut up. As she yapped on about family meals, he glanced in Abby's direction.

She was watching him with amusement. Mrs. Turner was quite the chatterbox when she got going, and the poor doctor looked ready to run. Abby had to admit, he was one fine-looking man. He was tall, and his body was muscular. He was wearing scrubs and tennis shoes, and the pants were hanging perfectly on his hips with the drawstring casually tucked to one side. His hair and eyes were dark brown, and his facial features were strong with a hint of stubble on his cheeks. Her eyes kept being drawn to his hands. They were graceful and long—as she would imagine surgeon's hands to be—and they were absently twisting around a form he was holding. She knew those hands were going to end up in a book of hers in the future.

The two finally finished the tour and headed back to the desk. Abby grinned at the doctor. "How was your tour?" she teased.

He gave her an amused smile. "It was good. I am impressed with this facility and all that is offered here."

Mrs. Turner interrupted. "Now, Dr. Turov. Let me go get you those information packets I was telling you about. You can pass them on to your patients when needed. Just give us a bit of time to throw some together. We had an outreach event this past weekend, and we used up the last of the ones we had."

Victor nodded at the woman and graciously said, "Take your time, Mrs. Turner. I'm going to run and grab a coffee at the Starbucks. Would you like me to bring you something?"

Mrs. Turner skipped a beat but then beamed before declining his offer. Victor turned to Abby. "And how about you, Mrs. Shea?"

She was way ahead of him and had already pulled some money from her wallet. She pushed a ten-dollar bill at him and asked for a venti latte. The caffeine would give her a good jolt and hopefully help her writing process.

Victor's eyes narrowed when he saw the money, and he thought about how much she would need to learn. Out loud he said, "No. No. It's my treat." When Abby protested, he cut her off with a stern, "I insist." She registered the tone of his voice and pulled her hand back. As she put the money back in her purse she thanked him, and he nodded his approval. She stared at his back as he headed down the hallway.

Dr. Turov returned in ten minutes and pulled up a chair to sit next to Abby at the desk. They sipped on their coffees, and he waved at the papers spread out. "What's this?" he asked.

She made a face. "This is my latest project, and it's not going well."

When he continued to look at her expectantly, she explained, "I'm a writer. And these are the notes for a book."

"Ah. So you're a writer? Interesting. And what kind of books do you write, Mrs. Shea?"

She thought about it. "Technically they're murder mysteries. But they're more about women than the actual mysteries. I guess you could call them chick lit with a twist."

"So one could say you kill people for a living?"

Abby laughed. "I guess you could say that. I am quite good at killing people on paper. Although," she frowned, "this one is giving me trouble." Then she looked speculatively at him. "You're a doctor. Maybe you can help me?"

"I would be happy to help. What is your problem?"

She sighed. "So, I want to stab this guy in the heart with a knife. But I want him to live for a while. Is that possible, or would he die right away?"

Victor snorted some coffee in surprise. "You paint quite the picture, Mrs. Shea. Generally speaking, I try to keep my patients alive and not kill them." He rubbed his chin while thinking. "A coroner could better answer this question, but I think you might be able to pull it off if you stabbed him in the stomach instead of the heart. He would bleed out slowly, and it would be a painful death. Will that work?"

Abby's shook her head. "No. I really wanted to use the heart as a symbolic gesture. I'm big on symbolism. Is there anything I could do to the heart to kill him, but slowly?"

Victor was amused by the conversation. "Well, you could poison him with a massive dose of beta blockers. It would slow down his heart and kill him within about an hour, depending on the dosage."

Abby's eyes twinkled. "That is actually perfect. I can work with that. Thank you!"

"So have you always been a writer?"

She shook her head again. "I used to be a social worker. I mostly worked with elderly clients."

He cocked his head to one side. "And what made you give up the social work job?"

She fidgeted. "I don't know." She changed the subject. "I wonder what's keeping Mrs. Turner?"

He shrugged. "I'm sure Nurse Ratchet is rushing to get those packets completed."

As Abby chuckled at the Nurse Ratchet comment, he continued. "And yet, you still work around the elderly here, don't you?"

She nodded but didn't meet his eyes. "Yes. I guess I can't give it up completely."

They were interrupted by a visitor slowly making his way to the reception desk. The man was ancient, with a face only a mother could love, and he was thrusting a walker in front of him as he shuffled along.

All they could hear was click, drag, wheeze, click, drag, wheeze. When he finally reached the desk, he breathlessly asked for a patient's room number. Abby looked it up and gave it to him. She had to repeat it twice before he heard her. Then the man shuffled on down the hallway.

When he was gone, Victor calmly looked at Abby. "Was that a visitor or a patient?"

She burst out with laughter, and the sound was like music to his ears. He looked over at her appreciatively. She had a beautiful face and big green eyes. Her hair was a golden mess on top of her head, and it gave the impression she had just been fucked. The thought sent a tremor through his groin. She had a long, slender body but curves in all the right places. He idly wondered if her breasts were real. A woman that tiny was not born with a rack like that. He really hoped they were real. Victor then noticed even her feet were tiny. Damn, she was beautiful. He looked back up at her face and saw she was staring at him with a flushed expression. The chemistry between them was obvious. Neither said a word, but then the spell was broken by Mrs. Turner's voice.

She was looking back and forth between their two faces with a look of displeasure. "I have your packets, Dr. Turov," was all she said.

Victor tore his glance away from Abby and smiled at Nurse Ratchet. He stood up and stretched as he thanked the older woman for her efforts. He took the bag of material she handed him and looked at the time on his cell phone. "Thank you, ladies. I need to get back now. I enjoyed my visit," he finished, as his eyes lingered on Abby.

Mrs. Turner nodded and walked away. Once she was gone, Victor asked, "Mrs. Shea, when will you be working here again?" He knew the answer, but it would not do for her to know that.

Abby hesitated. "Um, I'm filling in on Friday for someone. I'll be here from one to four. Why?"

He smiled. "I thought I would stop by again and pick up my jacket. That is if you still have it. You didn't lose it, did you?"

"Oh," she said. "No, of course, I didn't lose it." She reached for her phone. "Let me leave myself a reminder or I'll forget," she sheepishly admitted.

He smiled again. "Do you want me to text you a reminder?"

She realized he must have saved her number from last week. The thought was disturbing but also thrilling. She ignored it and replied, "No. That's okay. I'll remember."

"Very well then. I will see you on Friday."

As he walked away she thought about their conversation. What was that crack about her losing things? She did tend to misplace the occasional pen or sweater, but it was almost as if he knew. Such an odd, odd man. Abby looked down at her writing notes and tried to forget him. She was almost successful.

Chapter Nine

After her volunteer work, Abby headed to the downtown YMCA for a swim. She was hoping to beat the after-work crowd, so she wouldn't have to share a lane. She quickly changed in the women's locker room and headed out to the pool. Sure enough, there was one lane still open on the end. She headed toward it and noticed with trepidation that Brett was just getting in.

Abby sighed. Brett was a nice enough guy. He was about her age and single, with a strong muscular body due to the heavy weight lifting he did. He was also a good swimmer, and the two could pace each other well and easily share a lane. The problem was he liked to take breaks at the wall, and he attempted to chat with her when she came up to make turns.

Abby liked to lose herself in her swims. The steady pacing of the laps was soothing, and she reveled in the feel of the smooth water on her skin. It was relaxing, but chatty Cathy ruined that with his attempts at long discussions. Lately, he had been getting into tough mudder races, and that's all he wanted to talk about.

She sighed and hopped in the water. Maybe he would need an intense cardio workout today and leave her alone. She started swimming slowly and felt the familiar release of her tight muscles. She swam for a good thirty minutes before she noticed Brett stretching his legs at the shallow end of their lane. She approached and tried to make the turn, but he waved her down.

Abby stopped and said hello.

"Hi, Abby. How's it going?" he eagerly asked.

"I'm doing great, Brett. I need to get in another fifteen minutes, though," she hinted.

He nodded and seemed nervous. "Sure. No problem. I was about to get out. I just wanted to ask you something before I did."

She felt her heart drop.

Brett nervously looked at her. "I was wondering if you would want to go out to dinner with me sometime? I have a membership at the Foundation Room. Have you ever been? It's actually a very cool place."

Abby pressed her lips together. God, she hated this. She had never been good at being single. She had no interest in this man, but she didn't want to hurt his feelings. She also didn't know how to let him down easily. She hedged. "Oh, that sounds like fun. But actually, I'm busy right now working on a project. I don't really have the time to date..." she finished faintly.

Brett took it well. "Sure. No problem. When do you think your schedule will ease up?"

She realized he wasn't getting the hint and reluctantly replied, "Maybe in a week or two?"

He looked happy. "Sounds good. I'll hit you up again next week." He pressed his hands on the floor platform and effortlessly raised his body up and out of the pool. She had to admit, he had a nice body.

Brett gave her a wave and a grin. "See you around."

She waved back and continued on with her swim.

***

On Thursday, Abby finished her morning walk, ate a quick breakfast of yogurt and berries, and slapped on some old jeans. She was volunteering at the hunger center today, and she would be helping unload the truck full of food dropped off by the food bank. The volunteers would then sort through it and stack it on the shelves. Folks in need were able to visit the center three times a day for meals. Abby loved the work. It was more physical than her hospice gig, and she enjoyed organizing things on the shelves.

She arrived before the truck and found other volunteers drinking coffee, smoking cigarettes, and chatting. A lot of the "volunteers" came from the local prisons or court system. They were serving their mandatory community service time. Most were men who had been arrested for substance abuse charges. They were harmless enough, although some went in and out of prison frequently due to their inability to kick the habit. Abby was polite to them but kept her distance. In the past, several had given her lecherous looks, and a few had even grabbed at her ass. Fortunately, Paul was there to make sure they kept in line.

Paul was a manager for the Catholic Charities. He was a quiet man in his early forties, and he took his job seriously. He liked to start off each volunteer session with a quick prayer, and Abby found that endearing. She often saw him at an early morning weekday mass, and the two shared a common love of Father Daniel.

She quickly spotted him over by the loading bay. He was wearing an old t-shirt with stains, khaki pants that were frayed at the bottom, and scuffed tennis shoes. Paul was even more helpless with fashion than Abby, but he didn't care. He was one of those strange men that didn't really fit in the modern world. And yet, he had a compassionate soul that folks responded to. He gave Abby a shaky wave when he saw her and looked back down at his spreadsheet. She noticed his dark-rimmed glasses were dirty.

"Heh, Paul. You seem to be stressing. What's going on?"

He looked back up. "Hi, Abby. I just got the printout of what the food bank is bringing us. Their supplies are running low. We're going to be short on milk, eggs, and meat again."

Abby nodded. The food donations were hit or miss at best, and they never knew what they would get in their share of the handouts. Lately, they seemed to be short on the essentials, which was worrisome. This pantry fed thousands of people in the Tremont, Ohio City, and downtown Cleveland area. Many of them were children.

Abby patted his arm. "The holidays are coming. You know the donations will start to pick up. If it's really bad, I'm more than willing to write a check or buy some things."

Paul smiled at her. "Thanks, Abby, but you can't bail us out all the time. It's sweet of you to offer, though. You're right. The holidays should kick in the good stuff soon."

As they spoke, they heard the beep of the truck backing in. Paul took over and organized the troops. He had them say a quick Our Father, blessed the food, and then started flitting around telling the volunteers what to do. He reminded her of an anxious bird. Paul had the bigger men pull the heavy items out and place them by the shelves. The remaining volunteers were to cut open the plastic wrap, pull out the items, and stack them on the shelves. They all wore protective gloves, and Abby felt the usual thrill of organizing her section. Today she would be stocking canned soup and boxes of macaroni and cheese.

She worked quietly, and the men kept bringing her more items to stock. A few tried to strike up an awkward conversation with her, but she would thank them sweetly and go right back to her work. She took a break after an hour and noticed Paul hovering around her. She frowned as she headed to the kitchen area to pour herself a cup of coffee.

Paul followed her into the kitchen, and she wondered if he needed that donation after all.

They stood by the sink and drank their coffee in silence. Occasionally a volunteer would come and ask Paul where to put an item. He answered their questions like a seasoned pro and continued to sip his coffee. Abby was comfortable in the silence and glanced out the back window. It looked like it was going to snow. They really hadn't had much yet for a November in Cleveland. She commented on it to Paul, and when she turned she noticed he was staring at her intently.

"Abby, I've been meaning to ask. How old are you?"

She blinked in surprise. "I'll be thirty soon."

He nodded. "Ah, the thirties. Are you ready for that?"

She grinned. "I guess so. It's not like I have a choice."

He nodded again but wasn't looking at her, and Abby felt uncomfortable. He continued. "You know, I'm forty-one. It seems like just yesterday I was turning thirty myself."

She didn't know what to say, so she simply said, "Oh."

Paul was stroking his beard. "It's not often you find someone your age with a compassion for people and a strong Christian faith."

Abby shrugged. "I'm not sure I would categorize myself as having a strong faith."

He disagreed. "No, you're wrong. You volunteer, and go to church all the time, and you're sweet to the clients when they come in to pick up food. That is very rare in a single young woman." He had emphasized the last three words.

She needed to nip this in the bud. "Well thanks, Paul. I'd better get back to work," and she hurried out of the kitchen.

Abby worked for another hour, and several times she caught Paul staring at her with an amorous look on his face. When the food was stocked, she snuck out before he noticed her leaving.

***

Abby got home later that night and flopped down on the couch. She had eaten a quick salad from Panera and had put in several good hours of writing at the coffee shop. Now she was in a comfortable pair of flannel pajamas and snuggled under her mom's quilt. It was getting cold out, and there was a light snow falling. She surfed the channels on her television and settled in for the night.

Her phone chirped with an incoming text. Abby glared at the phone but then grabbed it from the coffee table to see who it was. She sat upright when she saw it was from Dr. Turov.

Mrs. Shea, don't forget to bring my coat tomorrow.

He had included a winking smiley face.

She groaned. She had forgotten about the intense doctor. She fired off a quick response.

No worries. Your coat will safely make the journey. Just in time for the snow.

His response was just as quick.

Thank you. See you tomorrow.

She noted he didn't use the 'cu' abbreviation. Why did that not surprise her?

Abby reluctantly got up from the couch and went in search of his coat. She found it hanging in her hallway closet. When she pulled it out, she noticed it still had the faint smell of him. She pressed it to her nose and breathed in deeply. Then she carefully set it on the kitchen counter next to her purse and keys. There was no way she was going to give him the satisfaction of forgetting the damn thing. She had the distinct feeling he had been laughing at her when he told her not to forget.

Abby was just settling back into the couch when her phone started ringing. It was Rachel.

"Heh, toots. What are you doing?"

Abby yawned. "Being lazy. Just sitting on the couch doing nothing."

Rachel laughed. "It's a good night for it. Heh, I wanted to run something by you."

Abby knew that tone of voice. Rachel was being all business-like. "Uh oh. What are you up to?"

Rachel tried to sound innocent. "Me? Nothing. It's actually Joel you should be mad at. He met some guy at work he thinks might be good for you. He wants to know if we can fix you guys up on a blind date. We could make it a double-date if you're more comfortable with that," she added.

Abby blew out her breath. "I knew it! I knew you guys were going to go there. Why are you so concerned about my dating status?"

Rachel calmly replied, "Because we love you. It's not healthy to be single this long. You need to get back out there."

Abby whined, "There's no way I'm going on a blind date, Rach, and you know it. It's bad enough guys are crawling out of the woodwork to ask me out, and now I have to worry about you two setting me up as well."

"Whoa! This is news. Who is asking you out?"

Abby groaned. She hadn't meant to tell her friends. They would push her to say yes. "No one really. Just a guy I see at the pool. Plus, there's Paul at the food pantry. He was sniffing around today. Oh, and I think this doctor from the clinic might be interested too. But he freaks me out. Actually, they all freak me out!" she ended on a wail.

Rachel was ecstatic. "Well, why didn't you tell us? This is excellent news."

She was interrupted by Joel in the background. Abby could faintly hear him asking where his book was. She used that as an excuse to get off the phone.

"Sounds like you're busy, Rach. I'll talk to you later."

"Oh, you're not getting off the hook that easy. I'll see you at the musical on Saturday. We will discuss this in more detail then."

Abby sighed as she clicked off. The last thing she wanted to do was discuss this with anyone. She hated being single, and she hated that Nate had died. But she knew this was her life now. Maybe she should consider a date. The thought made her feel physically ill.

***

It was Friday afternoon, and Abby was back at the reception desk of hospice. She had Dr. Turov's jacket safely hung up in the volunteer office, but she had yet to see the man. It was already going on three p.m., and she wondered if he had forgotten. It bothered her she cared.

Fifteen minutes later and she was interrupted from her book by a deep Russian voice.

"Mrs. Shea. How are you?"

He was standing there in his scrubs, and he wore a funny pair of eyeglasses around his neck. His hair was mussed, and he looked exhausted.

"Hi. I'm good. How are you?" she asked.

He pulled up a chair and sat down next to her. "I'm tired. It's been a long week. I'm glad the weekend is here."

She nodded at him sympathetically. Then she honed in on the glasses.

"That's a fancy pair of spectacles you've got there, doctor," she teased.

He grinned as he looked down. "I forgot to take them off. They're called loupes, and they help me to see tiny blood vessels better."

Abby looked at them curiously. "Cool. So you wear those when you're doing a surgery?"

He nodded and pulled them from around his neck. "You want to try them?"

She curiously took the glasses from him. Then she put them on and tried to look through them.

Victor laughed because they were way too big for her head. He gently reached over and tightened the ends, and he noticed how soft her hair was. Then he sat back and watched. She looked ridiculous and adorable in the glasses. She was holding up her book and trying to read the words through the lenses.

"They take practice to get used to," he explained.

They were both laughing when Mrs. Turner interrupted them. She did not look happy. "Dr. Turov, you're here again. Was there something I could help you with?"

Victor looked at the older woman in surprise. "No. I'm just here to visit Mrs. Shea."

Mrs. Turner's glance narrowed. "We don't really encourage our volunteers to have visitors while they're working, Dr. Turov."

"Really? I would think you would do your best to keep your volunteers happy, Mrs. Turner. After all, they are helping you out for free." There was a challenge in his voice, and the two stared at each other.

Abby was getting uncomfortable. She stood up and explained to the volunteer coordinator she had the doctor's jacket. She excused herself and went to get it. While she was gone, Victor calmly stared down Mrs. Turner. Neither one said a word, but he could tell she was uncomfortable. She finally spoke as she pointed toward the computer Abby used to check in visitors.

"That has our entire list of patients on it including their diagnoses. It is confidential information, doctor. Surely you can understand why we need to protect that."

Victor gave her a withering look. "But of course, Mrs. Turner. I would hope you would trust I have no interest in violating that confidentiality. I am, after all, a chief of surgery at this hospital." He was putting her in her place, and she knew it.

Just then Abby returned with his jacket. She quietly handed it to him and then pulled off the loupes and passed them back as well.

Mrs. Turner noticed the exchange but didn't comment. Instead, she said, "Well I had best get back to my work. It was nice to see you again, Dr. Turov." She walked away with a stiff posture, and there was no sincerity in her voice.

Abby watched her go and then turned to give Victor a bemused look. "What the heck was that about?" she asked.

Victor shook his head. "I believe Nurse Ratchet does not care for me." Then he frowned. "I wonder why?"

Abby shrugged. "Well, don't take it personally. She's kind of like that to everyone. She takes her job very seriously."

Victor stood up. "It's okay. I tend to have that effect on people." He grasped Abby's hand and gave it a small squeeze. "As long as you don't despise me, then we're good." He released her hand and smiled as he put the jacket on. As he walked toward the exit he called out, "Until we meet again."

Abby watched him go. The man always left her so damn unsettled. She sighed and played with a strand of her hair. She had under an hour to go, but she didn't want to read anymore. The place was slow, and she was looking forward to heading home. Mrs. Turner interrupted her thoughts.

"Mrs. Shea, can I please speak to you for a moment?"

"Sure, Mrs. Turner. What's up?"

"I don't mean to pry, but I wanted to ask you about Dr. Turov."

Abby interrupted her. "I know you don't like us to have visitors. He was just stopping in to get his coat. He usually doesn't stay long..." she ended on a weak note.

Mrs. Turner gave her a reassuring smile. "I really don't mind if you have visitors, Mrs. Shea. I just said that for his benefit."

Abby noted that even now the old woman could not use her first name, and wondered what it was with people and this damn formality lately. She said nothing, though, and waited for Mrs. Turner to go on.

The old woman hesitated. "It's really none of my business, but I wanted to warn you about Dr. Turov. If you two are dating, you need to know he has quite the reputation with women."

Abby raised one eyebrow in interest. "Really? What reputation does he have?"

Mrs. Turner hesitated again. "Well, most would say he doesn't date at all and leads a celibate and private life." She went on, "But I have it on very good authority from one woman that he treats females as second-class citizens. This woman was treated poorly by Dr. Turov before he dumped her completely."

"Okay. Well, thanks for the warning."

The older woman smiled. "I really like you, Mrs. Shea. You're a sweet girl, and I know you've been through a lot. I just don't want you to get hurt." She patted Abby on the arm. "Just be careful."

Mrs. Turner walked away, and Abby was left shaking her head. She had no intention of dating the good doctor, so the point was moot. And yet, she couldn't help but wonder what the hell that was all about.

Chapter Ten

Saturday morning found Abby up bright and early. The snow had given way to a crisp, blue, late autumn day. Abby poked her nose out her open bathroom window and breathed in the heady scent. She loved autumn! She rushed through her morning routine and threw on a pair of jeans, boots, and a green sweater. She worked her hair into a French braid and pulled on her wool jacket. She was heading to the Cleveland Museum of Art. It was one of her favorite places to hang out. She planned to spend the rest of the morning there, and she would grab something to eat at the museum café.

Victor was up early too. He was now well rested and wanted to play. He wondered what Mrs. Shea was up to. The doctor debated if he should try to find her and then gave in to the urge. He flipped open his cell and pulled up the GPS tracking app. He had already entered her cell number into the system and had determined she kept her GPS turned on. Now he punched in a few keys and watched the blip on the map. Mrs. Shea was on the move. She was heading toward University Circle, and he guessed where she was going. Jack's report had said she was an active member of the art museum. He grabbed his keys and headed out the door.

***

It was early, and there was still plenty of parking on the street. Abby parked her car close to the entrance and headed in. She stopped at the counter to grab a flyer on the current exhibit and declined the offer of a headset. Today she intended to wander around the museum and take in her favorites at a leisurely pace. She turned away from the counter and ran smack into Dr. Turov.

He reached out and grabbed her shoulders to steady her feet, and they looked at each other.

"Mrs. Shea, what a pleasant surprise. What are the odds of us running into each other?" He kept his hands on her shoulders and could feel them shaking.

Abby stared up at him and felt a twinge of fear run up her spine. She thought about what Mrs. Turner had said yesterday, and she gave him a cautious look.

"Hi, Dr. Turov. What are you doing here?"

He smiled as he released her shoulders. "I'm here to take in some art, of course. How about you?"

She hesitated. He really did have a handsome and disarming smile. "The same. I'm a member here," she added.

"That's fantastic. I've been thinking about joining. I wasn't sure it would be worth my while. I suspect I don't come as often as you do."

Abby shrugged. "I don't come that often."

Victor looked at her pensively. Then he reached out and softly touched her arm. "Perhaps you can show me around. Come, what is your favorite piece here?"

She looked bemused by his touch but then answered his question without hesitation. "The Heroic Head, of course!"

He raised his eyebrows. "That does sound interesting. Lead on, Mrs. Shea."

Abby silently led him to the stairs and headed up. The doctor followed, and he appreciatively watched her ass sway as she ascended. They passed the baroque exhibit and rounded the corner. There on a landing was a sculpture of a man's head. The features of the face, especially the eyes and cheeks, had been roughly cut and gave the entire piece an emotional and haunted look.

They both stopped and gazed. Victor made a slow circuit around the sides of the head before returning to Abby's grinning side.

"That is something."

She nodded. "I know. I don't know why I love it, but I do!"

"You know they say you can tell a lot about a person by the art they respond to. I wonder what this piece says about you?"

"I'm sure it can't be good."

He grinned. "Perhaps. I have a friend that's a psychiatrist. I'll ask him and let you know what he says." Then he asked, "Tell me, what else do you like here at the museum?"

She thought about it. "I really like the impressionist pieces. Oh, and I like the doors."

Victor nodded and took her hand. It was cool and tiny in his grasp. This time instead of a shock they both felt a warm, tingling sensation.

Abby liked it, but she wasn't going to go there. She pulled her hand away quickly.

They reached the impressionism room and walked around in companionable silence. When they reached the Gardener's House at Antibes piece, she stopped. He watched her and then couldn't resist commenting.

"You really like this."

"I do."

"Why is that?"

She tried to put it into words. "Um, I like the colors. They remind me of words when I'm writing. Plus, the house looks like somewhere I would live, and the city in the background reminds me of Cleveland." She looked away, embarrassed.

He stared at her and smiled. "Those are good reasons."

She couldn't tell if he approved or thought she was an idiot. To change the subject, she asked, "What's your favorite at the museum?"

Victor responded. "I really like the Armor Court. All that metal reminds me of surgical steel, plus the weapons are cool."

She shook her head in amusement. "Typical guy! Did you want to go see them?"

He nodded, and they continued on. They toured all of the second floor and finished up on the first with one of Abby's favorite doors from the late 1400s.

She explained, "I love old doorways. My imagination goes wild with where they might have led." She tried to touch the handle, and an alarm sounded.

Victor grabbed her arm and pulled her away. He laughed, "Are you trying to get us arrested?"

As a retired volunteer rounded the corner, they hurried away. "Sorry. I always want to touch the art. I keep forgetting that's a no-no. My mom was the same way, and we actually got kicked out of a modern art museum once." She looked thoroughly mortified.

He gave her a sly grin. "So you're very tactile?" The comment went right over her head as she continued to put distance between them and the security guard. He continued on a more serious note. "Am I to assume your mom is no longer here?" He knew the answer, but he asked to see her response.

She smiled wistfully. "Yeah. She passed away ten years ago."

Victor nodded. "Mine has been gone for ten years. My dad died when I was still a child."

"Oh! My dad is gone too. We're both orphans!"

They looked at each other.

"It is odd not to have parents, isn't it?"

She nodded.

They had reached the front entrance and stood in front of the upcoming exhibit display. The new work coming in was from Monet, and Abby was looking forward to it. "This one looks interesting," was all she said.

Victor glanced at the posters. "It says here as a member you will get to see the exhibit before anyone else. That should make you happy."

She smiled wistfully. "That's for VIP members. They throw them a special party. I've always wondered what those were like."

"You never know. Maybe you'll get lucky and get to go someday." He was about to invite her to lunch when his pager went off. It was the clinic. He excused himself to make the call.

Abby walked away to give him some privacy. She was getting hungry, and she could smell the aroma of food wafting over from the café. He finished the call and walked toward her.

"I'm sorry, Mrs. Shea. That was work. I have to go in and check on a patient." He made it sound like they were on a date. "I really enjoyed walking around the museum with you. Are you volunteering on Wednesday?"

"Yes. Every Wednesday from one to four." She didn't know why she told him. "I'm sorry about your patient. I hope everything goes well."

He nodded distractedly. "Sure. Sure. This happens on occasion. Hopefully, he will be fine." He started walking toward the exit, and Abby followed.

When they got to the exit, he opened the door and waited for her to walk past. When she stopped, he looked inquisitively at her.

"Aren't you leaving?"

"No. I'm going to stay and have lunch in the café."

Victor frowned. "Oh, I would have liked to have bought your lunch." He reached in his wallet and pulled out some money. "Here. Take this and buy a good meal."

"That's not necessary. I had fun showing you around." She pushed the money away in embarrassment and took a step backward.

Victor's eyes narrowed. He really had a problem with her not letting him pay. But there wasn't much he could do about it now. He put the money back in the wallet and tried to look unconcerned. "Very well, then. I guess I'll see you on Wednesday."

"You will?" she asked with a hint of panic in her voice. "I mean, you're coming back to the hospice again?"

He gave her a wolfish grin. "Yes, I am. I rather like spending time with you. Have a good day, Mrs. Shea," and he departed the building.

Abby watched him leave and then slowly made her way down to the café. She hated to admit it, but she was attracted to him. She briefly flashed back to the first time she had met Nate. He had been super aggressive in his pursuit of her, and she had fled him like she was fleeing the doctor now. But Nate had never made her feel this uncomfortable. There was something off about the good doctor. She entered the café line and tried to forget him.

***

It was nine thirty on Saturday night, and the girls had just left the State Theatre. They had seen *Mamma Mia!*, and Abby had loved it. She had laughed through the entire production and couldn't help but feel joyous afterward. The girls headed over to Parnell's for a drink and were excitedly talking about the Broadway show.

As always, the conversation turned to men. They discussed the actors, which ones were hot, and which ones were gay.

"Seriously," said Lindsay, "I thought the guy who played Skye was kind of a dud."

"Me too," said Abby. "Until he took his shirt off. After that...well... you know...oh my!"

They all started laughing and discussed the merits of each actor.

The girls then hashed out all of their current relationships. They started with Lindsay and Kent. The two were separated and trying to work things out. Kent was a jerk at times, and Lindsay was getting tired of it. Abby noted she ordered her third glass of wine in an hour, and she wondered if her friend was developing a drinking problem. She worried about Lindsay. Kent had always scared her a bit, and she didn't know how her friend could tolerate him.

Then they moved on to Rachel and Joel. Everyone knew Joel was a sweetheart, including Rachel, but that didn't stop her from bitching about him. "The man is like a five-year-old child sometimes. He can't do anything on his own. If I have to pick up one more book or pair of his shoes, I swear I'm going to kill him." They all laughed.

Renee then complained about her grown children. She was older than the rest of them and often assumed the mom role when they got together. Her husband was Don, an amiable but quiet guy. She told them how her twenty-one-year-old daughter had run up her credit card bills so much she had asked for their help. Don had told the girl no, and Renee was upset. Her friends commiserated, as it was a tough decision to make.

The conversation then swung around to Kate. She was divorced and dating. They loved to hear about all of her crazy dates. She told them about the latest fiasco she had endured at a car show. They were all laughing again, and Abby had to excuse herself to use the restroom.

When she returned, she was disturbed to see the conversation had turned to her single status. Usually, they left her out. No one liked to bring up Nate, and they knew she wasn't dating. But Rachel wasn't letting her off the hook this time. "Like I was saying, Abs needs to get out there and start dating. Joel found her a blind date."

The girls squealed in delight, and Abby sighed.

"He's in the engineering department, so he's probably a nerd, but Joel said he's good-looking," said Rachel.

Lindsay piped in, "Seriously, why is Joel checking out dudes at work?"

Abby interrupted them. "There is no way I am going on a blind date. I mean, come on!"

Rachel chided her. "If not a blind date, then you need to pick one of your many suitors and give it a whirl."

The girls cheered in excitement, and Renee asked, "Abs, you have suitors? You need to spill, woman!"

Abby sighed. "Yes. I apparently have a neon sign flashing that says I'm a pathetic loser. So now these guys are circling around, and I'm not interested in any of them."

Kate piped in, "Oh no you don't. Tell us about each one, and we'll help you pick your prince charming."

Abby hesitated, but they weren't going to let her off the hook. She told them about Brett, Paul, and Dr. Turov. They listened intently and asked questions.

When she was done, Lindsay summed it up for them. "So basically we have bachelor number one, a muscular stud that shares our dear friend's interest in swimming. Then there's bachelor number two, an older and serious gentleman with strong faith and zero fashion sense. Finally, we have bachelor number three, an intense Russian doctor that likes art."

Kate shouted out, "Go for bachelor number one. He has a hot bod, and that will help if he has the personality of a stick."

Rachel disagreed. "No. No. Abs needs a nice guy. I say she gives the Catholic nerd a try. They can help the poor and fall in love while doing their charity work together."

Abby shook her head as they continued to debate the merits of each one. She was surprised no one was going for the doctor, but they all worked in the medical field and had dealt with plenty of cantankerous physicians. In truth, if she had to choose, she would pick Dr. Turov, but she wasn't going to tell them that. She really didn't want to date anyone. Nate had only died two years ago, and she was just not ready to move on. But she enjoyed listening to their hysterical debate.

Finally, after a long discussion, a slightly tipsy vote was taken. The winner was bachelor number one, Brett. Abby laughed and explained, "Well that's good. He actually thinks we're going out in a week or two anyway."

The girls cheered. "Now we just have to get her to pull the trigger," said Rachel. "Promise me if he asks you out again you'll go. Just taking that little step will do wonders for you."

They all agreed, and Abby found herself promising them. She realized she was now going to have to go out with Brett, and the thought terrified her. She tried to tell herself she could handle one measly date, but it wasn't helping.

It was getting late, and the girls were ready to head home. Abby pulled out her phone and ordered an Uber. Her friends all lived in the suburbs and would be sharing a cab home. Her ride arrived before theirs, and she hugged them all before hopping in the car. She smiled as the driver took her home. As usual, it had been a hysterical night out with the girls.

Chapter Eleven

On Wednesday morning Abby went for a swim at the Y. Brett had been leaving when she arrived, and he nervously asked how her schedule was going. In a rare moment of caprice, she told him things were less busy. He looked relieved and quickly asked her out. The two agreed to meet on Friday night at the House of Blues. Brett had tried to get her to agree to let him pick her up, but she had refused. It had been years since she dated, but she clearly remembered it wasn't wise to let a guy pick you up at your house. Her father had taught her that. Her mom had taught her not to shave her legs before a first date. That way things wouldn't go too far. Abby grinned as she remembered the sage advice from her folks.

Abby pulled into her garage and headed inside. She had time before she had to leave for hospice. She grabbed a quick shower and spent extra time on her hair and clothes. She tried to pretend she was doing it because she was in the mood. In reality, she was anticipating seeing Dr. Turov and wanted to look good. She pulled on a soft tunic dress in warm autumn colors, a pair of brown tights, and knee-high brown suede boots. She let her hair hang down past her shoulders and added some curls to give it more bounce. She even put on a bit of eyeshadow and mascara, something she never did, and looked at herself critically in the mirror. She had been going for sophisticated and older-looking, but what she saw was a skinny girl with big green eyes. She sighed. It would have to do.

A glance at the clock told her she still had time before she had to leave. Abby was getting antsy. She had already had two cups of coffee, but she decided to swing through the Starbucks drive-through.

As luck would have it, the Starbucks drive-through was out of order. She would have to go inside if she wanted a beverage. Abby debated.

It was cold out, and she had left her coat at home. She decided to grab a coffee at the clinic instead.

Fifteen minutes later she had parked and headed into the building. She made her way to the coffee shop and stood in line. She still had forty-five minutes until she had to start volunteering. When it was her turn to order, she started to ask for her usual latte. Then she heard a familiar voice behind her.

"Mrs. Shea. What perfect timing. I was coming to pick you up a latte before I headed for the hospice."

Abby turned and smiled at him. "Hi, Dr. Turov. Guess I beat you to it. What would you like?"

He ordered a large black coffee and tried to hand the cashier some money. Abby pushed his hand away and gave the cashier her Starbuck's card. The two struggled while the employee watched them with humor. Finally, the cashier took Dr. Turov's money and gave Abby an apologetic shrug.

She scowled at him, but the doctor just laughed. "When are you going to learn that I must pay?" As she rolled her eyes, he took his coffee and went to add some cinnamon. "Do we have time to sit here, or do you need to get to the desk?"

She glanced at her watch. "We have time." She waited patiently for her latte and tried to ignore him. The doctor grabbed a table and sat down. He crossed his legs and watched Abby appreciatively. Her hair looked lovely, and those boots were doing glorious things to his groin area. He wanted to see her in nothing but those boots, with her hair hanging down her back.

Abby finally had her latte and went to join him at the table. She smiled shyly and noted his dress shirt and tie. "No surgeries today?"

He shook his head. "No. Today I have regular office hours."

"Do you alternate between the two?"

"I usually do procedures three days a week, and the other two are spent seeing patients in my office. The days rotate, and I also do rounds at the hospital. Sometimes on weekends."

"It sounds exhausting," said Abby.

He thought about it. "Well, it can be. But usually, I'm so busy I don't notice."

She nodded. "Busy is good."

He looked at her speculatively. She wasn't making eye contact, and he noticed her hands were trembling.

Abby was feeling odd. She felt like the blood was leaving her head, and her hands were shaking uncontrollably. That happened sometimes, but it seemed to be worse than usual. She tucked her hands under her legs in embarrassment and hoped he hadn't noticed.

He had. He reached out and gently pulled her hand out from under the table. He put his fingers on her wrist and looked at his watch. He was checking her pulse and was stunned to see it was 125 beats per minute. "Your heart rate is through the roof!" He grabbed her latte and threw it in the trash can.

"Heh! I wasn't done with that."

"How many coffees have you had today?" His tone was curt.

She thought about it. "This is my third. But it's no big deal. Sometimes my hands shake. My dad had the same problem."

"125 beats per minute is a very big deal, especially for someone your age. And did your dad by chance have heart disease?"

She looked away. "Well, yes. But he smoked and was overweight."

Victor sighed. "Mrs. Shea. This is serious. We need to get to the bottom of this and why it's happening. You're going to have to come to my office for some tests."

"What? Oh, no. If you're that worried about it I can see my primary doctor. She's well aware of the problem..." she tapered off.

He honed in immediately. "So this is something you've been dealing with for a while. Why didn't you tell me? I'm a heart doctor. This is what I do!"

She gave him an exasperated look. "You're a heart surgeon. This hardly qualifies as something serious enough for that. Plus, I'm not going to ask a complete stranger, heh, why don't you take a look at my heart?"

Victor was starting to get angry. "We are hardly strangers." He stood up and took her arm. His expression left no room for argument. "Let me walk you to the hospice. I'll find room in my schedule to see you after you finish your shift."

She started to argue, and he cut her off. "I will drag you there if I have to!" Then he spoke more gently, "I'm just going to run a few quick tests. It should only take fifteen to twenty minutes. I won't even bill your insurance, and I'll send the results to your primary." He stopped and looked at her. "Please. Otherwise, I will worry."

Abby silently nodded. They walked to the hospice entrance, and he let go. As she greeted the volunteer she was replacing, Victor started to walk away. He turned and pointedly said, "I'll see you soon."

Abby clasped her hands in frustration. Somehow she had allowed him to talk her into a medical appointment. Then she had a horrible thought. What if he's going to do the tests himself? She had undergone several heart tests in the past. They all involved a bare chest. She flushed as she thought about him seeing her naked. Abby's instinct kicked in, and she immediately went into escape mode. She was going to have to sneak out of there without him knowing. She didn't care what he said, they were in fact strangers, and to hell if he didn't like it. She called Mrs. Turner and said she had to leave early.

***

Victor walked into his office, and Rebekeh met him at the door. She handed him patient charts and told him who was in each examining room. He cut her off. "Who's working the labs this afternoon?"

Rebekeh stuttered. "Amanda."

He nodded. "Who's the medical assistant?"

"That would be Jennifer. Why?"

"I have a new patient coming in at four. I want Amanda to run an EKG on her and do an ultrasound. Make it work with her schedule." As he walked down the hall he ordered, "And send Jennifer to see me as soon as possible."

He disappeared into the first examining room, and Rebekeh was left stunned. She went back to her desk and looked at the schedule. She could shuffle around a few people, and Amanda should have no problem with the extra tests. But who was the patient? She had never seen her boss act this out of character before. When Amanda walked up she told her about his behavior. The two quietly speculated, and soon the entire staff was getting in on the conversation. They were wondering if it was a famous person, and they debated which actors might have heart issues.

When Jennifer rounded the corner, Rebekeh told her to go see the doctor right away. The poor girl had a deer-in-the-headlights look until the office manager reassured her she had done nothing wrong. They heard the examining room open, and Jennifer scurried down the hallway. They could hear them talking, and then the doctor headed into another room.

Jennifer returned to the front and grabbed a new patient kit. She hurriedly whispered to everyone he was sending her down to the hospice to get a chart started on a volunteer there named Mrs. Shea. As she headed out, the rest of the staff tried to find out who the mystery woman was. When Burt was freed up from the examining rooms, they filled him in as well. Burt was the nurse on staff and a bigger gossip than all of them put together. He was less afraid of Dr. Turov than the rest of them too, and they knew he would try to get information out of the physician.

Abby was quietly putting together packets at her desk when Jennifer arrived. She looked up and smiled at the young girl. "How can I help you?"

"I'm looking for a Mrs. Shea," came the hesitant reply.

"Oh, that's me," Abby smiled.

Jennifer was surprised. She had been expecting an older woman. "Oh. Well, hi. My name is Jennifer, and I work for Dr. Turov. He sent me down to get your medical chart started."

Abby hadn't anticipated this. She thought quickly. "Oh, I can't really do that now." She pointed at the packet material. "I'm really busy."

Jennifer's heart sank. "Oh, please. He will be so mad if I come back empty-handed. I promise it won't take long. And you can keep doing your work while I take down your information." She gave Abby a pleading look.

It would appear she wasn't the only one Dr. Turov intimidated, and this poor girl had to work with the man. Abby reluctantly agreed. "Oh, okay. I don't want to get you in trouble."

Jennifer smiled in relief and pulled out an iPad. "Thank you. We do everything electronically which makes it a lot easier." She started asking for basic information like address, birthdate, and allergies. Abby suddenly realized he would now have access to her private information. It was like playing into a stalker's hands.

While Jennifer asked questions, Abby went back to putting together packets. At one point Jennifer asked her to sign a consent form.

"What's this for?"

"This allows us to get your medical records from your primary doctor. It also allows us to bill your insurance company, but Dr. Turov said we wouldn't be doing that with you." She looked at Abby inquisitively.

Abby sighed. She signed the form with her finger and wondered what would be in her primary doctor's file. She knew they had run heart tests on her in the past. She supposed he should have that information.

Next, Jennifer pulled out some basic medical equipment. She took Abby's blood pressure, temperature, and pulse rate. "Oh, that's rather high."

Abby muttered. "That's why Dr. Dictator wants to see me."

Jennifer giggled. "You know that nickname?"

"Yep. His reputation is legendary." Then she looked at the girl curiously. "What's he like to work with?"

Jennifer didn't hesitate. "He's a good boss. He likes things done a specific way, and if you vary from that he gets a little crazy. Sometimes he scares me. But he treats us fairly, and he pays very well." Then she added, "He's very private about his personal life, and he never gets involved in the office gossip. We've only ever met one of his friends, and we don't even know if he's dating anyone." She ended on a questioning note. It was obvious she wanted to know who the volunteer was.

Abby skillfully changed the subject. "Do you know what tests he wants to run?"

Jennifer nodded. "An EKG, ultrasound, and maybe a blood test. They're easy unless you're afraid of needles."

"No. Needles don't bother me. But the other two…he's not going to do them is he?"

Jennifer reassured her. "No. Amanda does our lab tests. She's nice. You'll like her. The doctor will just review the results and then probably listen to your heart." She kindly added, "He'll be able to do that through your dress."

Abby wondered if her nervousness was that obvious.

Once they were done, Jennifer got ready to leave. "Thanks again for letting me do this. It will speed things up when you come down." Then she added, "Oh, that reminds me. Dr. Turov is sending me back to pick you up at four. That way you won't have to find the office on your own." She gave an apologetic smile. "He said you might try to sneak out, and he wants to prevent that. Please don't sneak out. He'll be a bear to work with if you do."

Abby was stunned, but then she laughed out loud. "Oh dear. Okay. I guess I'll be here when you come back. I don't want you to have to deal with Dr. Angry." They gave each other knowing smiles, and Jennifer departed.

When she got back to the office, Jennifer quickly whispered what she had learned about Abby. "She's really young and really pretty." They speculated on whether the two were dating, which fueled the gossip even more. They had never seen the good doctor in a relationship before.

Rebekeh nipped the gossip. They were, after all, busy on this Wednesday afternoon. She took Abby's chart and called up the primary's office. After a brief conversation with the nurse, and then emailing the consent form, she had Mrs. Shea's medical record added to the chart. This would please Dr. Turov to no end, and Rebekeh was all about keeping the doctor happy.

Victor walked his latest patient to the front and asked Rebekeh to schedule his surgery. She agreed and wordlessly handed him Abby's medical chart. He smiled when he saw it. He had a few minutes before his next patient, and he leafed through the chart. He realized he now had the one medical record Jack couldn't get. That made him smile more broadly. Victor noted she'd had an EKG, ultrasound, and stress test done in the past. They had all come back negative, and the primary had recommended medication. The patient had refused.

Victor pursed his lips in anger that the primary had even thought of using a drug. It was premature without first finding the cause of the problem. He was glad Mrs. Shea had refused, but it meant she had been walking around with an elevated heart rate for quite some time. Victor felt the familiar anxiety coming on, but he knew she would be in later for tests. It would have to do.

He saw Jennifer walking past and motioned her into his office. "How did it go with Mrs. Shea?"

"It went well, doctor. She's very sweet."

"Did she give you a hard time?"

Jennifer hesitated. "A little."

"Mmm hmm. And did you lay on the guilt like I told you to?"

"Yes. And you were right. It worked like a charm."

Victor smiled. "I knew it would. You'd best head back down there around three thirty. If she's not ready to go, you can just wait there until she is. I don't want her sneaking out the door while we're not looking."

Chapter Twelve

Abby had no intention of leaving, even though every bone in her body was screaming to run. She had made a promise, and so she stayed.

At three thirty Jennifer strolled in looking apologetic. Abby raised her eyebrows in surprise.

"I'm sorry, Mrs. Shea. Dr. Turov told me to come down early."

"Please. Call me Abby. He's not very trusting is he?"

"He's just worried about you."

"I'm sure it's nothing. Let me grab my purse, and then we can go."

The two headed down the hallway. When they reached his office, Abby looked around. She had seen it once before, but then it had been dark and she had refused to walk past the door. Now she took a good look around. It was your typical doctor's office. There was a glass partition at the front, and the window was rolled back. To her right was a large waiting room with several older and frail looking people. Abby felt guilty looking at them. She had no right being here, and she hoped they didn't have to wait longer because of her.

Jennifer ushered Abby into the back, and she passed the main office where the patient charts and staff were. There were several of them standing in there, and they were all openly staring.

Jennifer stopped in front of a scale and had Abby hop on. She weighed in at 127 pounds. Then they headed around the corner and into a back room. There was a middle-aged woman in there and two carts with fancy equipment on them.

"You must be Amanda. I'm Abby." She extended her arm to shake the woman's hand.

Amanda smiled at her in greeting. "It's nice to meet you, Abby. Dr. Turov said you've had these tests before, but let me refresh your memory on what we're going to do."

She shut the door and had Abby take off her shirt and bra and lie on the table. Then she chatted away as she hooked up the leads for the EKG. "I like to do this one first. The ultrasound is goopy, and it can mess with the stickers."

Abby nodded and tried not to look embarrassed. She hated all things medical. She listened to Amanda drone on and let her mind wander. Fifteen minutes later and they were done. Abby got dressed again while Amanda printed off the reports.

"How does it look?" Abby asked.

Amanda could tell she was anxious. "I'm not allowed to say anything, so please don't tell the doctor I did. But it looks pretty normal to me. Except for the heart rate. But he's the expert."

Abby sighed in relief. She knew she would be fine, but it was still scary. "Thanks for telling me. And don't worry, my lips are sealed."

Amanda finished up and led Abby out of the room. They went back down the hall, and she had the young woman sit on a table in an examining room. "I'm going to give him the results. He'll take a look at them and then come in to listen to your heart. It might be a while depending on who else he's seeing. Do you want a magazine to look at?"

Abby smiled and pulled a paperback out of her purse. "No need. I always have something with me to read. Thanks for doing the tests. It was nice meeting you."

Amanda smiled back. "It was nice meeting you too. Do you mind if I ask how Dr. Turov came to worry so much about your heart rate?" She knew she was overstepping her bounds, but they were all dying to know, and the girl seemed so easygoing.

"Sure. We were having coffee at Starbucks, and my hands started to shake. He checked my pulse, and here we are."

"Oh," was all Amanda said. "Well good luck. He should be with you soon." She shut the door and hurried up to the front. "Holy shit," she announced to the staff. "They were having coffee. I think Dr. Turov was on a date!" They all looked at each other in amazement.

Meanwhile, Victor was looking over her test results. Everything looked normal. It certainly didn't explain her tachycardia. He would have to do some more digging. He grabbed Burt and headed to the examining room. He knocked on the door and then walked in.

Abby was sitting on the table with her legs crossed. She had a book in one hand, and she was nervously twisting a strand of her hair with the other. She looked so sweet and beautiful. It was startling to see her in this environment, and he had to remind himself to be professional.

He introduced Burt. "This is my nurse. If you would prefer, I can get a woman to sit in while I listen to your heart."

Abby smiled at Burt and said hello. "No. I'm sure this will be fine."

Burt gave her a winning smile and commented, "Look at you, girl, rocking those Jimmy Choo boots in Cleveland!"

Abby looked down at her boots. "Jimmy Choo?"

Burt fake fanned his face. "Yes. You know, the designer? I would recognize a pair anywhere."

Abby shrugged. "Oh. They could be. My friend, Rachel, gave them to me. She's really into fashion."

Burt wasn't letting it go. "A friend who gives away Jimmy Choos in mint condition? How do I meet her?"

Abby giggled, and Dr. Turov scolded the nurse. "Let's try to keep it professional, Burt." Then he pulled out his stethoscope. "Mrs. Shea, I'm going to listen to your heart." Before he started, he muttered, "Those *are* nice boots."

Abby and Burt burst out laughing, and the doctor shushed them. Then he started on her back and had her breathe in and out deeply. When he moved to the front, Abby turned her head away and tried not to look embarrassed. Burt was in her line of sight, and he was making funny faces at her. It helped.

The doctor leaned in and listened more intently. Then he gently slid his hand under the V-neck of her dress. He listened some more and kept moving the stethoscope around her left breast. He was so close she could smell him. It was the same scent that was on his jacket—some kind of faint cologne and pure man. Abby could feel her cheeks getting red and hoped no one noticed. She was thankful she had worn a pretty white lace bra. She was hanging in there until he hooked the cup of the bra with his left finger and slid the stethoscope underneath with his right.

Victor noticed her heart rate jump when he did that and smiled faintly. He was focused on listening to her heart, though, and every now and then he was hearing a faint click. He moved the stethoscope around and finally settled in on the underside of her breast. He said to himself, "Right there." He stepped back and pulled the stethoscope out. Then he ran it quickly over her carotids to make sure they sounded okay. When he was done he gave her a reassuring smile.

"Did you find something, doctor?" asked a surprised Burt.

Victor nodded. "Yes. Mrs. Shea, your tests came back normal, but I can hear a very faint click on the second part of your heartbeat."

"A click?" Now he had her attention.

He patted her arm. "Yes, a click. Some would call it a murmur. It's actually quite common. It usually means one of your valves isn't closing all the way. The click is blood backing up in the chamber. I would guess it's your mitral valve. A lot of people are born with mitral issues."

Abby pressed her lips together. "So is it something I have to worry about? And would that explain the fast heart rate?"

He thought about her questions. "It's not something you have to worry about now. When you get older you may need a new valve. But that's a good thirty or forty years in the future." He went on, "It doesn't really explain the tachycardia, though. Tell me, how much coffee do you drink again?"

She explained, "Usually only one or two cups."

"Any other stimulants…pop, tea, chocolate, energy drinks?"

"Not really. Well, sometimes chocolate."

He frowned. "What about drugs?"

"Drugs?"

"You know—medications, marijuana, cocaine?"

Abby raised one eyebrow in disgust. "Hardly."

He was relieved at the prompt and negative response. "What about anxiety. Do you have any social anxiety, panic attacks, phobias?"

She shook her head.

"Chronic infections, gastritis, stomach issues?"

She shook her head again.

"How much water do you drink? Are you staying hydrated?"

Abby shrugged. "I think so." She reminded him, "My dad used to get this too. Maybe it's genetic."

Victor thought about it. "Maybe. What kind of heart disease did your dad have?"

"He had bypass surgery for blocked arteries. He also had high blood pressure." She knew hers was super low.

Victor sighed. "I guess this is something we're going to have to keep an eye on. I will follow up with your primary. I want her to put you on a heart monitor for a few days, just to be safe, and maybe we'll have her run another stress test." He helped Abby off the table and placed his hands on her shoulders. "In the meantime, you're going to have to be careful. That means no strenuous activity and no caffeine of any kind. No coffee, pop, tea, energy drinks, or chocolate. You think you can do that?" He looked at her sternly.

"No coffee at all? Not even one cup in the morning?"

"None," was the emphatic reply. Burt watched in amazement as the doctor tightened his grip and stared down at her.

Abby turned her head to Burt and joked. "Can you believe this man is telling a woman not to drink coffee or eat chocolate? That could make a girl downright homicidal."

Victor grinned and turned his head to Burt as well. "She *is* rather good at killing people."

Burt looked back and forth between the two of them. He had no idea what they were talking about, but the chemistry they shared was obvious. He backed out of the room, and they followed. Victor walked her up front and spoke to Rebekeh. "I'm going to walk Mrs. Shea to her car. How are we doing on time?"

"We're actually in good shape. It's snowing like crazy out, and a lot of patients have canceled." She smiled at Abby. "You've got time."

"Good." He looked at Abby. "Let me get my coat."

When he left, she turned to the office manager. "Let me give you my insurance card. It will cover the visit, I'm sure."

Rebekeh refused and pushed the card away. "No. He will kill me if I bill your insurance. Just let him do this. Please."

Abby was confused, but she put her card away.

Victor reappeared, and they headed out the door. "I'll be back shortly," was all he said.

As they walked, Abby turned to go right. Victor grabbed her arm and pulled her to the left. "You really have no sense of direction, do you?"

"Well, you can't blame me. This place is friggin' big!"

They continued on, and Victor halted at the entrance to the hospice. "Don't you need to get your coat?"

She didn't look at him. "Well, I possibly left that at home."

He rubbed his face in disbelief. "I see. Personal health and safety is a real issue for you, isn't it Mrs. Shea?" He pulled off his coat and wrapped it around her. He held the two ends at her neck and stared down. "That is going to need to change."

Abby met his gaze defiantly. "Well, being bossy seems to be a real issue for you, Dr. Turov."

He smirked. "You don't know the half of it. You would do well to listen to me. If I catch you drinking coffee, there will be hell to pay."

Her eyes got big. Somehow he had maneuvered her up against the wall, and he was still holding the coat at her neck. She wondered how he knew.

As if reading her thoughts, he said, "I've been a doctor a long time. I can tell when a patient has no intention of following my orders."

Now she was getting annoyed. "You don't know if coffee is causing this. I could drink a cup, see how my heart rate is, and go from there."

It was Victor's turn to be annoyed. He leaned in closer. "Who is the doctor here?!" His voice was tight and furious.

Abby shrunk back against the wall. "You are," she whispered.

"Good. I would suggest you remember that!" He hadn't meant to be so stern, but the woman was really pissing him off.

She tried to lighten the mood. "Well, I guess I have to add a heart surgeon to my growing list of doctors." She smiled tentatively at him.

He smiled back and then released her. As he stepped away, he shook his head. "No, I am not your doctor. I would much rather be your boyfriend than your doctor. I simply consulted on a case for your primary. Right now all I want to do is kiss you, and that would be very unethical as your doctor."

"Oh." She looked at him in confusion. "Um, I don't really date."

He continued to stare at her.

She looked away and self-consciously explained, "You see, I'm a widow. And Nate—er, my husband—he didn't die that long ago. I'm just not ready to date again..."

She ended on a whisper and peeked up at him.

Victor stared for a few more seconds. Then he sighed. "Perhaps when you're ready, then. I will still see you on Wednesdays." He opened the door and walked her out to the car. The snow was coming down hard. Once she was safely in her car, he headed back in. She wasn't going to make this easy on him, but Victor wasn't going to back down. As he headed inside he passed Mrs. Turner in the entrance of hospice. They nodded at each other, and the old woman looked angry. He idly wondered what that was about, but he was in a hurry to get back to the office and forgot her.

Mrs. Turner had witnessed their entire interaction in the hallway. She couldn't make out what had been said, but the doctor had clearly been angry and was intimidating Abby. He had also touched the poor girl, and that upset the older woman. She knew what she had to do. When Mrs. Turner returned to her office, she picked up her phone and made a call. Dr. Turov needed to learn a lesson.

Chapter Thirteen

It was Thursday morning, and Victor had two surgeries scheduled that day. He had just finished the first one and was taking a break in his office. He had already dictated notes on the surgery. Now he was going through his emails while eating a sandwich.

There was one from Kelly. She was an old girlfriend and worked in the clinic's human resources department. Victor had broken his rule to never get involved with anyone at work. At the time he had been bored, and Kelly had been more than keen. It turned out she was interested in his power and money, but not in him. She obliged his control issues well, but her heart wasn't in it. He had realized that early on and broken it off after only four months. Kelly had been furious.

After the breakup, Victor realized all of his relationships had been just as empty. The women were either in it for his money or his domination over them, and there had never been any true feelings. In the past that hadn't mattered. But more and more he was realizing the old ways were not enough. He needed more than just a plaything he could control. That's why he had not dated anyone since, and that had been over three years ago.

He clicked on the email with disinterest and then sat upright when he realized it was official business. Kelly was formally notifying him someone at the clinic was filing a sexual harassment claim against him. Victor was stunned. He barely even talked to women at work, let alone did anything that could be misconstrued. He wondered if Kelly was playing some kind of game, but she had only made a few attempts to get him back early on. Then she had taken the hint and left him alone.

Victor closed his computer and strode over to the human resources office in another building. Problems needed to be dealt with head-on, and he had time before his next procedure.

Kelly was in her office when he arrived, but she made him wait a good fifteen minutes before seeing him. She had dressed carefully that morning knowing he would show up. The tight animal print dress was low cut and showed off her best feature. It also shirred around the waist, effectively hiding the extra pounds she had put on. She had meticulously applied her makeup, and the efforts made her look at least five years younger than her actual age of forty.

When Victor strode in, she felt her breath catch and her heart beat harder. Damn, but he was good-looking. And the bastard hadn't aged a bit. She knew his career had really taken off, and the clinic kissed his ass to keep him there. But now she had some power over Dr. Turov, and she planned to take advantage of it.

Victor stood over the desk, crossed his arms, and looked down at her. "Who filed the complaint?"

Kelly raised her eyebrows. "Victor, it's been a long time. Please sit down and we can discuss it. I'm sure we can make this go away."

Victor remained standing, but his eyes narrowed. "Miss Pierce, I have to be in surgery in less than an hour. Tell. Me. Now."

Kelly felt the old rush at hearing his Dom voice. God, the things they used to do together. But she was in control now, and she let him know as much.

"Oh no you don't. I'm not your submissive anymore, Dr. Turov. And right now you're in a shitload of trouble. I can help you out of it, but you're going to need to lose the attitude."

Victor remained standing with impassive eyes. "I don't have time for games. Either tell me about the complaint, or I will go over your head."

She looked stunned. "You don't want this getting out. It could ruin your career. I haven't told anyone about it yet, and I won't. But if you take it to my supervisor there's nothing I can do for you."

Victor gave her a thin smile. "You think one sexual harassment complaint is going to ruin my career? Do you have any idea how many perverted doctors there are out there? I see it on a daily basis. And if the clinic is that concerned, there are plenty of other hospitals that would love to have me. Now give me the damn report, or I will leave here and go see Phil."

She realized her plan hadn't worked at all. Kelly reluctantly pulled out the file and handed it to him.

Victor opened it and started reading. He was stunned when he saw the complainant's name, Abigail Shea. He tried to hide his surprise, but Kelly noticed. How could he have misread the situation so completely? He had thought Mrs. Shea was shy but interested. That feeling every time they touched certainly showed there was chemistry between them.

He finished reading and looked at Kelly. "Mrs. Shea is not an employee of the clinic."

"Yes, she is. She volunteers for our hospice, and a volunteer is legally considered an employee."

He nodded while continuing to think. "When did she file the complaint?"

"Late yesterday afternoon."

His eyes narrowed. "And you were the one to take her statement?"

"Yes, I was. God, Victor. She's a child. Have you no morals?"

He didn't reply and was still thinking. "So you met her, then? She filed the complaint in person?"

Kelly hesitated for a second, but Victor caught it. He was a smart man, and he was starting to put together the pieces of the puzzle. He just needed to figure out who had tipped her off about Mrs. Shea.

"Yes, I met her. She's a sweet girl. Did you know she was a widow? And so young."

Victor gave a lascivious smile. "Yes, it was actually one of the things that attracted me to her. But she's not that young. She's almost thirty." Then he cruelly added, "Some women age better than others." He noted Kelly's angry look and set the bait. "I'm also drawn to her beautiful black hair. Have you ever seen hair that black and shiny before?"

Kelly glared at him and patted her own red curls. "Please. That color has to come from a bottle."

Victor was barely listening now. His mind went back to yesterday afternoon, and he thought about what had transpired. Could it have been anyone on his staff? He dismissed them one by one. Then he remembered Mrs. Turner in the hallway and the angry look on her face. That fucking cock-blocking bitch!

Kelly was still droning on. "I think I can appease the girl and make this go away, Victor, but you're going to have to stay away from her."

Victor glanced at his watch and gave Miss Pierce a bored look. "Really? How kind of you. And what is that going to cost me?"

She smiled at him sweetly. "There's no need to be sarcastic. I'm sure we can come to some kind of arrangement."

Victor picked up his phone and found the number. As he hit the call button he gave her a withering look. "That won't be necessary, Miss Pierce. I'm pretty sure I can rectify the situation right now."

She watched in confusion.

Before the line picked up he casually stated, "And by the way, Mrs. Shea has blond hair."

Kelly gasped.

***

Abby saw the call coming in was from Dr. Turov. She hesitated but then realized he was probably checking up on her heart. She picked up with a friendly hello.

"Mrs. Shea. It's Dr. Turov. I was calling to see how you're feeling this morning. No more shaking hands, I hope?"

She reassured him she was fine and thanked him again for yesterday.

"You're very welcome. And I trust you will follow up with your primary and avoid coffee like we discussed?"

"Yes, I will try."

His eyes narrowed. "Good. That's all I can ask. Listen, before I hang up I think you should be aware of something."

She listened as he explained the sexual harassment complaint. By the time he was finished, she was pissed off. "Who would do such a thing?!"

Victor stared at Miss Pierce as he answered. "I'm guessing our Mrs. Turner is behind the complaint." He watched Kelly and knew from her reaction he was correct.

"Why does she dislike you so much? I mean, I know she's an uptight old lady with a stick shoved up her ass, but this is going too far."

Victor grinned. "You do paint a picture. If you wouldn't mind, can you please contact our HR department and clear the matter up? I know you and I have had a few interactions, but I would never want to make you uncomfortable."

Abby didn't hesitate. "No problem. I'll take care of that today. I'm also going to have a word with Nurse Ratchet."

He laughed, and Kelly noticed the warmth in his eyes. "Thank you, Mrs. Shea."

He hung up and stared down at Miss Pierce. "Was this really necessary?"

Kelly glared at him. "Mrs. Turner called me with concerns, and I simply followed up on them."

"No. What you did was lie and take advantage of a situation that fell in your lap. I have half a mind to report this to Phil." Then he looked at her in exasperation. "Why would you do this? We broke up over three years ago."

She looked up at him and tried to flirt. "I haven't found anyone since that meets my needs the way you did. We were so good together. We could be again."

He shook his head in surprise. "I seem to remember you were always complaining about my work schedule and how bored you were. And we weren't really compatible. Hell, the sex wasn't even that great." As he walked out he turned back and gave her a disparaging look. "You're just looking for someone to pay your bills, Miss Pierce. Grow up and take care of yourself!"

Late that afternoon Abby drove over to the clinic. It took her twenty minutes to find the damn human resources department. She had studied the map carefully, but as usual, she had taken a few wrong turns. A kind orderly had shown her the way, and he gave her ass an appreciative glance as she disappeared into the office.

Abby was greeted at the door by a Miss Pierce. She hesitated. She really didn't know how to broach the subject, and the woman was looking at her with an odd expression on her face.

Abby said, "I'm sorry to bother you. It looks like you're getting ready to leave."

Kelly plastered on a fake smile. "That's quite all right. I suspect you are Mrs. Shea? Victor told me you might call or stop by." She emphasized the name, Victor, possessively.

Abby looked at her in confusion. "Um, do you mean Dr. Turov?"

Kelly was shocked to realize the poor girl didn't even know his name. The smile got thinner. "Yes. That's his name."

"Oh," replied Abby. "Well, he told me Mrs. Turner filed a complaint on my behalf. I just wanted to make sure the complaint was withdrawn. I really have no problem with the doctor. He was actually quite kind and took care of a health problem I was having."

"How sweet of him. I'm glad to hear Mrs. Turner overreacted. We don't want any of our employees to feel uncomfortable, even our volunteers," said Kelly.

Abby could sense the woman was angry and decided it was directed toward Mrs. Turner. "Well, she is old and does tend to worry about all her volunteers. Then the complaint will be withdrawn?"

Kelly pulled out a folder and tore it up. "Consider the issue resolved."

Abby beamed at her.

Kelly realized the girl was quite stunning. She would bet her right kidney Mrs. Shea was an innocent and had never encountered a submissive experience in her life. What the hell was Victor thinking? Clearly, he wasn't, and his dick was doing all the talking. The thought made Kelly vindictive.

"I did find the report rather odd." She whispered conspiratorially, "Victor and I used to date. You are hardly his type, and it did make me wonder."

Abby looked unconcerned and instead laughed. "I know, right? He's way too intense for me." She looked at Kelly curiously. "What was he like to date? Just being around him makes me nervous."

"Girl, you don't know the half of it!" said Kelly. "He was so controlling, and not in a good way if you know what I mean."

Abby didn't, but she pretended she did and nodded. Kelly realized the girl was absolutely clueless and explained, "He was lousy in bed and very selfish!"

They both laughed, and all Abby said was, "Men!"

She left the HR office and headed to the hospice. She found Mrs. Turner sitting in her office chatting on the phone. The older woman looked surprised to see her. When she hung up, Abby got right to the point.

"Oh, Mrs. Shea, I'm so sorry. I saw that man with you up against a wall, and it made me so angry."

Abby frowned. Had Dr. Turov had her up against a wall? She had no recollection of that.

"It's not your place to make that call, Mrs. Turner. I was perfectly capable of taking care of myself if the situation warranted it, but it didn't. Dr. Turov actually saw me in his office for free and ruled out serious heart issues."

"Oh, I didn't realize that," said the older woman. "It's just, you're so young, and your husband passed, and I just think you're so sweet and, well, so vulnerable. I thought you would be too afraid to say anything if you were uncomfortable."

Abby shook her head in disbelief.

Mrs. Turner continued, "He really does have such a bad reputation."

Abby cut her off. "Are you talking about the reputation he has with Miss Pierce?"

Mrs. Turner nodded. "Yes. Kelly is my niece."

Abby nodded. That explained a lot. "Has any other woman told you anything bad about Dr. Turov?"

"Well, no, but I trust my niece."

"Sometimes when there's a bad break-up people remember things differently than the way they actually occurred," said Abby.

Mrs. Turner nodded but didn't say anything.

Abby went on. "It doesn't matter now. Just be sure your niece drops the charges." Then she changed the subject. "I'm not going to be able to volunteer here anymore. My schedule is getting busy, and the parking has always been a challenge for me."

Mrs. Turner looked sad. "Oh, Mrs. Shea, I am so sorry. You were such a good volunteer. You will be missed. If you ever want to come back, you can start right up and not have to go through the training again."

"Well, that's good to know. Thank you, Mrs. Turner."

The older woman stood up, and the two hugged.

Abby headed to her car in relief. She hated confrontations, but that one had gone rather well. Sure, she hadn't told the busybody her real reason for quitting. Abby liked to keep her life private, and the old woman had crossed too many boundaries. But it was over, and now she could get back to her writing.

When she got home, she fired off a quick text to Dr. Turov.

Spoke to HR and the case was dropped. Spoke with Nurse Ratchet and quit volunteering for hospice. Your reputation is intact!

His response didn't come for several hours.

Thank you. Sorry to hear about hospice. I will miss our Wednesdays.

Abby read his text several times before deleting it. She hadn't thought about the fact that quitting hospice meant not seeing the doctor anymore. The realization made her sad, but it was probably for the best. She put her phone down without responding. A small voice inside her head pointed out she hadn't deleted his contact information. She ignored the voice.

Chapter Fourteen

Friday night hadn't come soon enough. Victor nursed a glass of bourbon and waited for Yuri to arrive. The two were finally getting together for dinner, and they would have plenty to discuss.

When his door buzzed, Victor threw it open and grinned at his friend.

Yuri took in the glass. "Drinking already, my friend? It must have been a bad week."

They embraced, and Victor waved him into the living room. Yuri walked right past and into the kitchen. He pulled the vodka bottle from the freezer and poured himself a shot. "My week was tough as well." He raised his glass. "To your health."

They both took a drink.

Once Yuri was settled in a chair, he told Victor about work. As a psychiatrist, he saw all kinds of interesting cases, and the job sometimes took an emotional toll. This week he had seen two suicide attempts and admitted six patients for safety reasons. Security had also been called three times when patients had gotten out of control in the emergency room.

Victor shook his head as he listened. He had no idea how Yuri could do that every day. He preferred surgery. He could control so much more of what he did than his friend could at his job. But when they were in med school, Yuri had loved the psychology courses and the psychiatry rotations. Victor had despised them.

"And how was your week? How many patients did you kill?" asked Yuri.

"None, thank you. I'm a damn good surgeon."

"And you have such a modest ego, too."

Victor snorted. Then he told him about his more difficult surgeries. Eventually, they got around to the subject of Kelly and the sexual harassment case.

"I told you not to fuck where you work, but you wouldn't listen to me."

Victor nodded. "I know, I know. I'll never make that mistake again. At least now I have something on the bitch. If she ever pulls a stunt like that again, I have some leverage."

It was Yuri's turn to nod. "And who was the woman she claimed filed the report?"

Victor's eyes lit up. "Ah, Mrs. Shea. I need to tell you about her."

"Mrs?"

Victor waved him off. "Don't get all sanctimonious on me. She's a widow. She volunteers at the clinic in the hospice unit. Well, she did volunteer. After the harassment fiasco, she quit, which is damn inconvenient."

He went on to explain how they had met, the chemistry between them, and the report he'd obtained from Jack. When he told Yuri about tracking her through her cell phone, his friend cut him off.

"Wait. That's stalking, Victor! You've never taken it that far before. And this woman doesn't even sound like a submissive."

Victor grinned. "Oh, she's definitely not."

"What the fuck are you doing messing with her, then?" Yuri was clearly stunned.

Victor stood up to refresh their drinks. He chose his words carefully. "For starters, I can't get her out of my head. This is the first woman I've met where I'm actually attracted to her mind as well as her body. I think I can have a real relationship with her."

His friend didn't say anything for a few minutes. "And will you have a *normal* relationship with her, or will you need to control and punish her?"

Victor handed him the vodka drink. He blew out his breath and rubbed his neck in frustration. "You know I'm going to need control, Yuri. But maybe I can tone it down a bit."

"Perhaps. But why change what you are? There are plenty of willing women out there. I told you I have one for you. Her name is Pamela, and I met her at the club. She is less needy than a lot of them, and I think she would be a good fit."

Victor shook his head. "I'm done doing that, Yuri. I don't want a woman from the club. I don't want or need all those bells and whistles anymore." He pulled out his cell and typed something in.

"Very well, then. You know I'll be there if you need help. Now, where are we going for dinner? I'm starving."

Victor read something off his phone, grinned, and clicked it off.

"How about the House of Blues?"

"Ah, that sounds good. We haven't been to the Foundation Room in a long time."

Victor shook his head. "No. I think we'll eat downstairs for a change."

"Why would we do that when you pay for that expensive membership every year? The food is much better upstairs." Then he stopped. "Wait a minute. You just tracked her to the restaurant, didn't you?"

Victor grinned as he grabbed his coat.

"You are one sick fucker, my friend."

Victor looked nonplussed. "The car is waiting for us. Come now. Don't you want to see what all the fuss is about?"

Yuri had to admit he was intrigued to see the girl that had captured his friend's attention. They headed out the door.

Chapter Fifteen

The restaurant was crowded. Victor walked around twice but could not find her anywhere. He pulled out his phone in confusion, but the blip clearly showed Mrs. Shea was in the building.

"Maybe she's up in the Foundation Room," said Yuri.

Victor thought about it. "Well, she can certainly afford the membership."

Yuri arched one eyebrow, "She has money?"

"Yes, she does."

They checked in at the podium and were quickly ushered into the elevator. It let them off on the second floor and into a darker and more intimate atmosphere.

The hostess greeted them immediately. Yuri explained his friend wanted to choose their seating, and Victor left them to walk around. The Foundation Room had several dining areas, and each had a different decorative theme. Some were tucked around corners.

Victor headed toward the far end and saw her immediately. She had her back to him and was sitting at a table close to a stone fireplace. She wore her hair up in a chignon twist, and soft strands were hanging down her neck. The dress she wore was sleeveless, with a fitted bodice and full skirt. It was made of a soft, silky material and ended just below the knees. She wore a pair of silver high-heeled sling-backs, and one leg was crossed daintily over the other. Even from the back she looked gorgeous, and Victor took in the view appreciatively.

Then he noticed the fucker sitting across from her. Shit. Mrs. Shea was on a date. The man looked to be about her age. He had short blond hair and a muscular body that made it obvious he spent a lot of time at the gym. He was talking animatedly and using his hands to emphasize points. Victor wanted to punch him in the face. Hard.

He walked back to the front and led Yuri to a table. It was further down and behind Mrs. Shea's back. It would afford them a perfect view.

After they were seated, Yuri looked around at all the tables. "Well. Where is she?"

Victor pointed, and Yuri started laughing. "Oh my god. Is she on a date?"

"It would appear so," was the curt reply.

Yuri continued to laugh. "You apparently are losing your charms." He took in the view. "She does look lovely, though."

Victor muttered to himself. "She told me she wasn't ready to date anyone."

"Clearly she lied. Come, my friend, why don't we go somewhere else and leave the couple be."

Victor shook his head. "When have you ever known me to back down from a challenge? No. I think we'll stay. I want to hear what Mrs. Shea has to say about this."

They were interrupted by the server, Raul. "Dr. Turov, it's nice to see you again. It's been a while, eh?"

They ordered drinks and listened to the specials.

"We'll order right away, Raul. I'll have the crab cakes. What say you Kopyev?"

"In a hurry are we?" came the sarcastic reply. Yuri chose the filet and closed his menu.

Before Raul could leave to put in their orders, Victor pointed at the young couple. "Tell me, Raul, who is the man sitting over at that table?"

Raul looked and readily replied, "That's Brett Masse." The Foundation Room staff knew all their members.

"And what does Mr. Brett Masse do for a living, do you know?"

"He's a pharmaceutical sales rep."

The doctors looked at each other. Drug reps were right up there with insurance agents as being royal pains in the ass.

"Thank you, Raul. I would like to pay for their meal. Put it on my account, but please don't tell them just yet."

Raul nodded. "Very good, Dr. Turov. I'll let their server know and bring your drinks right out."

After he left, Yuri looked curiously at his friend. "What was the point of that?"

Victor glared over at the table. "If I pay for their meal, the fucker can't expect anything from her later on this evening."

"Have you considered she might *want* to meet his expectations? After all, the girl *is* on a date with him."

"Don't use that psychological crap on me. I have not misread the signs she's been giving me. Mrs. Shea is interested, and this guy is just a minor inconvenience."

Yuri looked at his friend appraisingly. Then he looked at the couple. "Well, I think you might be right about him, anyway. Her body language indicates she has no interests there."

"Oh?"

Yuri was an expert on body language. "Yes. See how she's leaning away from him? And her arms are crossed. That's a protective stance. She's also not giving any of the signs of flirting like touching her hair or cocking her head to one side." His eyes narrowed. "Actually, she shows all signs of being miserable and wanting to flee. Maybe they're not on a date."

"No. They're on a date," came the sarcastic reply. "If you can drag your eyes away from my future girlfriend, you will see all the signals that asshole is giving off."

Yuri looked at the man. He kept touching her arm and hand and was leaning forward. He was also laughing a lot and subtly showing his muscles. "Oh yeah. He's in predator mode." Then he looked at Victor and saw his narrowed eyes and tight posture. "Shit. And so are you! This could get interesting."

Their entrees arrived, and they ate in silence. Victor kept his eyes on the other table, and Yuri watched his friend with growing interest and concern.

When it looked like the couple was finishing up their meal, Victor motioned for Raul.

"I wonder if you can do me a favor. Is there any way you can take Mr. Masse and keep him busy in another room for five to ten minutes?"

The server thought about it. "He's really into microbrews, and we have quite a selection at one of the bars over in the concert venue. Let me see if I can take him over there."

"Thanks, Raul. I appreciate it. Just make sure the girl stays. I'll make it worth your while."

Abby was relieved when a server arrived and took Brett away to sample beers. He had been talking non-stop for the past hour, and she was having a hard time feigning interest. She pulled out her phone to send a quick text to Rachel, but she was interrupted by an all-too-familiar Russian voice.

"Mrs. Shea. So nice to see you. You're looking lovely tonight."

Abby looked up in shock. Her mouth opened, but nothing came out.

"Mind if I join you?"

He waited for her to nod and then gracefully sank down into Brett's empty chair. He stretched his legs out, placed his hands on the table, and looked over at her. His right fingers were gently drumming the surface, and Abby had a hard time pulling her gaze away from them.

"So. Are you a member here?"

Abby struggled to find her voice. "No." She was surprised when she followed that up with, "Are you following me?"

"Following, no. Tracking, maybe just a little." He changed the topic quickly. "So, tell me. Are you on a date? Because I distinctly remember you saying you weren't ready to start dating again."

Abby gave him a shamefaced look. "Well—"

He turned to face her, leaned into the table, and cupped his chin in his hand. "Now why would you lie to me?"

Abby looked at him and sighed. "I wasn't lying, really. Well, maybe just a white lie. I mean, this whole thing wasn't my idea. I just went along with it to get my friends off my case."

"Your friends?" he asked.

"Yes. They were threatening to fix me up on a blind date. Instead, I agreed to go on this one, and they promised to leave me alone after that. They were the ones that picked Brett out of the three of you..." her voice trailed off as she realized what she said.

"Three of us? So I was in the running?"

She nodded and blushed.

Victor grinned. "I see. So tell me, why didn't your friends pick me?"

"Because you're a doctor, and they're all nurses," she explained.

"And was that the only reason?"

She hesitated. "Well, in truth you scare me. I mean, showing up here can't be a coincidence. And some of the things you say..."

He smiled. "Your instincts are good, but I promise I don't bite." He changed the topic again. "And how is your date going with the Ken doll?"

She burst out with laughter. "Ken doll?"

Victor said nothing, so she answered his question. "Um, not so good.

He keeps talking about triathlons and tough mudders. We met at the pool, and I think he thinks I'm a competitive athlete. But I'm not. I just like to swim."

Victor nodded in thought. "When was the last time you were on a date?"

"Nine years ago."

"A lot has changed in nine years. It used to be you dated a bit and got to know each other. Then if things were going well, on the third date you hooked up." He smiled at her. "But things are different. Couples now have sex on the first date, and then they decide after if they want to keep going out. I'm surprised your friends didn't tell you this."

She looked horrified. "Um, no, they didn't. But most of them are married, and the rest are recently divorced or separated."

He looked at her pointedly. "Your Ken doll took you to an expensive place. Between the drinks and the food, it's going to cost him a good two hundred dollars. He's going to expect something from you after all of this."

"Well, he's not going to get it!" She hurriedly looked around for their server and waved him over. "I would like to pay the bill now if that's okay?"

The server looked at her and then at an amused Dr. Turov in confusion. "Miss, the bill has already been paid. Dr. Turov took care of it. Was there anything else you needed?"

"Oh. Um, no thank you." When he was gone, she turned to Victor. "Seriously?"

He gave her a sheepish grin. "What? I thought you could use some help."

She shook her head. "You are unbelievable. But thank you. And I will be paying you back."

"When are you going to learn that I pay for everything?" He could see Raul and Brett approaching. "Would you like more help in getting rid of your date?"

She saw them too. Abby hesitated for a split-second before saying, "Yes, please!"

She didn't see his satisfied smile.

Chapter Sixteen

Brett was none too happy to see Abby sitting with a man when he returned to the table. He raised his eyebrows as he approached and looked at Victor with a tinge of jealousy.

"Hello. I'm Brett. And you are?"

Victor stood up and gave him a brilliant smile. "Dr. Turov. I'm Mrs. Shea's doctor. I stopped by to say hello, and she was telling me about your athletic events. I work with quite a few athletes and help them prepare. Perhaps I could give you some pointers?"

Brett's face lit up, and he eagerly shook Victor's hand. They both had a firm handshake.

"It's nice to meet you. If you wouldn't mind, I would love some pointers. The Cleveland marathon is coming up soon, and I am running in it." Then he turned to Abby. "I didn't know you saw a sports medicine expert. Are you entered in a race?"

Abby stifled a smirk and shook her head no. Brett barely noticed and started asking the doctor questions. Victor was listening to the younger man talk, but his eyes were on Abby. Finally, Victor said, "It looks like you're done eating. Why don't you join my friend and I at our table? Dr. Kopyev is a psychiatrist, and he specializes in sports motivation. I'm sure he'd love to chat with you as well."

Brett started to agree but then stopped. He looked at Abby. "Do you mind?"

She smiled. "Not at all. I'm quite looking forward to hearing what the doctors have to say." She gave Victor a mischievous smile.

He returned the grin.

They approached the table where Yuri was finishing up his meal. He had been watching Victor talk to the girl, and her body language had said it all. She had shied away from him and kept her posture closed off, but she had also cocked her head and twisted a strand of hair around her finger. The girl was attracted to his friend, but she was also scared of him.

Yuri stood as they approached. Victor introduced him to Brett first.

"Mr. Masse here is an athlete, and I was just telling him about your expertise in sports motivation, Dr. Kopyev."

Yuri raised his eyebrows at Victor but shook Brett's hand.

Abby whispered behind them, "Is he really a sports motivator?"

Victor laughed and whispered back, "No. Let's just call it a white lie. There seems to be a lot of those going around tonight."

Abby ignored him. She was waiting to be introduced to Dr. Kopyev, and she realized he was the complete opposite of Dr. Turov. Yuri was short, with a receding hairline, and he had a belly that indicated an over-indulgence in food or drink. His hair was light, and his eyes were a bright blue. He was talking to Brett, but those blue eyes kept looking over in her direction. His gaze made her uncomfortable.

Finally, it was her turn to be introduced.

"Mrs. Shea, this is my good friend Dr. Kopyev. He's a psychiatrist." Then he turned to Yuri. "Mrs. Shea is a writer."

They shook hands. Abby couldn't resist. "So is Dr. Turov really your friend, or is he secretly one of your patients?"

Yuri threw back his head and laughed heartily. "Well, he's not a patient. But it's not for a lack of trying!" He liked her immediately. She was younger and smaller than what Victor usually went for, and she had an air of innocence about her that was refreshing. He also liked her sense of humor. Yuri subtly glanced at her body, and his eyes lingered on her breasts. They were nice. When he looked up, he caught Victor glaring at him. It served the fucker right for telling that idiot he was a sports motivator.

At that moment Raul showed up and asked if he could get them anything else. Victor immediately ordered a round of drinks. He looked to Abby first, but she declined. He nodded his approval and then turned to the men. They agreed to do shots, and the first round went down quickly. Abby watched as two more rounds were ordered. Brett had tried to buy one, only to be told by his server that Dr. Turov had already paid his bill. Abby noted his look of irritation, but it was quickly replaced by a growing excitement at the sports conversation. This was fueled further by the alcohol.

Forty minutes had passed, and the men were chatting up a storm, laughing, and slapping each other on the back. Abby watched until she felt safe enough to leave. Then she pulled out her phone and ordered an Uber ride home. It would be there in ten minutes. Her plan was to leave and then text Brett when she was safely in the car. She would tell him she felt ill. She watched the men in amusement and then excused herself to use the restroom. They barely noticed her get up.

Abby was just getting into the elevator when Victor stepped in beside her. "Going somewhere?"

She cringed. "Yes. I'm heading home while Brett is distracted. Thank you for that, by the way. You guys sure are drinking a lot of shots."

"No. They're drinking a lot of shots. I'm drinking water. I don't want to be hungover for tomorrow."

She looked at him in confusion.

He explained. "I asked Raul to fill my glass with water."

She laughed. "That's so devious! Is Yuri drinking shots of water too?"

"No. My friend likes to drink." He changed the subject. "Tell me, how are you getting home? Did the Ken doll bring you here? Do you need a ride?"

"Oh, god no. I took an Uber here, and I'm taking one home."

Victor looked upset. "No. No. You can't take an Uber. Those are dangerous. Women traveling alone should never get in a cab with an unknown driver."

"They're not that bad. I take them all the time. Most of the drivers are normal."

"Most? Mrs. Shea, I must insist you take my car home. I have a paid driver on standby. Please cancel your Uber ride, and I'll call Vince."

She looked at him uncertainly. "But they're already on their way. And besides, I don't know Vince either."

He looked at her in exasperation. "Yes, but I know him. I ran a thorough background check before I hired him. He's a retired police detective. Please cancel the Uber, now!" His voice had gotten intense.

Abby hesitated. The man had a knack for freaking her out, but she finally pulled out her phone and canceled the ride.

Victor nodded in approval and called Vince. When he hung up, he smiled down at her. "Vince will be here in five minutes. Where's your coat ticket? While we're waiting, I can get your coat."

Abby didn't look at him. She had worn a small cardigan over her dress, but that was it. She knew he would be angry.

Victor leaned down and softly asked, "No coat again? What am I going to do with you?" He clasped her hand and led her to a small nook by the kitchen entrance. He pressed her up against the wall and leaned in. She still wasn't looking at him, so he cupped her chin and tilted her head up. When she finally met his gaze, he smiled.

"If ever there was a woman that needed a man in her life, it's you. I would like you to reconsider going out on a date with me."

She shook her head and worked to find her voice. "I don't think that's a good idea."

"Why not?"

"Because you scare me. And you're stalking me!"

He quietly cursed and released her. Then he pulled out his cell phone and punched in some numbers. He showed her the screen. "This is a tracking app. All I did was log in your cell number, and it showed me where you were. Parents use it all the time to keep tabs on their children."

Abby looked at the screen with interest. "Oh. I've heard of this. That's pretty cool." Then she looked up at him accusingly. "But I'm not a child."

"True. But it was a convenient way to run into you. Haven't you ever driven by someone's house in hopes of seeing them? This is a lot like that, only more high tech."

"Well sure, but that was when I was a teenager."

He smiled. "I'm hardly a teenager. But I knew you were nervous around me, and this was a way to run into you without scaring you."

"Um, it didn't work."

He laughed. "I guess not."

They looked at each other, and Victor leaned in again. He pressed his left hand up against the wall by her head. Then he took the index finger of his right hand and slowly traced it down her cheek. Abby felt the familiar spark and warmth.

"I know you feel that too. It's one of the reasons I'm having trouble staying away."

She said nothing and tried to shift away from him. He pressed his right hand up against the wall on the other side of her head and leaned in even further. She could smell his cologne and a hint of mint on his breath. Their bodies were almost touching.

"I tell you what. I'll make a deal with you. Let me kiss you just once. All you have to do is stand there and do nothing. Show me no reaction whatsoever, and I'll leave you alone for good. You have my word. But if you respond, then you have to go out on a date with me tomorrow."

She thought about it.

"What do you have to lose?" he whispered. "It's only one kiss."

She sighed and nodded in agreement.

Victor moved in slowly so his body was now gently pressed up against hers. He left his hands on the wall on either side of her head and held her gaze as he lowered his mouth. It hovered over her lips for a split-second before he gave her the softest of kisses.

Abby instinctively closed her eyes and willed herself not to respond. She could feel the warmth spreading from her lips and had to fight not to reach out and touch him. It had been so long since she had been this close to a man. His body felt hard and strong and oh-so-masculine.

Victor could sense her wavering. He kept his lips on hers but moved his left hand into her hair. He tugged gently so that her head tilted up. Then he deepened the kiss as his right hand lowered down and encircled her waist. He pulled her in tighter and gently teased her mouth open with his tongue. When he slipped it in, he felt her body begin to relax. God, she felt good. Her body was soft and feminine, and her waist was so tiny.

Abby wasn't sure when it happened. One minute she was passively standing there, and the next she had her hands on his chest and her tongue tentatively responding to his. The warmth was spreading rapidly through her body. The spark had deepened into a kind of magnetic pull that was drawing them toward each other.

The phone ringing startled both of them. Victor reluctantly pulled away to answer it, but he kept his arm around her waist. Vince was calling to let him know the car was waiting outside. They spoke briefly and hung up.

He smiled down at her. "Your ride is here."

She nodded.

"I would like to pick you up at eleven tomorrow morning. Will that work for you?"

She sighed but didn't protest. There was no denying what had just happened. "Sure."

"You should know I take dating very seriously, Abigail."

With a start, she realized he had called her by her first name.

"I have two simple rules, and Rule Number One is monogamy. When you date me, you do not date anyone else. That means no texting, no chatting on the internet, no accepting drinks from strangers, and no flirting of any kind. The same goes for me. We are a couple. Boyfriend and girlfriend. Is that going to be a problem?"

"Um, you don't have to worry. I've never been the playing around type. But isn't it a bit premature to be calling each other boyfriend and girlfriend?"

He looked serious. "No. When I do something, I give it one hundred percent. I already know how much I like you."

She nodded thoughtfully. "Okay. I like you too." Then she asked, "What's the other rule?"

Victor gave her a small smile. "I think we'll wait a bit longer before we discuss that one."

She eyed him suspiciously but didn't push it.

Victor walked her out to the car and opened the back door. He introduced her to Vince. "Abigail is going to Tremont. She'll tell you the address." Then he smiled and gave her a quick kiss. "I'll see you tomorrow."

As the car pulled away, Abby watched him walk back into the restaurant and wondered what the hell had just happened. She steadied her breathing and gave Vince her address. As she settled back in the seat, she was startled to realize her panties were damp.

When Abby was safely home, she sent Dr. Turov a quick text.

Thanks for the ride and helping me tonight! Can you do me one more favor?

His response was immediate.

You're welcome. What's the favor?

I never saved Brett's number. Can you please let him know I went home? And maybe make sure he's not driving.

He laughed when he read it and fired off a quick response.

With pleasure. Good night, Abigail.

Thank you. CU tomorrow!

The night ended quickly after that. Victor told the Ken doll Abby had left, paid the bill, called Vince, and got the two staggering men outside.

"Where do you live, Mr. Masse? We can drop you off on our way."

Brett drunkenly waved him off. "No need. I live above Flannery's." He pointed down the alley. "It will take me two minutes to walk there."

Victor was furious. The fucker had taken her to a restaurant within walking distance of his apartment. The Ken doll clearly had expected the night to end up there.

Chapter Seventeen

Victor was up early the next morning. His first thought when he opened his eyes was that he had a date with Abigail. That made him smile. He rolled out of bed and donned his workout clothes. Yuri was sleeping it off in one of the spare bedrooms down the hall, so he tried to be quiet.

As he headed out the door and down to the gym, he thought about where to take her on their date. He had tickets that night to the Monet exhibit, and he knew she would love that. Those had been purchased last week after their museum adventure. He had planned to use them to lure her in. Now he would use them at the end of what he hoped would be a perfect day.

Victor hopped on a treadmill to warm up. He put his cell on the stand and started searching for things to do in Cleveland. An hour later his workout was over. He had run thirty minutes and done a full body circuit. As a surgeon, Victor's free time was at a premium. He had learned long ago how to maximize that time, and fitness had always been a priority. He saw firsthand what happened to people that did not take care of themselves. It was a great motivator, and as a result, he had a fit body.

His workouts were also a good time to de-stress and think problems through. Today it had allowed him to plan the date. It had also given him time to think about how to handle Abigail. As a non-submissive, he was going to need to treat her differently than his dates in the past. Victor was on unfamiliar ground, and the thought made him anxious. The sooner he took control, the better. But he knew he couldn't push her too fast. She was already afraid of him, and he didn't want her to bolt. No, Abigail needed to be treated very carefully.

***

Abby was up early as well. She'd had trouble sleeping the night before because she was nervous about the date. As she was brushing her teeth, she idly wondered what she should call him. Dr. Turov? Victor? Vick? The last one made her snort. Somehow she didn't think that would fly. The man was so damn formal with her, but at least now he was using her first name.

Abby knew she should eat, but her stomach was too nervous. Instead, she decided to go for a swim. The exercise would calm her down. As she grabbed her swim bag she briefly thought about Brett and wondered if he was at the pool. Then she realized he was probably too hungover to be swimming right now. He was going to be a problem, and she dreaded seeing him again.

***

It was nine thirty, and Victor was pacing. He had things he could do, but really he just wanted to head over to Abigail's house now. He checked his tracking app and knew she was home. Maybe he could take her out to breakfast. Victor grabbed his coat and knocked on Yuri's door.

"What?!"

Victor walked in the room and took in his friend's disheveled appearance. "That looks like one hell of a hangover," he said with amusement.

Yuri glared at him.

"Listen, I'm on my way out. I left you some coffee. Just be sure the door locks when you pull it shut. And try not to puke in my spare bathroom."

"Fuck you! This is all your fault making me talk to that idiot all night long. I needed alcohol to get through it."

"You'd best have some alcohol in your office when he comes to see you on Monday, then."

"Wait, he's coming to see me?"

Victor laughed. "Yes. Don't you remember? You agreed to let him come in and discuss the new psychotropic drugs his company is putting out."

"You have got to be kidding me! All this I do for you, and you still didn't get the girl."

"What are you talking about? I got the girl. I'm heading over there now for our date."

Yuri sat up and winced when the room started to spin. "She agreed to go out with you?"

"Yes. I can be very persuasive."

"I hope you know what you're doing, Victor."

"No. I haven't a clue."

Yuri nodded. "Well if nothing else, the two of you will be fun to watch. So basically you get the hot chick, and I get the sales rep turd and a wicked hangover."

Victor laughed. "Sounds about right. Have a good day."

Yuri flipped him off.

***

Abby had just gotten out of the shower and thrown on a robe when her doorbell rang. She frowned. It was only nine fifty, so she knew it wasn't her date. She headed downstairs and opened the door. Victor was standing on her porch.

He scowled at her. "You need to see who it is before you open the door, Abigail!"

"Good morning to you too. Um, aren't you a bit early?"

He walked past her and took in the short robe and wet hair with a grin. She realized what she was wearing and pulled the robe tighter around her chest. He was carrying a cup of coffee and had her newspaper tucked under his arm. She followed him into her kitchen.

Victor took a seat at the table and smiled at her. "Sorry. I had nothing to do at home, so I thought I would hang out here while you got ready."

"I guess I shouldn't be surprised you knew where I lived." Then she took in his coffee. "You're seriously going to drink coffee in front of me?"

"Vince told me where you live. And why wouldn't I drink coffee? I love it, and it doesn't affect my heart like it does yours."

"I love coffee too! And the jury is still out on what it does to my heart."

"Nonetheless, you won't be drinking it." He opened the paper and ignored her.

She stuck her tongue out at him, but then she noticed his black dress pants and button-down white shirt. "Um, where are we going today?"

He looked up from his paper. "A couple different places. I want them to be a surprise."

"Okay. But what should I wear?"

He thought about it. "You certainly looked nice for the Ken doll. Something similar to that would be good. But keep your hair down. I rather like your hair down."

Abby headed back upstairs. He was making her feel uncomfortable again, but that comment about her hair was nice. She locked her bedroom door just to be safe and then looked in her closet dubiously. Abby had never been good with clothes, and she didn't have much in the way of dresses. Fortunately, Rachel had been over the other day and brought several potential outfits for her date with Brett. They wore the same size, but Rachel was a few inches shorter. The outfits were still hanging in the closet. Abby fingered each one, but she had no clue what to wear. She finally bit the bullet and called Rachel.

Her friend answered immediately, and Abby realized she had been waiting for the call. "How did it go last night?" asked Rachel.

"It was a disaster. The man wouldn't shut up. Then he got drunk with some guys. I finally left him at the bar and went home."

"Oh! That's awful. I'm so sorry. Don't let it keep you from going out on other dates, Abs. Some guys are jerks, but you know there's good ones too."

Abby grinned. "Actually, that's why I'm calling. Remember the doctor from the clinic that I was telling you about? Well, I'm going out with him today."

"Shut up! I am so proud of you. Two dates in a row. Is he good looking?"

"God, yes."

"Wait. What's his name? I can look him up on the clinic's website."

"Victor Turov. While you're looking, what should I wear? He won't tell me where we're going, but he said I should dress up."

Rachel had found his photo on the website. "Wow, Abs! He's the cardiothoracic chief of staff. That's huge! And he's hot too."

Abby was barely listening. She was desperately throwing clothes onto her bed. "Focus, Rach! What should I wear?"

Rachel thought about it. "Wear the burgundy dress. It's dressy but feminine. Is he tall?"

"Super tall. I feel short next to him."

"Perfect. Put on some gray tights and wear your high-heeled gray leather boots. Then wear your silver circle necklace and that gray jacket.

Not the fitted one, the loose one."

Abby pulled everything out and looked at it. Not bad.

"What about earrings?"

"The silver diamond hoops. And use your good clutch. What are you doing with your hair?"

"I was going to wear it down and curl it a bit."

"That might work. If he takes you somewhere fancy, though, put it up in a neat bun or coil. If he takes you somewhere casual, lose the jacket and throw your hair in a pony."

Abby's head was reeling, but she thought she had it all down. "Thanks, Rach. I've gotta go get ready. I'll call you later."

"Have fun. We'll be thinking of you."

Abby hurried into the bathroom and started drying her hair.

When Victor heard the blow dryer, he got up from the table and started walking around. He was already getting a feel for Abigail, and she had good taste. The furniture was all soft brown leather with pops of color in two upholstered end chairs. The decorations also had color, and she had framed nature scenes on the wall. Over the fireplace were photographs, and Victor looked them over carefully. He knew the people in them thanks to Jack's report. Most were of her late husband, but there were also some of her family and friends. Victor lingered over one of Nate and Abby on the beach. He had his arms around her possessively, and the two looked thoroughly in love. Victor felt a twinge of envy and realized he was jealous of a dead man.

He wandered into the kitchen and noticed the alarm system attached to the wall. It was lit up and appeared to be working properly. This made him happy. The freezer had French fries, frozen vegetables, a loaf of bread, and an ice cube tray. That was it. The fridge was better and was full of fresh produce, juice, milk, cheese, salad dressing, and coffee creamer. Victor scowled at the creamer and noticed the coffee maker on the counter. He opened the lid and saw what looked to be recently used grounds inside. "Oh, Abigail!" he whispered.

He poured the creamer out in the sink and threw the container in the garbage along with the coffee grounds. He then unplugged the pot and rinsed it in the sink. He wrapped up the cord and placed the whole thing on the table. Victor found the coffee beans in a nearby cupboard and packed it away in a bag. He put that on the table as well.

By the time she came down, he was innocently sitting back at the table. She noticed the coffee pot right away. They looked at each other, but Abby didn't take the bait. Instead, she sweetly said, "I'm ready. Where are we going?"

Victor gave her a knowing smile before taking in her outfit. She looked stunning. "You get ready fast, Abigail. And you look quite beautiful."

She gave him a shy smile. "Er, thanks. You look good too."

He stood up and took her hand. "Tell me, where do those mythical creatures, your coats, live?"

She shook her head in exasperation as she led him to the closet. When she opened the door he feigned shock and said, "They do exist!"

Abby rolled her eyes before pulling out a coat. He helped her put it on, and they headed out to his truck.

***

The Great Lakes Science Center was on the northern part of Cleveland and right on Lake Erie. Abby had only been there once before with Nate to see the NASA display. She clapped her hands like a little kid when they pulled into the parking lot.

"What are we going to see?"

Victor parked, and she was out of the truck before he could come around to her door. "You need to wait for me to open your door, Abigail!" he admonished. Then he added more gently, "We're going to tour the Mather steamship. We're also going to see a movie in the theatre. It's about Moscow." He grinned as he took her hand and led her into the center.

The movie wasn't starting for another hour, so they went over to the steamship first. It was Victor's turn to be excited.

"It's not a warship, but it still gives you a feel for what it would be like to live and work on one."

They took the tour, and Abby had to admit it was pretty interesting.

The movie was even better. It was in the dome theatre, which made Abby feel like she was soaring through the air. She got a bit nauseous, but the scenery in the film was spectacular. The movie portrayed the history of Moscow and showed all of its architectural beauty. Victor kept pointing out and telling her different things about his hometown. He was holding her hand, and he kept squeezing it in excitement. She found herself being drawn into his enthusiasm. When the movie ended, they headed back to the truck.

He opened her door. "Are you hungry?"

"Starving!"

"Good. Let's go eat."

They ended up going to Guarino's in Little Italy. It was two o'clock on a Saturday afternoon and the place was still busy from the lunch rush. The hostess said their table would be ready in fifteen minutes. The foyer was crowded, so Victor led them back outside to wait. It was cold, but the sun was out and they were standing under an overhang.

Abby's cell phone rang. She looked at the number but didn't recognize it. "I'm sorry. I'd better take this. It could be hospice calling."

Victor frowned. "I thought you didn't volunteer there anymore?"

"I still do vigils," she explained as she picked up. "Hi, this is Abby."

"Heh Abby. It's Brett. How are you?"

Abby's heart sank. She turned away from Victor, but he saw the look on her face as she did. "Um, I'm okay. How are you?"

"Feeling pretty embarrassed about last night. I'm so sorry I got that drunk. Did you get home okay?" asked Brett.

Victor walked around and was standing in front of her. She stared at his neck as she answered, "Um, yes, I did."

"Good. That's a relief. Again, I'm so sorry. I don't usually drink that much."

She tried to move away from Victor, but he reached out and put his right arm around her waist. Then he took his left thumb and pushed her chin up so their eyes met. He did not look happy.

Abby tried to get off the phone. "Don't worry about it. Listen, I've got to go."

"No, wait!" stammered Brett. "I wanted to make it up to you. Can we go out again?"

She sighed. Did this man ever take a hint? "Um, no, I don't think so. And I've really got to go."

Brett continued to talk, and Abby considered just hanging up on him. Anything was better than the looks Victor was giving her.

Before she could make a move, Victor had pulled the phone out of her hand. He kept his arm around her waist. "Hello, is this Mr. Masse?"

Brett paused midstream. "Er, yeah. Who is this?"

"Dr. Turov. We met last night."

There was silence as Brett digested this. "I'm sorry. Is Abby at an appointment?"

"No. Abigail is on a date with me right now. In fact, we have decided to date exclusively."

"What? Can I speak to Abby?"

"No, you cannot," was the serious reply. "In fact, I don't want you ever calling her again. Please delete her number from your contacts."

Now Brett was sputtering. "What the hell? She was just on a date with me last night."

"Yes, and you got quite drunk and forgot about her. One man's loss is another man's gain, eh Mr. Masse?"

"You're the one that got me drunk!"

"Indeed. But I don't remember putting a gun to your head to do those shots. I meant it when I said to delete her number. Goodbye, Mr. Masse."

He hung up and handed the phone back to Abby. She put it in her purse and gave him a sheepish look.

"Now was that so hard?" he asked.

Abby sighed. "I've never been good at that sort of thing. I didn't want to hurt him."

"I find it's best to be brutally honest with people. It may seem harsh, but when someone knows exactly how you feel, there is no room for confusion or pain down the road. That's a lot different than your little white lies, eh?"

"Maybe. I'm just not really good at confrontations."

He looked at her thoughtfully. "Lucky for you I am very good at them."

"Well, thank you for that. Now I'm going to have to find a new pool to swim in."

"Yes, you are," was his serious reply. She missed the tone of his voice because their buzzer went off at that moment.

Victor opened the door and led her back into the restaurant. They were quickly seated and were discussing the Moscow movie.

"Do you miss home?" she asked.

He thought about it. "A little. It's really cold there, but it's what I know. I like America, though. It suits me."

"Why did you leave?"

"For the opportunity. There are a lot of Russian doctors here because we can do so much more in the States than back home."

They were interrupted by the server and placed their orders. Abby went first and asked for the sweet potato ravioli.

"You forgot the protein," Victor said.

She looked at Victor in confusion and then said, "Oh. That's okay. This will be enough."

He shook his head. "No, it won't." Then he looked at the server. "Add some grilled chicken to her order, please. And I'll have the eggplant Parmesan with some grilled chicken as well."

The server nodded and walked away.

"Are you always so bossy?" asked Abby.

"When I have to be. Listen, you are not eating enough protein."

She thought about it. "How would you know?"

"I just do. I'm very smart," he teased as he tapped his head. "Protein is made up of amino acids. Your body needs those but can't produce them. You have to eat enough protein to get those amino acids into your system."

"God, you are such a doctor!"

He leaned back in his chair and smiled. "Yes, I am. Don't worry. You'll get used to it."

When their food came, they ate for the next hour and talked the entire time. Abby was really starting to like him, and the feeling was mutual.

When the bill arrived she eyed the check, and Victor gave her a challenging look. She smiled sweetly and thanked him for lunch.

"You're welcome." He looked at his watch. "We have time to kill. Let's go to Coventry."

They spent hours in Coventry bumming around. Abby dragged him into Mac's Backs, one of her all-time favorite bookstores. It was three stories of new and used books haphazardly wedged into every nook and cranny. She loved sifting through everything and always walked out with unexpected finds. Victor followed her around in amusement as she kept handing him books to hold. When they reached the checkout, she had eight of them and an excited look on her face.

The cashier asked if they had found everything okay. Victor's eyes twinkled. "Tell me, do you have any of Abigail Shea's books?"

The cashier nodded. "Yes. She's actually a local writer. I wouldn't have guessed her to be your taste, though."

Victor laughed. "You would be surprised."

Abby smirked as the cashier pointed him in the right direction.

"That's okay. Maybe next time." He pulled out his credit card to pay, and Abby frowned at him.

"I can buy my own books."

"I told you. I pay for everything."

The cashier was looking at them curiously.

She shook her head and whispered, "This is too much."

He signed the receipt and took her hand. As they walked out he explained. "I'm very well off, Abigail, and you're my girlfriend. I want to pay for your things."

She gave him an impish look. "Well, in that case, I would like a pair of diamond earrings and, um, a new car."

"Is that a challenge?"

The man was so serious. "No. I was just kidding!"

He smiled as they walked down to Phoenix Coffee. The scent hit her full force when they walked in. God was she jonesing for a cup! Victor put in his order for a large black coffee. Then he asked the staff member what decaf options they had available. The man happily rattled off a bunch of herbal teas, and Abby tried to look interested. When he was done, she ordered a decaf latte and glared at Victor.

"Good girl," was all he said.

They sat at a table in the window and looked out at the world. Victor glanced at his watch and explained they only had thirty more minutes to kill.

"Where are we going?"

"It's a surprise. I promise you'll like it."

His phone beeped, and Victor looked at the number. "I'm sorry. It's one of my attendings. Hopefully, I won't be long."

Abby listened as he quietly discussed lab results with the person on the phone. Then she pulled out one of her new books and started reading. It was about a young girl lost in Scotland, and she was hooked by the second chapter. She didn't even notice when Victor finished his call. He sat back and watched her, enthralled. She had one arm propped on the table with her head leaning on her hand. The other hand was idly twirling a strand of hair. Occasionally it would stop to turn the page, and sometimes she pulled the strand across her upper lip like a mustache.

A customer dropped a plate by the door, and the shattering noise caused Abby to look up. Then she looked over at Victor, startled.

"How long have you been off the phone?"

"Not long."

"I'm sorry. You should have said something."

"That's okay. I enjoyed watching. You love books, don't you Abigail?"

She nodded. "Since I was a little girl. I was reading before I could walk."

"And when did you start writing?"

"After I got married. Nate wasn't big on me working, and I needed something to do."

Victor looked surprised. "Mr. Shea had some pretty old fashioned views."

"Well, he traveled a lot for work, and he liked me to come along."

"Oh, I get it. I was just surprised is all." He finished his coffee and looked at his watch. "We can leave whenever you're ready."

She gathered her things, and Victor had to reach for the gray jacket she was about to leave behind. He handed it to her but said nothing as they walked out. His eyes were twinkling again.

Chapter Eighteen

When they pulled into the art museum parking garage, Abby's eyes got big. She looked at all of the chicly dressed people entering.

"Are we doing what I think we're doing?"

He grinned at her.

"How did you pull that off?" she asked.

"Your enthusiasm was contagious, Abigail. I decided to become a member of the museum like yourself."

She reached in her bag to pull out a hair tie and some bobby pins. Then she flipped down the vanity mirror and started arranging her hair. "Yes, but these events are for VIP members only."

Victor watched in fascination as she wound her hair up in the tie and began pinning it in place. Her fingers were as deft and graceful as a surgeon's. When she was done, it looked like she had spent hours at a hair salon. Then she pulled out a lipstick and started applying it to her lips. He felt his cock begin to stir.

"Well, that's okay because I joined as a VIP."

She looked over at him in amazement.

"Actually, you're a VIP now too. I upgraded your membership."

She started laughing. "Wha-at? I mean, um, okay. Thank you." She really didn't know what to say.

Victor started to get out of the truck and touched her arm. "Wait for me to open your door."

She dutifully waited as he walked around to her side. He opened the door and reached his hand in, and she shyly accepted it. He pulled her out of the Tundra and right into his arms with a tug. Then he gave her a long kiss, thoroughly ruining her lipstick, before leading them into the museum.

They spent the next two hours walking around. There were musicians from the Cleveland Orchestra there playing baroque music, and servers were navigating between the guests with glasses of champagne, wine, and hors d'oeuvres. The atrium was dimly lit, but there were sparkly white lights overhead. Abby felt like she had stepped into an enchanted world.

As for the Monet exhibit, it was pretty spectacular. The museum gave them complimentary headphones to put on, and they could enter the number of each piece to hear information about it. Abby was thrilled to see Victor take his time. Most people lost interest halfway through an exhibit, but he stuck it out to the end and seemed to be enjoying himself.

Victor enjoyed the exhibit, but he was more interested in covertly watching her. She had a childlike awe toward the art, but she also enjoyed observing the people and even struck up a conversation with some of them. He realized his new girlfriend was a genuinely optimistic and engaged person, albeit shy, and the thought pleased him. She also didn't drink much, which was rare for one of his dates, and she didn't seem to care at all about the obvious money around her.

And yet, Victor knew things would have to change. She was barely eating any of the food, even though their lunch had been a long time ago, and she steered clear of the meat options entirely. Victor knew they would need to discuss Rule Number Two soon, but he was worried how she would react. Maybe he could put the conversation off a bit longer.

When the event ended, Victor drove them back toward downtown. He suggested they stop somewhere for a drink and a bite to eat, and Abby agreed. He took her to Fahrenheit. It was very close to her house, and Abby tried not to get nervous. The date would eventually end, and she never knew what to do when the guy dropped her off. After their conversation last night, she was even more concerned. What if he expected sex? She was definitely attracted to him, but it was way too soon.

The restaurant was busy, but Victor asked for a quiet booth. They were taken to the back and tucked in against a wall. The server came immediately and offered drinks. Abby looked at the menu, but all she really wanted was a coffee. She was used to going to bed at this time, and the day was starting to take its toll. The caffeine would wake her up again.

She looked at Victor hesitantly. He had been laughing and in a good mood all day. Maybe she could broach the subject.

"What would you like, Abigail?"

She nervously clasped her hands. "Well, I was wondering if I could possibly have a cup of coffee?" She saw his scowl and rushed out the words. "You could check my pulse, and if it's not too high then maybe it would be okay."

He looked at the server. "She'll take a cup of hot herbal tea and some ice water. I'll have an iced tea." Once the server was gone he looked across the booth at her.

"I guess not, then." She was trying to be flippant, but he continued to stare.

With trepidation, he realized he could not put off the talk. He stood up and walked around to her side of the booth. Then he slid in next to her.

She smiled tentatively. "Um, hi!"

Victor took her hand and held it in both of hers. It looked so tiny in his strong grasp. Then he sighed before looking her way. "I think maybe it's time we talked about Rule Number Two."

"Okay."

"Actually, this is a rule I had to add. Now there are three rules."

"How come?"

He smiled. "Because you are special."

"Oh." She made a face. "Special good, or special bad?"

"Definitely good."

"Oh."

"So Rule Number Two. Let's call it the health and safety rule. I want you to try very hard to make your health and safety a top priority."

"Um, I thought I already did that."

He shook his head. "Oh, Abigail. If only. Let me spell it out for you. Take transportation for instance. I don't want you ever taking a cab or Uber again."

She frowned. "But then I have to drive. Parking is tricky sometimes, and if I've had a drink I really shouldn't be driving. I'm kind of a lightweight."

He was massaging the palm of her hand with his thumbs. "I have no doubt. But this one is easy. You can call Vince any time you like, and he will drive you. Here, give me your phone."

She wordlessly unlocked her phone and handed it to him. He punched Vince's information into her contacts. When he handed the phone back, she frowned. "But surely Vince isn't working all the time. And that could get expensive."

"He's on call for me 24/7, but I usually only need him at night or early mornings. If I've been working long hours, I'm too tired to drive myself home. You will probably only need him at night as well, right? And don't worry about the cost. That's my concern, not yours."

She sighed and looked away. Victor watched her carefully. "Look at me, Abigail." When she did, he explained, "This is very important to me. Do you think you can do it?"

She pursed her lips but nodded.

"Good. There's more. Quite a bit actually. Maybe it would help if I wrote it all down for you."

She stared at him in amazement.

Just then the server arrived with their drinks. She asked to take their order, but Victor asked for a pen and paper first. The server obliged, and then he ordered a few of the appetizers from the menu. He hadn't even asked Abby what she wanted, and she noted with irritation all the items had meat in them.

Once the server was gone, Victor resumed their conversation. He wrote each point down on the paper and explained them as he went. By the time he was finished, there were fifteen health and safety issues listed, and the food had arrived. Abby's head was reeling.

Victor was watching her closely. "It's a lot to take in, I know. Maybe you should read the list over. I want to be sure you're clear on all of these."

She looked at the paper and tried not to laugh. His handwriting was atrocious. She pointed out the third item. "What does this say? It looks like no fleeing or feeding."

He looked down sheepishly. "That says no speeding. Sorry. It's a hazard of my profession. Doctor's handwriting. Maybe I should type these out and email them to you."

She shook her head in amazement and continued reading. After four more writing clarifications she was done. She pushed the paper away. "Okay. These seem pretty reasonable."

He was still watching her intently. "And do you think you can follow them?"

She fidgeted. "Well, most of these I do all the time anyway. But some might be more challenging than others."

"Mmm hmm. Let me guess. Is coffee one of the ones that will be a problem?"

"Yes. And eating meat. And avoiding fast food. I don't really cook much, and I do love Taco Bell. Oh, is pizza considered fast food?"

"Yes."

"Dang. Yeah, then those are going to be hard."

He nodded. "There's more to Rule Number Two, and I think it will help keep you motivated."

She absent-mindedly forked a meatball and started eating while she waited for him to continue.

"If I catch you breaking any of these rules, I will punish you."

She choked on the meatball and her eyes watered, but then she laughed.

He wasn't smiling. "Have you ever been spanked before, Abigail?"

She snickered. "No."

"Your parents never spanked you?"

"Um, no. I was the baby of the family and the only girl. I was spoiled rotten."

"I see. And what about Mr. Shea, did he ever spank you?"

"God, no!" She looked at him, and he wasn't laughing. "Wait, are you serious?"

"Yes. Very serious."

"Oh." Her mouth had dropped open, and she had to mentally force herself to shut it again.

"Are you okay?" he asked.

"I guess. I mean, you just told me you're going to spank me." She looked at him with alarm. "So you are serious?"

"Yes, I am."

"Oh." She was thinking about it. "But only if I break a rule, right?"

"Exactly."

"And how do you do it? I mean, the spanking."

His lips started to twitch. "Well, Abigail, I usually use my hand and spank your bottom like this," he gently showed her on her arm. "If I have surgery scheduled the next day, though, I have to use a paddle. I can't risk hurting my hand before a procedure."

She looked at him nervously. "You mean you spank hard enough to hurt your hand?"

He hesitated. He didn't want to scare her, but he had to be honest. They were going to need to trust each other completely for this relationship to work. "Yes, sometimes. If you majorly break the rules."

"Oh." Her voice got small. "But why? That doesn't seem normal."

He sighed and tried to find the words to explain. "Well, there's several reasons. For one, I worry about things that are important to me. And you are rapidly becoming someone that is important to me."

She felt a thrill at that comment.

He went on. "If something is important to me, I try to control it. The more I can control something, the less anxious I feel. That's why I have rules. I do the same with my surgeries."

She nodded. It made a sick sort of sense.

"The punishment serves several purposes. It relieves my anxiety and anger when you screw up. It also gives you a physical reminder of what you did wrong, and hopefully, it's enough to keep you from doing it again in the future."

She was starting to look pale, and he worried he was losing her. But he had to be honest. "And finally, Abigail, I do it because it's a major turn-on for me."

She gasped. "What?!"

"Oh yes, little one. There is nothing more erotic than completely dominating another person and seeing their ass redden from my hand. Especially someone as sweet and lovely as you."

She couldn't look at him. Her face had heated up and was bright pink.

"I promise that you will like it too. You have a very submissive personality, Abigail."

"I do?"

"Oh yes. Your shyness…your use of white lies…the way you blush… these are all signs of a submissive."

Abby thought about it. "I can also be quite stubborn, you know." She went on, "It doesn't seem really normal to me. And I'm really big on being normal."

He waved her comment off. "What is normal? What we see of couples in public is very different than what is going on behind closed doors. I think my way is very healthy. It forces us both to be honest with each other, and that honesty leads to more trust and intimacy."

She munched on another meatball, and Victor took it as a good sign. At least she hadn't lost her appetite. "So you've done this with girlfriends in the past?"

He nodded. "They were different than you, though. They all knew the submissive role well and were comfortable with it. You, on the other hand, are a virgin, so to speak. I have to be careful with you and take it slow."

Her cheeks were now red. "God, the words that come out of your mouth."

He laughed. "I must say, Abigail, you are taking this better than I had hoped."

She thought about it. "Well, I'm fairly confident I can keep those rules, so I may never see the south end of your hand." She smiled at him sweetly as she ate another meatball.

Victor laughed in relief and started eating. "I like your attitude."

They finished up their food, and Victor took her home. After the conversation they'd had at the restaurant, Abby wasn't at all nervous when he walked her into the house. He walked around and checked to make sure all her doors and windows were locked. Then he grabbed the coffee maker and coffee from the table. "I think I'll take these with me to increase your chances of behaving." He had an amused grin on his face.

She sighed.

Victor set the items down by the front door and pulled her into his arms. "God, you smell good." He breathed in her hair and then claimed her lips with his own. The usual spark and warmth spread through both their bodies, and Abby completely melted in his arms. He briefly thought about taking her right then and there, but he knew she wasn't ready. So instead he pulled away and smiled down at her.

"Good night, Abigail. Make sure you lock up and set that alarm as soon as I leave."

She nodded.

"I'll type up the list and email it to you as soon as I get home."

She yawned and nodded again.

Once he was gone, Abby dutifully locked up and turned on the alarm. She headed upstairs to wash off her makeup and put on her pajamas. She had just climbed into bed when her cell pinged with an incoming email. Sure enough, it was from Victor. She opened the attachment and read over the list.

Rule Number Two – Health and Safety
- No cab or Uber rides.
- No driving in bad weather such as heavy snow, ice, fog, or rain.
- No speeding.
- No smoking.
- No heavy drinking (in your case, over 2 drinks).
- No drugs of any kind including prescriptions (unless I approve them).

- No caffeine of any kind (this includes coffee, tea, soda, energy drinks, chocolate, or pills).
- No fast food or junk food.
- Eat protein at every meal (the size of your fist).
- Exercise regularly (at least 3 to 4 times a week).
- Get plenty of sleep every night (at least 8 hours).
- House alarm is on at all times (even when you're home).
- No walking alone.
- No entering or driving into unsafe neighborhoods.
- For Pete's sake, wear a damn jacket when the temperature is below 70 degrees!
- This list is subject to change. I can, and will, add things when I see fit.

Abby snorted when she read the last bullet point. Leave it to the dictator to work in a contingency clause. She fired off a text to the good doctor.

Thanks. What do you consider an unsafe neighborhood? And how can I possibly not walk alone? I would have to have someone with me at all times to avoid that rule.

His response was immediate.

For starters, consider the neighborhood around the clinic unsafe. Good point on walking alone. Change that to no walking alone outside for exercise, especially with your iPod on when you're distracted.

She blinked and wondered how he could possibly know about that. Then she sent her response.

Okay. Fair enough. Thanks for today. I loved it!

Victor smiled when he read the text.

Good night, little one.

Abby curled up in her bed and thought about the day. It had been near perfect, aside from the crazy conversation at the end. Was she really willing to put up with Victor's control issues? Wasn't that a sign of future domestic violence? And, more importantly, could she handle being spanked? She just didn't know. What she did know was she liked the man. A lot.

Chapter Nineteen

Over the next three days, Abby received numerous texts from Victor. He was checking in and also telling her funny things about his job. On Monday he sent her a lovely bouquet of daffodils. They were her favorite, and she wondered how he had known. She toyed with the idea he was a psychic, but then she dismissed it as ridiculous. The man had probably just gotten lucky. Then again, it was a tough time of year to find the spring flower. Abby gave up worrying about it and enjoyed them. They made her smile and think of him.

On Tuesday Victor called and invited her to dinner Wednesday night. He explained he had gotten quite used to seeing her midweek. She agreed, and he said he would pick her up at six.

Abby had spent the day writing, and then she had to rush home to get ready for their date. She carefully reset the house alarm once she was inside. She knew Victor would be listening for it to click off when he came to pick her up. She had no intention of ever breaking a rule. He had been right. The threat of a spanking was proving to be highly motivating.

He arrived ten minutes early and was carrying a big shopping bag. Abby let him in and eyed the bag suspiciously. She was wearing jeans and a soft pale lilac sweater with gray leather boots. She was relieved to see he had on jeans as well. Her wardrobe was so limited, and she mentally made a note to call Rachel to go shopping.

Victor set the bag on her kitchen table and pulled her in for a kiss. He realized how much he had missed her. The feel of her warm body next to his was intoxicating, and he reluctantly pulled away.

She nodded at the bag and teased. "Are you cooking dinner?"

"No, silly. That is a gift for you."

She made no move toward the bag.

"It doesn't bite. Go on, open it!"

She sighed and walked over to the table. She peeked in the bag and then gave him an exasperated look. "Seriously?"

Victor walked over and stood by her. He had a boyish grin on his face. Inside the bag was an electric tea kettle and a large assortment of herbal decaf teas.

"What? I thought this would be a good replacement for your beloved coffee. It's a hot beverage, *and* it's healthy."

She grinned. "Well thank you. Your efforts to keep me from being punished are appreciated. But remember, I'm English. If my parents couldn't get me to drink tea, what makes you think you can?"

He gave her a wicked grin. "I can be very persuasive, Abigail."

"I have no doubt."

They headed to Mabel's for dinner. It was a restaurant owned by Michael Symon, and it had a reputation for outstanding barbecue. They were seated upstairs with a view of the kitchen and the long, family-style tables below.

Once Abby looked at the menu, she realized Victor was still pushing his health and safety agenda. They served nothing but meat in various forms. Even the sides had meat in them. She glared at him. "I thought meat was bad for the heart."

He looked up from his menu. "Oh, it is for the typical American. Most eat way too much and the high-fat varieties. But you, little one, are the exception. You need protein, and this meat is supposed to be the best."

She glared at him but continued to peruse the menu. She finally settled on a turkey sandwich.

Victor shook his head. "This is the best barbecue place in town, and you get a plain turkey sandwich?"

She shrugged. "It's meat."

He laughed. "You are going to be a challenge, aren't you Abigail? I'm getting the sampler platter. You can try some of mine to see if you like any of it." He set the menu down. "And how are you doing with the rest of rule two?"

"Good. They're easy for the most part. Even the tougher ones have been okay. I haven't had any coffee, I'm wearing my coat, and my house alarm is on at all times." She smiled at him sweetly. "Sorry to disappoint your hand."

"You're not disappointing me or my hand. Actually, I'm thrilled. Keep it up!"

That was not the reaction she was hoping for. She wanted to get a rise out of him, so she smugly added, "You do realize I can break all of these rules without you ever knowing."

He looked at her seriously. "That's true, but if you choose to go that route you will eventually slip up. Then there will be hell to pay." He buttered a piece of bread and continued. "If you break rules, then I get anxious. When I get anxious, I start tightening the reins and making more and more rules. Do you really want to go there?" He squeezed her hand. "We need to build this relationship on trust, Abigail. That means complete honesty with each other. I expect you to tell me when you've misbehaved."

She smiled at him but was thinking there was no way in hell that was ever going to happen.

"Okay," she said. But what about you? Do these rules apply to you too? I know you said Rule Number One did, but it seems to me you could benefit from most of Rule Number Two as well."

Victor was stunned. No other girlfriend had challenged him in this way before. On the one hand, she made a valid point. But he was the fucking Dominant, and she needed to remember that. He calmly responded.

"I naturally follow most of the health and safety rules, Abigail, because they make sense. But I don't have to follow any of them if I don't want to, because I am the man. Rule Number Two is for you, not me."

"Well, that hardly seems fair. And it sounds very sexist to me."

"That's because it is. I have very old fashioned views about gender roles. I'm the male, and therefore I'm in charge."

"I'm sure there are plenty of controlling females out there," she said dryly.

"Yes, but there's not one in our relationship, now, is there?"

She made a face at him, and Victor laughed. Just then their food arrived and they started eating. It was all delicious, and Abby ate more meat than she had in a long time.

They discussed their jobs. Victor had just seen a patient that had flown all the way from Japan to get his opinion.

Abby looked at him in amazement. "You're that good?"

He shrugged. "Yes, I believe I am."

"And so humble too," she teased.

He asked about her writing, and she explained her story had just taken a dramatic and unforeseen turn.

"What do you mean? Can't you just write what you want and stick with your outline?"

"I wish! But I learned a long time ago not to fight where the story takes me. My writing brain has a mind of its own."

Victor shook his head. "So you have no control over a story? I don't think I could do that."

"No," she laughed. "You probably couldn't."

They were interrupted by Abby's cell ringing. She apologized and looked at the number.

"Sorry, that's my friend, Rachel. I'll call her later."

"No. No. Take the call now. I don't mind."

Abby picked up. "Heh, Rach. What's up? I'm on a date with Victor."

"Oh, good. I told you there were decent men out there. Where did he take you? More importantly, what are you wearing?"

Abby groaned. "Is that all you called for? I'm hanging up now."

"No, wait! I want to meet this guy. Invite him over for dinner on Saturday night. I'll cook, and we can play games. I'll invite Renee and Don, and Lindsay and Kent too."

"I thought they were separated."

"Who knows with those two. One minute they're on, and the next they're off. Quit stalling and ask your date if Saturday works."

Abby groaned. She didn't want to put Victor on the spot like that, but her friend was stubborn. She might as well get it over with. She covered the phone and looked at him.

"Rachel wants to have us over for dinner on Saturday night with two other couples. If you don't want to go, that's fine, I can make up some excuse."

Victor smiled and raised one eyebrow. "More white lies, Abigail? No, that won't be necessary. I would be happy to meet your friends."

She looked at him uncertainly. "Are you sure? They can be a force to reckon with."

"I'm pretty sure I can handle it. Tell her yes."

"Okay." She uncovered the phone. "Heh Rach, we can make it. What time do you want us there, and what should we bring?"

Rachel was ecstatic. "Bring some wine. We can discuss what you should wear before then."

Abby snorted. "You know me well. Actually, I was going to tell you I need to go shopping. You in?"

"Of course!"

They hung up, and Abby smiled shyly at Victor. "Thanks. They're nice people. I think you'll like them."

"I'm sure I will."

***

Saturday came quickly, and Victor was getting ready for their date. He had already bought the wine they would bring. Abby had said she would pick it up, but he had nixed that immediately. She had also offered to drive, and he hadn't even dignified that with a response. He had brusquely told her to be ready by five forty-five.

The phone rang while he was getting dressed. It was Yuri, and Victor put him on speaker.

"What's going on, my friend? If you're not busy, I thought we could go grab some dinner."

"I already have plans, Kopyev. I'm going out with Abigail."

"Ah, and how is it going with the new submissive?"

Victor laughed. "I would hardly call her that. But it's going fine. She's well aware of two rules now and hasn't gone running for the hills. I'm taking that as a good sign."

"Really? I would have thought that after your obedience discussion she would have been done. Maybe there's a submissive in that girl after all."

"Maybe. But we haven't had the obedience talk yet."

Yuri was confused. "But I thought you covered the two rules."

"I did, but now there are three rules." He explained the health and safety addition.

Yuri listened quietly and then said, "You've never cared about that before."

"Well, I do now. This girl is different, and I need to protect her."

"Is it the girl, or is it you, Victor? Perhaps your need for control is getting worse."

"No. It's definitely the girl."

Yuri thought about it. "She *is* exquisite, and there's something almost fragile about her. Which leads me to believe that when you discuss obedience she's going to run."

"Not necessarily. I've already discussed punishment with her, and she took that very well."

"Really? There may be hope for you yet."

"I'm counting on it. I really like this one, Yuri. She told me she has no intention of ever breaking a rule. That pleased me to no end."

"Yes, but you know damn well she will eventually falter. Just be gentle with her when that happens."

"I will. I don't plan to screw this up. Now, if you'll excuse me, I have to go."

"Where are you two going?"

Victor chuckled. "We're going over to her friend's house. We're having dinner and playing board games with three other couples if you can believe it."

Yuri was stunned. "I never thought I'd see the day Victor Turov went in for a normal date. Maybe you'll get lucky, and the games will be kinky sex ones."

"They had better not be sex games. There's no way in hell I'm sharing this girl with anyone!"

"Such a shame. I have become quite fond of your Mrs. Shea."

"Fuck you, Kopyev." He hung up and grabbed his coat and keys.

Yuri was still laughing.

***

They were the last to arrive. Rachel greeted them at the door and gave Abby a hug before turning her attention to Victor. She gave him a quick assessment. He was older, tall, and intense looking. He was also hot as hell.

"Hi. I'm Rachel. It's so nice to meet you." She shook his hand and took the bottles of wine he handed her. Then she led them into the kitchen. The other couples were standing around the island, and Abby quickly introduced everyone.

Joel asked, "So Victor, you're a surgeon?"

"Yes. A cardiothoracic surgeon at the clinic."

"Oh no, Abs! Another medical person," said Joel. "Everyone in here works in the medical field except for me and Abby," he explained. "We get to hear a lot of gory medical stories. She doesn't mind, but I can't stand it."

Victor laughed. "No doubt Abigail likes it for the book ideas."

They all looked amused at the formal use of her name.

"Oh no. Is Abby asking you how to kill people? She asks me all the time!" said Lindsay.

"Just once I wish she would ask me. You know you can work an entire murder plot around money," said Joel.

"Yes, but I keep telling you no one wants to read that boring crap," countered Abby.

Rachel patted her husband's arm. "Poor Joel. He can't understand why we all fall asleep when he starts talking numbers."

The conversation continued, and Abby absent-mindedly picked up a potato chip and dunked it in some dip. She was about to bite into it when she caught Victor's glance. He had one eyebrow arched and was staring at the chip pointedly. Abby realized with a start she was eating junk food. She pressed her lips together, threw the chip in the garbage, and looked away.

Of course, Rachel noticed. "Something wrong with the dip?"

"No. Sorry. I'm just trying to eat healthier." Abby refused to look at Victor.

"Since when?" asked Rachel.

"If anyone can afford to eat junk, it's you, Abs. You're so thin." This was from Lindsay, who struggled with extra pounds.

"I don't think she's thin. I think she looks good. Maybe you should try to eat healthy too," said Kent, Lindsay's husband.

Everyone winced. Don jumped in to change the conversation and asked Victor if he liked microbrews. The men headed down to the basement to pick out beers, and the girls looked at each other.

Lindsay was getting ready to have a full-on snit about Kent, but Rachel cut her off. "We need to discuss doctor hottie first while we've still got the chance."

Abby smiled shyly at them. "So what do you think?"

"Gorgeous."

"Intense and confident."

"I would totally do him." That was from Renee, who was old enough to be his mom, and they burst out laughing. "What? I'm in my sexual prime now."

"Since the topic came up, are you two...?" Rachel trailed off.

Abby was embarrassed. "God, no! We just started dating. But we are kissing."

"And?"

"He's a damn good kisser!"

The girls cheered, and Lindsay opened one of the bottles Victor had brought. As she poured, Rachel looked the wine up on her Vivino app. "Your doctor has good taste. This stuff is highly rated, and it's expensive."

The conversation moved on to other things, and Abby relaxed. She had never been comfortable as the center of attention, even with her friends. As they discussed Kent's rude comment, she listened to the male voices coming up from the stairs. She could clearly hear Victor's accent mingled in with the other men. She realized he was completely comfortable talking to strangers, and she shook her head.

When dinner was served, they all gathered around the large high-top table. It comfortably seated the eight of them, and Abby sat right next to Victor. He squeezed her hand under the table and gave her a smile. Rachel was an excellent cook, and she had opted for a cozy meal of turkey meatloaf, mashed potatoes, green beans, cornbread, and cake for dessert.

She explained to Victor, "Abs and Don don't eat much meat, so I'm always struggling to find something to tempt them."

"I eat meat," said Abby.

"Me too," added Don. "Just not red meat. I'm sure Victor can tell you how unhealthy that is for the heart."

"Sure. It all depends on the patient, though. Some need the protein more than others." Victor was looking at Abby.

Meanwhile, Lindsay came around the table with a bottle of wine and was refilling glasses. She was pouring heavily, and when she got to Abby's glass, Victor frowned.

The dinner was delicious, and the conversation was lively. When everyone was done, Abby started to clear the plates.

Rachel explained to Victor. "Abby and I work well together. I do all the cooking, and she does the dishes."

Kent chimed in. "And Lindsay sits on her ass and does nothing."

The couple started arguing again, and everyone else was looking uncomfortable. Victor stood up and grabbed some things from the table. He brought them to Abby and made a funny face. She thanked him and half-suppressed a laugh.

Kent was on a rant. "I'm just saying there are certain household things that don't get done at home."

That got a rise out of Lindsay. "And what do you do at home? You don't help me at all. Even Victor is helping Abby, and they just started dating."

Kent snorted. "And that's why. Every guy jumps through hoops at the beginning just to get the girl in bed."

Victor swore under his breath. Don and Joel jumped up and took

Kent downstairs again.

"I'm so sorry," whispered Abby.

"Don't be. You didn't do anything wrong." Victor smiled at her and continued to clear the table. Once it was cleared they started playing games. The guys came back up, and Kent seemed more mellow. Rachel opened a new bottle of wine and started pouring. When she got to Abby's glass, Victor pulled it away.

"She's had enough."

Rachel looked at Abby in confusion. "Did you drive?"

Victor stood up as he answered. "No, I did. But Abigail is a lightweight."

He carried her wine glass to the sink and grabbed a water from the fridge. He set it in front of her and sat back down. They were all staring at him in shock.

He shrugged and explained, "Two is her limit."

Abby wanted the floor to open up and swallow her. Fortunately, Kent took the opportunity to make a snarky comment about Lindsay's drinking, and that pulled everyone's attention away.

The night continued, and, as more wine went down, things got more uncomfortable. Not only were Lindsay and Kent snipping, but Rachel and Joel were arguing with each other over the rules of a game. Don was slurring from the microbrews, and Renee was falling asleep at the table. Abby was embarrassed by her friends. She was used to it, but she knew an outsider like Victor was probably horrified.

Sure enough, he leaned over and quietly suggested they leave. She agreed, and the two said their goodnights.

Rachel pressed some leftover containers into Abby's hands and apologized to Victor. "I'm sorry things got a little heated tonight. Abs can tell you we've all been married a long time, and that sometimes means we're idiots. Have you ever been married, Victor?" She was digging, and it was obvious.

Abby glared at her, but Victor just smiled. "No."

"Oh." She was used to getting more out of people. She changed the subject. "Did you know Abby's birthday is a week from today?"

He looked at Abby. "I did not. Is this the big thirty?"

She groaned. "Don't remind me."

"Please. You're still just a baby."

Rachel honed in. "How old are you, Victor?"

"Well past thirty," was all he said.

Rachel was getting frustrated by the lack of information. "We're taking Abby out on Saturday to celebrate. You should come."

Abby quickly interrupted. "No. It's going to be a girl's night out. No guys are allowed."

Rachel looked at her in surprise. She said to Victor, "Never mind, then."

He nodded but was looking at Abby curiously. "You and I can celebrate another night." He took her hand and led her out to the truck.

Once they were safely in and on their way, he blew out his breath. "Well, that was interesting!"

Abby covered her face with her hands. "I'm so sorry! They were crazier than normal tonight."

Victor laughed. "No one is normal, Abigail. This is what I keep trying to tell you. At least in our relationship, the rules are very clear. I would never talk to you that way because I would never have to. With those two there are no boundaries, and their expectations are completely out of whack."

"Wait. Are you saying Kent had a reason to talk to her like that?"

He hesitated. "There's no excuse for what that prick was saying. But your friend was drinking way too much. I counted five glasses of wine, and those were heavy pours. She clearly has a drinking problem. Perhaps he is reacting to that."

Abby looked concerned. "I have noticed she's drinking a lot more lately."

He reached over and squeezed her hand. "You can't worry about your friends, little one. Just remember when it comes to you, two drinks are your limit."

"Yes, you made that abundantly clear at dinner," came the sarcastic reply.

They reached Abby's townhouse, and Victor walked her in. He did his usual lock check on all the windows and doors, but then he plopped down on the couch and motioned her over. She gave him a shy smile before sitting next to him. Victor pulled her into his lap and wrapped his arms around her.

"I think we should make out like teenagers," he whispered.

She grinned and whispered back, "Okay."

They spent a pleasant half hour pressed up against each other.

Abby forgot her shyness and had her hands on his chest and in his hair. Victor's hands were wandering too. One was cupping a breast, and the other was resting on her mid-thigh. He was kissing her all over her neck and face, and she could feel his obvious hard-on.

Finally, Victor pulled away and cupped her face. "You are intoxicating, little one. But I have to go. Don't forget I have to fly to Indianapolis tomorrow." He had told her about the trip on Wednesday. He was going to be in Indianapolis all week, consulting on surgeries.

Abby sighed and whispered, "No. I think you should stay."

Victor laughed. "Oh, Abigail. You are so not ready for that."

She looked at him in confusion. "I'm not?"

"No, baby. I'm not like your Mr. Shea. We need to trust each other more before we can go there."

"Oh." She wasn't sure she believed him. She wondered if he just wasn't that into her, and the thought was depressing.

Victor was watching her face closely. As if reading her mind, he stood and pulled her up with him. Then he captured both of her wrists in one hand and pinned them behind her back tightly. With his other hand, he leisurely caressed her. He started between her legs, causing Abby to gasp. Then his hand trailed up over her belly, circled around both breasts while teasing the nipples, before settling at the base of her head. Victor was watching her the entire time. He pulled her face toward his and then claimed her mouth in a rough and passionate kiss. His tongue invaded her mouth and left no room for argument. When he finished, Abby was leaning against him weakly.

She struggled to find her voice. "Oh."

Victor nodded. He was breathing hard and finally released her wrists. "Did that bother you?"

She thought about it. "No. I liked it," she whispered.

He laughed. "Oh, Abigail. We are going to have so much fun." He gently smacked her on the ass. "When you're ready."

She reluctantly pulled away and watched him get his coat. "I almost forgot to get the luggage tags you asked for. They're upstairs. I'll be right back."

Victor headed toward the kitchen. "Do you mind if I take some of the leftovers for breakfast tomorrow?"

She yelled down from the stairs. "Help yourself. There are bags in one of the drawers."

He rummaged through her kitchen drawers and found the bags. He also saw several keys that looked like duplicates of her house key. Victor didn't even hesitate. He grabbed a key and slipped it in his pocket. When Abby returned, he had the food in a bag and an innocent expression on his face.

She handed him the luggage tags and walked him to the door.

"Good night, Abigail. I had fun tonight. Don't forget to lock up and set your alarm."

He kissed her again and then headed to his car. Abby leaned against the door after he left. She set the alarm and sighed. The night had been eventful to say the least. She was on unsure ground with this man, but she knew she liked him. She also knew she wanted him. Bad.

Chapter Twenty

The week had gone by quickly. Abby was working toward a deadline on her book and spent a lot of time writing in the neighborhood library. She had wisely avoided the coffee shop. It would be too tempting to order a coffee, and she told herself she didn't want to disappoint Victor. In truth, she was more afraid of getting spanked. For the umpteenth time, she wondered just how bad it could be. She had no intention of finding out.

While he was gone the two had talked on the phone every night, and they had also texted each other throughout the week. Victor had finally flown home late Friday evening, but they had not seen each other. He had gone into the clinic early on Saturday to catch up on things, and now Abby was busy getting ready for her birthday celebration. They made plans to go out the following day.

"Have fun tonight but remember the rules, Abigail." Victor was feeling anxious, and his tone came across harsher than he had intended.

Abby had him on speaker phone while she was putting on her makeup. "Victor. We talked about this. Vince is picking us up here and driving us to the casino, and we will all stay together. Then we're going to dinner at Zocalo's, and I will order something with meat. Then I'm having one drink at the Chocolate Bar before Vince brings us back to my place. I will wear my coat, the alarm will be on, and I won't have any caffeine. You've got nothing to worry about."

He sighed. "Okay, little one. I am trusting you. Please stay safe."

They hung up, and Abby rushed to get ready. The girls would be there in ten minutes. Rachel had pushed for a dress-up night, but Abby had insisted they wear more casual clothing. It was, after all, her birthday. She put on a pair of leggings, a tunic sweater, and some boots.

Then she opened her jewelry box. Nate had given her a lot of nice things over the years, and many had been in celebration of her birthday. Abby got a little misty-eyed as she pulled them out. She ended up wearing a necklace, earrings, and bracelet in honor of her late husband.

The doorbell rang as she was pulling her hair up into a ponytail. Abby smiled at her reflection before running downstairs. It was going to be an epic night.

Twenty minutes later and Vince had deposited them all at the front entrance of the Jack Casino. It had been a lively ride. They had made him blast the radio and had sung along at the top of their voices. Abby could see Vince's grin in the rearview mirror. She hoped Victor was paying him well. She tried to give him a tip, but he refused. The man was as stubborn as her boyfriend.

They piled out of the Navigator and headed into the casino. The security guard let everyone pass but Abby. She had to show him her ID, and he looked it over carefully. Then he sheepishly wished her a happy birthday, and the girls cheered.

They headed up to the second floor where the high-end slots were. They had decided they were each going to put in a twenty-dollar bill and bet the max until they won or lost it all. As they were walking, they passed the main bar. Lindsay made a beeline toward it, and the rest of the girls followed.

"We should do a birthday shot to get the night started," said Lindsay.

Abby knew they were going to give her a hard time if she didn't drink. She debated doing one shot to get them off her back. If she made it a weak one, and just had the other drink at the Chocolate Bar, she would still be within her limits.

They ended up doing lemon drops. It barely tasted like alcohol to Abby, and she was feeling pretty smug. Her friends were appeased, and she was able to order a big bottle of water without anyone giving her grief. The rest of them ordered another round, and they carried their drinks to the slots.

On the way, Rachel busted Renee trying to send a text to her husband. She stopped the group.

"Listen. This is a girl's night out, and most of us need a break from our men. I vote we make it a no-guy zone, which means no texting or calling the boys. Let them wonder what we're up to."

Kate chimed in. "What about guys we meet tonight? You attached women don't care, but if I meet a hottie while we're out, I'm damn well going to talk to him."

"Amen, sister," said Lindsay, and they all rolled their eyes at her.

"Hell, I wouldn't mind talking to some hotties myself," said Renee, and they all laughed.

"That's fine. But anyone caught contacting their man has to do a shot," stated Rachel.

Abby chuckled at her friends. She knew some of them would have a tough time sticking to that rule. She also knew Victor wasn't expecting any contact from her that night, so she would be safe.

They continued on to the high-end section of the casino. It was tucked back in a corner and had a more subdued atmosphere. The place was pretty empty. There were a few elderly patrons sitting at various slots, and there was a group of guys sitting at a blackjack table in the corner. The guys watched them walk by, and one even called out to them. He was ignored.

The girls debated several machines and finally opted for one called Celebration. It had big diamonds for the bonus and bright pink and purple flashing lights. The maximum bet was $5, and they had $100 to ride. They each took turns pulling the lever and were talking and laughing as the reels spun. Each time the machine paid out credits, the girls cheered and clinked their glasses.

It was Kate's turn to spin. She was busy telling a story and barely paid attention to the reels. They all stopped talking when the machine got louder. The first two reels had lined up with diamonds, and the third was slowly spinning. Then a diamond clicked into the final place. The machine started playing loud music and showed graphics of pouring coins and shooting fireworks. The overhead light was also flashing.

Rachel was the first to recover. She was reading the payout graph at the top. "We just won six thousand dollars!"

They stared at each other, and then everyone started talking at once. Lindsay was jumping up and down, and Kate was laughing hysterically. Abby immediately thought of Victor and pulled out her phone to send him a text. Renee was attempting to do the same with Don.

Rachel busted them. "Ladies. We have our first offenders of the no-text rule." She motioned a server over and ordered two shots of tequila.

"Hell, I want one too after this," announced Lindsay. They all agreed, and the server left to fill an order of five shots.

Meanwhile, several casino officials approached the group, and a crowd had gathered around them. They reviewed the machine for fraud first, and then they congratulated the ladies on their win. One representative asked if they would like some complimentary champagne to celebrate, and another asked if they would be willing to have their picture taken.

Before Abby knew it, she had downed a shot of tequila and two glasses of champagne. They had all posed for a photo for the winners' wall, and the representative had also taken photos using each of their cell phones. Now they were heading to the cashier to get their money, and Abby could feel the effects of the alcohol. The room was a little fuzzy, and she was starting to slur her words.

Rachel noticed and linked her arm with Abby's. "This is the best birthday ever!"

As the cashier counted out their money, Abby thought about Victor. She knew he would be angry if he saw what she was doing. But then she realized he didn't have to know. It was her thirtieth birthday, after all, and she was a grown-ass woman. The alcohol had given her confidence and completely wiped out her fear of punishment. The excitement of the win also hadn't hurt, and it was pushing her toward more reckless behavior. The girls continued to drink and play games for another hour. By the time they left the casino, they were all thoroughly drunk.

They staggered down the street in search of Zocalo's. Somehow they ended up on Euclid Avenue by mistake, and they saw the Chocolate Bar looming in the distance. The girls headed in that direction, and Renee commented they could always just eat there. They pushed two tables together in the back and settled in.

Bobby was their server. He was a young kid with red hair and a winning smile. The girls were merciless in teasing him, but he took it well. They ordered a bunch of unhealthy appetizers including waffle fries, nachos, and fried ravioli. Abby vaguely noticed none of the food had meat, but she didn't care. She was beyond the point of having an appetite, and she barely touched the food.

The drinks, on the other hand, were going down easily. She knew she should stop, but something made her continue drinking. Her friends were as well. A group of guys had joined them at the table, and Kate and Lindsay were shamelessly flirting with the men. Abby hung out at the other end with Rachel and Renee. They were discussing their husbands in great detail, and Don was actually on his way to pick up Renee. When he arrived, he took one look at the girls and offered to take everyone home. Kate had already disappeared with one of the guys from the table, but Lindsay was still chatting up a storm with two others. She refused to leave, and Rachel and Abby said they would stay with her.

After Don and Renee left, the girls moved down to sit next to Lindsay. The men she was talking to immediately honed in on Abby. She was young and pretty. She was also oblivious to what was going on and was barely keeping her eyes open.

Rachel realized Lindsay was just as bad, and she knew something had to be done. She drunkenly told the guys, "Just so you know, this one is married, and this one has a serious boyfriend."

One of the men laughed. "Relax, darlin'. We're just having fun. I don't see the boyfriend, and I don't see a ring on either of their fingers. What their men don't know won't hurt them."

Now Rachel was getting pissed. She grabbed Lindsay's arm and whispered, "We have to leave! Abs is really drunk, and these guys are jerks."

Lindsay started to argue, but then she saw Abby's swaying figure. She reluctantly agreed.

Rachel turned to the guys. "We're leaving now. She picked up the pitcher of beer they had just ordered to get rid of it. She tripped on her heels and spilled the entire pitcher down Abby's front. "Oh my god, Abs, I am so sorry!"

Abby laughed and drunkenly waved her away. "S'okay. I won't melt."

It had missed her head, but the front of her sweater and leggings were soaked. She grabbed a napkin and attempted to dry off. One of the guys grabbed a napkin and was dabbing at her breasts.

Rachel swatted his hand away. "Leave her alone!"

The men stood up, and one said, "It's all good, sweetheart."

They left the table, and Rachel sighed in relief. She turned to Abby to let her know it was time to go.

Abby staggered to her feet. "I hath to go pay the bill. And I've gotta pee."

"Okay, let's pay the bill first. Again, I am so sorry."

As they started to walk away, Lindsay grabbed Abby's arm. "Wait. You need to call that Vince man for our ride."

"Oh. Okay." She struggled to find the phone in her purse. When she did, it took her three tries to unlock it. Then she scrolled down to the V's in her contact list and handed the phone over to Lindsay. "Juss tell him you're a friend of mine and where we're at. I gotta go pay the bill."

Rachel took her arm, and they headed to the bar to find Bobby.

Lindsay squinted at the phone until she found Vince's name. Then she hit dial and waited. She was as drunk as Abby, and she hit Victor's name by mistake. He picked up on the first ring.

"Abigail. I didn't think I would hear from you tonight. Are you home already? How was the girl's night?" He was thrilled she had called.

"Nope. Not Abby. Thish is Lindsay, her friend. I'm calling for Abs, and we need a ride, please."

Victor's eyes narrowed. The girl was obviously drunk. "Lindsay, is Abigail with you? Please put her on the phone."

"Can't. Not sure where sheesh at."

"Has Abigail been drinking?" He could feel his anxiety rising.

"God, yesh. She's trashed. It's her birthday," Lindsay explained.

He spoke slowly in an angry but controlled tone. "Please find her and put her on the phone, now!"

"K. I think sheesh in the bathroom." She put the phone down and walked away without hanging up.

All Victor could hear was background bar noises. He swore loudly and hung up the phone. He immediately dialed Vince. "I need you at my house as soon as possible."

Vince didn't hesitate. "On my way. Five minutes, tops."

The call clicked off, and then Victor pulled up his tracking app. Her phone was at the Chocolate Bar. He prayed she was there as well.

***

Abby and Rachel stood in line for ten minutes but still weren't helped. The place was packed, and the bartenders were furiously trying to place drink orders. Bobby was nowhere to be found. Lindsay stumbled up and announced their ride was on its way. Then she said she had to pee.

"I do too!" complained Abby. Rachel agreed to stay in line while the other two went to the restroom. She was still standing there when Victor walked in.

Despite the crowded bar, he spotted her immediately. Rachel was wearing a ridiculous pair of high heels, and she towered over the other patrons. When he reached her side, he tapped her arm to get her attention. "Where's Abigail?"

Rachel looked at Victor in surprise. "I thought the Vince guy was coming to get us."

Victor repeated the question with more force. "Where. Is. Abigail?!"

Rachel pointed to the stairs leading down to the restroom. "She had to pee. Lindsay took her."

Victor walked off, and Rachel followed him. She was drunk, but she knew an angry man when she saw one.

The restrooms were down the stairs and at the end of a long hallway. They could see Lindsay standing in the corner making out with a man. It was one of the guys she had been talking to at the table. Then they noticed the other man further back pulling on Abby's arm. She was pulling just as hard to get away from him.

"Let me go, asshole. Not interested!"

Victor rushed over and grabbed the man's arm. He twisted it behind his back and had it at an unnatural and painful angle. The man released Abby immediately.

Victor continued to twist his arm but looked at Abby. "Are you okay?"

She blinked at him in confusion. "Victor? Mmm hmm. I'm 'kay."

He noted her swaying and swore softly. He released the man and put his arm around Abby's waist. Then he looked at the guy.

"This is my girlfriend. I suggest you leave now before I break your fucking arm!" His eyes were black, and every inch of his body showed fury. The guy wisely backed away.

Victor turned to Rachel. "Get your friends so we can get the hell out of here."

Rachel grabbed Lindsay and explained, "It's just us. Everyone else left already."

He nodded and walked Abby back up toward the bar. She was still confused. "What are you doing here?"

He ignored her and spoke to Rachel instead. She was the soberest of the three of them, which wasn't saying much. "Where are your coats?"

Rachel led him to their table, and he saw Abby's phone sitting in a condensation puddle. He picked it up, dried it off, and put it in his pocket. Victor noted the large array of empty bar glasses and appetizer plates, and there were two women's coats on the floor. One was Abby's, and the other was Rachel's. Lindsay was already wearing hers.

Just then their errant server arrived with the final bill and Abby's credit card.

Victor asked, "Have you run the card yet?"

"Not yet."

"Good." He took her card and put it in his pocket. Then he pulled his own out from his wallet and handed it to the server. "I'm going to need an itemized receipt, please."

Bobby nodded. "I'll be back in two minutes."

While they waited, Victor went to help Abby on with her coat and realized she was soaking wet. "Abigail, why are you so wet?"

Rachel apologized. "It was me. I accidentally spilled a pitcher of beer on her."

Victor pinched the bridge of his nose between his thumb and forefinger. What little control he had left of his anger was rapidly dissolving. When the bill arrived, he wrote in a large tip and signed. He then thanked the server.

"No problem, sir. They were drunk but a lot of fun!"

Victor scowled at Bobby and led the girls out of the restaurant. Vince was waiting with the car illegally parked on the street. He quickly opened the doors. Lindsay hopped in the front, and Rachel scooted in the back to the far end. Abby slid in the middle, and Victor got in next to her. He had to assist Abby with her seatbelt, as she was too drunk to click it in place.

When Vince got in on the driver's side, the two men eyed each other in the rearview mirror.

"We're down two, Dr. Turov. Are you sure they're not still in there?"

Rachel responded. "Nah. Kate hooked up, and Renee went home a long time ago."

Vince nodded and started the Navigator.

"Drop me off first, Vince, and then you can take the women home," said Victor

The driver nodded and pulled into traffic.

Victor looked down at Abby. She was trying hard to stay awake. She was also rapidly losing color in her face.

Shit! "Abigail, are you okay?"

She nodded.

"Vince, do you have any garbage bags in here? I think she might be sick."

The driver quietly pulled out a plastic bag from the center console and handed it to Victor.

Rachel started pitching a fit. "Abigail Shea, you better not get sick! I cannot handle puke."

Lindsay was laughing in the front seat.

Abby swallowed hard and then leaned into Victor. "I'm 'kay," she whispered.

Victor watched her carefully, but it appeared she was just falling asleep. He noticed the wristlet she was clutching in her hand. He pulled her credit card and cell out of his pocket and went to put them in the purse. When he unzipped it, he saw the wad of cash inside.

"Abigail! Why do you have so much money in here?"

Lindsay started cheering and clapping up front. "We won at the casino, doc! We each won a lot of money."

Rachel nodded. "Twelve hundred apiece to be exact."

"And you carried it around in your purses all night?" His anger went to a white-hot fury.

There was no response from Abigail. He hoped she had merely fallen asleep and wasn't passed out. Victor started breathing deeply to try and calm down. Thank God they had called when they did!

Five minutes later Vince pulled into the parking garage at Victor's condo. The surgeon gently shook Abigail to wake her. She was in a stupor, but she responded enough to get out of the vehicle. She leaned into him and walked with a stagger. Once they were in the elevator, he picked her up to carry her the rest of the way. She snuggled into his chest.

Victor realized it was going to be a long night. His top priority was to get her into dry clothes and then drinking as much water as possible. He knew she was safe now, and his anxiety began to dissipate, but his anger remained. Tomorrow, Abigail was going to be punished.

Chapter Twenty-One

Once in the condo Victor carried Abby down to his bedroom and set her on the bed. She kept falling backward, and he had to put one arm around her waist to keep her upright. With the other hand, he grasped her sweater at the hem.

"Put your arms up in the air, little one."

She dutifully raised her arms, and he pulled the wet sweater up and over her head. He let it drop to the floor and gently eased her back on the bed. Then he pulled off her boots before grasping the waistband of her leggings. It took some doing, but Victor was able to pull them down and off her legs.

He gazed down at her body. She had soft, beautiful skin and a heart-shaped birthmark on her lower belly. She was wearing a see-through black lace bra and matching bikini panties. Victor was hard instantly. He realized how easy it would be to fuck her right now, and the thought just fueled his anger.

He turned away and rummaged through his dresser. He was looking for something for her to wear, but he was also trying to distract his thoughts. Abigail had put herself in a tremendous amount of risk that night. What's more, she had confidently made promises to abide by his rules, only to turn around and break them hours later. How could he trust her? And once he doled out a punishment, would she be able to trust him? The situation was less than ideal, but Victor knew he still had to move forward.

He found a sweatshirt and workout pants and carried them to the bed. He pulled her back up into a sitting position and realized her bra was wet as well. Victor had it off in seconds. Her nipples were reacting to the cold, and he desperately wanted to work them between his mouth and fingers. Instead, he pulled the sweatshirt over her head and maneuvered her arms through the sleeves. It was too big for her, and the word Russia was splayed across the chest. That made him smile.

The pants were more of a challenge. He had to kneel down and work one foot and leg through at a time. It was a lot like dressing a child. Then Victor had her stand while he pulled the pants up and around her waist. He left her panties on and tied the drawstring snugly at her waist. She was leaning into him and mumbling under her breath.

Victor led her into the bathroom and over to the toilet. "Abigail, you need to pee."

She peered up at him and said, "'Kay."

He helped her to get her pants down and set her on the toilet. She was holding her head in her hands. While she peed, he fixed her hair. He pulled it all together and tied it back in a low ponytail. Then he filled a glass with water from the tap and handed it to her.

"Drink," he ordered.

Abby was desperately trying to stay awake. She vaguely realized she was with Victor and should be embarrassed. But all she wanted to do was sleep. She focused on drinking and peeing as best she could. When the glass was empty she handed it to him, wiped, and tried to stand. The room was spinning, and he had to help her get her pants back on. Then he led her to the bed where she gratefully tumbled in. She was asleep within seconds.

Victor pulled the covers over her and sighed. She was so different from any other girlfriend he had dated. The truly submissive ones would never have dared such a blatant act of disobedience. They had known their role well, and if they accidentally screwed up, they took his punishment meekly but with pleasure. As for the women who had dated him for his money, they might have risked getting this drunk, because obedience was not in their nature. However, they put up with his punishment as a means to an end, and he had easily bent them to his will.

Abigail did not fall into either of these categories. As far as he knew she was dating him because she liked him. The attraction was mutual, and he really needed that in his life right now. He just didn't know how to go about making it work.

Victor continued to watch her and debate his next move. The punishment was going to occur because it was a non-negotiable part of who he was. But maybe he could tone it down a bit. He knew if she could handle that, then she would be ready for sex. That meant he had to prepare.

As a doctor, the importance of safe sexual practices could not be overlooked. All girlfriends in the past had undergone testing for sexually transmitted diseases, and he had done the same. Victor kept blood and gynecological test kits in his condo, and he did the testing himself. The kits were sent to an anonymous lab, and no one saw the results but him. Condoms were also worn at all times.

Victor knew from Abigail's medical records she had been tested for the standard STDs three years ago. Her symptoms had included discharge and itching, and he suspected the gynecologist had run the tests automatically and not because of a true concern. The results had come back negative.

What Victor did not know was her sexual history, but they would be having that discussion soon enough. His biggest concern was the three H's—HIV, hepatitis, and herpes. A blood test could easily check all three of these, and it would be so much easier if he did it now without her knowing. Abigail was passed out, and it would only take a few minutes. He knew this was stepping well outside of his ethical boundaries as a physician, and he could lose his license because of it. He was stunned to realize he was willing to take that risk. He wanted her to be at ease as much as possible with him, and this was one way he could do that.

Victor went and grabbed two blood kits from his office. He set everything up on the end table by the bed, and then he rolled up Abigail's sleeve. As he tied the tourniquet around her arm, she stirred a little and mumbled. He checked her eyes and saw she was definitely passed out. He drew her blood first, and because of the alcohol in her system had no problem getting enough in the vial. He labeled it "hers." Then he drew blood from his own arm and labeled that vial "his." Victor filled out the paperwork, sealed the envelope, and put it in the fridge. He would ship it out on Monday.

Victor was getting tired, as it was now well past midnight. He stripped down and put on a pair of pajama bottoms and t-shirt. He brushed his teeth and left the bathroom light on. He was certain Abigail would be sick later on, and this way she could hopefully find the toilet. Victor crawled into bed and tried to sleep. She looked so tiny next to him, and she wasn't moving. He rolled on his side so he could watch her better. Never in a million years would he have guessed he could have liked someone so much. He threw his arm across her body and slowly fell asleep.

Abby was tossing and turning. Her stomach felt like it was on fire, and her mouth was dry and cottony. She peered around the darkened room and tried to get her bearings. She was horrified when she realized it wasn't her bedroom. What's more, there was a warm body pressed up against her back. Abby immediately panicked. She turned to look, and her breathing calmed down when she realized the man sleeping next to her was Victor.

Her relief was short-lived, though, when she realized she had no idea how she had gotten there. What's more, the clothes she was wearing were too big and not her own.

Abby didn't have time to worry about it. Her stomach was making angry noises, and her mouth started to water. She knew she had to puke, and she saw a doorway lit up in the corner. Abby made a beeline for it. She didn't get there in time, and a little vomit hit the floor in front of the toilet. She was too sick to care.

Victor woke from a sound sleep when he heard the retching noises coming from the bathroom. He looked at the clock. It was 4:11 a.m. She had made it longer than he thought she would. He sighed and got out of bed.

He found Abby huddled over the toilet looking miserable. Some of her hair had come loose from the ponytail and was hanging in her face. She was vomiting and crying at the same time.

Victor grabbed a washcloth from the linen closet and ran it under hot water. Then he knelt down on the floor behind her. He pulled the stray hair back and saw there was vomit on some of the strands. He ran the washcloth over the hair to try to get the puke out. Then he re-tied her ponytail more securely in the band and wiped her face with the clean side of the washcloth.

"I'm so sorry, Victor," Abby whispered.

He said nothing as he stood back up. He rinsed the washcloth, filled the glass with water, and set them both on the counter. As Abby continued to retch, he sat down on the floor, straddled his legs on either side of her, and waited for it to end. He noticed some puke on the floor and grabbed a towel to cover it. Then he softly rubbed her back.

When she was finally done, Victor pulled her into his arms. She was shivering, so he grabbed a clean towel and threw it over her. He wiped her face again with the washcloth and then handed her the glass of water. "Drink."

Abby shakily took a sip and set the water down. Victor picked the glass up and put it back in her hand. "Drink all of it, Abigail." She could hear the anger in his voice, and she dutifully sucked the water down. It made her want to puke again, and she willed her stomach to calm down.

Victor pulled her back into his arms and leaned his head down next to hers. "Let's sit here a bit and make sure you're done."

She nodded and closed her eyes. They sat there for a good fifteen minutes. Abby was just dozing off when another wave of nausea hit her. She was up and puking again, and Victor refilled the water glass. They did this three more times before she was truly done.

Then Victor finally pulled her up to a standing position and handed her his toothbrush. While she brushed, he filled the glass up yet again. He made her drink all of it and then asked if she had to pee. When she said yes, he stood and waited. Abby blushed and looked away. Then she whispered, "I don't want you to see me."

"Abigail, I saw you pee earlier. I see naked bodies all the time. I'm a doctor." Then he added, "Yours is quite beautiful."

She bit her lip and blushed even deeper. "Please." She motioned him to turn with her hand.

Victor grinned and turned around.

Abby continued to stand there. "Um, I don't want you to hear me either," she whispered.

He shook his head in amazement. "I just heard you puke your guts out. What the hell is the difference?"

"It just is. Please."

He left the room, and Abby quickly peed.

When she came out of the bathroom she saw he had gotten into bed. She turned out the light and crawled into bed next to him. Abby snuggled under the blankets. She was freezing and knew it was because of the drinking. Victor gently pulled her on top of him. His body was radiating heat, and she sighed as she sank into his warmth. As she fell asleep she mumbled again, "I really am sorry."

"Good night, little one. We'll talk about it in the morning."

They both fell asleep.

Chapter Twenty-Two

The pager woke Victor up. He squinted at the number. It was the clinic.

"Dr. Turov," he mumbled into the phone. He realized just how exhausted he was. He listened to the scheduler explaining the attending had called off due to a family emergency. "You can't find anyone else?" The lack of sleep had made him cranky. He listened some more. "Very well. I'll be in as soon as I can."

Victor looked at the clock. It was six forty, and Abigail was sound asleep on top of him. He gently rolled her off and sat up in bed. Then he headed into the bathroom for a quick shower. As he surveyed the mess on the floor, he felt his anger rising. Victor thought about punishing her right then and there. Ideally, he would have punished her last night, but she had been in no condition for that. If he did it now, she would still be miserable from a hangover. He also knew he needed more time to do it right.

No, Abigail would be given a reprieve. But that didn't mean she could sleep in comfort while he had to go to work. Victor thought about how to handle her while he took his shower. By the time he had dried off, he knew exactly what he would do.

"Wake up, little one."

Abby fought to open her eyes. They felt like they were stuck together. She also had a massive headache, and the light in the room wasn't helping. Finally, she was able to focus on Victor.

He was sitting on the edge of the bed, and he helped her to sit up. Then he handed her two aspirin and a glass of water. She dutifully swallowed the pills.

Victor motioned to the pitcher of water he had placed on the nightstand. "I want you to drink all of this, fill the pitcher back up, and drink it all again. You're really dehydrated right now."

She nodded.

"I have to go into work. I should be home around noon. In the meantime, I want you to sleep for a few more hours."

She nodded again and drank more water.

His tone changed. "Then I want you to get up and clean that fucking mess in the bathroom!"

Abby's eyes widened in shock.

"When you're done in there, I want you to eat something. There are plenty of options in the fridge. Make sure you get something on your stomach, Abigail."

She nodded.

"Then clean yourself up and sit on the couch in the living room." He pointed to the door and the hallway. "When I get home, I want to see you sitting on that couch. Do you understand?" His voice was harsh and cold.

She nodded but couldn't look at him. She was fighting back the tears.

"Let me hear you say it, Abigail."

"Yes, I understand," she whispered.

He looked down and then clasped her face in both of his hands. He tilted her head up so she was looking at him. He could see the tears in her eyes but didn't care.

"Your behavior last night was fucking unacceptable. We are going to discuss it, and I am going to punish you. Be on that couch when I get home!" He kissed her forehead and left the room.

Abby stared at the door. She had never done well when people yelled at her. Nate had sometimes yelled when he was drinking, and she had always wanted to run and hide when that happened. She felt the same way now, and the threat of a punishment wasn't helping matters. There was no way she could sleep anymore.

Abby quietly got out of bed and tiptoed over to the door. She listened but couldn't hear anything. She decided to wait another ten minutes to make sure he was gone. In the meantime, she headed into the bathroom.

There were towels and puke on the floor. She cleaned up the mess and placed the towels in a pile by the bedroom door. Then she surveyed the bed. It was a king size on a raised platform with storage drawers underneath. She knew Victor was a neat freak. She decided to change the sheets as well since she had reeked of vomit and slept in them. She pulled them off the bed. Then she found her clothes on the floor. She was alarmed to find them wet, as she had no recollection of how they had gotten that way.

Abby tiptoed down the hallway and peeked around the corner. Everything was quiet. She ventured out further and confirmed he was gone. Only then did she breathe a sigh of relief. She had never been in his home before, but she was too distraught to take it in now. Instead, she started searching for the laundry room. When she found it, she quickly threw in a load and selected the speed wash setting. Then Abby rummaged around the closet to find cleaning supplies. She headed back into the bathroom to give it a thorough cleaning.

Three hours later the bathroom was sparkling, there were fresh sheets on the bed, and Abby had showered. She was waiting on the last dryer load to finish so she could get her clothes. She had put on Victor's robe in the interim so she could wash his Russia sweatshirt and pants as well. Abby had eaten a piece of toast, but it hadn't helped her stomach or her headache in the least. She had also drunk plenty of water.

Now that the cleaning was done, she had time to think. She looked at the couch and gingerly sat down on it.

Abby began to cry and then couldn't stop. She really liked Victor. He was fascinating, he saved lives for a living, he was hot, and he made her laugh. He was also the first man she had been attracted to since Nate died. But this intense side of him that talked about punishment and made crazy rules was way outside of her comfort zone.

The buzzer sounded on the dryer, and Abby went to fold the last load. She put everything away and got dressed. While she was in the bathroom she noticed his toothbrush and realized she had used it. She assumed that would bother him and rummaged through his drawers until she found a new one. Abby set it on the counter and tried to stop crying. She dried her face and looked at herself in the mirror. She looked like crap.

She had to get out of there. She had no idea what his address was, but she knew he lived in the Flats. She assumed she could find her bearings once she got outside. Then she realized it might be easier to call Vince. He would know the address and could easily take her home. Abby hesitated. Did she really want to leave and end the relationship? Then she remembered Victor's harsh voice that morning and made the decision. She called Vince and went in search of some paper. She wrote a quick note.

Victor. I'm sorry. I just can't do this. Abby

She left the note on the kitchen counter. Abby carefully pulled the door behind her and made sure it locked.

Vince was waiting at the front entrance. He held the door open and gave her a quick and concerned smile. It was obvious she had been crying. Abby vaguely remembered he had driven them all home last night, and she apologized for being so drunk. He just laughed.

"It happens. A thirtieth birthday is a big deal." It was the most conversation she had ever gotten out of him.

"If you don't mind my asking, how old are you Vince?"

He smiled at her in the rearview mirror. "I'll be fifty on Christmas day."

Abby smiled. "That's a big deal too."

When he dropped her off, she thanked him profusely and tried to leave a tip. As usual, he turned it down.

Abby was never so happy to be inside her house again. If felt safe. But then she realized Victor might try to come see her when he got the note. She debated just ignoring the doorbell if it rang, but then she freaked out and texted Rachel.

How u feeling?

Not bad. U?

Hungover. Mind if I crash there for a few days?

Sure. How come?

Need to get away from Victor. He wasn't happy about last night

Can't blame him. U2 still dating?

No

Ok. Should warn you Kent and Lindsay will be here to watch game

Ok. CU soon!

Abby packed some clothes in an overnight bag. Then she grabbed her laptop and a few books. She remembered he could track her through her cell phone, so she left it on her dresser. As she left her townhouse she set the alarm. She threw everything in the trunk and pulled out into traffic. She immediately started crying again. Happy friggin' thirtieth!

Chapter Twenty-Three

When she got to Rachel and Joel's, Abby was feeling sick again. She left her things in the car and rushed into their house. She flew by her friend and into the powder room. When she came back out, Rachel handed her some mouthwash.

"God, Abs. You really got trashed last night. That's the most I think I've ever seen you drink!"

"I know. What the hell was I thinking?"

"You weren't. None of us were after that casino win. But, heh, that was the most epic birthday celebration ever!"

They laughed, and Rachel explained they were going to watch the Browns game down in the basement. She was also making dinner to be served at halftime.

Abby was amazed by her friend. "I can't believe you can cook after last night. Aren't you the least bit hungover?"

"Oh, I am. I just hide it well. I also didn't drink as much as you and Lindsay. She, by the way, spent the night and is still sleeping it off upstairs. Kent is on his way over."

Abby nodded. "Hopefully that's not a big scene. I'm really starting to worry about her drinking."

"I am too. I think I'm going to talk to her about it."

Abby was glad. Rachel would be the perfect person to broach the subject. Lindsay wasn't going to be happy, but Rachel had never shied away from a difficult discussion. She was trying to have one with Abby now.

"Are we going to talk about Victor? Did you guys have a fight?"

Abby shook her head and fought back the tears. "I don't want to talk about it, Rach."

Her friend looked at her thoughtfully. "You know it was very sweet of him to come get us last night. And you can't blame him for being mad, especially after he saw that guy trying to grab you."

"What guy?"

"Shit, Abs. You don't remember?" Rachel filled her in on the events of the evening.

Abby sighed. "I don't remember any of that. I swear I'm never going to drink again!"

Just then Lindsay staggered down from upstairs. Her hair was a beehive mess, and she had mascara circles under her eyes. She nodded at Abby. "Girl, I don't remember much of last night. But I have no doubt it was spectacular."

Abby giggled. "Aside from all the puking, I did have a great time!"

Lindsay raised one eyebrow. "My puking or yours?"

"I think both."

They laughed, and Rachel explained to Lindsay, "Abs and Victor had a fight."

Lindsay poured herself a Pepsi and waved off the comment. "He'll get over it. They always do." Then she asked Abby, "You want some pop? It will settle your stomach."

Abby hesitated because of the caffeine, but then she realized she had broken it off with Victor. She would have dived into a cup of coffee if she thought her stomach could tolerate it, but she nodded and accepted the soda instead.

They headed down to the basement. Joel already had the big screen television set up, and he was fiddling with beers behind the bar. Lindsay made a beeline for the sectional couch and crashed on one end. Abby picked a spot at the curve and snuggled under a blanket. Charlie hopped up in her lap, did a few circles, and then settled down for a nap. Abby absent-mindedly petted him. It was the perfect atmosphere to relax and not think about Victor.

When Kent arrived, he laughed at the two hungover girls on the couch. He went to sit at the bar with Joel, and Rachel joined them. The pre-game was on, and Abby watched the announcers doing a spoof on fantasy football. After that, she dozed in and out. She thought of Victor and realized he should be home by now. She hoped he had taken the note well.

***

It was twelve thirty, and Victor was getting home later than he thought he would. There had been a lot of patient issues, and the nursing staff seemed slower than usual. He was bone-tired after a week of traveling and the events of last night. He was also on edge thinking about Abby. This would be her first real introduction into his lifestyle, and he wanted it to go well. She needed to know such behavior would not go unpunished. She also needed to learn he was in charge at all times. If done well, the punishment would teach her both these lessons. It would also help them to develop trust in the relationship.

When he unlocked the door, his eyes went immediately to the couch. She wasn't there.

Victor checked the powder room, but it was empty.

"Abigail?"

He headed back to the bedroom, but it was also empty. He noted the fresh sheets on the bed and then walked into the bathroom. It was spotless, and he saw the new toothbrush sitting on the counter. He frowned and walked back up front.

In the kitchen, he found the note. After reading it he swore softly. His first reaction was anxiety. He had lost her. But then the emotion quickly gave way to anger. She hadn't even given it a chance, and he deserved more than just a damn note.

Victor grabbed his cell phone and called her. It went straight to voicemail, and he hung up. Then he sent her a text.

Where are you? We need to talk.

He waited a few minutes, but there was no response. Victor was usually not a patient man. He pulled out his tracking app to see where she was. It showed her house. He debated and decided to give her more time. He hopped in the shower to rinse off, put on some casual clothes, and only then checked his phone again. There was no response from her, and the app still showed her at home. Victor didn't hesitate. He grabbed his keys and a coat and headed to Tremont.

When he got there he rang the bell. There was no answer. He rang it again and waited, but she didn't come to the door. The app clearly showed she was home. She was either sleeping or ignoring him, and he didn't intend to stand outside any longer. Victor pulled out the key he had stolen from her kitchen drawer. He tried it in the lock, and it turned easily. As he entered, he called out her name. The only answer he got was the chirping of the alarm system. He walked into the kitchen and looked at the console. Yuri had the same system, and he knew how to work it. He just needed to figure out the code.

Victor thought of what he knew about Abby. He needed a four-digit number, and fortunately, he had an excellent memory. He tried her birthdate first, but that didn't work. Then he tried the last four digits of her social security number. When that didn't work he punched in her street address, and the system shut off. Victor shook his head. That was probably the most obvious code she could have chosen, and he would need to talk to her about it in the future.

He looked around the first floor before heading upstairs. She wasn't there. When he saw the cell phone sitting on the dresser he exploded. She had known exactly what she was doing by leaving it behind. He picked up the phone and looked at the security lock. It required another four-digit code. Victor tried her house number again and gained immediate access. He shook his head in amazement. It took him two seconds of scrolling through her text messages to see where she was. Rachel and Joel's house would have been the first place he looked. At least now he knew the drive would not be in vain.

As Victor left, he reset her house alarm. She wouldn't be going back there tonight. He hopped in his truck and headed to Bay Village. He would be there in twenty minutes. His anxiety and anger had given way to determination. This girl was worth fighting for, and he would find a way to ease her fears and make it work.

Chapter Twenty-Four

Victor parked the Tundra right behind Abigail's car on the street. As he walked up the driveway, he saw Joel in the garage pulling beers out of a cooler. "Need a hand with those?" asked Victor.

Joel looked up in surprise. "Well, hi. I didn't think I would see you here today."

Victor shrugged. "Women."

Joel laughed and handed him some beers. "Come on in. Everyone is downstairs watching the game."

They walked into the house and ran into Rachel in the hallway. She scowled at Victor. "What are you doing here?"

Joel gave her an exasperated look. "It's none of our business, Rach."

"Oh yes, it is. She doesn't want to see him."

Victor ignored her and headed down the stairs. He could still hear them arguing behind him. When he reached the bottom, he saw Kent sitting at the bar. He surveyed the room and saw Abigail tucked in at the curve of the couch. It looked like she was sleeping. Her hair was in two loose pigtails down the sides of her head. He immediately felt relief at the sight of her.

Kent greeted him with a handshake. "Victor. It's good to see you. Can I get you a beer?"

Abby was startled awake by the greeting. She heard the all-too-familiar Russian accent and looked over at the bar. Victor was standing there talking to Kent, but he was staring at her. She quickly looked away. Abby felt her heart begin to pound. What the hell was he doing here?

The men talked about the Browns game for a few minutes. Then Victor grabbed a water bottle from behind the bar and casually walked over to his girlfriend. He wordlessly handed her the bottle and then noticed the glass of Pepsi sitting on the coffee table.

"Is this yours?" he asked in astonishment.

She looked at the glass with chagrin and then at Victor. "Um, yeah," her voice cracked. "It was only to settle my stomach with the syrup. I didn't think—"

She stopped. She wanted to say it didn't matter because they had broken up, but instead, she just looked away.

Victor grabbed the glass and walked it over to the bar. He deposited it on the counter and then walked back to the couch. "When you break the rules, Abigail, you really break the rules." He sat down and took a sip of his beer. Then he looked down at her, but she was staring at the TV screen.

"How are you feeling?" he asked.

"Better."

"Were you sick anymore?"

"Just once when I first got here."

He nodded. "And did you eat anything?"

"I had toast." She risked a look at him and saw the scowl on his face. "Rachel is serving dinner at halftime. I should be able to get something down then."

He considered what she said. "Good. We'll eat, and then we are leaving." His voice left no room for argument.

"But I thought..." her voice trailed off.

"What did you think, little one? That we would break up through a note?"

She didn't respond.

"You know, Abigail, you haven't even given it a chance. You're making it a lot worse in your head than it actually is."

She bit her lip. "I'm not really good with confrontation, Victor."

He put his arm around her shoulders and kissed her ear. "So I noticed. I'll try not to yell at you so much in the future."

They were distracted by the game. The Browns ran the ball in for a touchdown, and Kent and Joel were cheering loudly. Rachel came down the stairs to watch the replay. Then she looked at the couple on the couch.

"You okay, Abs?"

"Sure." Abby gave her friend a reassuring smile.

"Good. Dinner should be ready in an hour."

Abby nodded and unconsciously snuggled in closer to Victor. The guys came over and started talking to him about football. She started to drift off to sleep again. It was crazy how comfortable she could be in his arms after being so freaked out that morning.

When halftime came, Rachel yelled down the stairs for everyone to come up and eat. Lindsay finally surfaced from the end of the couch. She stretched and noticed Victor. "Heh doc!" she said before winking at Abby. She and Kent headed upstairs, and Abby went to follow them.

Victor pulled her into his arms from behind and nuzzled his face into her neck. Then he felt her phone in his pants pocket and handed it to her. She was stunned when she saw it. Abby's mind was going a mile a minute trying to figure out how he got it, but his words interrupted her thoughts.

"I think we need to add an item to Rule Number Two. From now on you must keep your cell phone with you at all times." He laughed as he took her hand and led her upstairs.

Rachel had put out a good spread. There were two different types of salad, a rice dish, cheesy potatoes, roasted chicken, and baked apples for dessert. Abby still felt sick, so she didn't take much food. Victor was right behind her and added more meat and salad to her plate.

Of course, Rachel noticed. "You know she's not feeling well, Victor."

He just looked at her but said nothing.

Joel interjected. "Leave them alone, Rach."

Abby sighed and grabbed a bottle of water from the fridge. She sat down and tried to eat. It wasn't going down easy, but she continued to chew and swallow.

Kent was asking Lindsay about last night, and she was recapping the evening in vivid detail. She started with their big casino win and told her husband he wouldn't see a dime of that money. Then she went on to tell him about the complimentary champagne, tequila penalty shots, and drinks at the Chocolate Bar. She was trying to goad him, but Abby realized Victor was listening to the conversation more intently than Kent.

Lindsay didn't know when to shut up. She was telling Kent how drunk they had all gotten, how Rachel had spilled the pitcher of beer on Abby, and how a guy had tried to dry her chest.

Victor's entire body tensed at that point, and he had to take in a few calming breaths. He was watching Lindsay with a thoughtful expression on his face. When she stopped talking he said, "You forgot to tell him what happened in the hallway by the bathroom."

Kent waited expectantly, and Lindsay shot Victor a dirty look.

Rachel quickly jumped in. "Nothing happened in the hallway. We just went and got Abby and got the hell out of there."

"That's not how I remembered it," said Victor. He stood up and took his plate to the sink. Then he looked down at Abby. "Are you ready to go?"

Before she could answer, Rachel angrily intervened. "She's not going anywhere! She wants to spend the night here, right Abby?"

The tension had risen in the room. Kent and Joel were whispering to each other, and then Kent said loudly, "If she doesn't want to go with him, then she doesn't have to go."

Abby knew Kent well enough to know he was looking for a fight. She would lay odds Victor would win that battle, but she didn't want to find out. Instead, she stood and quickly took her plate to the sink. She gave Rachel a hug. "Thanks for letting me sleep off my hangover. I'm going to go home." She reached down and gave Lindsay a hug as well. Then she took Victor's outstretched hand.

He smiled down at her. "Where's your coat?"

She realized with trepidation she had left it in the car. Lindsay must have read the expression on her face.

"I think I saw it in the hallway, Abs." She went and grabbed her own coat and handed it to Abby with a knowing look. Victor helped her put it on and didn't notice the grateful smile she gave her friend.

They headed outside and walked toward the vehicles. When they reached Abby's, she tried to get in, but Victor stopped her.

"Leave it. We'll take mine. Vince can bring you back tomorrow."

Abby protested, and he explained. "You might be tempted to drive to Canada." He winked at her, and she started laughing in spite of herself.

"At least let me get my computer out of the back."

She popped the trunk and he saw her computer bag, overnight bag, and coat. He gave her a piercing look. "Looks like you were planning to stay awhile." Then he mischievously pointed at the coat and asked, "Do you want to give Lindsay back hers?"

She pressed her lips together to keep from smiling. "I don't know what you're talking about, Dr. Turov."

He laughed and grabbed her bags. Then he opened the passenger door of his truck and helped her in. Once they were both situated in the car, he gave Abby a reassuring smile. Then he hit the seat warmers and pulled out. They chatted about mundane things the entire ride home, but they both knew what was coming.

Chapter Twenty-Five

When they reached Victor's building, he showed Abigail where the entrance was to the parking garage underneath. He gave her the code to the gate and had her save it on her phone. Then he pulled in to one of the parking spaces near the elevator. He touched her arm. "Wait for me."

Victor got out and came around to her side. He opened her door and then pointed to the two spaces next to his truck. "These are mine as well. When you come visit, you can park in either one." He grabbed her bags, took her hand, and led her to the elevator.

Inside Victor showed her how she needed a key fob to work the elevator. He pointed to the first-floor button and explained that was where the pool and workout room were. "I'll show you them later." Then he hit the top floor button, and they headed up to his condo.

Abby had been fine until then, but now she was getting nervous. He opened the door for her and let her in. She looked around the room she had vacated only that morning.

Victor put down her bags and then helped Abby off with her coat. He was carefully watching her face and could tell she was scared. That was good. He wanted her scared, but he didn't want her terrified. He tried to ease her discomfort.

"Do you need to use the bathroom?"

She nodded and headed to the powder room. Then she looked at him suspiciously. "You're not going to come are you?"

He laughed. "No. I only do that when you're incapacitated."

Abby stepped in the powder room and shut the door. She blew out her breath and stared at her reflection in the mirror. She had no idea why she had come back with him. She could have ended the relationship at her friend's house, and they would have had her back. But now she was stuck seeing this punishment thing through.

Abby thought she had left with Victor to prevent a scene with Kent. Now she realized she still liked the crazy bastard. She actually felt happy and safe in his arms, which made no sense at all. She finished peeing and washed her hands. She had stayed in there as long as possible. It was time to face her fears. She took one more deep breath and stepped back out into the living room.

Victor was sitting on the couch.

Abby looked at him and wondered what the deal was with the damn couch.

He motioned her over to him, and she found her feet moving of their own volition in his direction. They stopped when she was standing in front of him, and she risked a glance at his face. He was giving her a reassuring smile. Then he gently turned her around and pulled her onto his lap.

"When I give out a punishment, Abigail, I like to talk about what occurred. That way you're very clear about my expectations, and hopefully, the behavior doesn't happen again." He added, "Honesty is crucial to our relationship and to a punishment. If you're honest with me, then the punishment goes a lot quicker. Does that make sense?"

She nodded, and he continued. "There was a major disconnect between what you said to me on the phone yesterday afternoon and what occurred last night. We need to figure out what happened to cause that disconnect." He had his arms around her waist, and his face was leaning toward her ear. "Stand up, little one."

She did what she was told. Victor reached around and pulled the drawstring on her pants. Abby jumped in shock and then instinctively reached down with her hands to stop him. "What are you doing?" she asked.

He explained, "I like to spank a bare bottom. It stings more, and I get to see your ass redden from my palm."

"Oh," was all she said, but she did not remove her hands.

He reassured her. "You have a beautiful body, Abigail. Don't be embarrassed. I saw it all last night." He quickly grasped the hem of her pants and panties and pulled them both down in one quick motion. Abby was mortified. She didn't have time to think, though, as Victor half turned her and said, "Lay across my lap." His voice was calm but left no room for argument.

He helped her into position. She was lying face down with her ass centered over his lap. Victor had wrapped her pigtails around his left hand and was firmly holding her head in place. His right hand was resting on her bare butt, and he gave her a test smack. The sound was loud, and Abby flinched.

"Did that hurt?"

She thought about it. "Kind of."

"Good." He was now rubbing her ass. "I think we'll go over the five W's and see what we can discover. Let's start with the when since that is the easiest. When did the misbehavior occur?"

Abby quickly responded. "Last night."

"Good. And where did it occur?"

"At the casino and then the Chocolate Bar," she replied.

He continued to rub her ass. "And who were you with?"

She rattled off her friend's names.

"Anyone else?"

Abby frowned. "No. Just the girls."

Victor gave her a hard smack. "Try again, Abigail. Who else was with you?"

She was confused. "Oh, do you mean the guys Kate and Lindsay were talking to?

"Yes. That's who I mean. How many were there?"

Abby tried to concentrate. "I don't know. I wasn't paying attention." She tried to look at Victor to explain, "I wasn't talking to them."

He smacked her again.

"Ouch! I said I wasn't talking to them."

"Yes you were, Abigail. You were talking to one of them at the end when I got there."

She sighed. "I don't remember any of that, Victor."

His voice got terse. "And is that safe? Is it safe to be so drunk you don't remember a man molesting you in the hallway?"

"No, it's not." Her voice was small.

He smacked her twice. "Let's move on to the whats. Tell me what you drank last night."

She started with the lemon drop at the casino bar while he quietly rubbed her backside. Then she told him about the tequila shot, and his hand stilled but he didn't spank her. When she got to the champagne toasts he spanked her twice.

"Why am I spanking you, Abigail?"

"Because I went over my two drink limit."

"Correct. And what happens when you go over your limit?"

"I get drunk."

"Yes. *And* you put yourself at risk. *And* you get sick!"

He was angry now, and Abby knew the drinks she had later in the evening were going to send him over the edge. Her butt was starting to sting a little too. She told him about the vodka cranberry she drank while gambling, and he gave her another smack. Then she tried to move on to the Chocolate Bar, but he wouldn't let her.

"You're forgetting something, little one."

She frowned. "No. That was everything I drank at the casino."

"I'm not talking about drinks. What else happened while you were gambling?"

She tried to look at him, but her head was face down. "I'm not sure what you—oh, you mean that we won money?"

"Yes, and what did you do with the money?"

She frowned again. "Put it in my purse."

He smacked her hard and fast. "Is it safe to carry that much money around in your purse?"

She swallowed hard. That one had really hurt. "No. But what else could I have done?"

Victor could not believe she was arguing with him. No girlfriend had ever dared before. He wasn't sure if that pleased him or made him angrier.

"You could have asked the casino to cut you a check. Or you could have called Vince to pick up the money. Carrying around that much cash, especially when you were drunk, was just asking for trouble. People saw you win that money, Abigail."

She sighed. "I never thought about it. I'm sorry."

They moved on to the Chocolate Bar, and Abby pretended she didn't remember what she ordered. She was annoyed when Victor pulled out an itemized receipt. "Let me read what was ordered, and maybe it will jog your memory."

"How did you get the receipt?"

"I paid the bill."

"Of course you did," she muttered, and he laughed.

He started reading down the list. He tilted her head so he could see the side of her face while he read. When he got to the vodka Red Bulls, he noticed the quick facial change. "Abigail, please tell me you did not order that drink." His voice had gotten deathly quiet.

"I did," she whispered.

Victor closed his eyes and breathed deeply. "Are you trying to give me a stroke?"

She explained. "I was tired."

"Perhaps you should have taken that as a sign to quit drinking and go home."

Abby said nothing.

"Why is a vodka Red Bull so wrong?"

"Because of the alcohol and the caffeine."

"Mmm hmm. And did you drink both of the ones on this list?"

"Yes," she whispered.

He spanked her ass four times, and they hurt like hell.

"Is that all you drank?"

Never was she so happy to say yes.

"Jesus, that's a lot of alcohol. No wonder you were sick! A man would get sick on that, and you're much smaller than a man."

He was rubbing her ass again, and it was warm and tingly.

"Let's move on to the food." He read off the list. "This sounds like junk food to me."

"I didn't eat any of it."

Victor sighed. "So you didn't eat anything at all? How about water? Did you drink any water?"

She thought about it. "I got a bottle of water at the casino."

"That's it?" He smacked her twice. "Always eat some food and drink plenty of water when you're drinking, Abigail. It will protect your stomach and prevent dehydration."

"I know. I just wasn't thinking."

"Hopefully your sore ass will help you to remember in the future."

Abby smiled. "That's it. I didn't drink anything else. And then you came to get us." She tried to get up, but he gently pushed her back down.

"We're not through yet, little one. We still have to discuss the why. The why is usually the most difficult. Your butt has to be getting sore. Do you want to take a break?" He would never have offered this in the past.

She thought about it and shook her head no. "I'd rather just get it over with."

"Very well, then. It's important to understand the motivations behind behavior. Why do you think you drank so much?"

"I don't know."

Victor gave her a smack. "I think you do."

"I just got caught up in the moment with my birthday and the casino win, I guess."

He smacked her again. "Try thinking about why you didn't want me to be there. I think that will help."

Now she was confused. "Um, I wanted it to be just the girls."

This time he gave her two smacks. "Try again, Abigail."

"We had these plans set before I even knew you."

"Quit lying to me. Why couldn't I come?" He spanked her hard three times.

Now Abby was crying. "I don't know."

Victor hesitated, but then he gave her four very hard whacks. "Come on, little one. Just let it go. You can do this. Please just tell me."

Those had really hurt, and Abby continued to cry.

Victor whispered, "Why, Abigail? You'll feel so much better when you tell me." He pulled her hair so her head tilted toward him. They were staring at each other, and her eyes were wide and brimming with tears.

Then suddenly the words rushed out of her. "Because birthdays were Nate's thing. I didn't want you there because I didn't want to hurt him. Because I still love him. And I feel like I'm cheating on him when I'm with you!" She was bawling now.

Victor had suspected as much. He helped her to stand, pulled her pants up, and then pulled her into his lap. He put his arms around her and rocked her until the crying subsided. Then he grabbed some tissues from the end table and wiped her face. "Do you feel better?"

"Yes. I'm sorry. I don't know where that came from."

He put his hand over her heart. "From here."

She smiled at him. "So you fix all kinds of heart problems, huh?"

He laughed. "No. That's Yuri's department, not mine. I just had a hunch."

"Guess I'm a little crazy."

"No, little one. You were married a long time, and now you're moving on, which is difficult. But he's dead, Abigail. And even though I never met him, I think your Mr. Shea would have wanted you to be with someone like me."

She raised one eyebrow. "Really? Because I'm pretty sure he would have kicked your ass if he had seen you spanking me."

He gave her a wry smile. "I have no doubt. But I would lay odds he was as controlling as I am. He just used a different method than me is all."

She thought about what he had said and asked, "How can you be so sure?"

He stood up and pulled her up with him. "Because it's obvious you need someone to protect you, and men like me notice. You attract Dominant men, Abigail."

"Oh."

He took her hand and led her into the powder room. She was facing the mirror, and Victor was standing behind her. He had her turn so she was facing him, and then he pulled down her pants and underwear again. He explained. "I'm an extremely visual person. I want you to look at your ass and see how red it is. It got that way because you broke the rules, Abigail. Remember that. I am hoping it will remind you to behave in the future."

She looked over her shoulder at the reflection in the mirror. Her butt was red, but it got like that after a hot shower too. She was damned if she was going to tell him that, though.

Victor pulled her pants back up and put his arms around her. He leaned his forehead against hers and sighed, "Do you still want to break up with me?"

"No. But this whole punishment control thing is super weird. And don't think that I didn't notice you were turned on while spanking me."

He pulled away enough so he could look down at her. "Of course I was. I told you, domination is extremely sexual." Then he added, "You were turned on too."

"I was not!"

He laughed. "Your ass was right in my face, Abigail. I could smell your arousal. It's nothing to be ashamed of. Submission can be very releasing and sexual as well."

She was horrified but then quickly dismissed his words. There was no way she had been turned on, right?

Victor looked at his watch. "We have time to go see the pool now if you want. It's open until five."

She agreed, and they headed down to tour the fitness facility. It was nice. There was a men's and women's locker room at the entrance. A key fob was needed to get into the locker room, and then one entered the pool or weight room from there.

Victor handed her a key fob and key. "These are yours. The key is to my condo. Go in and see if the locker room is empty. If it is, then come get me."

It was empty, and Victor walked in to look around. There was a wall of lockers, two shower stalls, and two bathroom stalls. There was also a sauna and hot tub in the corner along with a door leading out to the pool and weight room.

"I don't want you hanging around in here too long, Abigail. It doesn't seem safe. If you need to shower or change, do it up in my condo. Don't ever use the hot tub or the sauna."

She nodded, and they headed out to the pool. It was twenty-five meters and had five lanes. There was a lifeguard on duty, and Victor explained it was only busy during certain times of the day. The pool was surrounded by an indoor track that also looped around the workout room. The latter could be seen through a wall of windows and had cardio machines, free weights, and weight machines. It also had an attendant on duty at all times. Abby was impressed and wondered what he paid in HOA fees.

They headed back up to the condo, and Victor had her use her key to be sure it worked. When they were back inside, Abby looked at him curiously. "By the way, how did you get in my house?"

He actually looked embarrassed. "I saw some keys sitting in a drawer when I was looking for a kitchen bag. I helped myself just in case there was ever an emergency."

She raised one eyebrow at him. "Mmm hmm. Can you say stalker?"

He laughed and plopped down on the couch. "Do you want me to give it back?"

"If I said yes, would you?"

"Nope."

"That's what I thought. But how did you get past the alarm system? I'm positive I set it."

"It took me three tries to get in. Your house number? Really? You're going to need to change that when you get home."

He turned on the Vikings game, and Abby looked at him. "Do you want me to call Vince to drive me home?"

"What? No. You're not going home tonight. You were just punished. I can't leave you alone or you'll think too much. You don't do well when you think."

"Okay." She flopped on the couch next to him. "Are you a Vikings fan?"

He nodded. "Minnesota is cold like Russia. When I moved here, I picked them as my team."

She giggled. "You know it gets cold in Cleveland too. Did the Browns win?"

"They lost. And it doesn't get nearly as cold here as in Russia, or Minnesota for that matter."

He pulled her down on the couch next to him. Then he threw a blanket over her. Abby snuggled in and was sound asleep within minutes. When her phone chirped with a text, Victor had to wake her up. He handed her the phone.

She squinted at the screen. "Rachel is checking in to make sure I'm okay."

Victor grunted. "Now that is a woman that does *not* attract Dominants."

Abby laughed as she continued to scroll. "She wants to go shopping this week."

He looked at her with alarm.

Abby started to send a reply, and Victor stopped her. "Wednesday night and next weekend are out. We have plans."

"Okay. What are we doing?"

"I'm not sure. I'm just calling dibs."

She nodded and went to text.

He stopped her again. "Where are you going shopping? Who are you going with? And will there be any drinking involved?"

She gave him a bemused look. "I don't know."

He pulled the phone away from her. "I guess now is the time to discuss another add-on to Rule Number Two, Abigail."

She looked at him in alarm.

"I want you to check with me before making any plans with your friends."

Abby was sitting up now. "You mean I have to ask permission?!"

He shrugged. "Yes. I don't trust them anymore. I warned you if you broke the rules I would tighten up the reins. You have no one to blame for this but yourself."

She shook her head at him. "These are my friends we're talking about, Victor. I've known them a lot longer than I've known you. And none of them forced me to drink, you know. I chose to do that all on my own."

"Oh, believe me, I am well aware of that fact. The problem is, Abigail, that you have a hard time saying no to people. And your friends don't seem to care about your personal safety the way I do."

She glared at him, and he quietly returned her stare.

Abby finally broke her gaze and fired off a text to Rachel. After some back and forth she had his answers. "She wants to meet on Tuesday after work in North Olmsted. We're going to hit the discount stores and a consignment shop. It will just be the two of us, and she wants to grab dinner at the Wild Mango while we're out." She looked up at him. "I usually get a glass of wine during dinner."

He thought about what she had said. "Okay. Pay attention to your surroundings, especially in the parking lots. Make sure you order something with meat. If the weather is bad, take Vince." Then he added, "And if I find out you had more than one glass of wine, I will beat your ass!"

Abby rolled her eyes and sardonically replied, "Gee. Thank you, Sir!"

He just laughed.

At bedtime, Abby found herself back in the Russia sweatshirt and workout pants. She was in the bathroom washing her face when Victor came in. He noticed the new toothbrush and asked her about it. "Why did you get me a new one?"

She shrugged. "I know how neat you are. After I used your old one, I figured you would want a new one."

Victor laughed heartily. "Abigail, you can use my toothbrush. We're going to be sharing all kinds of bodily fluids. A few mouth germs aren't going to matter."

She blushed as he continued to laugh.

They got into bed, and Victor opened the drawer to his nightstand. "Before I forget, here is your jewelry back. I took it off last night so it wouldn't get lost or damaged."

Abby took the jewelry and thanked him. She had completely forgotten about it.

Victor was watching her carefully. "I'm afraid I have to add another item to the rules, little one."

Abby groaned.

"This one gets tacked on to Rule Number One."

She looked at him in surprise.

"Don't wear another man's jewelry while you are dating me."

She looked puzzled. "Why?"

"Because that's one way men mark their territory, and you no longer belong to Mr. Shea."

She thought about his choice of the word belong but let it pass. Instead, she asked, "How did you know they came from him?"

"Diamonds almost always come from a man, Abigail. It's actually what helped me figure out why you got so drunk last night. You don't usually wear this much jewelry. I realized you put all this on in honor of him. You also put yourself at serious risk by flashing that kind of wealth around."

Abby sighed. "Okay. But I'm not much of a shopper, Victor. Almost all of my jewelry came from Nate."

He gave her a wicked grin. "Then we will have to buy you some new things."

Chapter Twenty-Six

The next day Abby was working in the library when an email came through on her cell from Victor. It was simply titled Revised Rules. She shook her head as she opened the attachment.

Rule Number One – Monogamy
- No flirting with men.
- No text messaging men.
- No chatting on phone or internet with men.
- No accepting drinks from men.
- No dating men.
- No wearing another man's gift of jewelry.

Rule Number Two – Health and Safety
- No cab or Uber rides.
- No driving in bad weather such as heavy snow, ice, fog, or rain.
- No speeding.
- No smoking.
- No heavy drinking (in your case, 2 drinks).
- No drugs of any kind including prescriptions (unless I approve them).
- No caffeine of any kind (this includes coffee, tea, soda, energy drinks, chocolate, or pills).
- No fast food or junk food (this includes Taco Bell, pizza, and chips).
- Eat protein at every meal (the size of your fist).
- Exercise regularly (at least 3 to 4 times a week).
- Get plenty of sleep every night (at least 8 hours).
- House alarm is on at all times (even when you're home).
- No walking for exercise alone.
- No entering or driving into unsafe neighborhoods.
- Wear a coat when it's under 70 degrees.
- Carry cell phone with you at all times.
- Get permission before going out with friends.
- This list is subject to change. I can, and will, add things when I see fit.

The man had some serious control issues. When she was done reading she fired off a smart reply.

Thanks for the revision. I really shouldn't be responding, though. I'm forbidden to chat with men on the internet!

He replied promptly. *I admire your commitment to the rules, but it's okay to chat with your boyfriend. It keeps him from getting anxious.* He added a distraught smiley face to the text.

She laughed and went back to work.

***

Victor was reviewing emails in his office when his phone rang. It was Yuri.

"What's going on, my friend?"

Victor responded, "Just catching up on work correspondence. How about you?"

"The usual. Helping the mentally distraught of the world. Naturally, I thought of you."

Victor grunted.

The two discussed their jobs and the Browns game. Then they moved on to Victor's relationship.

"And how is it going with the lovely Mrs. Shea? Or did she dump your ass?"

"Not yet. Actually, it's going quite well. I had to punish her yesterday, and she took it better than I thought she would."

"Really? That soon? And did you go easy on her as I suggested?"

Victor thought about it. "No. I actually spanked her twenty-five times."

"Twenty-five times?! What the hell did she do?"

"She went out with her friends to celebrate her birthday and got drunk."

"That's it? Victor, that's normal behavior. How old is she now? Twenty-one?"

He laughed. "She just turned thirty. And it wasn't normal behavior because she broke the rules. She has to learn that's not acceptable in our relationship."

"You never gave a rat's ass what your girlfriends did when they weren't with you. Why the change with this one?"

"I keep telling you. She's different."

"I hope she's not too different, Victor. She needs to be able to handle your obedience rule. Have you discussed it yet?"

"No, but we will soon. I think we're ready for sex. We just need to have the history conversation. I've already tested her blood."

"She agreed to a blood test?"

"No. I drew a sample when she was passed out drunk."

"Fuck, Turov! What the hell were you thinking?"

"I was thinking it would be easier on her if she didn't know I checked."

"You could lose your license."

"If she found out, I doubt she would push the issue. She's not the type. Plus, there's no way she could prove it."

"You're probably right. But I'm starting to worry about you. It's like you're trying for a normal relationship, but you're veering even further down the path of control to get it."

"No. What I'm trying to do is convince a sweet girl my lifestyle is something she can like and also live with. I don't believe there is such a thing as a normal relationship, and neither do you."

Yuri laughed. "That's true. Listen, I have to go. Just have the obedience talk with her. That's all I'm asking."

"Quit worrying. We'll have the talk. I am looking forward to having it done and over with. Then I can enjoy that delectable body as much as I want."

Yuri groaned. "As usual, I will be living vicariously!"

Victor laughed, and they hung up.

***

It was Wednesday night, and Abby was getting ready for their dinner date. She had the music blasting and was holding up one dress after another in front of the mirror. As usual, she had no idea what to wear. Victor had mentioned going to a new trendy steakhouse called Red. She had never been, but she knew it was fancy and some of the Cavaliers hung out there. Abby had it narrowed down to a red sweater dress that was casual but sexy or a chic black cocktail dress.

"Definitely the red one," came the male voice from the doorway.

Abby jumped in fear until she saw Victor leaning against the wall. He must have let himself in, and he had a huge grin on his face. His eyes were moving up and down her body, and she realized she was standing there in nothing but a blue bra and matching silk panties. She ducked into her walk-in closet and pulled the red dress over her head. She could hear Victor chuckling.

When she came out, he was sitting on the edge of the bed surveying the pile of clothes she had discarded.

"Tough decision?"

She sighed. "Fashion has never really been my thing."

"You're probably just overthinking it."

"Yeah. Someone told me I have a tendency to do that."

He laughed. "You always look nice to me, especially in your undergarments."

She ignored him while she fixed her hair, but her cheeks were still red. "Do you always show up early to everything?"

"Not everything." He gave her a knowing look. Then he added, "You still need to change your alarm code. We can do that before we leave."

When she was ready, and the code had been changed, they headed to the restaurant.

They were seated in a booth along the wall. Abby looked over the menu and then ordered the salmon.

"I bring you to one of the best steakhouses in town, and you order fish?"

"I like salmon."

He sighed and ordered a steak for himself. When the server was gone, he got up and slid around to her side of the table.

"Oh no. Am I in trouble again?"

"Not at all. Salmon is an excellent source of protein."

She looked at him suspiciously. "But—?"

"But nothing. I just wanted to sit closer to you." He ducked his head under her hair and started kissing her neck. "You smell nice."

"So do you." They were leaning in toward each other and gently kissing when the server interrupted them with their food.

Victor reluctantly pulled away and ran his hand through his hair. They were getting so close. He knew he needed to have the history conversation, but not at dinner. They ended up talking about their days instead, and Abby told him she had followed up with her primary. This made him happy. She also told him about yesterday's shopping expedition with Rachel. She was a great storyteller, and he laughed at her comments about being buried under a pile of clothing.

After dinner Victor excused himself to go talk to a fellow physician at the bar. While he was gone, the server came with the check. Abby gleefully handed over her credit card and was just signing the receipt when he returned.

He stood over her with his arms crossed and a scowl on his face. "I told you I pay for everything, Abigail."

She gave him an innocent smile. "Oh, I'm sorry. I forgot."

He pulled her up to a standing position and helped her on with her coat. Then he whispered, "Do you want to be punished?"

She looked at him in surprise. "No. But it's not a rule."

"It is now."

"Oh." She thought about it. "How does that possibly fall under monogamy or health and safety?"

"It doesn't. It falls under Rule Number Three, which we will discuss later." He led her out of the restaurant and to the valet stand. Once they were safely in his truck, he looked over at her. "I think we'll go back to my place for a drink."

Abby looked at him in alarm. "I'm not poor, you know. I can afford to pay for some things. I don't think I should be punished for that."

He was driving and looking at the road. "I'm not going to punish you. Pull a stunt like that again, though, and I will." Then he glanced over at her and smiled. "I just want a drink."

It was close to eight when they got to Victor's condo. He went into the kitchen and poured himself a bourbon. He offered Abby a glass of wine or a beer. She declined both, and he frowned at her. "I really think you should have a drink."

"I just went through the worst hangover of my life. I don't want to drink."

"Very well then." He led her to the couch. "You can always change your mind."

He plopped on the couch and pulled her down next to him. She snuggled in, and Victor absent-mindedly wound a strand of her hair around his finger. He took a sip of his drink, set it down, and then gave her a long kiss. When he pulled away, he said, "We need to talk about sex."

"Oh." She smiled tentatively at him.

"I really want to fuck, and I'm pretty sure you do too, but we need to know each other's past before we can do that safely.

She pressed her lips together and tried not to laugh at his choice of words. The man had a one-track mind when it came to safety. She merely said, "Okay."

"I'll go first," said Victor. He proceeded to tell her his sexual history starting with losing his virginity at sixteen, to the nine girlfriends that followed.

"Nine?" Abby was horrified.

"Yes, nine. That's not counting all the one night stands in my youth either. But really it's not many when you consider I'm thirty-seven years old. I was too busy during medical school for any relationships. Once I became a doctor I had more time, but none of the relationships lasted very long. While they did, though, you should know I always used a condom. I've also been tested, and I have the results right here." He pulled a piece of paper out of his pocket. He had ordered the tests results be rushed, and they had been emailed to him earlier that day.

Victor handed her the lab report. She looked at his face and then the paperwork. It listed all of the STDs she had heard of along with some she hadn't. Her eyes got big when she saw HIV on the list. All of his results were negative. She quietly handed the paper back to him.

He was watching her carefully. "I just had those tests done."

She nodded. "So you want me to get tested too?"

"Maybe. It all depends on your history."

When she didn't say anything, he tried to help her along. "Let's start with your virginity. When did you lose it?"

She sighed and answered, "A lot later than you. I was twenty-one."

The answer thrilled him more than he cared to admit. "And how many partners have you had?"

Abby was embarrassed to answer. Instead, she held up one finger.

He looked at her hand. "Are you telling me Mr. Shea was the only man you have ever been with?"

She nodded.

"My God, Abigail. Do you have any idea what that does to me?"

"No."

He rubbed his forehead with his hand. "It's a major turn-on."

"It is? I thought it was kind of pathetic."

"No, little one. The only man that ever had you is gone. That means you're mine solely to possess. That's a huge turn-on!"

Possess? She chose to ignore the comment. "I'm pretty sure

Nate never cheated on me. He was very loyal. Oh, but actually my gynecologist tested me for some stuff right before he died. I had an infection. But those all came back negative."

"Good. And what type of birth control did you use?"

"We didn't use anything."

He frowned. "Why not?"

"Lots of reasons. Nate didn't like condoms, and I wasn't allowed to use hormones. I was told I couldn't get pregnant too, but then I ended up having an ectopic pregnancy and hysterectomy. After that, we didn't need to use anything."

He kissed her cheek. "I'm sorry, Abigail. That must have been tough."

She shrugged. "I never really thought I wanted kids, so it wasn't as bad as it sounds. The surgery was scary."

Victor continued to hold her hand. "I've never wanted kids either. The potential worries they would cause would probably be more than I could bear."

"I bet," she laughed. Then she shyly added, "I have no problem going to get tested if you want me to."

He thought about it. He already had her blood test results, and they were all negative. Of course, he couldn't tell her that. Instead, he said, "I don't think testing is necessary."

"Okay. Are we having sex now?"

He laughed. "We don't have enough time tonight."

Abby looked at the clock. It was only eight thirty, and she wondered how much time the man needed.

Victor stood up and went into the kitchen. He filled a tall glass with water and then poured a glass of wine. He brought them both into the living room and set them both on the coffee table in front of her. "In case you get thirsty," he explained. Then he added, "We have more to discuss. I need to know what your preferences are in bed."

She turned crimson and grabbed the wine. After taking a sip she half stated and half asked, "Um. I don't really have any?"

He laughed. "Of course you do. All women do. There are some things you like more than others, and possibly some things you won't do at all."

Abby took another sip of the wine but couldn't look at him. She also wasn't saying anything.

Victor watched her with interest. He noted the flushed cheeks and apparent discomfort. He played with the idea her husband had been a prude, but then he dismissed it immediately. From what she had told him, Nate Shea showed all the signs of having been a Dominant. There was no way in hell he stuck with the missionary position. He decided she was just timid and needed help opening up.

"Are you shy, little one?" He put his arm around her. "Okay. We'll both just stare straight ahead while I ask you some questions. All you have to do is answer them. I promise I won't even look at you."

She sighed.

"Let's start with your mouth. Did Mr. Shea ever put anything in your mouth?"

She started giggling nervously. "Um, yes."

"And did you mind?"

She thought about it. "No. Actually, Nate said I was pretty good at that."

Victor grinned, but they still weren't looking at each other, so she didn't see. He thought about how to phrase his next question.

"And did Mr. Shea ever leave anything behind in your mouth?"

She snorted but finally said yes.

He nodded. "And what did you do with it?"

"Oh my God!" She covered her face with her hands. "I'm not answering that."

He was amused. "Yes, you are. Just tell me."

He was looking at her now, and she was shaking her head. He handed her some wine.

After a long sip, she whispered, "I swallowed it."

Victor laughed out loud. "Good to know. Let's move on to your breasts. What did Mr. Shea do with those?"

Abby looked at him in confusion. "I don't know. Played with them?"

He was trying hard to keep a straight face. "How did he play with them? With his hands?"

"Sure."

"Mouth?"

"Yes."

He hesitated. "Dick?"

"I forgot about that. Yeeesss."

"Did he use anything else?"

She frowned. "No. What else could he have used?"

"Not important. Did you mind what he did?"

She shook her head. "Not really. He didn't spend a whole lot of time there."

Now it was Victor's turn to look confused. She had lovely breasts, and he realized with surprise her husband must not have been a boob man. He moved on and quickly tapped her crotch area.

"Now I know Mr. Shea put things in here. The question is what kind of things."

Abby slugged down the remaining wine. "I'm going to need a refill."

He handed her the water glass. "No getting drunk, Abigail. You can do this without more wine."

She stuck her tongue out at him.

"That's a good place to start. Did Mr. Shea put his tongue down there?"

She shook her head in disbelief. "Do we really need to have this conversation?"

"Yes. The more I know, the better our first time will be. Now quit stalling and answer the question."

She shrugged. "Yes. Mr. Shea put his tongue down there."

"And did you like it?"

She wrinkled her nose. "Not really. It didn't do anything for me, and I didn't like the smell on his face afterward." She got up. "I'm getting more wine."

He got up with her. "Let me pour it for you. I don't want you going overboard. That would lead to a spanking."

She arched one eyebrow and sarcastically replied, "How thoughtful of you."

He handed her the wine and kissed her on the forehead. "Now quit deflecting and sit back down. We're almost done."

Abby sat down and drained half the glass.

He glared at her but continued. "What else did Mr. Shea put down there?"

"Um, the obvious."

He smiled. "Anything else?"

She frowned at him. "What do you mean? Oh, are you talking toys and stuff?"

He nodded.

She finished the wine. "Nope. But I do have my own rabbit." She gave him a wicked grin. "That's a vibrator."

He looked at the empty glass and then at her. "I'm well aware of what a rabbit is. I have one of my own."

She looked surprised. "What can a man possibly do with a rabbit?"

"Use it on you, silly."

"Ohhhh." Abby was feeling tipsy now. "Mine's pink. What color is yours?"

He shook his head. "I don't remember. Drink some water."

She dutifully picked up the glass and started drinking. "I think that was the most bizarre conversation I've ever had, and I'm glad it's over."

Victor leaned over with a grin and gave her a kiss. "Sorry to disappoint you, little one, but we're not quite done."

She frowned. "We're not?"

"No. We still need to talk about your ass."

"Oh, God!" She spilled a little water.

He helped her wipe it off. Then he leaned in again and whispered, "Did Mr. Shea ever put anything in there?"

"Yes," she whispered back. She couldn't look at him.

Victor laughed. "Of course he did. Finger?"

She nodded.

"Dick?"

She nodded again.

"Toys?"

This time she shook her head no.

"And did you mind?"

Abby gave a tipsy shrug. "Not really, because I didn't know you could put toys in there."

Victor was alarmed to realize how fast she had gotten drunk.

"No, silly. I meant did you mind the finger or dick in there?"

"Oh. No."

This pleased him, and he realized Mr. Shea had been an ass man. He pointed at the water glass. "Drink up, and I'll get you more water."

She drank and then pointed at him. "You should know I'm not really that good at sex."

He frowned. "And why would you say that?"

"Because I don't always, um, you know, have an orgasm."

He got her more water. "Okay. Let's take a closer look at that. When you did have orgasms, what was different?"

She thought about it. "Don't really know. One time we had fooled around in a lake on vacation. Nate said it was because I love water. It was the best orgasm of my life."

She was really opening up now. Victor smiled at her. "No doubt it was one of the best of Mr. Shea's life too."

"Really?"

"Yes. Nothing gets a man off more than knowing he gave his woman a good orgasm."

"Oh." She blushed.

"And for the record, not having orgasms means your Mr. Shea dropped the ball, not you."

She didn't say anything.

"I'm serious, Abigail. Men are easy. All a woman has to do is show up and be willing. If they do that, a man is going to get off."

She made a face. "Well, that's true."

"Women are much more complicated creatures. Each one is different, and the circumstances all have to line up right for a woman to have an orgasm. That takes time and patience on a man's part. It's also where skill and experience come into play." He gave her a wicked grin. "Lucky for you I have both of those."

"Oh, really?"

"Yep. I can pretty much guarantee you will always have orgasms with me."

She looked at him. "You're awfully sure of yourself."

"I would go so far as to say I am a better lover than I am a surgeon."

She shook her head in disbelief. "You are like no man I have ever met."

"I could say the same about you. Since you're so open to talking now, tell me, did your Mr. Shea ever tie you up?"

She slugged down some water. "You mean like with handcuffs and stuff?"

He nodded.

"Nope. He liked to pin my arms down, though. Why? Do you? I mean, tie your girlfriends up?"

He grinned and nodded again. "Do you think that will bother you?"

"Probably if you left me tied up."

"I would never do that," said Victor.

"Okay. Then sure."

The conversation was going better than he had hoped. "Drink the rest of that water, Abigail." While she did, he asked one final question. "Since birth control isn't an issue, do you need me to use a condom?"

"As long as you're not fooling around with anyone—"

He interrupted her, "—which I won't be because we are both following the monogamy rule."

"Then, no, I don't see why you would have to use one."

He looked like he had just won the lottery. "I have never had condom-free sex in my life, Abigail. You have no idea what that is doing to me."

She finished her water and went to get more. She looked over her shoulder at him. "Are you sure you just don't want to have sex now? I'm horny from all this talk."

Victor laughed and pointed at his bulging crotch. "You and me both! But I already told you, we need more time than this."

She made a pouty face. "Good lord, how much time do you need?"

"Little one, you have no idea!"

She ended up sleeping over that night, but they didn't have sex. She fell asleep with Victor's hard-on pressed up against her ass.

Chapter Twenty-Seven

The week following the sex talk was busy for both of them, and they had missed their standing Wednesday night date. On Friday Abby had theatre tickets with her friends. Victor had begrudgingly given his permission to go, but he made her check in at intermission and after the show. She had also gone home early just to keep him happy.

Abby knew eventually she was going to have to fight back on his control issues. For one thing, it wasn't going to take Rachel long to figure out what was going on, and her friend would pitch a fit. Abby was also uncomfortable with how much freedom she was giving up. She idly wondered how far he would push it, but for now, she was content to go along with his requests.

Abby was looking forward to Saturday. They had discovered a mutual love of the outdoors and had decided to start hiking the Metroparks together. Victor was going to show her one of his favorite trails at Brandywine Falls. Saturday morning was cold, and she had dressed accordingly. She had worn some of her sexiest underwear underneath all the layers just in case. The hike would kill the morning, but they would have plenty of time in the afternoon and evening if he wanted to fool around. The thought made her nervous but also excited at the same time.

Abby rang the bell, and Victor opened the door almost immediately. "Why didn't you use your key?"

She shrugged. "I don't know."

He sighed. "Abigail. I want you to be comfortable here. You can always just let yourself in."

"Okay."

He helped her off with her coat and hung it up. "You know it's really getting cold out there. I'm not so sure a hike is a good idea today."

She gave him a teasing smile. "I thought Russians could handle the cold?"

"But of course we can. I was more concerned about you, little English girl."

"It's cold in England too. Besides, I wore a ton of layers. I should be fine."

He fingered the flannel shirt she was wearing. "Hmmm. I'm not sure this is going to be warm enough. Let me take a closer look." He nuzzled her neck and started unbuttoning the shirt. Then he pushed it off her shoulders and let it drop to the floor. He pulled her in for a kiss.

While they were kissing, Victor grasped the Henley shirt she was wearing underneath. "I think this material is way too thin," he murmured. "It will never keep out the cold." He grasped the shirt and pulled it up over her head. It hit the floor next to her flannel, and now she was down to a silky cami and a bra.

Victor guided her over to the couch and had her sit down. Then he lifted one of her legs and slowly unlaced the boot. He pulled it off and dropped it to the floor before unlacing the second boot. The entire time he was watching her with a grin on his face. "Abigail, how do you expect to go on a hike when you're not properly dressed?"

She laughed. "I was dressed just fine, Dr. Turov, until you started fiddling with my clothes."

"I don't know what you're talking about. But since you are half naked already, we should just keep going." He kissed her as his hands undid the buttons on her cargo pants. He pulled them off along with the silky thermal leggings underneath. He whispered in her ear, "I think a hike is entirely out of the question now. We should just have sex instead. Much warmer."

Abby looked at her watch and then teased, "I don't know. Are you sure we have enough time?"

Victor looked at his watch as well. "We'll be cutting it close, but I think we can manage."

He pushed her down on the couch and half lay on top of her. They were kissing with abandon now, and their hands were wandering all over each other. Victor had her cami pushed up and was cupping both breasts as Abby started unbuttoning his shirt.

Suddenly he stopped her. "We are moving way too fast, little one. We need to slow it down and do things right." He sat upright and pulled her up with him. He smoothed her camisole back down. "This is our first time. I want to explore your body slowly and possess every inch of you."

Abby gave him a bemused look.

Victor didn't seem to notice. He ran a hand through his hair and was half talking to himself and half talking to Abby. "It's been so

fucking long. I'm going to blow my wad before we even get started."
He abruptly stood up and took Abby's hand. Then he started walking
through the condo and looking at various walls and pieces of furniture.
At one point he grabbed a hand mirror from the bathroom and carried
it with him. As he passed the thermostat, he turned the temperature
up. Abby followed along looking confused and wondering what the
hell he was doing.

Finally, Victor stopped in front of the breakfast nook by the kitchen.
It jutted out from the wall and had a countertop for eating. There were
four barstools lined up in front of it, and a two-foot space underneath
the nook that ran the entire length of the wall. This was presumably to
give it a more modern feel. Victor squatted down and checked the space.
It was deep enough. He smiled triumphantly as he stood back up. Then
he looked at Abby and tried to explain. "I've never had a girlfriend in
my condo before, so I'm trying to figure out what's going to work best."

She was looking at him like he had lost his mind.

Victor ignored the look. He continued, "Normally my goal is to bring
you pleasure before taking my own. But there's no way I'm going to be
able to concentrate right now. You are just too damn sexy, and I have
wanted you for way too long." He reached over and gently traced her
lips with his thumb. "That's why we're going to have to start with your
mouth. Is that okay?"

Abby rolled her eyes. She knew she should be embarrassed, but
this was one area she actually had some confidence in. She gave him a
quick nod. "Sure."

His eyes lit up. "Good. Kneel down, little one."

She looked at him uncertainly. "Huh?"

He kissed her. "Trust me. If you don't like anything we do today,
just say the word and we will stop."

Abby hesitated but then kneeled on the floor. He had positioned
her so she was to the left of the barstools. There was no countertop
there, just the wall.

Victor smiled down at her. "Good girl. Now back up."

She looked behind her and slowly scooched back until she felt her
back and head pressed up against the wall. Her feet and lower legs were
tucked in the space underneath. When she could go no further, she
looked up at Victor expectantly. She was wondering why he had gone
to all this trouble for a blow job.

He slowly walked over until he stood right in front of her. Then he took a throw blanket and tucked it under her knees for support. When he stood back up, Abby noticed her gaze was just about at eye-level with his crotch. She eyed it curiously.

Victor slowly unbuttoned his jeans before pressing one palm against the wall above her head. With his other hand, he freed his bulging penis. It was long, thick, and clinging to his belly.

Abby's mouth fell open in shock. The words were out before she could stop them. "Where the hell have you been hiding that thing?!" She looked down at his feet and then up at his face. He was watching her with an amused expression on his face.

"What did you expect? I wear size fourteen shoes."

"Oh my god. How did I never notice your shoe size before?" She was covering her mouth with her hands and was laughing.

Victor's eyes were twinkling. "Well, I am tall. They probably blended in with the rest of me."

"Uh huh. And exactly how were you planning to get that inside of me?"

He laughed. "Trust me. It can be done. Right now it just needs to fit in your mouth." Then he gave her a wicked grin. "Now quit talking and start sucking."

She rolled her eyes and feigned shock. "You are unbelievable!" Then she grabbed hold of his penis with a determined expression on her face. She brought the tip to her mouth and rolled it around on her tongue. She could hear the sharp intake of his breath. She smiled as she continued to work his tip before licking the length of his shaft. Then she slid the whole thing into her mouth. It was long, and the tip was hitting her throat. She willed herself to relax so she could take more in.

Victor was watching her with a deeply aroused expression. Her mouth felt so good around him. It was wet and hot, and she was intent on what she was doing. He found that endearing. Her tongue was doing amazing things to his senses, and she was sucking him with abandon. He could feel the familiar increase in pressure. When she grabbed his balls and gently squeezed, he knew he wasn't going to make it much longer. But he wanted to test her limits, so he started rocking his hips and pushing his dick in further.

Abby naturally tried to move back, but her head came up against the wall behind her. It was then she realized why he had chosen this spot.

She looked up at him, and he was staring down at her intently.

"If this gets to be too much, just tell me to stop."

She nodded, and he continued to press his hips toward her head. As he did so, his dick was sliding further and further down her throat. Occasionally she would gag, and he would stop. Then she would take his penis back in her mouth, and they would continue.

Victor's breathing was getting deeper now. He grabbed the mirror off the counter and held it out to the side of her face. "I want you to look at what you're doing, little one. Look where my cock is. Your mouth belongs to me now."

She glanced at the mirror as she continued to suck. It was rather erotic to see his dick disappearing inside his mouth. What he said to her was even more sexy. She gave in to the emotion and sucked him harder.

Victor pulled the mirror away and braced both of his hands on the wall above her. "I'm about to cum, baby. Are you ready?" She nodded, and a few sucks later he exploded inside her mouth. The salty stream hit the back of her throat with force. Abby fought to stop the choking and brought both of her hands up. She pressed them around her mouth so that nothing would spill out. Then she worked to swallow his ejaculate. There was a lot there, but she managed. When she was done, she let his dick roll out before wiping her mouth with the back of her hand. She looked up at him, pressed her lips together, and smiled shyly.

Victor was still trying to recover. She hadn't been kidding. She was damn good at blow jobs, and her husband had taught her well! He looked down at her sweet smile in amazement. Then he gently pulled her away from the wall and up into his arms. He kissed her deeply and could still taste his cum on her mouth.

"See. I knew you were good at sex. That was an incredible orgasm you just gave me!"

She smiled.

Victor picked up the blanket from the floor and set it on the counter. Then he lifted Abby up and set her on top. Her legs were dangling off the edge. He poured a large glass of water and handed it to her. "Drink." She dutifully sipped on the water. He set the mirror next to her and then went to leave the room. "Stay put," he ordered, as he headed to the bedroom. She swung her legs in contentment and continued to drink the water. She had been nervous, but now she was feeling pretty smug. The feeling was short-lived.

When Victor returned, he was carrying some rope.

Her eyes got really big, and she felt a quick pang of fear.

Victor gave her a reassuring smile and quick kiss before fiddling with the faucet behind her. She looked over her shoulder, and he appeared to be testing it for sturdiness. He was muttering to himself, and she heard him say, "This should work." Then he walked back so he was standing in front of her.

He took the glass from her hands and set it aside. When she glanced at the rope, he shrugged and said, "Just in case." He grabbed the hem of her camisole. "Lift your arms up, little one."

She did, and he pulled the cami up and over her head. Then he placed his hands on her shoulders and slowly slid her bra straps down her arms. His hands were strong and warm against her soft skin. He unclasped the bra in the back and pulled it the rest of the way off. Victor fingered the satiny material.

"This is pretty." Then he looked at her breasts and brushed his knuckles across the peaks. "But these are much lovelier."

Abby blushed as her nipples hardened.

Victor tipped her head up with his hand and noted the pink hue on her cheeks. "Always so shy." Then he reached down and put his hands around her waist. He was able to wrap them completely around so both thumbs were touching up front, and both sets of fingers were touching in the back. He looked at her.

"How is it you are so tiny here…" and he raised his hands to cup her breasts… "But so large here?"

She sighed. "It's genetics. My mom was the same way. I really wish they were smaller."

"Nonsense. They're perfect. And I really want to see what they can do." He began to massage her breasts as he kissed her face. He tugged her hair to tilt her head to one side and trailed kisses down her exposed neck. When he reached her shoulder, he kept going until his mouth reached her right breast. He cupped it with his hand, closed his mouth over the nipple, and started sucking hard.

Abby was startled by the intensity, and her back arched. She instinctively reached her hands out and pressed them against his arms.

Victor paused briefly but then continued sucking. He pulled his hand out of her hair and began kneading her other breast. He was gently working the nipple between his thumb and forefinger, and Abby felt the sensation shoot straight to her pelvis. She was surprised at how her body was responding. Once again she put her hands on Victor's arms and unconsciously was pushing him away. She was also squirming on the countertop.

Victor paused again. "Quit deflecting." He resumed what he was doing, and now his tongue was circling her areola while his teeth gently nipped the tip.

Abby felt her clit begin to pulse, and a slickness was forming between her legs. She moaned and squirmed on the counter. She wanted to kiss him, but his mouth was intent on her breasts. Instead, she ran her fingers through his hair.

Victor pulled away so he could look at her. "If you sit still, you will enjoy this so much more."

"Okay." She couldn't help it, though. She grabbed his face and started kissing him instead.

Victor pulled away and sighed. He looked down at her and appeared to be debating something. Then he said, "You're still deflecting. I'm going to have to tie you up."

Abby gave him a stunned look as he grabbed the rope.

"Put your hands behind your back." He wasn't looking at her now and was unwinding the rope.

She hesitated for a second but then did what she was told. Victor kissed her nose and then quickly bound her wrists together. He took the loose end of the rope and stretched it back to tie it to the faucet. Her arms were pulled back toward the faucet. Victor walked around to stand in front of her and grasped her legs. He pulled her quickly toward the edge of the counter. This stretched her arms back tightly, and her back was arched with her breasts thrust forward.

He gave her a wicked grin and ran his hand across both nipples. "Much better."

He parted her legs and moved in so his body was pressed up against hers. "I know you're feeling this. Don't fight it, baby. Just let it happen."

He kissed her hard and slipped his tongue into her mouth. Both of his hands reached down and started massaging and kneading her breasts. He was pinching and pulling her nipples, and the sensation was almost more than she could bear. He was a lot rougher than Nate had ever been, but her body was still responding to his touch. Her back arched even more, and her arms pulled tightly against their bindings.

Victor patiently continued until he knew she was getting close. Her breathing was more shallow, and her thighs were squeezing against him. She had also stopped deflecting. He grabbed the mirror with one hand and held it out by her side. "Look at what I'm doing to your breasts. You are so beautiful. See how they look in my hands and my mouth. They are mine now."

Abby looked through half-closed eyes, and the sight made her moan. It was so erotic seeing him possess her like that. He put the mirror down and grasped both breasts. He ran kisses on the underside of one before taking the nipple into his mouth. He sucked hard and then reached down with his right hand. He cupped her pussy and massaged her clit area with his thumb through the fabric of her panties. It didn't take long. Within minutes she arched up and cried out, and he let her ride it out until her body collapsed.

Victor put one arm around her waist as he reached back and untied her. When the rope came off he pulled her arms around front and gently massaged her wrists. She was staring down at her hands. He forced her head up so she was looking at him. There was a telltale flush across her face again, and he grinned. He held up a finger. "That's one!"

She gave him a shy smile. "Wow!" Was all she could say.

He laughed and pulled her off the counter. Then he gave her a big bear hug. "You have very reactive breasts, baby. That was fun." He refilled the glass of water, took a long drink, and then handed the glass to Abby.

She took a sip and was surprised by how thirsty she was. She eyed her boyfriend. He still had his shirt on, but he was naked from the waist down. His hard-on was back and a sight to behold, and she realized he had enjoyed that as much as she had.

Victor took the glass from her hands and set it down. "You are exquisite."

She smiled at him. "You're not so bad yourself."

He took her hand and grabbed the rope. Then he led her back to the master bedroom, stopped at the bed, and pulled the comforter off.

"Lie down, little one." She did so, and he had her scooch to the center of the bed. He gazed down at her in appreciation before slowly taking off his shirt. Abby forgot to be embarrassed as she took in his naked body. He was all lean muscle, with a slight amount of hair on his chest, and a tight core. Her gaze headed south, and he chuckled.

Victor spread her legs and crawled onto the bed between them. Then he reached up and hooked his index fingers into her panties. He slowly pulled them down and off her body. He held them in one hand and gave her a smug look.

"Hmmm. These are soaking wet. Somebody wants me bad."

She scrunched her face in mock disgust.

He laughed and tossed the panties on the ground. Then he trailed one hand up her left leg and stopped at the mid-thigh. He trailed kisses there before reaching for the rope. Victor tied the rope around her thigh and threw the loose ends over the side of the bed. He got up and walked around to that side. Then he kneeled down and tightened the rope so her leg opened out. He secured the end tightly to a post under the bed.

Abby was too shocked to say anything.

Victor walked around to the other side of the bed. He opened the drawer underneath, and she could hear him rummaging around. Then he pulled out more rope and went to tie her right leg.

Now she was getting anxious and asked, "Is that really necessary?"

He quietly shushed her. "Trust me. I'm about to put my mouth all over your pussy. I suspect you're not going to like it, but I'm hoping to convince you otherwise. I need to keep you from deflecting to do that."

She covered her face with her hands. "The things you say!"

He laughed. "What? Do you prefer the word vagina?"

"Maybe just don't say anything at all."

"Very well. Let's see if you can keep quiet too."

After her right leg was secured, Victor crawled back on the bed and over her body. He was holding himself up by his arms, and his face was inches from hers. He gave her a luxurious kiss. "I want you to stay very still so you can absorb exactly what I'm doing to you. Do you think you can do that?"

She nodded, and he started working his way down her body with his mouth. He was kissing as he went, and occasionally he would lick or nip around a sensitive area. When he reached her belly, Abby began to fidget and reached down to grasp his shoulders.

"Be still!" he scolded.

She tried, but he was getting too close to her sensitive area. Her legs were wide open and pulling on the restraints, and she felt completely exposed. She put her hands in his hair and started tugging.

Victor stilled and then looked up at her in exasperation. "Oh, honey, you're still deflecting. That is simply not going to do."

He got up off the bed and went back to rummage in the drawer. He pulled out more rope and padded leather cuffs. He grabbed her right arm and wrapped one cuff around her wrist all the while smiling at her. He tightened the buckle and tested it, but she could not pull through. Then Victor grabbed her other arm and did the same thing to her left wrist. He secured both wrists together with a clasp and gently lifted her arms up over her head. Then he tied them tightly to the wrought iron headboard with the rope. She was now completely tied down with her legs spread wide apart and her arms over her head.

Victor stood up and looked down at her with satisfaction. She was glaring at him and trying to squirm, but the ropes were holding her tight.

"I don't like this!" she whimpered, and there was fear in her voice.

"Trust me. I'm not going to hurt you. You need to relax so the ropes don't bite into your skin." Then he pointed to the ceiling. "Look at how lovely you are all bound up."

She looked up and was startled to see a mirror on the ceiling. "When did you put that in?"

He laughed as he crawled back on the bed. "This past week. I did it myself. I thought it would help with your orgasms." He started massaging her belly. "Now where were we?" He kissed her belly button and then started licking it as his hand headed south.

Abby was anxious but couldn't move, so she started talking instead. "Well, I hope you did it right. What if that mirror comes crashing down on us?"

Victor shushed her as his mouth followed his hand to the apex of her vagina. Before he could do anything, her body lurched beneath him and she started talking again.

He sighed and looked up at her. "You're really not comfortable with this, are you? Just try it once. If you don't like it, then we won't do it again."

She pressed her lips together in frustration before looking at him. "Okay."

He took his thumbs and stroked her labia as his mouth came down on her center. When his tongue darted inside, Abby lurched again and started talking.

Victor sighed and stopped what he was doing. He got off the bed and went to rummage in the drawer. He came up holding some silky fabric in his hand, and she eyed it nervously.

He smiled reassuringly at her as he gently placed his hand over her mouth. "Can you breathe? Show me you can breathe through your nose."

She anxiously nodded and breathed. When he was satisfied, he took the silk fabric and gently guided it under her head. Then he wrapped it around her mouth and tightened the gag in place. "How about now? Are you still breathing okay?"

She nodded with fearful eyes, and he whispered, "Trust me, little one. Just blink rapidly if you want me to stop." He crawled back down between her legs and picked up where he had left off. Abby tried to squirm, but he hadn't left her much room to move. She also tried to speak, but the gag was tight, and all she could get out was a muffled noise. She realized she was completely at his mercy now, but oddly enough she trusted the man.

Victor kept an eye on her face as he slowly stroked her with his tongue. His fingers were gently probing her slit, and he suddenly stopped to get a closer look. He was touching her and muttering to himself about her clit being more hooded than normal.

Abby squirmed in embarrassment. It felt like he was giving her some sort of freaky gynecological exam!

Once he was satisfied with what he saw, he inhaled deeply. "God, you smell good!"

Abby gargled out a reply, but he ignored her.

He pulled on her pubic hairs. "You don't have to shave for me. I like a natural woman."

Abby was mortified. She tried to explain she kept trim for swimming, but again it came out incoherently.

Victor shook his finger at her. "Shh. No talking!"

Then his mouth was on her in earnest. He was working his tongue over her clit before stroking it down to her opening and back. He was taking his time, and the pressure was light at first. It felt good, and she relaxed ever-so-slightly. Victor noticed and slowly picked up the pace while increasing the pressure. He gently inserted a finger into her wet slit and stroked her on the inside while his tongue worked her outside.

Abby realized he knew what he was doing, and her body was responding. But she was embarrassed and didn't want to cum in his mouth. For some reason, it seemed so much worse than him cumming in hers.

He sensed her resistance. "Quit fighting me. We're not going anywhere until you cum. I'll stay here all day if I have to. Look at the mirror. It will help."

She looked up and realized he was on to something with the whole visual thing. All she could see was his head between her legs, and the rest of her was bound up. Her breasts looked huge with the nipples hard, and her eyes were deep green and full of arousal. It was erotic.

Abby's breathing was getting deeper and faster. She was getting close, and Victor knew it. "You are so beautiful, little one, and you taste so good." He continued his tongue lashing of her pussy, and now he was hitting her clit with a calculated precision.

Abby was finding it harder and harder to resist him. It felt so good and so right. At some point, she forgot to be embarrassed, and she finally relaxed completely.

That's what Victor was waiting for. He reached up and squeezed one of her breasts hard, and she went over the edge and cummed in his mouth. He waited until she was done and then untied her legs. Then he crawled up so his face was above hers. He was grinning as he pulled the gag off of her mouth. He kissed her hard.

She wrinkled her nose in disgust and tried to turn her head. "Gross."

He laughed. "I love that smell. And you're going to learn to love it too." Then he held up two fingers. "That's two." He massaged her legs and then held up her head and offered some water.

She took a sip and glared at him as some spilled down her neck. "You know this would be a whole lot easier if you untied my arms."

"I can't. We're not done yet. And since it's now clear you're a deflector, this is necessary." He yanked on the rope. "It will keep you focused." He put the water down on the nightstand and then crawled back on top of her. He was holding himself up by his arms and looking down with a lustful expression.

Abby looked up at him and licked her lips nervously.

Victor followed the movement with his eyes. "I've always been old-fashioned, and the missionary position is my favorite." He caressed her cheek. "Nothing portrays male dominance over a female more than this."

Now she was panicking again, and her legs began to squirm. "Um, exactly how were you planning to get that porn star dick inside of me?"

Victor laughed and tried to reassure her. "I'm really not that big. Plus, I already examined your anatomy, and I'm sure it can fit."

If anything that comment made it worse. She started telling him as much, but Victor swiftly raised his hand so it was covering her mouth. "Can you breathe, baby?"

She nodded.

He sighed and looked around for the gag. "No more deflecting. Blink rapidly if you need me to stop." Then he pulled the gag on and tightened it. He settled back and slowly started caressing her body. "You are so soft and sweet." He pressed his hips against hers and spread her legs out wide. Then his hand reached down and stroked her pussy. It was soaking wet. "See, little one. Your body is smarter than your head right now. We're going to take this really slow, okay?"

She nodded.

Victor knew he needed to be gentle since it had been so long for her. He slipped two fingers in first to ease the way, and she flinched as she watched his face.

Once Victor was satisfied, he pulled his fingers out and guided his tip to her entrance. He gently pushed her legs wider and pressed his cock in until he met resistance. Then he stopped and waited. He was focusing on her response and trying not to think about his own. It had been a long time for him as well. Abby was hot, wet, and tight, and the lack of a condom was doing amazing things to him. He could feel her wrapped around his member, and he had to take a deep, calming breath to continue.

Victor pulled out slightly and then pushed in again. This time he could go further. He smiled reassuringly at Abby and caressed her face as he continued to ease in and out of her. The deeper he went, the more uncomfortable it got, and he could see the tension on her face.

"I promise this will get easier with time. It's just been a while for you, and your body needs to wake back up."

She nodded, and he kept going. He was kissing her and caressing her body, and Abby realized just how gentle and sweet he could be. The thought helped her relax even more.

Finally, he was in all the way, and they lay there and stared at each other in wonder. Victor was caressing her face and gradually moved his hands down to her breasts. He started caressing them, and he could feel her body responding. When he thought she was ready, he said, "I'm going to start moving now."

Abby nodded. He slowly pressed in and out, and the movement

burned and stung along her inside walls. In spite of this, she was enjoying the closeness with Victor. He was big, and he filled her completely. His body pressed against her was warm and hard, and she remembered just how good a man could feel. She looked up at the mirror on the ceiling. Watching his tight posterior muscles as he rocked in and out of her was a major turn on. She slid her legs up and wrapped them around him.

Victor's hand wandered down between their bodies, and he placed his thumb strategically and started rubbing. He explained, "Your clit is shy like you, and it likes to hide. This will help."

It sure as hell did!

He continued to rock in and out of her. When he thought she was aroused enough not to deflect, he reached up and pulled the gag off of her mouth. Then his lips came down on hers.

Victor was getting close, but he needed to hang on for her. He used every ounce of willpower he had as he started to pump her harder. His thumb was also working her clit in a pounding and circular motion. She was now raising her pelvis to meet his, and he knew she was getting close. Finally, her back arched up and she grabbed onto him hard.

"Are you cumming?" he asked.

"Yes!"

That's all he needed. He exploded inside of her and rammed harder than he meant to. When the last of his semen had pumped out, he collapsed on top of her. Then he reached up and untied her arms. Victor rolled over and pulled Abby with him. He undid the cuffs and massaged her wrists and arms. She watched him and tried to catch her breath.

"Damn," was all she said.

He laughed and then held up three fingers. Abby snuggled into him, and they lay there awhile in silence. They could both feel the connection. It had become much stronger now and felt like an invisible magnet binding them together.

Victor pointed up at the mirror. "Look how well we fit together, Abby."

She was thrilled to hear the informal name.

"Your pussy belongs to me now."

Abby snorted. "You and that mouth!"

He grinned before sitting up. "You hungry?"

She nodded, and he pulled her to a standing position. Then he smacked her lightly on the ass before picking up his crumpled shirt. He wiped her with it first before wiping himself. They noticed the trace of blood and then looked over at the bed. Sure enough, there was a few spots on the sheets. Abby was mortified, but Victor just laughed.

"Well, that's a first. I'm sorry, baby. I was rougher than I wanted to be. But you felt so damn good, I couldn't help myself."

She giggled. "You weren't that rough. This was caused by that anaconda dick of yours."

He continued to laugh as he took her hand and led her down the hallway.

Chapter Twenty-Eight

They staggered into the kitchen and started heating up leftovers from the fridge. Abby went to grab some of her clothes to put on, but he wouldn't let her.

"I want you completely comfortable with me and your nakedness."

She gave him a disgusted look before standing by the counter. "Seems unsanitary."

He laughed as he pulled out a barstool for her. "Sit. If anything seeps out, we can clean it up later."

She was beginning to think she would always blush around this man. "Sometimes you are just too much!"

"You'll get used to me. Your body is already fitting with mine nicely."

He sat down next to her, and they began eating. Abby was starving and she said as much to Victor.

He responded, "Well it is lunchtime."

"What? We've been fooling around that long?" She was stunned.

He grinned. "I told you we needed time."

"I was thinking you meant about an hour."

"I'm not usually a patient man, Abby. But when it comes to you and sex, I'm willing to take my time and do it right." He would lay odds she thought they were done, and he didn't want to tell her differently, so he let her eat in peace.

When they finished, Abby went to clear the dishes. She had almost forgotten she was naked, but when he sidled up behind her, she felt his warmth against her skin.

"Leave the dishes. We'll get them later." He took her hand and led her back to the master bathroom. He brushed his teeth while she stood awkwardly in the doorway. Then he handed her the toothbrush. While she brushed, he started fiddling with a long narrow table pushed up against the wall. She was standing close to it, and he realized it was the perfect height.

He smiled at Abby. "Do you have to pee?" She nodded, and he left her to it while he went down the hallway and used the guest bathroom.

When he returned she was sitting on the edge of the bed. "Do you mind if I take a shower?"

He sighed. "Not yet, baby. We'll take a bath when we're done."

Her eyes widened in surprise. "We're not done?"

He walked over until he stood above her. "No. I still have your ass to claim." Victor reached for her hand and walked her back into the bathroom. He pulled the table out so it was at an angle, grabbed some towels, and threw them over the top. Then he had her bend over the table. She looked beautiful with her perky rear end sticking up at him, and he was hard instantly.

He left to get some lube. "Stay put," he ordered. But as soon as he was gone, she stood up. When he returned, she was standing over by the sink.

"Uh oh. Someone is deflecting again."

She eyed him nervously. "Victor. Maybe we should put this one off for a while. I'm not sure I'm ready."

He pulled her in for a hug. "No, baby. I need to claim all of you. I promise I'll be gentle and take it slowly. You need to trust me."

She sighed as he led her back to the table. He had her bend over again and started caressing her cheeks. "Relax and take some deep breaths. It will help."

Abby tried to breathe deeply, but she was anxious, and her lungs wouldn't cooperate. She felt Victor's hand leave her ass and looked in the bathroom mirror. She saw him pouring lube onto his index finger. Then his hand was back, and the finger was gently circling her opening. She felt pressure as he eased the finger in, and her sphincter muscle immediately tightened in protest.

"Keep taking deep breaths, baby. You're doing great."

Abby stared at the mirror and sucked in some air. His finger wasn't hurting, but it felt uncomfortable inside of her.

Victor used his other hand to massage her lower back and spoke softly as he continued to ease his finger in and out. He was stroking her inside walls in a circular motion, and the muscle started to release.

Victor pulled his finger out and added more lube before reinserting two fingers. Abby felt more pressure, and she let out a groan. He suggested she push back a bit against him. When she did, her muscle contracted tightly around his fingers. She was now quietly panting but still doing okay.

Victor was taking his time. He slowly eased out again, added more lube, and then inserted three fingers at a glacial pace. He was preparing her as best he could for what was to come. He spoke softly. "You are doing so well, Abby. I am so proud of you." He watched as her opening got bigger.

Finally, Victor felt she was ready. He gradually took his fingers out and poured a generous amount of lube on his cock. She was watching from the mirror, and she started to whimper when she saw him guide it toward her opening.

"Shhh. Trust me, little one. Keep breathing deeply. It will help."

Abby nodded and tried to steady her breath. She watched in the mirror as his penis started to disappear inside her.

The pressure was intense. She felt very full and uncomfortable, and her sphincter tightened in response. With careful persistence, Victor was able to slide past the constricted muscle, though, and felt it tightening around his member. He smiled as the pressure stimulated the sensitive nerve-endings along his shaft. He held her still at the hips and quietly waited for both of them to acclimatize.

Victor felt his member moving more freely, so he took his right foot and pressed it against her instep to spread her legs wider. Then he inched in even more and stopped. He waited again and massaged her back. He could feel her legs quivering, but she was not crying or asking him to stop. He could see she was staring at him in the mirror and there was trust in her eyes. That about disarmed him, but he held on to his control for her sake.

Finally, he said, "Grab onto the table legs and don't let go."

Victor pulled on her hair with his left hand and started rocking his hips. His cock was easing in and out of her, and Abby moaned as he settled into a slow rhythm. He released her hair and reached down to massage her clit. He began tapping it with precision as his dick continued to slip in and out of her derriere. Victor glanced at the mirror, and the sight was glorious.

Abby was trembling from the intensity. Her back end was tight and uncomfortable, but his finger on her front was feeling unbelievably good. She began to press back against his hips on each thrust, and it wasn't long before she felt a delicious arousal in her entire pelvic area.

Victor watched her face with satisfaction. He picked up the pace with his hips and stroked her clit even harder with his finger. "Do you see me inside of you, baby? Your ass belongs to me now."

She nodded and whimpered as he continued to drive into her. She was barely listening to him, as the sensations began to take over. Her legs were shaking uncontrollably, and she realized she was at the brink of a powerful orgasm. Normally she would have been too embarrassed to vocalize, but this was unlike anything she had ever felt before. Abby came, and when she did she screamed out his name.

That was all Victor needed. He pulled her back tightly against his hips and pumped his seed into her ass. When he finished, they were both panting and covered in sweat. He eased out and pulled her up to a standing position. Her legs felt like wet noodles, and she sagged against him. Victor held her up and led her over to the toilet. He had her sit down and then grabbed a towel to wipe himself. She could feel a dull ache deep in her pelvic floor, but mostly she felt wonderfully sated.

Abby looked up at him in awe.

Victor was grinning down at her. "That's four, little one. And now that lovely ass belongs to me."

"I can't believe we just did that," she said breathlessly.

He grinned as he reached down to turn on the tub faucets. "It will get even better with time. Our bodies are just starting to figure each other out."

Abby nodded and watched him appreciatively. She couldn't believe she was lucky enough to have him as her boyfriend. She also couldn't believe all the orgasms he had given her. Dating him had been the right choice, albeit a crazy one to make.

While they waited for the tub to fill, he asked how she was feeling.

She smiled at him shyly. "Good, but everything is sore."

"A little sore is okay. You will feel better in time, and it will be worth it."

Once the tub was full he helped her in. Then he slid in behind her. Abby leaned back against him and closed her eyes, and Victor wrapped his arms around her.

"Our bodies are so damn compatible. And yours is wonderfully reactive."

Abby teased him as he began to wash her. "Maybe it's just beginner's luck."

He arched one eyebrow. "I am hardly a beginner, and you were definitely a challenge. You put up a fight at every turn. I've never seen a woman deflect as much as you!"

"And here you thought I was submissive."

He kissed her head. "Oh, you are very submissive. You just need to learn how to embrace it."

When they were done, they got out of the tub and dried off with clean towels. Then he wrapped his arms around her in front of the mirror.

"You are mine now, Abby. I need you to say it."

She snuggled against him. "Yes, Victor. I belong to you." Then she mischievously added, "And you belong to me!"

He grinned as he kissed her neck. Then he led her out and handed her some clothes to put on. They headed to the living room and snuggled on the couch. Victor turned on the television to a football game. He smiled down at her. "If you want, we can go out to dinner later on or catch a show."

She gave him an alarmed look. "Do we have to? Can't we just stay in and order food and watch movies or something?"

He was thrilled. His other dates would have wanted him to spend money on them after all of that. But she just wanted to cuddle. Abby was like no other woman he had ever met. "Of course we can."

They ended up ordering takeout and watching a comedy later on that night. When they finally went to bed. Victor pulled her against him.

"Good night, little one."

"Good night."

Just before he fell asleep, she asked him, "Victor, were we ever going to go on a hike?"

He laughed. "Hell, no!" He was certain she was rolling her eyes in the dark.

Chapter Twenty-Nine

The next day over breakfast Abby noticed there was a brand new electric kettle in the kitchen. It was just like the one Victor had bought for her. She pointed to it and shook her head. "Really?"

He opened a drawer while eating his cereal and showed her where the herbal teas were located. "Yes, really. I don't want you drinking any coffee. This is a healthy alternative." Then he reached over and checked her pulse. "You're still running at the high end of normal."

She teased him. "Maybe my heart rate is up from all the sex I've been having. Are you going to limit my sex too?"

"God, no. I'll put you on medication before I do that."

She shook her head. "Typical man."

He grinned and continued to eat his breakfast. Abby sighed and fixed herself a cup of tea. She was developing a taste for it, but there was no way she was going to tell him that.

When they were done eating, Victor helped her with the dishes. Then he led her to the couch. "I think it's time we talked about Rule Number Three." They sat down, and he took her hand.

"You know how I like to be in control."

She smiled. "That's an understatement!"

He shrugged. "It's who I am. And Rule Number Three epitomizes that part of me."

She looked at him expectantly.

Victor was actually nervous. He needed this to go well. She belonged to him now, but this rule would push her to the outer limits of her comfort zone. He took a deep breath. "Let's call this rule the obedience one." He waited, but she was still watching him calmly. He continued, "I want you to comply with any request I make of you."

She stared at him.

"That means if I tell you to do something, or not do something, you will obey me without hesitation or question. Do you think you can do that?"

Abby frowned. "I thought I already did that. I mean, I have to ask permission to see my friends for Pete's sake."

He nodded. "Certainly Rule Number Two is about obedience. But this goes beyond that. I don't just want you to follow a set of rules. I want you to submit to me at all times, regardless of what I ask or when I ask it."

She looked thoughtful. "What kind of things are we talking about?"

"It could be anything, really. My primary goal is always going to be your safety. If I feel your choices are putting you in danger, I will step in and command you to make changes."

She sighed. "Okay."

"I may also ask you to do things simply because they please me."

She swallowed hard. "Are you talking sexual things?"

He nodded. "Yes. Or it could be other things. So far you don't seem to have a problem with the sex."

She blushed. "But I could in the future. It all depends on how crazy you get."

"Don't worry about that. Whatever we do I promise we'll always take it slow, and I will always bring you pleasure."

She pressed her lips together. She wasn't looking at him, so he tugged on a strand of hair and turned her head his way. "Tell me what you're thinking, little one."

She hesitated. "I don't mind listening to you, Victor, but I'm worried about how far you will take all of this. I mean, I'm not exactly thrilled about giving up my freedom."

"You aren't giving up all of your freedom. Once we're settled, I will rarely make commands and only when absolutely necessary. If you're honest with me, and we trust each other, then it won't be a problem."

"But you said I couldn't argue or question your commands. If I'm uncomfortable with something, how is that being honest?"

He sighed. "You're overthinking this. I have gotten good at reading you, and that will only get better with time. You blush easily, and always when you're uncomfortable. Plus, I'm pretty sure you were obedient your entire marriage."

She gave him a confused look. "Why would you say that?"

"Didn't Mr. Shea ask you to do things you didn't want to do?"

She thought about it. "Well, sure. But those were little things."

"What about your job? I remember you telling me he asked you to quit your social work job so you could travel with him."

"Well, yes..."

"And that was a big thing, wasn't it? But you did it anyway because you trusted him and wanted to please him." He stroked her cheek and leaned in to kiss her. "I think you like having someone take control. You're a natural submissive."

"You keep telling me that, but I don't believe it." She was hugging her legs close to her chest and looking sullen. "And why do you get to be in charge? Why can't I tell *you* what to do?"

She was challenging him again, but this time he was going to enjoy the conversation. "Okay. Let's take a look at that. Who is older, Abby?"

"You are."

"Yes, by seven and a half years. One could argue with age comes wisdom, which makes me better able to make decisions than you."

"Not necessarily."

He cocked an eyebrow at her. "Okay. Then who is smarter, you or I?"

She glared at him but begrudgingly admitted, "You."

He grinned. "Mmm hmm. And who is bigger?"

"You are."

"Yes. I'm a good eight inches taller than you and weigh at least 100 pounds more. That means I am better able to provide protection from danger."

She was still glaring, but he was on a roll now.

"And who is stronger, Abby, you or I?" He put his arm around her so their biceps lined up next to each other.

She glanced down at his arm and sighed. "Of course you are."

"Yes, I am. Which again makes me better equipped to provide protection."

She shook her head in disbelief. "And what exactly would you need to protect me from?"

Victor gave her a pointed look. "With you, who knows? Recently I had to pull you away from a drunk man who was molesting you in a hallway."

She looked down and rubbed her neck in embarrassment.

"Finally, baby, and I can't emphasize this point enough, men are biologically made to dominate women in a relationship." He pulled her onto his lap. "Think about it. Men get to invade and enter a woman's body, not the other way around. Not only that, but we get to mark our territory by leaving our semen behind."

Abby was appalled by the conversation. "Fine. You're in charge. But we just started dating, Victor. It's too much to take in this early in a relationship."

He looked contrite. "I know. But this is who I am, and the only type of relationship I can have."

"So all your other girlfriends agreed to this?"

He nodded.

"Didn't you tell me none of them lasted that long? Maybe this is why."

"Maybe. But I'm the one that broke all of them off. It was more a question of compatibility than my rules, I think."

Abby sighed. "So what if I'm not willing to do this?"

He rubbed his temple with his hand. "I'm really hoping you are. I think we work well together. I also think you are dating me because you like me."

She frowned. "Well, yeah. Why else would I date you?"

"Let's just say some women in the past were in it more for my money."

"Oh." She gave him a wicked smile. "I would have guessed your body, but heh, money works too."

He grinned and kissed her neck. Then he whispered, "Is that why you're dating me, little one, for my body?"

Abby burst out laughing. "No. But it certainly doesn't hurt! But you didn't answer my question. What if I can't do this?"

Victor got serious immediately. "If you find you can't follow this rule, then we won't be able to date anymore."

Now she was upset. "Really? I don't understand why."

"Because I can't be in a relationship without controlling it."

She tried to pull away, but he wouldn't let her.

"Just try it, Abby. I promise the reality isn't as bad as what's going on in your head."

She was staring at the wall. "Can I think about it before I decide?"

He nodded. "Sure. You're actually going to get a feel for obedience over the next few days. I'm going to be taking a closer look at your life to see if any changes need to be made."

She gave him a worried look. "Oh?"

"Yes. So tell me, what's a typical Sunday like in the life of Abby?"

She grinned. "Well, Dr. Turov, my Sunday usually starts off with church. Does that mean you're coming with me?"

"Absolutely."

She gave him a smug look. "Okay, but I should warn you, it's a Catholic church."

"Well, Mrs. Shea, you should know I was raised in a Russian Catholic church, so that won't be a problem." He laughed as he went to change.

***

Abby drove to her place with Victor right behind her. She changed, and then he drove them to the church. Victor looked around with interest once they were seated. It was old, with beautiful stained-glassed windows, and rustic pendant lights hanging by chains from the ceiling. The church wasn't that big, and the place was packed. He had thought the Catholic religion was on the decline in America, but the crowd there said otherwise.

Abby was kneeling next to him in the pew praying. She was wearing a pretty skirt and sweater with her hair up in a bun. She looked like an adorable little librarian. Oh, the fantasies he could have on that one! He idly wondered if she was confessing her sins from yesterday. The thought made him smile.

Victor continued to look around and noticed a group of questionable men sitting in the back. He nudged Abby and nodded his head in their direction. She looked over and then leaned in to whisper, "They're homeless. They come in to get warm, and they also visit the hunger center when it's open."

Victor frowned, but his thoughts were interrupted by the start of mass. As they stood for the processional, he noticed a man a few pews up who kept turning around and surreptitiously looking at Abby. He had the look of a lovesick puppy dog. Victor's eyes narrowed.

The mass itself was nice. The readings were familiar ones, and the choir sounded good. It had been years since he had been to a mass, and he was surprised at how much he was enjoying himself. He looked over at his girlfriend, and she was singing along with the choir quietly. Victor grinned and put his arm around her. Then he noticed the asshole puppy dog watching her again. The two men eyed each other, and Victor stared the other man down.

When it was time for communion, Abby stepped out into the aisle with Victor and let the other people pass. Then she stepped back in and kneeled to pray. Victor eyed her with amusement. When she finally sat back in the pew, he leaned in and asked, "No communion?"

"Not today. It would appear you have ruined me for all men *and* for communion too!"

Victor laughed. "The men part is a good thing. But you can always go to confession and profess your sins."

She shook her head. "There's a problem with that solution."

"What's that?"

"You actually have to be *sorry* for your sins for that to work."

This time Victor laughed loudly, and several parishioners looked over at them including the puppy. Victor raised one eyebrow at the man, and he turned away.

While they were waiting for communion to end, there was a commotion from the back of the church. Everyone turned around to see two of the homeless men throwing punches at each other. The fight was intense. The men fell over a pew and crashed into a statue before falling to the ground. Several people, including the priest, ran to the back to break it up. When it was over, the priest returned to the altar and apologized. He finished the mass, and then they were singing during the recessional.

Victor was furious. She had to pick the one church that attracted a dangerous element. He looked down at her and scowled, and she studiously looked away. This was the first thing he was going to change.

They headed out to the vestibule, and several people stopped to talk to Abby. Victor stood to the side and waited. He was scrolling through his emails when he noticed the puppy dog sidling up to her. Oh, hell no!

Victor immediately walked over and put his arm around Abby. Then he asked, "Who's this?"

Abby smiled. "This is Paul. He works for Catholic Charities, and he manages the hunger center at the church." Then she turned to the puppy dog, "This is Victor, my boyfriend."

Hearing the word flow easily from her mouth delighted him. Victor shook the other man's hand and noted the weak grip.

"It's nice to meet you, Paul. You have an admirable profession."

The puppy dog gave him a half-smile. "It's nice to meet you too, Victor. And thanks. I'm pretty proud of what I do." Then he turned to Abby. "I didn't know you were dating someone."

She blinked. "Um, yeah. We just started dating a few weeks ago."

The puppy dog nodded. Then he looked at Victor with more confidence and asked, "And what is it you do?"

"I'm a heart surgeon at the Cleveland Clinic," was the smug reply.

Paul's eyes got big. "Wow. That's an admirable profession too!"

Victor smiled but didn't say anything. He was watching Abby, who was just clueing in to the pissing match they were having. She eyed them both nervously.

The puppy dog kept talking and was telling Victor what a wonderful volunteer Abby was. "I really don't know what I would do without her. In fact, we've got a big delivery coming in tomorrow morning." He turned to her, "You are going to be there, right Abs?"

She winced at the familiar nickname and tried not to look at her boyfriend. "Sure. Of course, I'll be there."

Victor quietly commented, "And I will be there too."

They both looked at him in surprise. Abby beamed, but Paul was frowning.

"We are always happy to have the help, Victor, but all our volunteers need to go through a screening process first."

Victor wasn't fazed. "I'm sure you can make an exception, Paul. I just want to come and see what it's all about." Then he added with steel in his voice, "I also need to make sure it's safe for my girlfriend."

Paul was stunned, but he recovered quickly. "Er, sure. That's understandable. I guess I can allow it this one time." He looked at them speculatively. "I guess I'll see you both tomorrow, then."

Once he was gone, Abby looked at Victor with amusement. "Was that really necessary?"

"Yes, it was. He wants what's mine." He grabbed her hand and led them out of the church. Then he asked, "Am I to assume he was one of the men in the running?"

Abby had forgotten about that. "Oh, yeah, I guess he was."

Victor shook his head. "That was my competition, and your friends picked me last?"

She thought about it. "Well, you were the most dangerous choice of the three."

Victor looked serious. "No, little one. The other two were more dangerous. The Ken doll had date rape written all over him, and the puppy dog has some serious screws loose."

"Puppy dog?" she laughed out loud. "You should be a writer with your play on words."

He opened the door for her. "I'll leave the writing to you. Now, where to next in a day in the life of Abby?"

She thought about it. "I usually go work on my book a bit, and then I swim before the football game."

Victor nodded. "Let's get your computer, then."

They headed back to her house, and Abby asked, "What are you going to do while I'm writing?"

Victor pointed to the briefcase in the back seat of his truck. "I have plenty of work to do."

She nodded. "Oh, good." Then she thought about it. "Do you swim? Do we need to go pick up your swimsuit?"

He smiled. "Yes, I do swim. But I think today I'll just observe. I'll be better able to pick up on things that way." Then he asked, "Do they have a place for me to sit?"

"They have windows looking into the pool with chairs by the windows.

"Good. That will work."

She was thinking too. "How are you going to come help out at the hunger center tomorrow? Don't you have to work?"

"I have a meeting tomorrow afternoon, but my morning is wide open."

"Oh." She looked at him suspiciously. "That doesn't sound like your normal schedule. Did you plan all of this in advance?"

He gave her a wolfish grin. "Yes, baby, I did."

She sighed and mumbled, "I should have held out longer."

Victor laughed all the way to her house.

***

They pulled up next to the coffee shop fifteen minutes later. It was right across the street from Lincoln Park and within walking distance of her church. Victor noted the homeless men sitting on benches in the park. They seemed to be everywhere in her neighborhood, and it was seriously starting to honk him off. Victor had nothing against the homeless, but if they had an addiction problem they could be dangerous. Certainly, the fight earlier at mass did nothing to ease his mind.

They walked into the shop; the staff all knew Abby. They asked if she wanted her usual, and she hurriedly told them no and ordered an herbal tea. A hint of rose crept across her cheeks. Victor noted it and looked at her thoughtfully. When it was his turn to order, he told them he would have her usual. They promptly made a fully-caffeinated latte. Then he asked the last time they had fixed it for her, and the barista told him on Tuesday.

Victor drew in a quick breath and gave her a sharp look. She refused to meet his gaze and instead busied herself getting the computer set up at the table. He waited until she was done and then leaned in to whisper, "You will be punished for that later."

Abby sighed and risked a look at him. "I know," was all she said.

They worked for two hours. Victor noted how engrossed she was in what she was typing. That meant she was oblivious to everything else around her, which was a problem. She needed to be more aware of her surroundings. He sighed before mentally adding it to the list.

They headed to the downtown YMCA next. Victor noted the three-lane pool and found a seat by the windows. She had gone into the women's locker room to change, and he soon saw her walk by on the other side of the glass. She looked stunning in her swimsuit, and he realized he wasn't the only one admiring her figure. Again, Abby was oblivious. She walked by and gave him a smile and wave before hopping into the pool.

Victor watched her swim laps. She had a strong and graceful stroke, and she glided through the water making it look easy. He was impressed. He had learned to swim as an adult, and he generally splashed up a storm as he swam. He noted the other swimmers coming and going. Since there were only three lanes, Abby had to continuously share one. At times that meant she had to slow her pace, and at other times she was being passed by stronger swimmers. The whole thing seemed rather tedious to him, especially considering how much roomier the pool was at his condo building.

After forty minutes she was done, and they headed back to Tremont. Victor took her to Fat Cats for lunch. It was right up the street from her townhouse. She considered ordering one of the vegan options on the menu, but she knew he wouldn't like it. He was already going to spank her for the coffee incident, and she decided she didn't want to add fuel to the fire. Instead, she ordered a salad and added grilled steak. He ordered the same.

They talked about the mass, and Victor explained the differences between the church he was raised in and hers. Then they talked about her plans for tomorrow. He would accompany her in the morning on her errands, but then he had to go to an M&M meeting in the afternoon.

Abby was intrigued. "What's an M&M meeting? Do you sit around and eat the candy?" she teased.

He chuckled. "It stands for morbidity and mortality. We review any surgical cases that didn't go as planned to see if we can prevent problems in the future. It's a way for all the surgical teams to learn from each other."

She thought about it. "So, if a patient dies, you review that?"

"Definitely. We also review any case that had to go back in for more surgery or problems that came up in the ICU. Remember the man I had to open up the night we met? That case had to be reviewed at an M&M."

"Oh. It sounds kind of like an editorial review in my profession. Although in your case it's much more serious."

"It is definitely a critical review, and some of them can get quite heated. We surgeons have big egos, and we don't like it when our mistakes are pointed out to us."

"What? You have a big ego? I would never have guessed."

He laughed, and they continued their meal.

When they got back to her place, Victor made a beeline for the couch. He sat down and beckoned her to join him. She slowly walked over and stood in front of him.

Victor had her skirt up, her panties down, and her naked ass sprawled over his lap within seconds.

"Why am I spanking you, Abby?"

"Because I drank some coffee."

He was rubbing her ass and thinking. Finally, he asked, "And how many times have you done this since I set up Rule Number Two?" Before she could answer, he added, "Think long and hard before you answer, little one. Remember that honesty is crucial to our relationship."

She thought about it. "Um, twice. No. Wait. Three times, I think."

He spanked her hard and fast eighteen times. When he was done, he smoothed her skirt back down and pulled her onto his lap. Her panties were still dangling at her ankles.

She leaned her head against his chest. "I'm really trying, Victor. But some days I just need the caffeine."

"I know. You have an addiction. Every time I catch you, though, I will punish you harder. But I'll go easier on you if you tell me right away when you slip up."

She didn't say anything, but she was thinking there was no way she would ever do that. She would rather take her chances.

They turned the game on, and this time the Browns won. Then they ordered a delivery from a local sushi restaurant.

While they were eating, she tentatively asked, "So how did today go?"

He looked at her. "As far as me assessing your life?"

She nodded.

"You sure you want to discuss this now? I'm still going to take a look at tomorrow."

Abby thought about it. "Will that change your thoughts on today?"

"No," was the gruff reply.

"Oh. Then I'd rather hear what you have to say now."

"Very well then." He put his chopsticks down. Then he gave her a serious look. "Remember, there is no room for argument on anything I say."

She nodded.

"Good. First and foremost, you need to find a new church. I don't want you ever going back to that church"

She interrupted. "But we're volunteering there tomorrow."

"I'm aware of that. We'll still go to the soup kitchen in the morning. I'm keeping an open mind. But the church definitely has to go. Find a new one, and let me know what you pick." Then he added, "I will be going with you from now on."

Her face lit up. "You will?" Nate had never gone to church with her.

Victor smiled. "Yes, baby. I rather enjoyed the mass. It brought back fond memories.

"That's awesome! No one ever goes to church with me. They all think I'm crazy."

"Well, I'm not sure how much I believe. But it can't hurt. As for the coffee shop, I'm still debating that one. You are so engrossed in your writing you tune out everything else. That can be dangerous, especially with the park across the street. Not to mention there's too much temptation there. Let me think on that one a bit longer."

"Okay. And what did you think of the pool?"

He shrugged. "I think you'd be much more comfortable at my pool.

There are more lanes, and if you avoid the early morning hours it's never crowded. Plus, you won't have to worry about running into the Ken doll."

She nodded. "I'm definitely going to give yours a try." Then she smiled at him. "This wasn't so bad."

He laughed. "Things are always worse in your head, Abby. You have quite the imagination."

She grinned. "I know. It makes me a good writer, but not such a good submissive, eh?"

He reached over and gave her a hug and kiss. "Oh, I don't know. I think you make a fabulous submissive."

They were in bed by nine thirty with Victor sleeping in his boxer shorts. He was spending the night at her house to see what it was like at night. He threw his arm over her and pulled her back against his warm body. He explained they would not be having sex that night. "We need to wait until you are less sore."

She was disappointed, because damn, but she fell asleep within minutes.

Chapter Thirty

They were up bright and early the next morning. Abby did her grocery shopping at the Westside Market on Mondays, and she liked to get there early before the crowds. She took a shower and ate breakfast before heading to Victor's place. He had already driven home to get ready, and she was to pick him up at seven. He had told her he wanted to assess her driving.

Victor was waiting by the elevator when she pulled in. He was wearing black dress pants, a white dress shirt, and a red tie. He was carrying his briefcase in one hand, and his jacket was slung over his other arm. Abby had always been a sucker for a man in business attire. They looked so powerful.

Victor folded himself into her car and gave her a quick kiss. His tall frame took up the entire passenger side, and he looked uncomfortable. Abby grinned as she drove them to the market. There was no parking on the street, so she pulled into the lot.

They headed to the outdoor produce stands first. Abby had her favorite vendors, and they bantered back and forth as she loaded up on fruits and vegetables. Of course, Victor insisted on paying for everything, and he also carried her bags to the car. Then she dragged him inside where all the meat and cheese vendors were located.

In truth, Abby didn't visit the indoor stalls too often, but she knew Victor would be watching to see if she purchased any protein. They wandered around looking at all the selections, and she eventually bought some chicken breast and sausage. He didn't comment but had noticed she did not know any of the meat vendors.

Victor was enjoying himself. For as long as he had lived in Cleveland he had never visited the Westside Market. It had an amazing variety of food for sale, from homemade pasta to fresh seafood, and just about every ethnicity you could think of was represented. On impulse, he bought some Czechoslovakian kolaches to take to his M&M meeting. He also paid for Abby's meat purchases, and he was delighted when she didn't complain. She was getting used to his ways. An hour later they headed back to the car loaded down with more bags.

She drove them back to her house. Victor sat at the kitchen counter while Abby washed and prepped the produce. She was happily chatting up a storm and not paying attention to what she was doing. He was nervously watching her, as the knife was getting dangerously close to her fingers. Victor finally couldn't take it anymore and took over the chopping duties. Abby watched in amazement at the speed of his hands.

"Wow!"

Victor shrugged. "What? I'm a surgeon. I handle knives all the time."

"I hope you don't move the scalpel that fast over your patients!"

He laughed and kept on working. They had everything prepped and in the fridge in no time.

Next up was volunteering at the soup kitchen. It was located in the basement of the church. Abby parked the car in the lot, and then they stood around with the other volunteers waiting for the truck to arrive. Victor looked around at the crowd. It was a motley crew of senior citizens, high school kids, and sketchy looking men smoking cigarettes. The puppy dog was also there with a clipboard walking around and talking to people.

Victor frowned. Nothing about this scene pleased him. He asked about the teenagers first. It was a group of five or six boys who were clowning around and throwing things. Abby explained they were from St. Ignatius, and they were putting in their required charity hours. He nodded, but his attention was already being drawn to the men smoking in the corner. Abby tried to walk away, but he touched her arm to stop her. He quietly asked, "And where did those men come from?"

She sighed and drew him away from the group so they wouldn't be overheard. "Okay. Look. Don't make a big deal out of this. They get a lot of volunteers that need to put in mandated community service hours."

Now he was scowling. "Uh, huh. So what you're saying is they're ex-cons."

She stared at the sidewalk. "Well. Not exactly. Most of them are actually still in prison. A van brings them over."

"What? Who supervises them? Where is the corrections officer?"

"They don't need one. They're low-level offenders. Mostly just drugs and driving under the influence."

Victor furiously pinched the bridge of his nose. "Jesus, Abby. What do you expect me to do with that information? There's no way in hell I'm going to let you continue volunteering here!"

Her mouth fell open. "You haven't even seen what it's like, yet."

"I've seen enough." He grabbed her hand and walked over to where the puppy dog was standing.

"Er, hi, Abby. And Victor, right? Good to see you both," said Paul.

Victor didn't acknowledge the greeting. "I'm afraid we won't be staying. This is not the type of environment I want my girlfriend to be in." He pointedly looked at the men in the corner.

Paul looked at Abby, who was too appalled to meet his gaze. Then he motioned them to follow him into the church.

Once they were inside he said, "I assure you, Victor, she is perfectly safe here. These men come from a halfway house, and I supervise them. I would never let anything happen to Abby."

"I don't see how you can guarantee that. Addicts fall off the wagon all the time, and they can be quite dangerous."

Paul was astounded. "But surely this is Abby's decision to make, not yours."

"No. It's my decision. And I have made it."

Paul made one last effort, "Don't these men deserve a second chance?"

Victor sighed. "Of course they do. But not around my girlfriend. She won't be volunteering here anymore." He led her out of the church, and Abby gave Paul an apologetic look as she followed behind.

She was shaking when they got in the car and had to take a few deep breaths to calm down. As she pulled out, she looked at him.

"That was so embarrassing! We could have just left without saying anything."

"No. It had to be said. This way he won't bother you to come back. And how dare that skinny little prick think he could protect you from those men!"

"You're completely overreacting, Victor!"

Now he was getting angry. "Am I? Are you saying none of these men have ever harassed you before?"

She looked away and pressed her lips together.

"Mmm hmm. That's what I thought. And let me remind you this is my call to make, not yours. You are to obey me without question."

She was getting angry too, but she didn't say anything. Instead, she pulled onto the freeway and headed to Bay Village. They needed to let Charlie out for Rachel and Joel.

They drove in silence, and Victor watched her face. He knew she was angry, but it was causing her to drive faster than he would like. He leaned over to look at the speedometer. "You're going ten over the speed limit. You need to slow down."

She glared at him. "Everyone drives ten over in Cleveland. I won't get a ticket." She continued to speed.

"I'm not worried about tickets. I'm worried about your safety!" Then, more calmly, he said, "I don't want you driving more than five over the speed limit."

"Oh, come on! Are you saying you drive that slow? And I know Vince doesn't. Only old people drive that slow."

His tone got deathly quiet. "We're not talking about anyone but you."

She glanced over, saw the expression on his face, and slowed down. "Nate was the safest driver I knew, and he still got killed. You can't control everything, Victor. Bad stuff just happens."

He was rubbing his temple. "I know, little one. But it doesn't stop me from trying."

She gave him a tentative smile as she pulled into Joel and Rachel's driveway. They let Charlie out and played fetch with him for a good half hour. Then they went to grab a quick lunch. When they finally pulled back onto the freeway, the traffic was barely moving. They turned on the radio and learned there was an accident ahead. Victor only had an hour to get to his M&M meeting, and it was looking like he would be late.

Abby made a quick decision and crossed three lanes of traffic to get onto an alternate freeway. Then she hit the gas and started dodging in and out of lanes. She was trying to buy some time, but all she was doing was making him angry.

"Slow down!"

She glanced at him briefly. "I'm a good driver, Victor. I can get you to your meeting on time."

"I don't care about the meeting. What I care about is your safety, and mine for that matter. Slow down!"

"Quit being such an old man!"

She wasn't sure what was compelling her to drive so fast. Possibly her anger over the whole volunteer incident? What she did know was that he would spank her, but she didn't care. He would have to do it after his meeting, and that small amount of cushion made her more reckless than she would normally be.

Victor was furious. He was trying to read her facial expressions to gauge what was going on in that pretty little head of hers. She looked determined, angry, and stubborn. He calmly said, "You will be punished."

Abby ignored him and kept on speeding. When she pulled off the freeway, she finally slowed down for the city streets. She risked a glance at her boyfriend, but he was leaning back in the seat with his eyes closed. He looked relaxed, but she could see a muscle in his lower jaw tensing. She smiled because the man looked so damn hot in spite of everything.

Victor had already thought through her punishment. It would be pleasurable for both of them, as he was still taking it easy on her. He had also come up with a plan to assure her safe driving in the future. That was doing wonders to ease his anxiety. He was feeling pretty smug about handling his new girlfriend. Yuri would be proud.

Abby finally pulled up next to his truck in the condo building. She looked at her watch and noted he would still get to his meeting on time. She gave Victor a triumphant smile.

He finally opened his eyes and looked calmly over at her. Then he pulled his cell phone from his pocket. He found the number he was looking for and held Abby's gaze while he waited for it to connect. "Hello, Dr. Jenkins? This is Dr. Turov. I'm going to be late for the M&M. Please start without me. Just leave the Mitchell case for last." He listened a bit. "Sure. That sounds good. And thank you."

When he hung up, he slowly reached over and turned her car off. Then he took her keys and motioned to her. "Come with me. You need to be punished."

The color drained from her face. "Well, crap!"

Victor laughed as he opened her car door and led her to the elevator. Once they were in his condo, he pinned her up against the front door. He traced her collarbone with his finger.

"Did you enjoy defying me?"

She tried to fake nonchalance. "Um, yes, I think I did."

His hand lowered down between her breasts as his thumb skimmed a nipple. He leaned in so his eyes were right in front of hers.

"Good. Because I'm rather going to enjoy punishing you."

He kissed her firmly and then led her by the hand to the bedroom. Victor stopped on her side of the bed and opened the drawer at the base. Abby's eyes got big as she saw it was full of ropes, paddles, and canes of various shapes and sizes.

"Are you kidding me?"

Victor laughed. "Would you like to pick which one I use?"

Her lips were pressed together in a frown, but she nodded. Then she knelt down and wordlessly started pulling out options from the drawer.

"Do I even want to know what's in the other drawer?" she mumbled.

Victor laughed. "That side is all about pleasure. This one is all about pain."

She turned around and came face to face with his hard-on. It was straining against the fabric of his dress pants. She licked her lips and looked up at him.

"So you get to sleep on the pleasure side, and I'm stuck on the pain side? Talk about symbolism!"

He smirked. "Technically this side brings me a whole lot of pleasure too." His mouth was twitching as he tried not to laugh.

She glared at him and went back to rummaging through the drawer. Finally, she settled on a little leather paddle that looked like it could be used for ping pong.

"This one."

He nodded. "Good choice." Then he helped her up and led her into the bathroom.

"Take off everything from the waist down." His voice was autocratic.

She sighed but did what she was told. Meanwhile, Victor was pulling the table from the wall. This time he didn't pad it down with a towel. When it was situated, he reached out for her hand.

"Bend over the table, and hold onto the legs. This is going to hurt."

Abby was regretting her earlier rash behavior. She bent over and hugged the hard surface.

Victor didn't give her time to think. He brought the paddle down hard on her ass, and the thwack echoed through the bathroom. It hurt, and she winced.

"Why am I punishing you, Abby?"

"Because I drove too fast."

He spanked her again.

"And did I ask you to slow down?"

"Yes." Her voice was softer.

Thwack! This time he used his whole arm instead of just the wrist. The paddle left a bright red mark on her rear end, and Victor felt his cock stiffen at the sight.

"And is it okay to disobey me?"

"No," she whispered.

He spanked her again even harder. This time he gave five rapid-fire hits, alternating one on each cheek, and ending in the center.

Abby moaned.

Victor was watching her face closely in the mirror. She wasn't crying, but she looked to have reached her limit. He certainly had spanked her hard enough. He set the paddle on the counter and gently pulled her up. Then he spun her around so she was facing him, and her ass was facing the mirror.

Victor rubbed it softly. "Look at your ass, little one. That redness is the mark of my anger. Each time you defy me, I will punish you harder. Do you understand?"

She looked up at him and nodded. He noted she wasn't looking particularly upset. Instead, she was looking aroused. That was a welcome surprise. He quickly asked, "You want to fuck?"

She nodded shyly.

Victor unzipped his pants, lifted her, and slammed his dick inside in record time. He had her pressed against the wall with her legs wrapped around his waist. Her pussy was gloriously wet, and he had no problem plunging in all the way.

Victor was pounding her hard but knew he needed to slow down so she could cum. "Do you need help with your orgasm, baby?"

"Yes, please," was the shy reply.

He reached down between them with one hand to play with her clit. His other arm was holding her up by her ass, and Abby realized just how strong he was. Then Victor slowed down and was rocking in and out of her with deliberate precision. She had her hands on his shoulders and was lifting her hips to meet his on every thrust.

"Take off my tie," he ordered.

She paused for a second and then fumbled to undo the knot. When she finally had it off she went to unbutton his shirt, but he stopped her. He took the tie from her hand and shoved it down where his fingers had just been.

"This will give you something to rub on," he explained.

Abby was shocked to realize how good that felt. She started rocking so she could hit the tie at the perfect angle, and Victor chuckled. She was a fast learner.

He took his now free hand and stroked her lips with his middle finger.

"Suck on my finger, little one."

She shook her head and turned it away. "Gross. That was just down there."

"Suck, Abby."

She dutifully opened her mouth, and he slid his finger in.

"Good girl. Get it good and wet."

She sucked his finger and coated it with saliva.

Finally, he pulled it out, reached around her, and eased it up and into her ass. It hurt for a second, but then it felt wonderful. The feeling of both openings being full caused a tremor deep in her pelvic region. Abby was trying to hold on, but the sensations were all too powerful. She came quickly, and Victor chuckled before joining her seconds later.

When they were done, he pulled out and handed her a towel to wipe off with. He did the same and washed his hands. Then he grabbed the tie from the floor and put it back on.

"Oh my god, you're wearing that?!"

He gave her a sinful grin. "Yes. It smells of your arousal."

She snickered. "You are such a pervert!"

He arched one eyebrow. "I'm a pervert? You were just soaking wet from a hard paddling."

She frowned as she thought about it.

They got in the elevator and headed back to their vehicles.

Victor gave her a quick kiss. "I'll see you after my meeting. Make sure you're here by six. And bring your calendar."

She nodded. "How come?"

"We need to coordinate our schedules."

As she was getting into her car he yelled over at her. "And Abby. Don't you dare drive more than five over the speed limit." His voice was angry again.

***

Victor was greeted with the smell of cooking when he opened his front door. Abby was in his kitchen amidst a mess of pots and pans, and she was humming to herself. She hadn't seen him yet, and he watched her appreciatively. She had her hair up in a ponytail, and her humming was off-key.

She jumped when she saw him. "Heh! I'm cooking dinner. I hope you like pasta."

He grinned as he sauntered into the kitchen and pulled her in for a kiss. "I love pasta." Then he lifted the lid on the pot to get a closer look as his other hand loosened his tie. "Looks good. How soon until it's ready?"

She eyed the tie with embarrassment. "Fifteen minutes."

"Good." He kissed her again before going to change.

When he returned, she dished out the food. It was penne in a sausage broth with vegetables. She topped it with some fresh grated Parmesan cheese. It tasted great, and Victor told her as much. "I didn't know you could cook."

She sighed. "Well, only certain things. I'm really good with casseroles and salads, but meat can be a problem."

This did not surprise him in the least.

She explained, "I once cooked a turkey for my family for Christmas, and both my brothers got sick. Now I tend to overcook meat because I'm afraid I'm going to give everyone food poisoning."

Victor was thrilled. Some of his girlfriends had cooked for him in the past, but only when he asked them to. She had taken the initiative to do it on her own. He wasn't sure if she was trying to make up for her disobedience earlier, or just taking care of him. Either way it was a nice gesture.

As they ate, they talked about their afternoons. Victor told her the kolaches were well received. He also explained how two doctors had gotten into a shouting match over a mortality case.

Abby listened with obvious interest. She had always been curious about medical stuff and frequently quizzed her friends. Now he was giving her inside information on a whole new world—that of a surgeon. She found it fascinating.

When he was done, she told him about Paul. The puppy dog had called her with concerns she was a victim of domestic violence. Abby found the whole thing hysterical and joked she wanted to tell him about the paddle drawer.

Victor was not amused. "I don't want that prick calling you, Abby.

The next time he does, just let it go to voicemail. If he continues to bother you, let me know, and I will take care of it."

She shrugged. "Okay."

He continued. "What I do to you is not domestic violence. We're consenting adults, and we have very clear boundaries. You are choosing to be punished every time you break a rule. Plus, I control it so you're not hurt badly, and you can stop me any time it gets to be too much."

She gave him a reassuring smile. "I know. I trust you."

He smiled back at her. They were finished eating, and he carried their bowls to the sink. Then he asked, "Did you bring your calendar?"

Abby nodded and pulled a big planner from her purse.

Victor laughed. "That's very old school of you."

"I get teased about this all the time. But it's big and visual, and I apparently need that to stay on top of my appointments."

He could give her a few kinky responses to that statement, but he let it pass. Victor couldn't resist teasing her, though. "What happens if you lose it?"

She feigned irritation. "I don't know why you keep implying I lose things!"

He grinned as he sat down on the couch and pulled her next to him. His calendar was on his cell phone like any normal person under the age of fifty. He pulled it out and explained, "Let's finish our obedience discussion before we get into our schedules."

Abby waited expectantly.

"Just to reiterate, no more going to that church or volunteering at the soup kitchen. I also don't want you doing any vigils at night for hospice. Only daytime ones."

Abby grumbled. "I'm running out of volunteer options, and I really need to volunteer. It keeps me focused."

"There are plenty of safe volunteer options you can choose from. The clinic alone has plenty of opportunities."

She gave a snarky reply. "Yes, but I thought you deemed the clinic in an unsafe neighborhood."

His eyes narrowed at her tone. "You can always have Vince drive you. He told me he is liking the extra income." Then he added, "Speaking of Vince, I want him to take you to the Westside Market from now on."

"Sure. Can I ask why?"

"I'll just feel better if he's with you. He can help carry your bags, and he'll pay attention to the surroundings better than you will."

Abby shrugged. "Okay. Is there anything else that needs to change?"

He was pleased she was offering no resistance. "Yes. I've thought about it, and I don't want you to write in that coffee shop anymore."

Abby sighed. "Well, it's probably for the best. But I need to write somewhere. When I try at home I always get distracted."

"You can try writing here if you like. The library is fine too. There are usually more people there and more emergency exits."

Abby quietly shook her head at the emergency exits comment. "Good. I can definitely work in the library."

He nodded. "That's it, little one. Just remember that all existing rules still apply. You should also know I'm not happy with your neighborhood. I think it's unsafe. That means if I find the alarm off even one time, you will have to move. No discussion. Do you understand?"

She looked at him in open disbelief. That was a huge thing! "I'll be careful, Victor," was all she said.

He clasped her hand and smiled. "Good. Let's talk about our schedules now. I'll go first."

They hit an issue on the very first event. The heart center's holiday party was on the same night as Abby's annual Christmas Carol show with the girls.

She explained, "It's tradition. We go every year as a way to kick off the holiday season. Plus, I love Dickens. He's one of my favorite writers."

Victor considered what she said. "Can you switch the tickets and go a different night?"

"Possibly. It might be hard to get everyone on the same page, though."

He sighed. "I'm the chief of staff, baby. I have to be there, and now so do you."

She made a face but agreed.

Victor continued, "Speaking of Christmas, I would like to take you somewhere and spend the holiday together."

She beamed, but then her face fell. "Oh. I'll be down in Florida. I spend every Christmas with my in-laws."

He looked at her curiously. "Surely the Sheas will understand. They can't expect you to give up a major holiday, especially now that you are moving on."

Abby was looking distraught and uncomfortable. "You don't

understand. It's complicated. They're difficult people, and I feel obligated to help them."

He continued to gaze at her face. "Very well, then. Send me the hotel and flight information. We'll probably have to change them, but I will be going with you."

She looked at him hopefully. "Really? I should warn you they're awful people. And they live in a sketchy part of Tampa."

He shrugged. "We'll make the best of it. I'll get us a suite and find some fun things for us to do while we're down there."

She grinned. "Thank you! That will be awesome. You have no idea how much I dread that trip every year."

Victor mentally filed the information away before moving on. "New Year's Eve is all mine. I'll plan something for the two of us and let you know."

She nodded. Then he told her about a week-long conference he was doing in Boston in January. "You are coming."

She dutifully wrote it in her calendar.

Victor finished with a clinic gala ball in February, and Abby made another face.

"I have to do a lot of this PR shit, baby, so get used to it. As my girlfriend, you are expected to come with me." Then he made his own funny face. "If it makes you feel better, I hate it too."

"Did you take your other girlfriends to this stuff?"

"No."

"Why not?"

"I never wanted to before."

"Oh." Then she mumbled, "Lucky me."

Victor laughed.

"You know I will have no clue what to wear to something like that," she grumbled.

"Not to worry. I will help you with your wardrobe. I know how much you struggle." He was teasing her, and she wrinkled her nose in mock disgust.

He threw his arm over the back of the couch. "Your turn, little one. What's on your schedule?"

She reminded him of the play she had on Saturday. He had already given his permission. Then she mentioned Thanksgiving. She was spending it at her brother's house, and she invited him to come.

"I would love to, baby, but I'm on call that day. If there's no emergencies I will be there." He added, "I need to meet your family."

Abby mentioned the musicals and plays coming up the next year.

Victor begrudgingly nodded. "Okay. But my work schedule comes first. And you will be following the rules closely when you're with your friends, including getting permission."

Abby was barely listening. She was eyeing the last thing on her calendar and wondering how he would react. She cautiously told him about the Cancun trip scheduled in April. It was a girl's trip, and they were going to celebrate the finalization of Kate's divorce. She would be rooming with Rachel. When she finished, she looked up to see a deep scowl on Victor's face.

"The fuck you are!"

"Seriously?"

"Yes, seriously. A girl's trip. To the party capital of Mexico. In the heart of the drug cartel wars. There is no fucking way you are going on that trip!"

"But I've already paid."

"I will reimburse your money," came the emphatic reply.

She wasn't looking at him, and her face was flushed. "What am I supposed to tell my friends?"

"Tell them the truth, Abby. Tell them I forbid it."

"Like that would go over well," she muttered.

"You might be surprised. Eventually, they're going to figure out what type of relationship we have. Why not beat them to it?"

She sighed and finally looked at him. "It's not that easy, Victor. They're not going to understand."

"I know for you it's not easy. If you like, I can tell them. And who cares if they understand or not? It's no one's business but ours."

She gave him a horrified look. "Um, no. I don't want you to tell them."

"Suit yourself." He knew he had pushed the obedience issue hard today. He wanted to get her in bed fast, to remind her of the special connection they had.

"Come, little one. Let's go play."

She gave him a thoughtful look before slapping her planner shut. She was not happy he had nixed the trip, but she still wanted to fool around. "Okay," she finally said.

They went and spent a pleasant hour between the sheets. When they were done, Victor pulled her naked body next to his in a hug and promptly fell asleep.

Abby lay awake a little longer. She was thinking about all his rules. The Cancun trip had really annoyed her, but she had to admit he was right. It probably wasn't safe. But still, she wasn't sure she could handle all his demands. Then she remembered the sex and decided to at least try. Because, damn!

Chapter Thirty-One

On Saturday Victor showed up at her house promptly at eleven. He had told her they were going to lunch. That was true, but he had other plans for the afternoon and knew she wouldn't like them. He, on the other hand, was rather looking forward to it and smiled in anticipation.

Abby opened the door and then pointedly shut off her alarm with a dramatic click.

He laughed and merely said, "Good girl."

Then he showed her the shopping bag he was carrying. It contained some kind of technical equipment.

She eyed it suspiciously. "What's that?"

He smiled. "This, little one, is my latest way of ensuring you follow my rules." He took her hand and led her to the garage. Then he opened the box and showed her the gadget before inserting it in one of the ports in her car.

"What does it do?"

"It sends me a report of your driving habits. How fast you're going. Where you're driving. All the stuff I care about. How cool is that?"

She stared at him like he had sprouted a second head. "Are you friggin' kidding me? That's not cool. That's not cool at all."

"I told you. When you break the rules I always find a way to tighten the reins." He fiddled with the object and set the controls before getting out of her car.

Now she was glaring at him. "I can always just disconnect it."

"Yes, but I will know, and then you will be punished. Really, Abby, it would be much easier if you just followed my rules."

She sighed and went to get her coat.

Victor stopped her. He tugged on her shirt front and looked down at the bra she was wearing. It was hot pink. "I need you to change your undergarments. Go put on something beige or nude in color."

She blinked at him. "Why?"

He wagged his finger at her. "Yours is not to question, remember. Yours is simply to obey."

She eyed him nervously but went to change.

They headed to Crocker Park, and Victor let her choose the restaurant. Abby picked the Yard House. They had a good selection of eclectic options she would like, plus she knew the beer selection would thrill him.

While they waited for their food, he asked how she was doing with Rule Number Three. "You've gotten a good feel for my obedience requirement. Do you think it's something you can do?" He sounded calm when he asked, but on the inside he was quaking waiting for her response.

Abby thought about his question. "Well, it doesn't seem natural to me, but I think I can live with it." When she saw his grin she quickly added, "But I'm not sure about long-term. It will depend on how far you push it."

She had meant it as a warning, and he picked up on that. His eyes narrowed, and he knew he had to be very clear with her. "I will only push it if you misbehave. Usually, I'm a reasonable man. But I can, and will, order you to do whatever I want whenever I want." His voice was serious, "As my girlfriend you will have no say in the matter. What's more, you will like it."

She stared at him. "When you talk like that it scares me, Victor."

He eased his tone. "Don't be scared. We are slowly learning to trust each other, and that will only get better with time. You should know every fiber of my being is geared toward protecting you, not hurting you. I just need control. Once you get comfortable submitting to my will, the rest will be easy."

Abby thought about what he said and tried not to laugh. His words sounded like they came straight out of a gothic novel. She started to reply, but then the entrees arrived. The conversation should have put her off her food, but Abby tucked in and started eating with gusto. She realized just how comfortable she was with the man in spite of all his crazy talk.

They ate in companionable silence. Victor was giving her surreptitious looks, but she seemed fine. Not for the first time he marveled at her easygoing nature. Even his truly submissive girlfriends had balked on occasion. But then again, he was much easier on Abby then he had ever been on any of them. He worried about having to take it further, but Victor never wasted time on worry. He would cross that bridge if and when he came to it.

When they were done eating, he casually suggested they do a bit of shopping. He was surprised when her eyes lit up and she agreed. She tucked her arm in his and led him down the street. When she turned in at Barnes & Noble, he realized what kind of shopping she had in mind.

He shook his head. "Oh, honey. I meant clothes shopping. You are always complaining about needing more things to wear. I thought I could make a few purchases for you."

Abby made a face. "Ugh. I hate clothes shopping. But there's a new book out by one of my favorite authors." Then she tilted her face up and gave him an adorable and pleading look. "Can we go in, please? I promise I'll only grab the one book. I'll just be a few minutes."

He gave her an amused smile. "Mmm hmm. Only a few minutes, eh?" Then he looked at his watch and realized they had some time. "Okay, little one. I am timing you. Go!"

She squealed in delight and ran into the bookstore, and Victor chuckled as he followed behind her.

Forty minutes later they left with a large bag of books. Victor pointedly looked at his watch and tutted, and Abby had a sheepish half-smile on her face. "Well, someone once told me I'm good at white lies."

Victor chuckled. "Hmm. Wonder who that was?" He was purposefully steering her down a road toward a department store. When he held the door open, she looked suspiciously at him.

"I really don't want to shop for clothes."

He mimicked her words, "I promise we'll only be in there a few minutes."

She snorted with laughter.

Then he added, "I need to pick up a new red tie. Somehow my old one got worn out."

Abby gasped and turned scarlet. Victor laughed and ushered her into the store. He led them past the tie selections and to the escalator at the back. On the second floor, he steered her over to the tailoring department and stopped to ring the bell on the desk.

"Why are we here?"

He looked down at her. "I told you, I want to do a bit of shopping."

Just then a chic brunette breezed around the corner followed by a mousy looking woman. The brunette's face lit up when her eyes landed on Victor, and she looked him up and down with obvious appreciation. Abby felt a twinge of jealousy. It turned to embarrassment when those eyes turned to her and did the same thing.

The she-bitch spoke. "Are you Dr. Turov?" She was back to looking at him and put out her hand.

Victor smiled and shook it. "I am. You must be Tricia. It is nice to meet you." Then he put his arm around Abby. "And this is my girlfriend, Abby."

Tricia beamed and shook Abby's hand. "You are lovely, dear. Let me get a good look at you." She tugged Abby's coat off and handed it to Victor. Then she started circling around as she whisked out a tape measure and pulled it firmly around Abby's breasts. She did the same to her waist and hips as she shouted out numbers to the mousy woman.

Abby glared at her boyfriend with a murderous expression on her face.

When the she-bitch was done, she smiled at Victor. "I must say, Dr. Turov, when you gave me her measurements I didn't believe you. But she has the perfect model's body. That is so rare." Then she turned to Abby, "It's going to be such a pleasure to dress you. Follow me. We have everything set up in the back." As she started to walk, she looked back. "You wore neutral undergarments, correct?"

Abby nodded but didn't follow the woman. She turned to Victor instead and furiously whispered, "What did you do?"

He smiled benignly at her. "Tricia is a personal shopper. She comes highly recommended. I hired her to fit you with some new clothes."

Abby looked dismayed. "Oh, god. This is so embarrassing!"

"Why? You heard the woman. You have a perfect model's body."

"Please, Victor. Let's just leave."

He gazed impassively at her before speaking. "This is not up for discussion. We have quite a few social engagements coming up and you need clothes." He grabbed her arm. "Your boyfriend has generously arranged a personal shopper for you. I suggest you show him some gratitude and get your pretty little ass back there for your fitting." He was trying for a light tone, but Abby could hear the edge in his voice.

"Oh, Victor, I am grateful. It's just…this is so outside my comfort zone."

He smiled. "I know. I rather enjoy doing that to you."

She arched an eyebrow at him. "Really? Maybe I should return the favor sometime."

Now he was laughing and shaking his head. "Oh, little one, you do. On a regular basis."

She frowned at him but was distracted when they reached the fitting area.

It was a circular room with a raised platform in the middle. Along the walls were doors leading to separate changing rooms. There was also a sitting area with a love seat and two chairs, a full-length mirror, and two full racks of clothing. Abby eyed the racks nervously.

Tricia waved them in. She escorted Abby to the platform and had her stand on top. Then the mousy woman scurried over and helped her remove her clothing. She was left standing there in just her bra and thong, with her hair up in a ponytail. She glared at Victor. The bastard hadn't even told her to wear normal panties!

Meanwhile, Tricia escorted Victor to the love seat. She offered him something to drink, and he accepted a bottle of water. Then he threw one arm over the back of the sofa, stretched his legs out, and gave Abby a lazy grin. She looked so damn sexy standing there in that thong. With those green eyes flashing she looked like a hell-cat ready to strike. Victor could feel his cock stirring.

Tricia interrupted his thoughts. "I think we'll start with the evening gowns, Dr. Turov, since you mentioned that was your most pressing engagement." When he nodded, she motioned to the mouse to bring out the first dress. It was a full-length black number with lace and tiers. It looked like a dream on Abby's curves, and Victor sat up straighter. That one had potential, and he told Tricia as much.

She nodded. "I agree. She is stunning in it. But black is so overdone. Let's look at some bolder options."

She snapped her fingers at the mouse, and the black dress was whisked away to be replaced by a red chiffon number. It was low cut and showing off more cleavage than Victor would like.

"Jesus, I'll be fighting the men off with a stick." He nixed that one, and they continued on.

When they got to a green satin gown with a fitted bodice and a low cut back, Victor could no longer contain his hard-on. She looked like a goddess, and the green was bringing out her eyes and golden hair to perfection. He quickly grabbed a newspaper to hide his arousal.

Abby was silently fuming. No one bothered to ask what she thought of the dresses, and she was starting to feel like a recalcitrant child being dressed by her parents. It was infuriating. She also didn't like the dynamic between the she-bitch and her boyfriend. The woman was clearly flirting with him by tossing her hair and giggling at his comments. Plus, she had noticed him cover himself with the newspaper. Abby felt a sharp pang of jealousy. She wondered if he was attracted to the personal shopper, and the thought was deeply upsetting.

After trying six other gowns, they settled on the green one. Tricia had the mouse bring out shoes to go with the dress, but Abby interrupted.

"I like the black dress better," she stubbornly declared. She was looking at Victor, and there was a challenge in her eyes.

He looked nonplused. "Okay, baby. Then we'll get both. We'll certainly have the opportunity to use them."

That was not the reaction she was looking for, and she realized she was spending even more of his money. Not only that, but the she-bitch was cooing in delight over the added sale.

The onslaught of clothing continued. The mouse brought out one cocktail dress after another. When Victor approved one, shoes and bags were also chosen. They even had her try on some casual clothing including jeans, sweaters, tops, skirts, and sleepwear. Over an hour later there was quite a collection of clothing on the 'yes' rack, and Abby was getting fatigued.

Tricia was ready to move on to undergarments, but Victor stopped her. He knew he had pushed his girlfriend far enough for one day.

"Abby already has a great selection of underwear. I think we've done enough damage for one day."

Tricia nodded. "Very well, Dr. Turov. We'll get these rung up and boxed for you. Can I get you anything while you wait? More water perhaps?"

Victor was watching Abby closely. "I think my girlfriend could use a water," was all he said. One was quickly handed to her, and then the women were gone.

Abby sat down on the platform and took a swig of water. "It was like I wasn't even in the room," she muttered.

Victor nodded. "She was catering to the one paying. I'm sure it's a fairly common occurrence. I imagine a lot of her clients are wealthy men outfitting their mistresses."

"Yep," she snarked. "That's how it felt. Not a good feeling. And you do realize that green dress alone was over two thousand dollars?"

He stood up and walked over to her. "And your point is?" He reached down to pull her to a standing position.

She finished her water as she stood and glared at him. "My point is, it's too much to be spending on a girlfriend you just started dating! What if I break up with you tomorrow?"

His eyes narrowed as he cupped her face with his hands. "Are you planning on breaking up with me tomorrow?"

She sighed. "No. But it's too much, Victor. Did you do this with your other girlfriends?"

Now he was angry. "Of course not. Why the fuck would I? I have never taken one to a work event before."

She was just as mad. "Well, I don't see why I have to accept, then. I am perfectly capable of paying for all of this myself." She pulled a credit card out of her wallet and started walking toward the hallway.

Victor snaked his arm around her waist and pulled her body up against his tightly. "Don't piss me off, Abby." His voice was low and menacing, and she felt a tremor run up her spine.

"You're the one pissing me off," she whispered.

Now Victor was furious. He guided her into a changing room and shut the door. "Is that right, baby? I think maybe you need to be reacquainted with our rules." He pressed her body against the wall and leaned in so his face was right in front of hers. "What is Rule Number Three?"

She averted her eyes. "To obey you," she whispered.

"Yes. And are you obeying me right now?"

She didn't say anything.

He pulled the Georgian chair out from the corner and sat down on it. Then he threw her over his lap. The first slap was loud, and Abby cringed.

"They're going to hear us," she whispered.

He was still furious. "I don't give a fuck if they do! You will learn to obey me."

He continued to spank her hard, fast, and loudly. Abby cringed and absorbed each slap with a quiet moan. This was the angriest she had ever seen him, and her ass was starting to feel the effects. She had had enough. "Okay, Victor. I'm sorry. I will obey you. I promise!"

His hand stilled, but he was still very angry. He helped her up and held her at the hips. He then looked at her with a challenging glint in his eyes. "Show me."

Abby looked at him in confusion.

"Step out of your thong, little one."

Her eyes got big as she realized it wasn't over. She quickly kicked her thong off to the side.

"Good girl. Now kneel down." As he spoke, he unzipped his pants and pulled his cock out.

Abby eyed the door nervously as she kneeled down. "They're going to hear us, Victor."

He scowled at her. "I told you. I. Do. Not. Care. Now show me your obedience." He guided her head toward his penis.

Abby whimpered a little but dutifully encircled his cock with her mouth. She sucked the length of it in and massaged the sensitive tip with her tongue. She knew she should feel humiliated and angry, but oddly the whole thing was starting to turn her on.

Victor let out a loud groan on purpose, and she glared at him but continued to work his penis. She decided to go fast and furious to get him off as quickly as possible. He was having none of that, though, and tapped her on the head to stop.

"That's enough, baby. I think I would much rather have you bent over in front of that mirror." He stood up and moved the chair. Then he had her lean over so her ass was sticking up and back, and her hands were on the seat of the chair.

He sidled up behind her and massaged her ass. He was taking his damn sweet time, and Abby was terrified either Tricia or the mouse would walk back in.

"Now then, which opening do I go for?"

"Just hurry up, Victor," she pleaded.

He pinched her ass hard.

"You do not tell me what to do, Abby. Do you understand?"

She nodded and was close to tears. God, he was being such a dick! But she still wanted him inside of her. What the fuck was wrong with her?

Victor continued to massage her ass, but then his hand reached lower and his fingers dipped into her slit. As usual, she was drenched with desire, and he smiled in relief. He encircled her opening a few times before inserting two fingers inside. Once he was satisfied she was ready, he thrust into her with his cock.

Abby's back arched, and she moaned before pushing against him. She was hanging onto the chair for dear life as he started to pound her from behind. He was not holding back, and it felt so good. She clamped her mouth shut to keep from calling out.

Victor realized what she was doing, and he grabbed a fistful of her hair and pulled hard. The pain made her gasp, and she opened her mouth.

"I want to hear your orgasm!"

They stared at each other in the mirror in a silent battle. Both their eyes were blazing in equal parts anger and desire. Abby held out as long as she could, but then she quit fighting him. He was in charge, he was her man, and he was feeling so damn good inside of her. Fuck those women. She opened her mouth, and seconds later she came loudly.

Victor grinned in amazement. He continued to thrust inside of her for several more minutes until his own orgasm swept him away.

Afterward, they dressed quickly, and Abby could feel his semen begin to seep out of her. The thong was sticking to her and doing nothing to help.

He was watching with a knowing smile. "Everything okay?"

She nodded shyly.

He put his arm around her. "Good. That was an enjoyable punishment!"

Abby sighed as they headed down the hallway and rounded the corner.

The women were finishing up with the packages, and she noted Tricia looked anywhere but at them. Abby felt a tinge of guilt but then realized she had finally shut the she-bitch up. That made her smile.

Victor was looking impassive again as he paid the bill. It was well over ten thousand dollars, and he looked down at his girlfriend before handing over his credit card. Abby met his glance but then smiled. "Thank you," she meekly whispered. He gave her a satisfied nod before signing the slip.

The mouse woman ended up helping them carry everything to the truck. She hadn't said much more than "lift your arms" or "step into this" the whole afternoon. But now she gave Abby a knowing and lascivious look. "Thank you. That was the best entertainment I've had in a long while!"

As she walked away, Victor and Abby looked at each other.

Victor chuckled. "It's always the quiet ones."

Abby was beyond mortified. A small part of her had hoped they hadn't heard and were just busy with the order. Now that she knew they knew, she wanted to cry.

As Victor was closing the back of the truck, he noticed the expression on her face. He pulled her in for a hug.

"It's okay, little one. They will eventually forget about it."

"I just can't believe I did that," she whispered.

He nodded. "I'm glad you did. It shows me you are truly in this relationship and willing to give it a try. Now if only you could learn to accept my gifts."

She sighed. "Your gifts are a bit extreme."

"Oh, baby. Everything about me is extreme!"

Abby decided to tease him. "I know. Tricia was practically drooling all over you. And don't think I didn't notice you trying to hide your rocket-sized woody under that newspaper!"

He glanced over at her. "Of course I had a hard-on. Seeing you in that sexy green dress about undid me. I'm not sure I'm going to let you wear it out in public."

She was pleased it had been for her. Then she admitted, "I was getting jealous."

He grinned. "Now you know how I feel. Men seem to hit on you all the time. But women aren't usually attracted to me. I've been told I give off a scary vibe."

"What? You? No way!"

They both laughed.

When they got back to Abby's place, Victor helped hang everything up in the closet. He noticed she was fingering some of the fabric and smiling. That made him happy. She had a play that night with the girls, and he asked her what she was going to wear.

She gave him a deer-in-the-headlights look and shrugged her shoulders. Victor shook his head before pulling out a pretty cocktail dress. He handed that to her along with a pair of high heels and a wrap. "Try these."

She gave him a grateful smile.

"You really are helpless when it comes to fashion, aren't you?"

Abby ignored him as she rushed to get in the shower. She was running late. Victor sat on her bed and thumbed through a magazine while he waited. She was out in record time, and he helped her zip up the dress while she started on her makeup. When she was ready, he pulled her back against his hard chest and sighed. "You know every time you go out with your friends I worry."

"I know, Victor. You don't have to worry. I'm going to go home right after the show ends."

He thought about it. "No, little one. I have to start trusting you again. Go out for a drink, but make sure you don't exceed your limit," he added sternly.

"Well, we usually just walk over to Parnell's. It will probably be easier for Vince to pick me up there once the theatre crowd has cleared."

He nodded and gave her a long kiss before they left. Once he dropped her off at the Hanna Theatre, he was still feeling anxious. The more time he spent with this woman, the more she got under his skin. He found he wanted to spend all of his free time with her, and he was resentful of the girls for claiming her on a Saturday night. Victor tried to shake the feeling, but it wasn't going away. He finally gave into it and pulled up Joel's number on his blue tooth. The men had exchanged numbers last weekend in hopes of winter golf. Now Victor was planning to persuade him to do something entirely different.

Two and a half hours later and the girls were heading down the street to Parnell's. They were deep in discussion about the ethical implications of the play they had just seen. It was cold out, and they rushed into the warmth of the bar. They were shocked to see familiar faces sitting at a table. Joel, Kurt, Don, Victor, and Yuri were all grinning at them with drinks in hand.

As usual, Rachel was the first to recover. "What the hell are you guys doing here?" She was trying to sound annoyed, but she couldn't keep the amusement out of her voice.

Joel explained, "We were tired of you ladies having all the fun." He nodded at Victor, "Plus, the big guy here was missing his woman."

Victor ignored the comment and went to help Abby off with her coat. Then he blatantly kissed her in front of all of them. When he was done, he introduced Yuri to the girls. Kate immediately honed in on the psychiatrist's single status and started flirting. A round of drinks was ordered for the women, and the group settled in for a fun night.

Abby leaned in to her boyfriend. "I thought you were going to trust me," she whispered.

He gave her a sheepish grin. "Baby steps."

She laughed.

Eventually, the conversation made its way around to the holidays. Everyone discussed their plans, and the girls gave Victor a hard time about his work party trumping their Christmas Carol event. He shrugged and explained it was an inevitable part of his job. This appeased everyone but Rachel. She continued to try to goad the doctor, which caused Joel to get mad. They started a heated argument about Rachel's meddling, and Abby knew she had to intervene. She told Rachel about Victor going with her to Florida.

Sure enough, Rachel quit arguing with her husband and grinned at the Russian. "You have no idea how nice that will be for Abby. Those people are nasty!" Rachel continued to talk about the Shea in-laws, and Victor quietly noted what she said. He looked down at his girlfriend, but she was studiously ignoring him. The topic was making her very uncomfortable.

"What's everyone doing for New Year's Eve?" interrupted Kate. She had her hand lightly on Yuri's arm.

They all looked at each other.

"We don't have any plans," piped in Renee.

"We can have a party at our house," offered Kent. "Well, that's if Lindsay gets off her ass and sets it up."

Lindsay glared at him and turned to Abby. "What are you two doing?"

"I don't know," she hesitated. "Victor is going to surprise me."

They all looked at the doctor expectantly and he shrugged his shoulders. "I'm not sure what we're doing yet."

Joel piped in. "Take her to Hocking Hills. She loves it down there."

Renee nodded. "Oh, that's such a romantic place!" She touched Victor's arm. "You can get one of those secluded cabins with a fireplace and hot tub." Then she turned to Don. "Honey, we should do that too!"

Don considered it. "I'm not opposed to some hiking."

Rachel looked at Joel. "We should go too! We can get one of those big cabins and make it a group party. I can plan all the meals and bring all the food."

"We have a ton of firewood we can bring," offered Kent.

Yuri was eyeing up Kate before he commented, "Well, I'm not much of hiker, but I'm all for the hot tub. Does anyone play poker?"

The men all nodded, Kate said she was in, and they all looked expectantly at Victor.

Victor was irritated, as this was not what he wanted. He explained, "I was really planning on ringing in the new year alone with Abby." Then he looked over at Yuri. His friend was smiling and cocking his eyes in Kate's direction. Victor sighed. "I guess we can all go together. I'll look into booking the cabin. It will be my treat."

They all cheered, and Rachel immediately started planning the menu.

Abby leaned in to Victor and giggled. "I told you they were a force to reckon with. Besides, you owe me a hike!"

He grinned and whispered, "I do owe you a hike, but I'm only doing this for Yuri's sake. He needs to get laid."

Abby rolled her eyes and looked over at her single friend. "Men! But don't count on it. He's not Kate's type."

Victor frowned. "She seems interested enough."

"Well, maybe. But Kate usually goes for unavailable men."

He raised an eyebrow. "Unavailable?"

Abby grimaced. "You know—married men or those with steady girlfriends."

Victor gave her a speculative look. "Ah. One of those, eh? Well, we'll just have to create a 'steady girlfriend' for Yuri before we head down there."

Abby laughed. "That just might work!"

They sat back and leaned into each other. Victor put his arm around her, and they watched their friends. All three couples were now arguing over stupid stuff related to the trip, and Yuri was telling Kate an animated story while she hung on his every word.

Victor started to massage Abby's neck, and the sensation shot straight down to her pelvis. She looked up at him, and he was giving her a lustful look.

He nipped her ear lobe with his teeth and quietly asked, "You want to get out of here?"

She nodded, and they said a quick goodbye. The others barely noticed them leaving.

On the ride home, Victor pointed out how much her friends fought. "It just proves my point that no couple is normal. They all have issues, and none of them are in a position to judge us should they learn the true nature of our relationship."

Abby nodded but was barely listening to him. All she could think about was getting naked.

When they got to Victor's condo, he led her by the hand straight to the bedroom. He could tell she was horny, and he was already sporting a serious hard-on. Victor walked her backward until her legs came right up against the bed. Then he gave her a lustful grin before pushing her onto the bed. She squealed as she landed on her back with her blond hair splayed out around her.

"My god, you are beautiful!" Victor said. He started pulling off his shirt as he looked down at her.

Abby smiled and licked her lips slowly to tease him. She scooched further up so her head was resting on a pillow.

Victor crawled on the bed so he was kneeling between her legs. He took one sleeve of his shirt and tied her hands together in front of her body. Then he pulled them up over her head. With the other sleeve, he tied her arms securely to the headboard. "This will keep you from deflecting," he said. Then Victor pushed up the hem of her dress and slowly pulled down her panties and hose. When her legs were free, he spread them wide, leaned down, and inhaled deeply. "You smell so good!"

"The words that come out of your mouth!" She was squirming on the bed, so Victor pinned her hips down with his hands. He kept them there while his thumbs reached down and started to stroke her opening.

"I'm going to put my mouth to good use right now, so quit fidgeting." He leaned down and ran his tongue along her crease. Then he teased her clit with it before settling in for a good long tongue lashing. Abby briefly tried to move, but her arms were secured, and he had her pinned down. She quickly gave up and settled in to absorb what he was doing. It felt so damn good, and she couldn't help but try to grind herself into his mouth. It didn't take her long to have an orgasm, and Victor smiled in satisfaction.

He slid off the bed and started rummaging in the drawer beneath.

"Whatcha doing?" she asked. When he didn't answer she mumbled, "I guess I should be thankful you're not going through the paddle drawer."

Victor looked up. "Why, Abby? Have you been misbehaving?"

She gave him a mock look of shock. "Of course not! You know what a good girl I am."

He eyed her suspiciously. "Mmm hmm. You do seem rather energetic this evening. You haven't been drinking coffee again, have you?"

She gave him an innocent look. "Nope. I'm just having a good time. Can I look in the drawer?"

He debated but then stood up and untied her hands. Abby leaned over so she was lying on her stomach on the bed with her chin in her palms. She was looking down at the drawer and the array of objects inside with an obvious and intense curiosity.

Victor watched her with amusement. "See anything in there you like?"

She gave him a wary look and began to pick through the items. "Somehow I just thought it would be full of dildos," she muttered. Then she pulled out a butt plug and looked at Victor in confusion. "This one is kind of small, isn't it? And where's the on button?"

Now he was laughing outright. "Oh, honey. That's not a vibrator. That goes in your butt."

She frowned. "For what possible purpose?"

"For your pleasure. Do you want to try one?"

She looked at him, shook her head, and then continued to rummage through the drawer. She finally settled on a beaded item with clips that looked like a necklace. "This is pretty. Let's try this."

Victor took it from her hand. "Are you sure? These are nipple clamps. They hurt."

Abby looked wary. "You mean they go on your nipples?"

"Not mine, silly, yours."

She thought about it. "I'm pretty good with pain. And you'll take them off right away if I don't like them?"

"Of course."

"Okay, then."

Victor grinned at his girlfriend. She never ceased to amaze him. He pulled her into an upright position so her legs were dangling over the edge of the bed. He lowered her dress so it pooled around her waist and removed the bra underneath. Then he had her clasp her hands behind her back. "Don't move your arms no matter what."

She nodded as Victor reached down and started massaging her breasts. Her nipples were already erect, but he continued to massage, pinch, and tease them in preparation. When he thought she was ready, he gently reached down and clamped one nipple.

As he tightened the screw, Abby sucked in some air. "Ahhh!"

Victor stopped. "Too tight? I can loosen it if you like."

She continued to breathe deeply. "No. It just took me by surprise is all. It should be okay."

He nodded and waited while she took a few more deep breaths. Then he fastened the second clamp to her other nipple. Abby squirmed on the bed, but she kept her hands behind her back and continued to stare at her boyfriend. He was so proud of her. She hadn't complained once.

When her breathing was more steady, Abby looked down at her chest. Her nipples were erect, and the clamps hung down with the beaded necklace running loosely down between them. It was actually very pretty, and the pain wasn't as bad as she thought it would be. What's more, it was making her ultra-sensitive but in a good way. She looked up at him. "What's the point of these, if you'll excuse the pun?"

Victor laughed as he pulled her arms back around front. He raised them over her head and eased her down on the bed. Then he positioned his body between her legs. "The point is they free my hands up to do other things, while these babies work their magic on your breasts." He gently grabbed the necklace part and raised it to her mouth. "Open up and hold this with your teeth, and keep your hands above your head." He slid his cock inside her. She was smiling at him with a look of part amusement and part arousal on her face.

As he began to rock inside of her, Abby felt her own body move, and the necklace pulled her breasts up and out with each thrust. This intensified the pressure on her nipples but in a good way. What's more, the sensation was shooting straight to her groin area. She realized in shock she wasn't going to make it much longer.

Meanwhile, Victor had one hand in her hair and was pulling hard. His other hand was between them working his usual magic on her button. She felt so damn good with her tight pussy wrapped around his dick. Her boobs were swaying to the rhythm, and she looked like quite the vixen. "You let me know if this starts to hurt, okay?"

She nodded at him as her breath continued to speed up. Her head was being pulled back by his hand, and she suddenly felt herself being swept away by an orgasm. As she came, she screamed out his name. Victor started to really slam into her body at that point, and he came a minute later. He collapsed on top of her but then realized she still had the clamps on.

He propped himself up on his arms and looked down at her. "Sorry. Did that hurt?"

She was trying to catch her breath and just shook her head. He caressed her face and showered kisses on her neck as he waited. Victor knew the most painful part of clamps was when you took them off, and he didn't want her to suffer. He continued to kiss her and caress her face until her breathing returned to normal. Then he gently reached down to one breast. "This is going to hurt, baby. I want you to breathe in deeply and then exhale as slowly as possible."

Abby nodded and did what she was told, and he gently loosened the first clamp. She couldn't help it, she hissed in pain as the blood rushed back into her nipple.

"You okay?" he asked with concern.

She was feeling a burning sensation that had startled her, but it wasn't too terrible. "Yah, just don't touch it," she whispered.

Victor nodded. He had her take a few more deep breaths and then released the second clamp. This time she knew what to expect and only let out a soft sigh.

Victor set the clamps on the nightstand and then lay on his back next to her. He gently pulled a blanket over both of them and held her hand. "You did so well with those. I am so proud of you."

Abby slowly rolled onto her side and grinned at him. "That was actually a lot of fun. And intense. How do you know about all this stuff?"

"I keep telling you. I'm a doctor."

She laughed and snuggled under the covers deeper. "Somehow I don't think my dermatologist, Dr. Humble, has this same knowledge."

Victor chuckled. "Probably not." As she was drifting off to sleep he teased her, "You know, little one, those clamps can also be used down between your legs."

She opened one eye and looked at him. "Seriously?"

Victor laughed and rolled over to go to sleep.

Abby was alarmed to realize she was turned on by the thought. Yah, she would try that with him in the future. Definitely.

Chapter Thirty-Two

On Thanksgiving Day Victor was able to go for dinner with Abby's family. He had wanted to see what her brothers were like, and he was surprised at how much he liked the older one, Jonathan. The man had a level head on his shoulders and was obviously protective of Abby. That made Victor happy. His kids were also well behaved, and the wife was nondescript.

Her younger brother, Henry, was another story. He showed up late, was drunk, and spent the afternoon complaining about everything. He also made Abby cry when he wouldn't shut up about their parents. Henry was a selfish man, but Victor also realized Abby adored him. He mentally filed the information away.

In late December the couple were on a flight to Tampa for Christmas. Victor had bought them first class tickets, and Abby was taking advantage of the free in-flight drinks. This worried him. Sure she was staying within her two-drink maximum. But it was not like her, in spite of her recent birthday binge, to consume any alcohol. Victor realized the Sheas were to blame. He began to wonder what he was going to find when they got there, and he went into protection mode without even realizing it.

They pulled the rental car into the Shea driveway four hours later. The house was a rundown ranch with discarded tires in the yard and an obvious air of neglect. Victor glanced over at Abby and saw she was nervously wringing her hands together. He reached over and placed his larger hand over hers. It was warm and comforting, and she gave him a weak smile.

"You know I will always protect you," was all he said.

She nodded but didn't say anything.

They walked up to the house together, and the smell of cigarette smoke hit them full force at the door. An old woman met them and motioned them inside. She gave Abby a hug but didn't say a word, and Victor found the entire encounter odd.

They walked down a narrow and dim hallway to the kitchen. There they found an old man sitting at a table. A cigarette was hanging out of his mouth, and there was an overflowing ashtray in front of him. Victor noted the yellow-stained walls and an assortment of empty liquor bottles on the floor. It would appear the Sheas liked to drink.

Abby valiantly plowed ahead and made introductions. The older couple nodded at Victor and eyed him with a surprising lack of interest. He had thought they would be upset their son's wife had moved on. Instead, they said a quick hello and turned their attention back to Abby.

She walked over to the fridge and pulled out a can of beer for each of the elders. Then she rummaged in a cupboard and pulled out some dish soap. She began to attack the dishes piled in the sink while simultaneously asking the Sheas questions about their health. That did the trick, and the couple promptly began rattling off their ailments.

Victor realized Abby was an old hat when it came to dealing with them. He let them chat and went in search of trash bags. Then he silently began to haul out the empty liquor bottles. It took him quite a few trips. By the time he was done, Abby had the dishes clean, dry, and put away. She had even started a load of wash in the laundry room.

Abby now stood at the counter organizing the elder's mail, and Victor went to stand next to her. The old man was explaining the cable and heat were about to be shut off, and Abby sorted through the pile until she found the bills. They had red 'past due' stamps on them.

Mr. Shea spoke. "We need more money. What did you bring us for Christmas, girl?"

Abby reached into her purse and pulled out an envelope. She wordlessly handed it to the older man. He ripped it open, and his wife rushed over to see what was inside. The Christmas card was tossed to the floor without a glance. Then they both looked up at Abby with reproach.

"This is it? You call this a Christmas gift?"

Abby sighed and glanced at Victor before responding. "It's five thousand dollars. That should more than cover your bills."

The man pounded his hand on the table. "It's not enough! You owe us. That money you got for our boy's death should have come to us, and you know it."

Victor was momentarily stunned by the conversation. He looked over at his girlfriend and saw her chin quivering. She stood her ground, though, and replied, "I gave you one hundred thousand dollars when he died. Where did that money go? I also know you get a good pension from the electric company. I can't keep giving you money like this. You need to learn to live within a budget."

The old man's face twisted into an ugly grimace. He ground his cigarette out in the ashtray and stood up. "We gave that boy life and raised him. It wasn't easy either. He was always getting in fights and trouble. But we did it and never complained." Then he pointed an angry finger at Abby. "All you did was marry the boy and fuck him. I don't see how that gives you the rights to his money."

Abby physically shrank back as if she had been hit, and Victor realized it was time to step in. He turned his back on the couple and gently grabbed her arms. When she looked up at him, he quietly said, "Little one, I need you to go out to the car and wait for me. Lock yourself in and wait. I'll be out shortly."

She hesitated. "But—"

Victor tightened his grip on her arms and gave her an uncompromising look. "This is not up for discussion, Abby. You will do as I say. Now go!" He fished the keys out of his pocket and handed them to her.

Abby stared at the keys with big eyes before clutching them in her hand. Then she gave the old couple one last hesitant look before leaving the house. Once she was in the rental car, she locked the doors and tried to calm down.

Inside the house, Victor was scowling at the Sheas. He walked over so he stood right in front of them at the table. Then he crossed his arms and fixed his gaze on the senior man. His voice was deathly quiet. "What gives her the right to that money is the legal system. Had he wanted to, I'm sure Nate would have left you some money."

They started to argue with him, but Victor cut them off. "I need to make something perfectly clear. Abby will no longer be visiting or helping you out in any way. I am forbidding her from having any contact with you whatsoever." He put his palms on the table and leaned down. "She is no longer with your son. She's with me. And she owes you nothing."

The old man started sputtering. "How dare you! How dare you come into my house and disrespect me and my dead son. You are nothing but

Russian garbage, and you just want that money for yourself. She does not have to listen to the likes of you, and neither do we!"

Victor gave a wry smile and shook his head. "I don't need her money. I have plenty of my own." He noted the old man's look of surprise. "And Abby does have to listen to me. Let me put this into words you will understand. If I find out she has had any contact with either one of you in any way, then I will beat the living shit out of her."

Mrs. Shea gasped, and her husband sank back down in his chair. Victor walked around and grabbed the check from the table. Then he leaned down and whispered, "This 'Russian garbage' owns that woman now. She will do as she's told. And you will never see her again!" As he walked out, he heard expletives and glass shatter against the wall.

Victor shook his anger off as he headed to the car. He knew Abby would anxiously be waiting to hear what happened, and he didn't want to upset her any more than she already was. When he reached the door she hit the auto-locks, and he slid inside. As he clicked his seatbelt on, he looked over at her.

She was close to tears. "I'm so sorry! I told you they were awful. I had no idea they would get that nasty, though."

Victor gave her a reassuring smile as he put the car into reverse. As he pulled out of the driveway he tried to reassure her. "No need to apologize. It's not your fault, and you certainly didn't make them that way. I'm just glad you'll never have to see them again."

"I won't?"

"No, baby. I told them you won't be visiting or helping them out anymore."

She stared at him in disbelief. "I know they're terrible, Victor, but I can't just abandon them. They have no one else. And you saw what it's like in there."

"Yes, I did. Which is why I am forbidding you from having any contact with them ever again."

"You can do that?" she whispered.

He nodded. "I can, and I just did." As he merged onto the freeway he risked a brief glance at her. "I mean it, Abby. If I catch you interacting with them in any way, you will be severely punished."

She sat quietly and tried to digest what he said. Then she looked at him. "I don't want to be punished, but they are very persistent. I'm sure they'll be calling me."

"When they do, I want you to ignore their call. Just let it go to voicemail. Then give the phone to me, and I will take care of it." He reached over and squeezed her hand. "They are no longer your problem. They are mine now."

She sighed but didn't say anything. He realized he needed to be clearer. "And Abby, don't you dare send them any more money. You're just enabling them when you do that. Plus, I will be furious, and you don't want to see me that angry."

She nodded and looked down at her clasped hands. Her hair fell forward and hid her face from his view.

They drove in silence for a while, and Victor began to worry about her frame of mind. "Tell me what you're thinking, little one."

She looked up at him hesitantly. He could tell she was weighing everything he had just said. Then her face relaxed into a tentative smile. "I'm thinking you just took away one of the biggest worries in my life. I've always been afraid of those people, but I felt guilty about just abandoning them. Everyone told me I should. Even Nate didn't have much to do with them. But I couldn't say no." Then she leaned over and kissed his cheek. "Now I don't have to. You did it for me. Thank you!"

Victor smiled in relief. "You're welcome. You're finally seeing the advantage of our type of relationship. My job is to protect you and handle all of these issues so you don't have to. It makes your life easy and more secure, wouldn't you agree?"

She nodded in response, and they drove the rest of the way to the hotel in silence. They stopped at the front desk to see about dinner and then headed to their room. Once inside Abby launched herself at Victor. She wanted to thank him for what he had done. After passionately kissing his face she knelt down and began to unzip his pants. His dick sprang out like a jack-in-the-box, and she took it in her mouth and started sucking.

Victor was thrilled. She was looking up at him with a look of complete adoration on her face. It was a subtle shift in their relationship, but he knew it was an important one. She was starting to trust and appreciate what they had. He smiled and stroked her hair. Then he gently pulled her up and held her in his arms.

"I love the feel of your mouth on me, baby, but I have a different way I want you to do it this time."

He led her to the bed and had her take her top and bra off. Then he had her lie down on her back. Victor slowly crawled up her body until he was staring down into her eyes. He gave her a chaste kiss on the nose and sat upright. Then he straddled her rib cage with his legs and placed his cock on her chest. It was wedged between her ample breasts, and the tip was nudging her chin.

Abby tried not to laugh as Victor slid his cock up and down. Then he took her hands and guided them to her breasts. He had her press them together and said, "Hold your hands here and keep the pressure on." She did what she was told, and he nodded in satisfaction. The pressure was providing just the right amount of friction. Then he reached up with one hand and slid it under her head. He tilted her head down and ordered, "You can resume sucking now."

Abby sighed at the autocratic command, but she took his penis back into her mouth all the same. As he moved, it was sliding in deeper and hitting her throat. She tightened around him and closed her eyes to concentrate. She wanted to please Victor and give him the best tit fuck of his life.

She was succeeding. He was looking down at her with half-hooded eyes and a rapt expression on his face. Abby increased the pressure in her mouth, and Victor picked up the pace. When he was close, he pulled back and clasped the base of his cock with his hand. Then he blew his wad all over her chest and face. It was running down her neck and pooling in the cleft between her breasts.

God, she looked glorious lying there with his seed all over her. Victor was feeling a deep sense of connection with Abby that he had never felt with any other woman. He marveled at it as she continued to gaze up at him. Something unspoken passed between them before he broke the moment by cleaning her face and chest with his shirt.

Abby raised her eyebrows in amusement. "Why is it we always ruin your clothing?"

Victor grinned and pulled her off the bed. "Your shirts are too tiny for the messes I tend to make. Now hurry up. We have just enough time for you to shower before we head to dinner. Then I'm taking you to a Christmas Eve mass. If you're a good girl, maybe I'll let you open your presents tonight."

She headed to the bathroom but cast him a devilish look over her shoulder. "I thought I just opened my present. It was big...and wet... and quite delicious." She scurried in and shut the door behind her. His deep laughs followed her into the shower.

***

They had a buffet dinner at the hotel. It was actually a lot better than either one had expected, and the place was packed. Then they headed to a local Catholic church up the street. The mass was done by candlelight, and a full choir was singing from the balcony. Abby was enthralled by the service, and she held Victor's hand through most of it. When he started singing along to "First Noel" with his deep baritone voice, her heart melted. She realized she was falling in love with him, and she ached with the realization. After Nate died, Abby never thought she would love someone again.

They spent the rest of their time down in Tampa seeing the sights and fooling around. By the time they returned to Cleveland, they were both well rested and ready for their new year's adventure. Yuri was going to drive down with them, and the rest of their friends would meet them there.

Chapter Thirty-Three

On the day they were to leave for Hocking Hills, Yuri got an emergency psychiatric case at the hospital that held him up for several hours. He didn't arrive at Victor's condo until after five p.m. He apologized profusely, but Victor waved him off.

"No worries. It gave me time to get some things done. We still have to pick up Abby, but then we can hit the road."

They headed over to Tremont in Victor's truck. Yuri was looking forward to seeing where Abby lived. His friend had made some complaints about the safety of her neighborhood, and he wanted to see for himself. He also wanted to observe their interactions more closely now they had settled into their relationship.

When they arrived, they found Abby frantically running around trying to pack. Victor scowled at her. "You had all afternoon to do this. Why are you just getting to it now?"

Abby blew her bangs off of her forehead and gave him a sheepish look. "I'm sorry. I got caught up in my plot and lost track of time." She walked over and gave Yuri a quick hug before throwing the last items into a bag. Then she folded up her laptop and started putting it in the bag as well.

Victor stopped her. "Why are you taking that?"

"Well, I thought I could write a little in the early morning or when you guys are playing poker."

Victor shook his head. "No, Abby. This is a vacation, and you know how you get when you're writing. You'll forget everyone else is around. Leave the computer at home."

She sighed and put her laptop back on the desk. "Okay, but do you mind if I write in the car in a notebook? I'm right in the middle of a good scene, and I don't want to forget it." She gave Victor a pleading look. When he appeared to be thinking about it, she tried to bargain with him. "You and Yuri can talk in Russian while I'm working, and I won't even mind."

He chuckled as he took her bag. "Very well, then. But when I tell you to put the notebook away, I don't want to hear any arguments."

She nodded and looked at Yuri nervously, but he had a mild expression on his face.

They headed to the truck, and Abby got in the back. She chatted with the men for a bit but then became engrossed in her writing. It was a long drive, and she planned to crank out the scene well before they arrived at the cabin. Two hours later she was startled when Yuri tapped on her knee to get her attention. She looked up to see his apologetic smile.

Then she saw Victor's glare in the rearview mirror. "I've been trying to get your attention for the past minute. It's time to put the notebook away."

"Okay," she nodded as she furiously continued to write. "Just let me jot down a few more notes."

"No, Abby. Now!"

She looked up and saw the anger in his eyes.

"This is why I didn't let you bring the computer." He reached his hand back, "Give me the notebook."

She sighed and handed it over, and he tucked it under the front seat. To ease the tension, she asked, "Are we almost there?"

Victor nodded and looked at his GPS. "It's a few miles up the road." Then he added, "Now is probably a good time to remind you of our rules. With your friends here you may be more tempted to break them."

Abby was horrified. She hurriedly looked at Yuri and then back at Victor. "Um, that's okay. I remember them."

Victor caught the look. "It's okay. Yuri is well aware of the type of relationship we have. He and I have been friends a long time. He understands."

Yuri turned around and looked at her. "Please don't be embarrassed. As a psychiatrist I can assure you a BDSM relationship is perfectly normal. It is also a lot more common than you think."

Abby forgot to be embarrassed. "Really? And what exactly is BDSM?"

Yuri raised his eyebrows in surprise. Before he could answer, Victor cut him off in Russian. *"Why the hell did you bring that up? You'll scare her!"*

Yuri looked nonplussed and responded back in Russian, *"Why? She's already in the lifestyle. She deserves to know how far it can go."*

Victor scowled at him. *"That is for me to share with her, not you. Besides, I'm not going to take it that far with this one. Now shut the fuck up!"*

Yuri's eyes narrowed, but then he nodded his assent. To Abby, he simply said, "It's nothing. What's important is your relationship is normal, as long as you're both consenting adults, which you are."

Abby nodded but looked at him skeptically. She mentally filed away the acronym and would look it up later.

Just then they arrived at their destination. Victor turned the truck down a narrow lane surrounded by trees. It ended at a circular driveway in front of a large cabin. It was a two-story wooden structure with a wraparound porch and large windows. There were rocking chairs on the porch and a wood pile close to the door. They could smell the smoke as they got out of the truck, and Abby looked up to see it coming out of a chimney. She grinned at her boyfriend.

As they were getting their bags from the truck, Rachel and Joel came out to help them. The girls hugged, and Rachel excitedly started telling them about the cabin. The bags were carried inside, and then a tour was given.

The first floor had a large living room with comfy leather couches and chairs arranged around a stone fireplace. A big screen television was mounted on the mantle. Next to the living room was a modern kitchen and long wooden table with twelve chairs. A door past the kitchen led out to the side of the cabin where a grill was situated. Further back on the porch was an eight-man hot tub. When she saw it, Abby's grin got bigger.

Toward the back of the cabin was a narrow hallway and two sets of stairs. One led down to a basement, and the other led up to the second floor. Rachel showed them the three guest rooms on the main floor first. They were small, but each had a queen bed and its own private bathroom. She explained the married couples had claimed these rooms.

They then headed down the stairs to the basement. There were two more rooms down there, also with private bathrooms, and those were for Yuri and Kate. Rachel explained the rooms were bigger, but the beds were smaller, and that was why they gave them to the singles. Yuri threw his bag in the unoccupied one and gave Victor a happy smirk.

They headed back to the first floor, and Rachel handed Victor a key.

Abby was confused. "I thought we were staying here with everyone else."

Victor nodded. "We are. We're staying upstairs. The cabin is set up so the second floor can be rented as a separate unit, or as part of this one. There's an entrance inside but also one on the outside."

Rachel pointed to the wall with the fireplace. "There's an outdoor staircase on the other side of the cabin. It leads up to a balcony and another entrance. You even have your own private hot tub up there." There was a hint of annoyance in her voice.

Victor put his arm around Abby and kissed the top of her head. "This way we have a little more privacy, but we can still be part of the group."

They headed up to the second floor and unlocked the door. It opened into a large room. There was a king-sized bed next to a gas fireplace along one wall. In one corner was a sitting area and television, and another corner held a kitchenette. There was also a bathroom and French doors leading out to the balcony. Abby could see the hot tub out there. It was perfect, and she told Victor as much.

He laughed. "Well, I would hardly call this a five-star hotel, but it will have to do."

"I'm going to have to find a way to thank you," she whispered.

He grinned, "I'm sure that can be arranged. But for now, we had best get back downstairs. We don't want to piss Rachel off any more than she already is. I think she likes control even more than I do."

Abby giggled. He was probably right. They quickly unpacked and headed down to join their friends.

That night the group soaked in the hot tub, played games, and partied. The drinks were flowing freely, and everyone was drunk except for Victor and Abby. She had carefully stuck to her two-drink limit under his watchful eye. He had opted to sip on one bourbon. They both watched their friends get wilder as the night wore on. At one point they were dashing from the hot tub to the snow to make snow angels. Then they would jump back into the hot tub while screaming from the cold.

It was hysterical, but Abby was starting to get tired. Victor noticed and took her upstairs. They could hear the group partying below them as they crawled into bed. As Victor's hand slid down into her pajama bottoms, Abby got nervous.

"What if they hear us?"

Victor was amused. "They're too drunk to notice." He pulled her on top of him and continued to explore her body with his hands. She realized he was right. Their friends were drunk as hoot owls, and those magic hands were causing her to rapidly forget about everything else.

***

The next day they woke to a silent cabin. It was still dark, and Victor suggested they go on a sunrise hike. They quickly dressed and headed out. The air was cold and crisp with a fresh scent of pine. The sky was black and dotted with stars and a sliver of moon. It was just enough light to see by, and Victor led them down a trail near the cabin.

The trail meandered through the woods and down into a gorge. They crossed over a stream on a little log bridge and then circled around a pond. As the sun began to rise, so did the wildlife. They saw numerous rabbits and a few cautious deer in the distance. They also heard the early morning calls of a cardinal.

An hour later the sun was up, and the two had circled back to the cabin. They headed in through the front door and found most of their friends up and looking hungover. Rachel was in the kitchen making breakfast.

She gave them a reproachful look. "You guys couldn't wait? We're going to hike right after breakfast. Now we won't all be together."

Abby reassured her. "We're still going with you." Then she sniffed the air. "Do I smell bacon?"

Rachel grinned and handed her a cup of coffee. "Breakfast should be ready in about twenty minutes."

Abby could feel Victor's eyes on her. She handed him the cup. "I don't drink coffee anymore, Rach."

Just then Lindsay walked in. "Since when don't you drink coffee? You're a worse addict than I am!"

Abby shrugged. "I'm trying to be healthier."

Rachel snorted. "Good luck with that." She went back to the eggs on the stove, and Abby snuck a look at her boyfriend. He was smiling at her while sipping the coffee. Abby rolled her eyes and went to fix an herbal tea.

After breakfast, the group hiked a long trail on one of the state parks. Then they had lunch as they debated their options for the afternoon. There was a mess of wet boots on the floor by the fire, and a pile of coats, hats, gloves, and scarves thrown over a bench.

Yuri was tired. He wasn't used to physical activity, and he was alarmed to hear the group might be heading back out to do another trail. He glanced out the window and noted it was starting to snow. Fuck that! He decided to use his psychiatric skills to sway the group. It was easy to plant a seed, and within minutes the men had decided to stay in and play a game of poker.

The women were less than enthused. Rachel, in particular, was not happy with the turn of events. "We came here to do things as a group. You guys are going to waste the rest of the day on a stupid poker game?"

"You can always join us," pointed out Don. The other men glared at him.

Rachel looked at the women. "I don't know about you ladies, but I'm not going to sit inside and be lazy all afternoon. I came here to take in some nature." She leafed through the state park brochure and found a trail close to the cabin. "This timber one looks good. Let's do that. It's only six miles, and then we can hit that general store on the way back." Leave it to Rachel to throw shopping into the mix.

Victor was watching Abby closely, but she had her back to him drying dishes by the sink. The women had agreed to meet in five minutes and had run off to their rooms to get ready. While they were gone, Abby grabbed a bottle of water from the fridge and the brochure. She casually walked over to the table and handed Victor the water. Then she pointed to the trail on the brochure.

He smiled at her, took the brochure, and read over the trail description. It was listed as one of the harder ones and had four little stick men to denote difficulty. The description also included a warning about dangerous cliffs and narrow and treacherous paths. He pinched the bridge of his nose in frustration. They had to pick a fucking dangerous one!

Victor looked over at Joel. "What's the weather forecast for the rest of the day?"

Joel pulled out his phone and quickly answered. "Heavy snow. Up to six inches. Tonight it's supposed to get really cold."

Victor thanked him and turned back to Abby. "I'm sorry, but you're not going on that hike. It's too dangerous, and with the snow coming in you're just a slip away from getting seriously hurt. You'll stay here."

She blinked in surprise but then quietly said, "Okay." She was self-conscious as she left the room. He hadn't even tried to whisper, and she was certain all the men had heard.

Sure enough, as soon as she was gone Kent leaned toward Victor. "Did you just tell her what to do and she listened? Dude, you're going to have to teach me how to do that."

Victor ignored Kent. It was his turn in the game, and he concentrated on that instead. Out of the corner of his eye, he saw Abby return to the room. She had a book in her hand and was curling up on the couch. That made him smile.

Soon the other women were back and ready to leave. Lindsay noticed Abby first. "Girl, you better get your butt in gear or Rachel is going to be pissed. You know how she gets."

Abby looked up from her book. "I'm not going. I'm going to stay here and read."

Just then Rachel entered the room. "Abby Shea, you can read anytime. You came here to hike, and you love it more than any of us. Get your butt off that couch!"

Abby sighed. "I don't feel like it, Rach."

"Oh, come on. Once you get outside in the fresh air you'll perk up."

Joel yelled from the table, "Rachel, what's the big deal? Just leave her alone!"

Rachel glared at him. "I don't understand why she won't go." Then she turned to Abby, "Are you sick?"

Kent chimed in. "She's fine. Victor just told her she wasn't allowed to go."

Abby wanted to die. Everyone was staring at her, and Rachel had a horrified look on her face. She turned to Victor in confusion. "Why?"

Victor calmly replied, "Because it's not safe."

Rachel didn't miss a beat. "She'll be fine. We'll all be together." Then she turned back to Abby. "So he tells you what to do, and you actually listen to him? What kind of relationship is that?" Her voice was part shock and part disdain.

Abby felt the shame deep in her belly. "He's just being protective, Rach."

"My God, Abs. It's the twenty-first century!" She glared at Victor. "I just don't see what the big deal is."

Victor responded, "It's really none of your business."

Now Rachel was pissed. "Fine. Then Abby can stay here and be a good little woman. She can cook the dinner too! Perhaps you would like her barefoot and pregnant in front of the stove?" With that, she stomped out of the cabin.

The room was silent after she left.

Kate was the first to move. She gave Abby an apologetic look and followed Rachel out the door.

Meanwhile, Renee was reading the brochure on the table and announced she was staying behind as well. "It does look dangerous, and my legs are sore from this morning. I'm going to soak in the hot tub and then take a nap." She gave Abby a kind smile.

Lindsay was the last to leave and took her time. She cracked a few jokes about chivalrous doctors to get Abby to laugh. Then to Renee, she said, "I'll let the angry girl know you're staying too. You're probably going on her shit list, but at least you're in good company!" With that, she made a face and left the cabin.

Joel was muttering under his breath and looking angry. The rest of the men wisely went back to the game without saying a word. Victor stole a glance at Abby. She looked upset, so he stuck his tongue out at her and made a funny face. She gave him a weak smile and went back to her book. Inside she was a quaking ball of anxiety. Eventually, she was able to calm down and get back into the plot of her book.

Two hours went by and the men finally finished their game. It was now snowing heavily, and Don announced he was going to join his wife for a nap. Joel put on a sweater, and a leash on Charlie, and said he was going for a walk. He was still in a foul mood, and they wisely let him go. Kent suggested a movie and found one on the satellite. The men joined Abby on the couch, and Victor put his arm around her. He let her read for five more minutes and then suggested they take a nap too.

She looked at him skeptically. "You're tired?"

"Yes. Exhausted." He had a deadpan expression on his face.

Abby rolled her eyes but snapped her book shut all the same. "Okay. I could use a nap."

The two left the room and headed upstairs.

Kent looked at Yuri. "You think they're actually taking a nap?"

Yuri snorted. "Hell no. The last time that man took a nap he was still in diapers. They're going to fuck."

Kent laughed. "We'd better turn the volume up, then."

"Why would we do that? Don't you want to listen?"

Kent couldn't tell if the psychiatrist was serious or not. "Um, I have always wondered if Abby was a screamer."

Yuri nodded. "I would lay odds she is. Put it on mute, and let's see if I'm right."

Kent hesitated for a second but then muted the volume.

Upstairs Victor had Abby on his lap with his arms around her. "I can't tell you how happy I am by your obedience, little one, especially in front of your friends. Are you okay?"

She nodded. "I just don't see why Rachel was so angry."

Victor was nuzzling her neck while his hands massaged her breasts. "I suspect there is more going on there than we know. Try not to worry about it. Our lifestyle is not for everyone."

Abby sighed. "I'm not sure it's right for me either."

Victor smiled as he eased her back on the bed. As he pulled her cargo pants and panties off, he murmured, "You may not like the control part, baby, but you sure like the sex part." Then he grabbed her legs and quickly pulled her ass to the edge of the bed. Victor knelt down and buried his face between her legs.

Downstairs all was quiet. Aside from the bed squeaking a little, there was no sound from above.

"Maybe they really are taking a nap," said Kent.

Yuri laughed. "Give it time. I'm sure our boy is taking care of her needs before he gets to his own. We Russians are nothing if not generous lovers."

They continued to listen, and after ten minutes they started to hear soft female moans.

Yuri grinned at Kent. "Showtime."

As they listened, Kent was embarrassed to feel his hard-on. He gave the psychiatrist a surreptitious glance and noted the pup tent in his pants as well.

Upstairs the soft moans had given way to louder ones punctuated by shouts of "God, yes" and "Victor!" Then there was silence.

Yuri commented, "Nice job, Dr. Turov. Now I suspect it's your turn."

Sure enough, they heard the bed start to squeak in a rhythmic pattern. The pace gradually picked up, and then it sounded like the bed was going to come through the ceiling.

"How the hell does he get away with that? He's pounding the shit out of her!" Kent was shocked but also completely turned on.

Yuri ignored him and was concentrating on the noise. He had his hand down his pants and a lustful expression on his face.

The pounding continued and then gave way to more female shouts. Finally, all was quiet again, and they could hear the murmur of Victor's deep voice from above.

Yuri pulled his hand out of his pants and stood up. "Well, that was highly enjoyable. Now I need a shower." He noticed the look on Kent's face as he headed out of the room. He tried to reassure the man. "Voyeurism is perfectly normal behavior. They probably wouldn't like it if they knew we listened in. But what they don't know won't hurt them. Plus, if they were that concerned, they could have been quieter."

Kent wasn't sure he agreed, but he put the incident out of his mind. He needed a shower as well, and he headed to his room.

At dinner time the girls still had not returned. The weather had turned downright ugly, and everyone was getting concerned. Renee and Don got started on dinner, and Joel and Kent tried to reach the women by phone. They weren't picking up.

They finally rolled in an hour after dinner was over. The three were obviously drunk, and Kate was limping on a pair of crutches. They explained how she had slid off the trail and sprained her ankle. That had resulted in a trip to the urgent care center followed by a visit to a bar to ease the pain.

The girls were laughing hysterically as they told their story, but no one else was laughing. Joel was furious and commented on how Rachel drove them back drunk. The two stalked off to their room to have a shouting match, and Charlie hid on the couch by Don and Renee.

Meanwhile, Kent was watching Lindsay scarf down the dinner leftovers. She was drunk and spilling food everywhere, and he made a nasty comment. That started them fighting as well.

Kate also ate some dinner and then said she was going to go lie down. Yuri gallantly offered to help her down the stairs and check her ankle. They overheard him telling her he was, after all, a doctor and could tend to her needs.

Victor and Abby gave each other knowing smiles. They ended up playing cards with Don and Renee that night, and everyone headed to bed early.

The next morning the group went on a short hike around the property. Yuri stayed behind with Kate, and the two hopped in the hot tub together. The group was much more subdued, but it was a lovely hike all the same. When they returned to the cabin, Lindsay suggested a shopping trip for the women. She teased Victor, "Don't worry. We'll protect your girl for you."

Abby looked at her boyfriend. He was eyeing up the women and obviously thinking about it. Then he pulled her off to the side and said, "You can go, but absolutely no drinking."

She nodded.

"I mean it. If they start to get out of hand, call me and I will come get you."

She thanked him and gave a quick kiss before hopping into Renee's SUV.

The girls spent two hours shopping and then ended up in a quaint little café by a river. Once their orders had been placed, they started gabbing.

Rachel started off by apologizing to Abby. She explained she and Joel were having problems. "He really wants kids. But I honestly have no desire, and he can't understand that. It's like he wants me to be something that I'm not."

The girls commiserated. Only Renee had kids, but hers were grown adults. The rest of them were childless.

Eventually, the conversation moved on to Abby and Victor's relationship.

Rachel led the charge. "I really like Victor, Abs, and the two of you seem great together. I just want to make sure things are okay between the two of you. Does he tell you what to do a lot?"

The other women were watching her expectantly, and Abby could feel her stomach turning. She chose her words carefully. "He's used to ordering people around, Rach. I'm sure you know what doctors are like."

They all nodded.

She went on. "He can be quite bossy, but he's also very protective of me, and I like that."

Lindsay spoke up. "But is he safe? I mean, he's not hurting you or anything, is he?"

Abby didn't hesitate. "God, no. I feel completely safe with him."

That reassured the girls. Abby decided to go for broke. "I should tell you that he wasn't happy with our Cancun trip. He doesn't want me to go, and he's offered to refund my money. He said Cancun has a drug cartel issue." She looked at them worriedly.

Kate looked bummed. "Does that mean you're not going?"

"Probably not. But I'll be there in spirit!"

The girls looked at each other but said nothing. Instead, they chose to move on to another topic. They were soon dishing about Yuri and the sex he'd had with Kate the night before. Apparently, it had gone well. The girls continued to discuss, but Abby got lost in her own thoughts. She was relieved to get the Cancun discussion over with, but part of her felt uncomfortable about the safety issue. Was she really safe with Victor? She thought she was, but who knew?

The girls returned to the cabin later that afternoon. Victor was relieved to see Abby come in, and he eyed her up carefully. She gave him a reassuring smile and went to help her friends. It was New Year's Eve, and they were setting up for their celebration. Renee had brought streamers, balloons, hats, and horns.

The party got started at seven that night. They were playing games and also watching the city celebrations on television. Everyone seemed to be getting along well, and the group was having one of those rare and magical moments together.

At ten thirty Victor put his arm around Abby and announced they were calling it a night. The group was not pleased. They argued it was a holiday and they should all be together. Victor just shrugged and led his girlfriend up the stairs. After they were gone, Yuri tried to appease the crowd. He explained it was a Russian tradition to ring in the new year by making love. He was looking at Kate pointedly while he explained this. The group was just drunk enough to take it in without too much complaint. They continued to party.

Meanwhile, upstairs, Victor and Abby slid into the hot tub naked. It was the first time they had taken advantage of their private space, and the two curled around each other like long lost lovers. They enjoyed the fresh cold air and the stars above until it got too hot to stay in. Then they crawled into bed and fooled around. There were no ropes involved and no bondage. Instead, they made love slowly, enjoying each other's company, and the connection they felt was deep. The two were sound asleep before the ball dropped in Times Square, with Abby's back tucked up against Victor's chest.

Chapter Thirty-Four

Victor and Abby fell into an easy and comfortable routine when they got back from vacation. They saw each other every Wednesday night and weekend, but Victor found that wasn't enough. He quickly mandated his girlfriend block out the lunch hour on her schedule so they could talk on the phone. She was only allowed to miss the call when she had something scheduled, but even then she had to run it by him first.

Their conversations were about everything. He would tell her about work, the people he dealt with, and funny stories from his childhood. She would tell him about her writing struggles, her volunteer adventures, and the school events she went to for her nephews. It was an easy way for them to connect, and Victor often used it to reinforce rules.

"Where were you going this morning in such a hurry? Your average speed was sixty-six miles per hour."

"Oh. I forgot you could check that. There was a guy driving while texting, and I wanted to get around him."

"Mmm hmm. And it took you the entire driving time to do that? I told you I don't want you going any more than five over the speed limit." His voice was stern.

She sighed. "I know. But I was only six over. A police officer would let me off for that, you know."

Victor laughed. "A police officer would let you off because you're beautiful, but I am not that easily swayed. You will be punished."

They moved on to his schedule, and he explained he would be working the entire weekend. She took it well, and Victor commented on it.

"You are the first woman I have met who doesn't mind my work schedule. Why is that?"

She thought about it. "I don't know. I guess I've always done well with solitude. Even when I was a kid my mom said I didn't mind playing by myself. I can stay busy for hours with reading, writing, crafts, and even napping."

"And is that what you plan to do this weekend?"

"I guess. Lindsay and Kate asked me to go dancing with them at Club 9 on Saturday night. I told them no, of course. But if you're not going to be up for anything, maybe I could go?" She could hear the doubt in her own voice.

Victor's response was immediate. "Absolutely not!"

Abby rolled her eyes.

"And stop rolling your eyes. You know damn well that place isn't safe. It's in the news all the time for gang-related events. Not to mention what your friends are like."

Abby switched the phone to her other ear. "There was only one incident there, Victor. And my friends are going through a hard time right now. Plus, I really love to dance. Maybe I could go for just an hour?"

"No. You can never go. I forbid you from going to any of those dance clubs, do you understand?" His voice was uncompromising.

"Yes," she sullenly responded. Then she stuck her tongue out at the phone.

"And stop sticking your tongue out at me. Honestly, Abby, you need to work harder on being submissive." There was humor in his voice.

She looked at the phone in amazement. How did he know?

They moved on to other topics and eventually hung up.

On Wednesday they got together for their usual dinner. Victor picked her up at her house with a bag tucked under his arm. She eyed it suspiciously and wondered if there was a paddle in there. Sure enough, he pulled out the same leather one he had used on her the last time she had sped in her car. He took her by the hand and led her to the couch.

After a thorough and painful spanking, Victor led her back to the counter. He pushed the bag toward her and explained he had gotten her a gift.

Abby touched the bag and looked at him inquisitively. Then she reached in and pulled out a blood pressure monitor. "Um, thank you."

Victor laughed. "This not only checks your blood pressure; it also measures your heart rate. It even keeps a record of your numbers so I can check on them when I visit. I want you to start using it every day."

He pulled the cuff out of the box and showed her how it worked.

She smiled at him. "Okay. This is actually a good thing."

"Oh?"

"Yes. I can sneak some coffee in and then prove to you it does nothing to my heart rate."

"I would suggest you rethink that, little one. Breaking a rule because you get caught up in a moment or forget is one thing. But purposefully breaking a rule to make a point to me will cause a punishment I'm not sure you can handle."

She gave him an amused look. So far his spankings had hurt but were tolerable. They also made her horny as hell, which was something she didn't mind in the least. To change the subject, she said, "Okay. You are fond of gadgets, aren't you?"

He was still scowling at her but then pulled her into his arms and smiled. "I do when they help me to protect you."

She rolled her eyes.

"Now if only there was a gadget that could prevent you from doing that! A pair of goggles, perhaps?"

She snorted with laughter, and they headed to dinner.

***

Winter in Cleveland was particularly rough that year, and by February the couple was going stir crazy. Victor's surgery schedule had been unrelenting, and Abby had been working toward a deadline on her latest book. They needed to unwind, and Victor thought about another vacation someplace warm. They couldn't get away for longer than a weekend, but it would be better than nothing. Unfortunately, they still had several clinic public relations events to get through before that was possible.

That night was one of the biggest ones. It was the annual surgery center gala ball, and Victor knew Abby was dreading it. He was scheduled to pick her up later that morning, and he thought about ways to help her relax. They didn't have to leave until seven p.m., and he eyed the drawers under his bed thoughtfully.

The two had gotten closer over the past few months and were starting to trust each other more and more. She had taken all of his punishments well, and she was very open to anything he suggested sexually. She was also much more obedient and seemed to be adapting to the submissive role. He decided it was time to take it further and give her a glimpse of what their lifestyle could really be like.

Victor walked over to the drawers and opened them. He sorted through the contents on both sides and debated on what he should use. He also walked around his condo and assessed the rooms. His eyes landed on the ceiling beams in the living room. They would work perfectly. He could feel his groin begin to stir as he planned out a scenario.

Abby was in her closet when he arrived at her townhouse. She was holding up both evening gowns and trying to decide on which one to wear.

Victor chuckled at her. "Why don't you bring both of them, and you can decide later?"

They loaded up both gowns along with the shoes and jewelry to match. Abby had also packed an overnight bag, as she would be spending the night at his place.

Victor took her to lunch. She was drilling him about what to expect at the ball, and he realized she was more nervous than he had thought. He assured her he would be by her side for most of the night. Yuri was also going, and she could sit with him while Victor gave his speech.

"Wait, you're giving a speech?"

"Yes. I'm the chief of their biggest money-maker. It's expected of me."

Abby gave him a look of awe. "You can do that? I mean, you can talk in front of three hundred people with no problem?"

Victor shrugged. "Yes. I don't think about it or plan anything out. I just get up there and say some bullshit, and the crowd is happy. Plus, if I get nervous, I'll just picture you in your birthday suit." He winked at her.

She laughed. "Don't you mean the crowd? You're supposed to picture the crowd naked."

He made a face. "Why would I want to see that? But you naked, that's a whole other story." He wiggled his eyebrows at her.

"Well, you're a braver person than me, Dr. Turov."

He suddenly got serious. "Oh, I don't know. You can be very brave yourself, Abby, when the situation calls for it."

She frowned at him in confusion, but just then their server arrived with the bill.

They headed back to the condo, and Victor could feel his excitement begin to mount. As soon as they were in the door he pulled her onto his lap on the couch. He loved how she always curled right into his body as if there was nowhere else she would rather be. Victor stroked her hair and smiled down at her.

"You trust me, don't you Abby?"

She nodded.

"And you seem to be adjusting to my control issues well."

She raised one eyebrow at him but nodded.

He cupped her face and tilted her head up. "I want to try something way outside your comfort zone, little one, but I think you will like it. It will also help us blow off steam before the ball."

She looked at him expectantly.

"It requires you to trust me completely, and you'll need to tell me to stop if I get too rough. Do you think you can do that?"

Now she looked worried. "Yes," she whispered.

He grinned at her. "Good." He stood up and pulled her off the couch. Then he pushed all the furniture to the outer walls of the room.

Abby stood by with her arms crossed and watched him with growing concern. When he was done, he took her hand and led her to the center of the room.

"I need you to take off all of your clothes, little one."

She did so without hesitation, which pleased him. Once she was naked he had her kneel down on the floor. Her hair was hanging down her back, and he had her wind it up and pin it on top of her head. When she was done she looked at him expectantly. She looked shy, nervous, embarrassed, and aroused all at the same time.

Victor was hard instantly. She was a sight to behold, and she was all his. He had to take a deep breath to steady himself. He explained to her, "This is one of the most submissive positions you can be in. You have no idea what it is doing to me."

She smiled at him, and he watched with interest as the flush spread across her cheeks.

"Now stay put!" He headed out of the room, and she watched him go. When he returned, he was carrying rope, padded cuffs, and some other things she didn't recognize. He had also taken his shirt off, and she chose to focus on his tight muscles instead of her growing nervousness.

Victor set the items down on a table. Then he walked over with the cuffs and rope. "Put out your hands."

She did, and he quickly placed the cuffs on her wrists. Once they were buckled and secure, he attached them to the rope so her wrists were bound together. Then he tossed the rope in the air so it looped over a wooden beam on the ceiling. Victor helped Abby to stand and then pulled the rope taught so her arms were pulled up above her head. He secured the loose end of the rope in a slip knot. He explained he could easily release the rope if the need arose.

Victor then walked over to the table and grabbed what looked like a long metal rod. When he brought it over, she could see it also had padded cuffs on it. He knelt down in front of her and attached the cuffs to her ankles. Then he grasped the metal rod in the middle with both hands. He quickly pulled his hands apart, and the rod expanded causing her legs to spread wide.

Victor grinned and explained, "It's called a spreader bar. Aptly named, wouldn't you say?"

She grinned in spite of herself.

"Would you like to hear some music? It might help you relax."

She nodded, and he went to turn on the sound system. Soon she could hear soft and sultry jazz music playing in the background.

Victor returned to the table and picked up what looked like a rod with fringes on the end of it. He walked over to Abby and showed her the fringes. They had little plastic balls on the end of them.

"This is called a flogger. He let her look at it and then draped the fringes over her right shoulder. He slowly ran it down the front of her body. Then he said, "I'm going to hit your body with it."

Abby looked at him in dismay. "Am I being punished?"

"No, baby. This is for pleasure. There is a fine line between pain and pleasure, and we're going to explore that gray area. Remember, if it gets to be too much, just tell me to stop."

She looked at him uncertainly but nodded.

Victor continued to drag the end of the flogger over her body. When he ran it up the side of her neck, she tilted her head toward the flogger and closed her eyes. He smiled and continued the sensual touch on her body. When she appeared relaxed, he pulled his arm back and snapped the flogger across her ass. It made a funny sound, and she was shocked by the impact.

Victor walked around to stand in front of her and rubbed her behind. "Did that hurt?"

She looked at him in confusion. "Yes. No. Maybe?"

He nodded in satisfaction and continued. Victor was in no hurry, and he ran the flogger over her body like an artist brushing strokes on a canvas. If felt like he was gently tickling her. Then when he slapped the flogger against her body, it sent shivers up and down her spine. Abby closed her eyes and kept them closed. She liked not knowing when the next hit was going to come, and her entire body tingled and almost hummed in anticipation.

Victor continued with the flogger until her skin had a soft pink glow all over. Then he set it down and picked up the riding crop. He had her open her eyes to look at the crop.

He explained, "This one is smaller but has more of a bite. I want you to relax and take it in without thinking too much about what I'm doing. It can be very releasing if you let it."

Abby looked at the riding crop in relief. It was smaller than the flogger or even the paddle he had used on her in the past. She was sure she could handle it and told him as much.

Victor knew better, but he was hoping she would find pleasure in what he was about to do to her. He started running the leather flap of the riding crop over her body as he had done with the flogger. Abby closed her eyes again and was breathing deeply. She moaned when he ran the edge up between her legs.

When he slapped the crop sharply over her left breast, her eyes flew open. The pain was exquisite. She looked at him in wonder, but he was already running the crop down her right thigh in concentration. Victor was completely in the moment. He alternated between caressing strokes and quick hits of the crop. He aimed the hits at sensitive parts of her body including her breasts, buttocks, and the juncture of her thighs. The hits were just quick enough to elicit a sharp lick of pain followed by a warming sensation. Abby gave in to the sensation, and her body felt wonderful as she started releasing more and more tension.

This went on for a while before Victor finally put the riding crop down and sidled up behind her. He pulled her against his hard body and released the rope from above. She melted into his arms. He held her briefly as her head lulled back against his chest. Then he told her to bend her knees as he gently lay her down on the ground. He pulled the rope away from the wrist restraints, and she opened her eyes and gave him a lustful look.

Victor lay down next to her and massaged her arms back to life.

Then he crawled around so he was in front of her legs. He grasped the spreader bar and told her to keep her knees bent as he raised the bar toward her body. Her legs were flexible and took the stretch well. Victor had her grab the bar with her hands to hold it against her body. In this position, her ass was up with her sex wet and gloriously exposed. It was ripe for the picking, and Victor wasted no time pulling his cock from his pants. He slid it into her opening, and Abby came almost immediately.

"You never cease to amaze me, little one!" He let her ride out the waves of her orgasm as he continued to rock in and out of her. Eventually, he felt his own body began to let go, and he exploded inside of her.

Victor collapsed on the floor next to her and lay there a moment to catch his breath. Then he looked over and saw she had returned her feet to the ground. He quickly sat up and undid the cuffs around her ankles. Then he pushed the bar away, lay back down, and pulled Abby on top of him.

They lay there for quite some time not saying anything. Finally, he asked, "How are you feeling?"

She snuggled in more and sighed in contentment. "Pretty amazing." It was true, too. Her body was still warm and tingling all over. She felt like she had just worked out and released all her tensions and stress.

Victor nodded in satisfaction. He had rolled onto his side, and Abby's head was now resting on his arm. He ran his other hand down her body and noticed the red marks. They really stood out on her fair English skin.

"I think tonight you will have to wear the black dress," he chuckled. "There's no way you can wear the green one. It has a low back and would show all these marks."

Abby looked down worriedly at her torso. "Are you sure the black one will cover everything?"

He leaned in and gave her a quick kiss before pulling her up. "Don't worry, we will make sure it does. Now off to the shower with you while I put this room back together." He gave her a smack on the ass as she headed out of the room.

Abby stood in front of the mirror in the bathroom and looked at her body. There were red marks everywhere, and she touched them gingerly. Most did not hurt, although a few were tender as though a bruise was forming. She stared at her reflection in confusion and wondered in what universe this was normal. She didn't have time to think about it, though, as she had to get ready for the ball.

Two hours later and they were at the Rock and Roll Hall of Fame. It had been rented out by the clinic and was elegantly decorated. Abby looked beautiful in the black gown with her hair up. She had braided sections of it back and left soft tendrils down to frame her face. Her heels were chic with a subtle sparkle, and she was wearing a diamond pendant at her neck and diamond earrings. Both had been gifts from Victor.

He looked just as good in his tuxedo, and the couple were drawing the eye of many a person in the room. Abby felt like they were at prom, and the thought of a teenaged Victor made her secretly smile. She made a mental note to check out any childhood photos he had.

Victor was true to his word and kept her close by his side as he mingled with the clinic community. Those who knew him were curious, as he had never brought a date to an event before. They bombarded Abby with questions, and she surprised herself by keeping up a steady stream of chit chat. The glass of wine Victor had given her when they first arrived had helped. She could have used another, but he had told her no, which was annoying.

When Yuri arrived, the three grabbed a table and sat down. Several other surgeons joined them, and then dinner was served. Abby was content to let the conversation flow around her while she ate her meal. She was sitting between Victor and Yuri, and she soaked up the ambiance and mentally noted some of the quirkier personalities in the room.

After dinner, it was time for the speeches, and Victor left the table to go stand by the stage. He squeezed her hand reassuringly before he left.

Once he was gone, Yuri leaned in to make conversation. They whispered back and forth about the Hocking Hills trip and his ongoing relationship with Kate. The psychiatrist was not holding out hope it would last, but he said for now it was fun to go along for the ride.

"And how are things going with you and Victor?"

She smiled and told him it was going well.

Yuri noted the faint marks on her chest that were only partially covered by her dress. To the inexperienced eye, they would go unnoticed, but he was trained to observe. He also knew Victor well, and the thought of what his friend had done to elicit those marks made Yuri angry. Normally he didn't care about Victor's girlfriends. They were seasoned pros who could handle anything he dished out. But Abby was different. Victor had coaxed her into the lifestyle, and Yuri wasn't sure she belonged there. There was something sweet and vulnerable about her. Then he thought back to the sex scene he and Kent had overheard at Hocking Hills. There had been nothing innocent about that, and he felt the blood rush into his cock without any warning.

Yuri realized with surprise he wanted Abby. He watched her clap when Victor strolled onto the stage, and he noted the way her perky breasts bounced with the movement. He thought about how those breasts would feel pressed up against his face.

Victor's speech was short but entertaining. The audience responded well, and Abby was grinning and listening to her boyfriend with a look of pure adoration on her face. That irritated Yuri to no end. He wanted her to know just what his friend was capable of, so he leaned in to continue their conversation.

"I'm glad things are going so well for you. I wasn't sure you would be able to handle a BDSM relationship," he whispered.

Abby looked over at Yuri uncertainly. He had mentioned that acronym again, and she really needed to look it up to see what it meant. To him, she simply shrugged and said, "So far so good."

Yuri could tell she had no idea what he was talking about. He could see Victor watching them from the side of the stage now, but he didn't care. He leaned in again and whispered, "Just make sure you tell him no if he pushes you too far. I don't want to see you get hurt. Normally Victor can control himself well, but he is different around you."

Abby bit her lip and glanced at the stage. Victor was staring at them, and she felt uncomfortable knowing he was watching. She kept her eyes on him but whispered to Yuri, "What do you mean?"

He smiled in satisfaction, as she had taken the bait. He whispered back, "When you first started dating he drew your blood without you knowing."

She gasped and looked at Yuri. "What! Why?"

The psychiatrist explained, "He does that with all his girlfriends. To make sure they're clean before he touches them." He noted her visibly recoil at the words. "But normally he gets their permission. With you, he just drew the blood when you were passed out from drinking."

Abby felt like she was going to be sick. She was startled when Victor suddenly appeared at her side. "Is everything okay?"

She looked up at him, gave a weak smile, and nodded. She grabbed her water glass to take a sip and averted her eyes. Victor looked back and forth between the two of them with a thoughtful expression on his face. Yuri met his look calmly, but Abby was staring straight ahead.

The band started playing as soon as the speeches were done, and Victor asked her to dance. They headed out to the dance floor where he pulled her in close. The warmth of his body immediately calmed her.

"What were you and Yuri talking about?"

She stared at his neck. "He was telling me about his dates with Kate. He doesn't think it's going to last very long."

Victor tipped her head up so he could look into her eyes. "Was that all?"

She hesitated, but then a neurosurgeon asked to cut in. Victor scowled at the man and watched Abby be swept away. He was stuck with the idiot's date, a slutty looking thing who was simpering up at him.

Victor kept an eye on Abby as she chatted with the neuro dick, but then she pulled away and headed to the restroom. He quickly excused himself to follow her but kept being waylaid by people wanting to talk. Many were the wealthy of Cleveland who donated thousands to the clinic. He had to stop and politely chat with them, but he inched closer to the restrooms and kept an eye on the women's door. She did not come back out.

Abby was relieved to escape into the quiet of a back stall. She plopped down on the seat and pulled her cell out of her clutch. She thought about texting Rachel to vent, but what could she possibly say? Instead, she started typing out notes of what she had observed at the party. Writing always soothed her, and she was soon relaxed again. She knew she would have to ask Victor about the blood draw, but for now, she was content to hide in the restroom. Yuri had made her very uncomfortable, and not just about what he had said. He gave off a pervy and creepy vibe she couldn't quite place, and she realized she didn't even like it when they gave each other a friendly hug. Abby gave an involuntary shudder.

Meanwhil,e Victor was growing impatient. She had been in there for over ten minutes, and he was starting to worry. He pulled out his cell and sent her a quick text while listening to an octogenarian drone on. The old man was so caught up in his story, he didn't even notice Victor texting.

How long are you planning to stay in there? Are you sick?

She groaned. He couldn't even give her a few minutes alone. She fired off a quick response.

I'm fine. Just taking a break.

Break's over. Time to come out.

She glared at the phone.

Okay. 5 more minutes. I'm writing down some notes.

He scowled at the phone and fired off a text.

No. NOW!

Abby groaned. Sometimes he made her so damn mad! She exited the stall but took her time washing her hands. Then she checked her makeup before finally heading back out. She found Victor leaning against the wall right outside the restroom door. He looked pissed.

"When I tell you to do something, you do it, do you understand?" He grasped her upper arm and steered her back toward the ballroom. Then he added, "I think it's time to leave."

She nodded, but they were soon accosted by more donors. They had to endure another hour of political chitchat before Victor was finally able to pull them away. Yuri had long since left the party, and the two headed out to the valet alone and in silence.

It was past midnight when they got back to Victor's place, and they were both exhausted. His anger had subsided along with any urge he had to punish her. He thought about making her kneel and ask for permission to get in bed, but his gut told him now was not the time. Something had occurred between Abby and Yuri, and he needed to know what.

He waited until she was in bed before broaching the topic. "You seemed upset after talking to Yuri. What did he say to you?"

She curled into his side and debated if she should tell him. As the night had worn on, Abby had realized she didn't care about the blood draw. She would have given him permission to do it anyway, but she was curious why he chose to sneak one in without her knowing, so she told him.

"Yuri is apparently worried I might not be cut out for our relationship. He told me you drew my blood when I was drunk. I think he was trying to make a point."

Victor sat up in bed in anger.

She continued. "What I don't understand is why you did it behind my back. I told you I had no problem getting tested."

He ran his hand through his hair. "I know. I ran the tests before we had that conversation. I saw an opportunity and took it. At the time I thought it would be easier if you didn't know."

"Well, now you can just order me to do stuff, so it really doesn't matter."

Victor grinned, but she couldn't see it in the dark. He pulled her into his arms. "I'm sorry Yuri felt the need to discuss that with you. It's really none of his business, but I'm glad it's out in the open. Part of trusting each other is not having any secrets. That's why you should know I also hired a private investigator to find out more about you when we first met."

"No kidding. Well, that sure explains a lot."

They both laughed, but then Victor got serious. "You are okay in this relationship, aren't you, Abby?"

She didn't even hesitate. "Sure. I really enjoy spending time with you, even when it's at some fancy, stuffy, political ball."

"Good, because I enjoy spending time with you too. Fuck Yuri."

He started tickling her, and she squealed in delight.

"No, Dr. Turov. I would much rather fuck you," she teased. And that's exactly what she did.

Chapter Thirty-Five

The weather finally started to warm up in mid-April. The birds were singing, the flowers were blooming, and Abby had a bad case of spring fever. Her book was finished and had been sent off to the publisher. It was due out in the fall, and she wasn't ready to start on another one just yet. That meant she had a lot of free time on her hands.

Abby tried to stay busy, but Victor had nixed the few volunteer gigs she found any interest in. He claimed they were too dangerous. She was beginning to think the man thought everything was dangerous, and the thought irritated her. She was an adult, after all, and more than capable of taking care of herself.

To make matters worse, Abby's friends had just come back from their Cancun trip. They had been perfectly safe at the resort and regaled her with stories of their fun adventures. Abby felt completely left out and sorry for herself, and she was resenting Victor's control issues more and more. That's why when Lindsay called and invited her to go dancing at Club 9, she said yes.

It was a Thursday night, and Victor was tied up at the clinic with a valve replacement surgery. He had called earlier to tell her, and he had said he would call again the following morning. She still left her cell phone at home in case he checked the tracking app. She also tried to follow as many rules as possible. That meant the alarm was on, Vince was driving, and she would not be drinking. But there were plenty of other rules she was breaking. Abby rationalized her capricious behavior as an inevitable reaction to her controlling boyfriend. She also figured she could handle any punishment he dished out. Heck, they usually led to fabulous sex after, and that was worth the pain if nothing else.

The girls had a fabulous night. They danced their asses off and worked up quite a sweat. The club was packed, and the DJ was playing great music. It was just what Abby needed, and she sighed in contentment on the ride home.

Vince commented on how happy she looked in the car.

Abby smiled at him. "I forgot how much I like to dance!"

"Just be careful. Those places can be dangerous."

"You sound like Victor." Then she looked at him nervously. "Does he ever ask where you've taken me?"

Vince met her eyes in the rearview mirror. "No. Our arrangement is pretty casual. I just text him the total amount of time I spent driving at the end of each week, and he pays me an hourly rate. He also takes care of my gas and any repairs that need to be done on the car."

Abby sighed in relief. She was so used to Vince driving her, she had almost forgotten he worked for Victor.

As if reading her thoughts, Vince commented, "If he ever asked me for a list, though, I would give him one."

Abby nodded. It was a risk she hadn't considered, but Victor rarely changed his behavior, so she was probably in the clear.

Sure enough, when she got home she saw he hadn't called or texted. Abby went to bed feeling euphoric. She had pulled one over on Dr. Dictator, and she was surprised how much she liked it. She couldn't wait for the opportunity to do it again.

That chance didn't come for another two months. It was a warm Saturday night, and they were planning to go to an event at the zoo. They were finishing a late dinner at Abby's townhouse when Victor's pager went off. One of his patients had just been admitted and needed an emergency bypass procedure.

"I'm sorry, little one. This type of surgery will take at least four hours. It's going to be a late night for me. We'll have to cancel our plans."

Abby smiled. "That's okay. We can still go to the zoo tomorrow if you want."

He nodded and gave her a quick kiss. "Sounds good. Don't stay up too late."

Once he was gone, Abby debated what she should do. She really didn't feel like dancing, but it was rare to receive a get-out-of-jail-free card. She finally grabbed her phone to see what Lindsay was doing, and within an hour they had made plans to meet at Club 9. Kate was going to join them as well. She had finally broken it off with Yuri and wanted to vent.

Abby set up a ride with Vince and then ran to take a shower. She remembered how hot it was dancing the last time, so she put on a sports bra, tank top, mini skirt, and a pair of cute tennis shoes. She then tied her hair in two long pigtails and hurried out the door.

The girls met outside the club and only had to wait in line ten minutes. Once inside they discovered all the tables were taken. It didn't matter. None of them had brought purses, and they really weren't there to drink. They hit the dance floor instead and joined the mob moving as one to the beat of the music.

Meanwhile, Victor was about to head into surgery. He had already spoken to the patient, the family, and the team and was looking over the labs when a nurse called to say the patient had gone into cardiac arrest. Victor rushed in to find the anesthesiologist bagging, and another administering chest compressions. They suspected there was a rupture, so Victor quickly opened the patient up. He worked to contain the bleeding for quite some time before they finally gave up. Victor noted the time of death at 20:47 and looked sadly down at the woman. Then he went to clean up before breaking the news to her family.

An hour later and he was ready to leave the hospital. He had called Vince for a ride and was debating whether he should call Abby. It was getting late, but he realized he really wanted to see her. Losing a patient was awful, and normally Victor had to deal with it alone. This time he had someone to talk to and lean on. He slid into the backseat of the car and dialed Abby's number. She didn't pick up. Victor frowned at the phone and tried again.

"Home sir?" asked Vince.

"I'm not sure yet. I'm trying to reach Abby, but she's not answering."

"She probably can't hear her phone. I dropped her off at Club 9 over an hour ago. It gets pretty loud in there."

Victor was stunned. Surely he had heard wrong. "Did you say Club 9?"

The driver nodded.

Victor started cussing loudly in Russian. He could see the look of alarm on Vince's face and tried to rein in his anger. "I'm sorry. I don't want her going to that club, and she knows it!" Then he more calmly explained, "It's too dangerous."

Vince murmured, "It does tend to attract a gang element."

"Exactly. Looks like I'm going to Club 9, then." Victor pulled up his tracking app and plugged in her cell number. When he saw it was at her house, he had to physically stop himself from punching the seat. It would appear his sweet girlfriend was a lot less obedient than he had thought. This day kept getting worse and worse, and Victor felt his control slipping away. He couldn't save the patient, but he could damn well regain control of Abby.

While they drove, Victor thought about the punishment he would dish out. He knew it needed to be a lot tougher if he wanted her to stop this unacceptable behavior. He pinched the bridge of his nose and closed his eyes in frustration. Victor wasn't sure Abby could handle something rougher, and he knew it could send her running from their relationship.

He was still worrying about it when another thought occurred to him. He looked thoughtfully at Vince. "Tell me, has Abby had you drive her to Club 9 before?"

Vince met his eyes in the mirror and nodded.

Victor couldn't believe what he was hearing! He tried to remain calm as he asked, "How many times?"

"Just one other time. A couple months ago."

Victor sighed. "I think from now on we'll have you send me a text whenever you take her somewhere. Just a quick note about where you took her so I'll know. I'm very protective when it comes to Abby."

Vince nodded. "That's fine with me. Will you tell her?"

"Oh, I'll make sure she's well aware."

They pulled up at the entrance to the club and saw the long line. Victor was still wearing his scrubs and wondered if it would help his cause with the bouncer. Fortunately, Vince knew the security guard at the door and he was able to get him in immediately.

The place was mobbed. The music was so loud he could feel it thumping in his chest. The lights were dim, and it took him a moment to adjust. He scanned the tables looking for Abby but didn't see her. Then he headed to the dance floor and saw her in the corner. She was dancing with her two friends, but there were also several young men circling around. Victor's anger went to a white-hot rage when one of the men leaned in and attempted to put his hands on her hips.

Victor strode onto the dance floor, snaked his arm around Abby's waist, and pulled her up hard against his chest. She attempted to fight her way out of his arms until she realized who it was. Then she went very still. Her eyes widened in shock as she looked up at him.

Victor's eyes were so dark they were almost black. He looked furious, and she could feel the anger pouring off of him. He released her waist only to wrap his hand around her upper arm in a death grip. Then he turned around and marched her off of the dance floor and toward the exit without a word. Abby gave Lindsay and Kate a quick wave goodbye as she hurried to keep up with him.

At the door, he stopped and looked down at her. "Do you have everything? Did you bring a purse or a coat?" His voice was clipped.

Abby was breathless from dancing. "No. Neither."

He nodded and whirled back around to lead her out of the club. Vince was parked a few feet away. Victor guided her to the car and opened the door for her. As she went to get in, their eyes met, and for the first time, Abby felt afraid. She had never seen that look on his face before.

Once she was in, Victor slid in beside her. All he said was, "Put your seat belt on." Then to Vince, he said, "Abby's place first, Vince. We need to pick up her phone." He glanced pointedly down at her.

They rode to the townhouse in silence. She considered asking him about the surgery, but instead, she stared at her lap. Her skirt was shorter than she thought, and she hoped he didn't notice. When he reached his hand over and rested it on her thigh, she knew he had, and she realized just how much trouble she was in.

At the townhouse, Victor went to walk toward the porch, but Abby stopped him. "I didn't bring my keys," she shakily explained. She walked over to the garage and punched in the code on the panel. He didn't comment but waited with her for the door to raise up. Once they were in the house, Abby started walking up the stairs to get her phone. Suddenly she felt Victor's arm around her waist again. He lifted her effortlessly and carried her to the kitchen. Then he set her down in front of the alarm system. It wasn't on.

"Are you fucking kidding me with this?!" he shouted.

Abby looked at the panel and then closed her eyes as if in pain.

Victor tugged on a pigtail so she opened her eyes and looked up at him. His voice was now eerily quiet. "I want you to go upstairs, get your phone, and pack a bag."

"Victor, I—"

He cut her off. "We have much to discuss, but we will do it at my place. Now go!"

Abby hurried up the stairs and grabbed her phone. It had blown up from all the texts Lindsay and Kate had sent her. They had seen the look on Victor's face and were worried. She sent them each a reassuring response and then grabbed her bag. She threw random things in but wasn't paying much attention. Her mind was racing with what she would tell him. She really had no excuse for her behavior other than being tired of his rules. Somehow she didn't think that would go over well.

As she turned to leave the room, she saw Victor towering in the doorway. A chill ran up her spine. He took her bag and then followed her down the stairs. On the way out, Victor set the alarm. He then guided her to the car. Once inside they sat in silence, and Abby tried to calm herself. He was scaring her, but deep down she knew she trusted him. She breathed deeply and thought about what she should say.

The ride was over too quickly, and before Abby knew it she was in Victor's condo and sitting on his couch. She watched as he went to the kitchen to get a drink.

Victor considered pouring himself a bourbon, but he knew he needed to keep a cool head. Instead, he filled two large tumblers with water and brought them back to the couch. He handed one to Abby and then sat down next to her. She was staring at her lap and wasn't saying anything, and he could see the slight tremble. He clasped her chin and turned her head. She still wouldn't look at him.

"Look at me, Abby."

When she did, he started his questions. "Did your friends call you after I left, or did you call them?"

"I called them." Her voice faltered at the end.

Victor scowled. "So this was pre-meditated." He noted she wasn't looking at him again. "Eyes on me, baby. Did you drink?"

"No."

"Good. Did you know those men that were dancing with you?"

She rolled her eyes. "They were hardly men. They didn't look old enough to be in there."

He grabbed a pigtail and yanked it hard. In a tight voice, he said, "Do *not* challenge me right now. Just answer the fucking question!"

Her eyes watered, and in a small voice, she said, "No. We didn't know them."

He nodded and released her hair. "They may have been young, but one was still man enough to try to put his hands all over you."

Abby didn't say anything. She was wringing her own hands

nervously in her lap and trying not to cry.

Victor took a sip of his water while he thought about things. Then he looked at her and said, "Let's count off the rules and see how many you broke, shall we? That way I know how many times I need to hit you."

Abby gasped.

"You broke rule one when you danced with another man." He held up his left thumb. "Then from rule two you did not get permission to go out with your friends, left your phone at home, and did not turn your house alarm on." He held up three fingers, one at a time. His voice was getting harsher. "Then from rule three you blatantly disobeyed me by going to Club 9." He held up his last finger. "That's five hits, Abby." His voice was ominous. "Am I forgetting anything?"

There was a flash of anger in her eyes, but then she meekly said, "No."

Victor took another sip of his water before looking back at her again. "Good. Now tell me, have you done this before?"

Abby bit her lip and then nodded.

Part of him was relieved at her honesty, but part of him was furious. "How many times?" he asked in a tight voice.

"Just once," she whispered.

"And did you dance with men then?"

She nodded.

"Did you leave your phone at home then?"

She nodded again.

"Was your alarm on the last time?"

Abby frowned. "I'm pretty sure it was. That's usually a habit with me. I was rushing tonight and forgot."

Victor blew out his breath and then held up the four fingers on his right hand as well. "That's nine hits, baby. Do I need to add any more?"

She hurriedly shook her head no.

"Okay, then. Let's move on to the why. Why did you feel the need to blatantly defy me?" His voice was deceptively quiet again.

Abby shrugged. "I don't know."

"Oh, I think you do. And one way or another you're going to tell me. Now I can certainly punish it out of you, but I would much rather hear it now while I'm calm."

She looked at him, rubbed her eyes, and then looked away. "I guess I was willing to take the risk. I figured I could handle the punishment if I got caught."

Victor sighed. "I am partially to blame for that. I've been going way too easy on you. I wanted to introduce you into this lifestyle slowly, so you could get used to it. I didn't want to scare you away." He leaned in and whispered in her ear, "But that's about to change. Now tell me the real reason why, or I will continue to hit you until you do. And baby, it's going to hurt!"

Abby surprised herself when she turned and looked him straight in the eye. She was scared by his threat but also angry, "Because I think your rules are stupid! Usually, I don't mind them, but sometimes they make me really mad!" Then she added more calmly, "When I didn't get caught the first time I felt a huge rush. I don't know. It was exciting to get away with it. But I also felt a thrill at what would happen if I did get caught." She blew out her breath and looked away again in embarrassment.

Victor thought about what she had said and smiled. The first part made him angry as hell, but the second part sounded very much like what a sub would say if she was bored or feeling neglected by her Dom. It gave him hope.

"I see. Well, let me explain something to you. We are in a Dominant/submissive relationship. I'm the Dominant, and you're the submissive. That means I don't give a *fuck* what you think of my rules! Your only job is to obey them without question. When you don't, I will punish you. And from now on it's going to hurt like hell!"

She glared at him.

"You can be mad all you want, little one, but I will always be in control."

"And I have no say whatsoever?"

"None."

"Do you hear how barbaric that sounds?"

"Certainly. That's because it is barbaric. Now you're getting the full picture. But I think we've done enough talking. It's time for me to show you exactly what I mean." Victor stood up and pulled her off the couch. Then he led her into the kitchen area. "Arms up," he commanded, and his voice sent a shiver up her spine.

She lifted her arms without hesitation, and he pulled her tank top off. Then he laughed at her sports bra before unzipping it.

"What? I was dancing. That's a lot like a workout," she explained. There was a trace of a smile on her lips.

"You weren't wearing much, were you?" Now he looked pissed again.

"I get really hot and sweaty when I dance."

He ignored her comment and instead commanded, "Kneel."

Abby knelt down on the ground and looked up at him. She was naked from the waist up, and her pigtails were hanging down either side of her face. They were brushing the tips of her breasts, and she looked like a contrite little schoolgirl.

"Stay." He walked away and into the bedroom. When he returned, he was carrying some twine and a long white rod. He had her lift her hands and tied her wrists together with the twine. The rough edges were cutting into her skin.

"I think we're done with padded cuffs for a while, don't you?" Before she could answer, he placed the white rod in her hands and told her to hold it on her lap. "This is called a cane," he explained.

Abby stared down at it doubtfully. It didn't look that menacing to her.

Victor went into the living room and turned the couch so the back was facing out. Then he walked over and helped Abby to a standing position. He took the cane from her, led her over to the couch, and bent her over the back of it. She had to stand on her tippy toes to keep her balance. Victor flipped her skirt up and pulled her panties down and off. Then he rubbed her rear end with his palm and quietly explained, "Our goal is nine hits. If it gets to be too much, tell me to stop, and I will. Do you understand?"

"Yes," she whispered.

Victor took a deep breath. Then he pulled his arm back all the way like he was swinging a tennis racket and brought the cane down forcefully on her ass. It made a loud thwack, and Abby was so startled she cried out. He ignored her. "That's one," was all he said.

Victor pulled his arm back again and hit her directly below the last hit. The pain was so intense that Abby's eyes immediately began to water. She was breathing fast and trying to get her bearings. She vaguely heard Victor say, "That's two."

On the third hit, Abby began to cry. The pain was incredible and like nothing she had ever felt before. Bright red and vicious looking welts were forming on her ass, but he didn't stop. Hits four and five alternated between her upper thighs and her ass. By this time Abby was sobbing, and snot was dripping from her nose.

Victor hesitated. When she didn't say anything, he hit her again.

He wasn't bringing the cane down nearly as hard, but he knew at this point it didn't matter. It would still feel like hell to her.

"Please stop!" she finally called out, and he immediately dropped the cane. It clattered loudly on the floor.

"Okay, little one, no more. But I still need to punish you. I'm going to fuck you instead, and I don't want you to cum. This is about punishment, and you are not to gain any pleasure from this, do you understand?"

She sobbed out a yes, and he gently inserted a finger into her vagina. She was barely wet, so he began to massage her opening and clit. Eventually, she was wet enough for him to enter. As he slid in, he grasped her hips and pulled her back against his pelvis. Victor moved slowly at first and gradually built up momentum. He knew she was at her breaking point, so he tried to get off as quickly as possible. After the punishment he had just given her, it shouldn't be a problem. His cock was stiff and ready.

Meanwhile, Abby felt like her ass was on fire. Her mind was numb from what had just happened, but she vaguely registered Victor was fucking her from behind. She felt helpless, humiliated, and totally at his mercy. Then she realized with alarm she was also starting to feel aroused.

Abby knew he had told her not to cum. She fought the building sensation in her pelvic region as best she could, but she soon realized she wasn't going to be able to stop an orgasm. She clamped her mouth shut tightly and tried not to breathe as her stomach tightened. She came at the exact same moment he did, and she prayed he hadn't noticed.

When he was done, Victor pulled out and then helped her to stand up straight. He led her by the arm to the master bathroom to show her the welts on her backside. They were bright red and ugly.

His voice was harsh. "This is what happens when you defy me!"

Abby began to cry again while he untied her hands. He ignored her tears and said, "Brush your teeth, use the toilet, put on your pajamas, and then get into bed. I'll be in soon."

Once he left the room, she stared at her reflection. She wasn't sure she recognized the person in the mirror. She also hadn't recognized her boyfriend. Gone was the teasing, protective man she knew to be replaced by a tightly controlled and furious stranger. Upon further thought, Abby realized he had always been there, had even warned her of this side of him, but she had chosen to ignore his warnings. Now she knew.

Abby snapped out of her reverie and hurried to follow his orders. When she sat on the toilet, the pain from where he hit her was bad, and she ended up having to squat. She realized there was no way she could sleep on her back, so she crawled into bed and lay face down on her belly. She turned her head so it was facing away from Victor's side. She couldn't stop the tears from flowing, and she hoped he would leave her alone when he came to bed.

Meanwhile, Victor had gone out and put the living room back in order. He gathered her clothes and the cane and set them on the breakfast nook. Then he poured himself a bourbon and thought about what had occurred. He was still angry at her behavior, but the punishment had helped. It had gone better than he thought it would, and he was proud of how many hits she had taken. He knew she would not disobey him like that again for a very long time, and he started to relax. He also realized he could trust her to stop him when he got too rough. It was another turning point in their relationship.

Victor finished his bourbon and went into the bedroom. He could see she was already in bed. He went to use the bathroom, brushed his teeth, and then grabbed some salve from the medicine cabinet. Victor stripped down and got into bed. Then he reached over to pull the covers off of Abby. He explained, "I'm going to put something on your backside. It will make it feel a little better and will help the healing process." He gently reached into her pajama bottoms and started to rub in the salve.

She didn't say a word, and he could hear an occasional quiet sniffle.

When he was done, Victor pulled the covers back over her, kissed the top of her head, and shut the lights off. Then he lay down and waited. He knew she needed to process what had occurred, and he gave her time instead of trying to force a conversation. Fifteen minutes had gone by and she still hadn't said a word, but he could hear her sniffling. That made him feel bad, which in turn made him angry.

"I make no apologies. You knew the rules and broke them."

She started to cry harder.

"This is as bad as it gets, Abby. If you can handle this, then you can handle me."

The crying continued, and Victor ran his hand through his hair in frustration.

"You're still here. You could leave at any time. Why are you still here if it's so bad?"

He heard her whisper in the dark, "Because I love you."

Victor's heart melted. He had suspected as much, but to hear her say it made him all warm and glowing inside. "I love you too, little one." Then he asked with a smile, "Did you cum?"

Abby's voice quivered. "Ye-es. I'm sorry. My vagina has a mind of its own."

He laughed. "My penis does too. It's why they get along so well."

She started to laugh, but then her voice broke into a sob.

Victor was distraught. "I don't understand why you're still crying. Are you hurting that badly?" He didn't think he had hit her that hard, but maybe he had.

"No."

"Then what's upsetting you?"

She rolled over to face him and winced in pain as her backside hit the mattress. "Am I a masochist? How could I like sex after that?"

Victor sighed in relief as he realized she was still processing. "No, little one. You hated that punishment. You were barely wet when I touched you. Your body was just responding to mine. I told you, they like each other." Then he added. "You're not a masochist, you're a submissive. A submissive does not necessarily like pain, but they'll put up with it when someone else has taken control and is leading them."

Abby thought about it and hoped he was right. She moved closer and snuggled into him, and Victor threw his arm over her. Then she asked about his patient, and he realized how much she cared. He told her what had happened at the hospital and how it made him feel, and she listened with compassion. They fell asleep facing each other, and that warm connection they always had grew more intense.

The next morning Abby woke feeling wonderful. Her ass still hurt like hell, but she felt like she had shed a huge burden. She commented on it to Victor while he was brushing his teeth. He spit in the sink and then grinned at her. "That's normal. You will always feel wonderful after a good hard punishment."

She shook her head in disbelief and headed to the kitchen. She decided to make breakfast and looked to see what was available. Eggs and toast would have to do, and she pulled a frying pan out while turning on the coffee maker for Victor. He came out and sat at the breakfast nook to read the paper, and she brought him a cup of coffee. When the food was ready he motioned her to sit.

"I'm going to stand. It hurts to sit."

"No," he sternly replied. "You will sit. You are still being punished."

She gaped at him as he pulled out the stool. As she gingerly sat down, she could feel the pain shoot through her backside and winced.

Victor murmured. "You're in pain because I punished you, Abby. And why did I punish you?"

"Because I disobeyed you."

"And will you do it again?"

She pressed her lips together. "I'll try not to."

He laughed at her honesty. "Good."

They ate in companionable silence, and when they were done Abby cleared the dishes. Victor motioned her back to his side but let her stand as he put his arm around her.

"You have two new rules we need to discuss. Do you want to do that now or wait until after church?"

Abby squirmed in his arms. There was no way she wanted to go to church with all that sitting, standing, and kneeling. She tentatively suggested they skip mass.

Victor frowned and thought about it. "That's fine, but I don't want you to make a habit of it. Our relationship should not be interfering with your faith."

When she nodded, he continued. "From now on Vince is going to text and let me know where he's taking you. If you're driving, then I want you to do the same. I need to know your location at all times."

She wondered what Vince had made of that. Abby didn't have time to worry, though, as Victor's next rule was a bombshell.

"I also don't want you living in the townhouse anymore. That neighborhood is dangerous, and I can't trust you to leave the alarm on."

She gaped at him. "Are you serious?"

"Very. I warned you this would happen if you forgot to set that alarm, but you didn't listen to me."

"It was an honest mistake. Everyone forgets something like that once in a while. I bet even you would forget!"

"And your point is?"

"You can't just force me out of my house, Victor."

"Oh, but I can. And the sooner you understand that, the better. Again, I'm not forcing you to stay in this relationship. If you can't live by my rules and want out, just say the word."

Her eyes welled up with tears. "Do you want me to break up with you?"

He looked startled and put his arms around her. "God, no. I told you last night, I love you, Abby. That's why I have to keep you safe."

She wiped her eyes in relief. "Where am I supposed to live?"

"Well, we can shop for a place that's in a safer neighborhood if you like. Or your other option is to move in here with me." He added, "Of the two I would prefer you live here. But I'm not going to force you."

She thought about it. "It would be nice if you wanted to live with me, Victor, not because of your need to control me, but because you really wanted me here."

He looked confused. "I can control you from anywhere, baby. There are Doms thousands of miles away from their subs that do it all the time. I really want you to live with me. I think it would be nice."

She thought about it some more. "Have you ever lived with someone? Because it changes things, you know."

He shrugged. "I never have, aside from my parents and a few college roommates. I'm sure we would adapt. We get along pretty well together."

Abby was still thinking. "And will there be more rules once I live here?"

He had noticed she used the word 'once' but didn't comment. Instead, he said, "I'm not sure what you mean."

"Nate insisted I take care of certain household tasks. He used to get really angry when I would forget them."

Victor rubbed his chin in thought. "Well, I have a housekeeper. But I like the idea of you having chores. It would emphasize my dominance over you. Let me think about it."

Abby went to shower and change. She faced the water from the front only. Her backside was just too sore. Once she was ready, she went back out and heard Victor on the phone. He was talking to his real estate agent. When he hung up, he informed her they were meeting the man in an hour to discuss the sale of her townhouse. Victor went to take a shower, and Abby stood looking out the back windows at Lake Erie. Everything was moving so fast. She was stunned by the turn of events over the past eight months, but she knew deep down she wanted to live with Victor.

Soon they were at her townhouse and talking to the realtor. Abby was shocked at the value of her home, as it had gone up quite a bit. The man suggested an asking price and also told her how to stage the place. She would need to remove some of the furniture.

Once he was gone, Victor smiled at her and suggested she pack more of her clothes. He explained, "You will need to live with me until you make a decision either way. It will be a good test run for us."

She agreed and went to grab a suitcase. "What am I going to do with all my furniture?"

He thought about it. "Some of it we'll have to store, but a lot of it will fit in my condo. I have an entire spare bedroom that's empty, and I like your kitchen table a lot better than mine. We can figure out what to bring and what to store."

She looked at him and sighed. "That's assuming I move in permanently."

"It is. But I've always been an optimist."

They took quite a few of her things back to his place, and she began to unpack. While she was arranging her closet in the master bedroom, Victor came in and lounged on the bed. He had a huge grin on his face.

She noticed and laughed. "What?"

"Nothing. I was just thinking I could get used to this."

Abby smiled and continued to put her clothes away.

"If it helps your decision, little one, I've thought about what household chores I would assign if you choose to live here permanently."

She looked over her shoulder and raised one eyebrow at him. "Oh?"

"Yes. For starters, you would be in charge of changing the sheets every time we mess them up."

Abby gave him a wry smile.

He went on. "If we use any toys, you'll be the one to clean them and put them away."

She shook her head in amusement. "You have a one-track mind!"

"Not at all. I also want you to pack my lunch every day and make sure the coffee pot is set-up and ready to go. I know you're an expert at that."

Abby rolled her eyes.

"You would also be required to cook dinner three nights a week. Maybe we can enroll in one of those programs where they ship the ingredients and recipes to you. I rather like when you cook for me." He thought some more, "Oh, and it will be your job to get the mail from the lobby. Every time I go down there I get accosted by a pack of sickly old people and all their inane health questions."

Abby laughed as she tried to picture that. "Okay, those all seem reasonable. Anything else?"

Victor shook his head no. "I think that's more than enough, don't you? I plan to keep my housekeeper, Mrs. Sokolov. She comes in once a week to clean the place and prep meals. I'll tell her you're moving in, and the two of you can discuss the menu. I think you'll like her."

Abby glared at him. "Let me guess. She's super-hot and you make her dress in a French maid costume."

Victor laughed. "Not if I want to live. She's a tough old Russian woman, and she would beat me with a rolling pin if I ever got out of line."

"Oh. I think I love her already!"

They both laughed.

Victor went to leave the room. "And Abby?"

She looked up.

"I've decided these chores go into effect now. It will give you good practice for when you decide to make it permanent." He winked at her.

Later that night Victor's phone started to ring, but he was in Abby's closet trying to hang her jewelry safe. He yelled for her to grab the phone.

When she did, Yuri was on the other line. He was momentarily startled to hear her voice. "Well, hello Abby. How are you this evening?"

She made a face. "Pretty good, Yuri. How about you? I heard you and Kate aren't seeing each other anymore."

He laughed. "No, that ended last weekend. I told you it was a doomed relationship."

She commiserated and then handed the phone over to Victor.

The two began talking, and Abby went back to the kitchen to put more of her things away.

"What's up, Kopyev?" Victor asked.

"Nothing. Just calling to check in. I'm surprised Abby is there so late on a Sunday night."

"Don't be. She just moved in. We're going to try living together."

Yuri was stunned. "What? When did that happen?"

Victor explained the events of yesterday.

"And your logical solution was to force her to move in? God, what the hell are you doing to her?"

Victor was pissed. "I didn't force her. She chose to move in. It was either that or find a new place to live in a safer neighborhood. She may still go that route, too, but for now, she will live with me." He went on in a snarky voice, "And for the record, her punishment was a strong beating with a cane followed by a hard ramming from behind. Tell me she's not a submissive when she could take that and still cum!"

Yuri sought for words to calm down his friend. "Okay. That's good. Just be careful with her, Victor. She's a nice girl."

"Is that why you told her about the blood draw, asshole?"

Yuri was surprised. "Oh, so she told you. I didn't think she would. And yes, I was just trying to protect her. I am concerned with where this relationship is going. She needs to know exactly what you're capable of now, Victor, so she can make a fair choice."

"Mind your own business, Yuri! I will handle Abby as I see fit. And if I catch you telling her any more pertinent details about me or my lifestyle I will kick your fucking ass!"

Yuri sighed and hung up the phone. He knew Victor would eventually calm down and forgive him. He always did. What worried Yuri was his own growing interest in Abby. He was now sporting a serious hard-on just thinking about her being caned and fucked. He knew it was wrong, but that didn't stop him from putting his hand down his pants to rub one out. Abby was fast becoming his favorite fantasy and he didn't fight it.

Meanwhile, Victor had slammed the phone down on the dresser. He took some deep breaths and then went in search of his girlfriend. She was curled up on her side on the couch reading a book. She hadn't noticed him come in, and he realized she hadn't heard the argument on the phone either. Victor caught the same air of vulnerability surrounding her as he had that first night in the hospital. It gave him pause. What the fuck was he doing to her? Was Yuri right? He just didn't know. What he did know was he was incapable of stopping. She was his, and he intended to keep her.

Chapter Thirty-Six

Domestic life suited Victor. He liked coming home to a warm body every night, and the added control he gained over Abby was an unexpected bonus. It had been three months since she had moved in, and she had all but forgotten about looking for a new place to live. The two had quickly and easily settled into living together.

Each morning they got up and worked out. Then Victor showered and got ready for work while Abby fixed breakfast and got his lunch ready. The two would sit side by side at the breakfast nook, eat, and discuss their schedules for the day.

Once the dishes were cleared, Abby grabbed a shower while Victor lay out the clothes he wanted her to wear. It was a rule he had started a month ago when he punished her for repeatedly forgetting the mail. He had sent her down to the lobby that night in heels, one of his t-shirts, and nothing else. The shirt had barely covered her ass, and she had returned completely mortified. That emotion quickly turned to passion when he lifted the shirt and banged her on the kitchen table. Now he chose all her outfits, which suited the fashion-inept Abby just fine.

After Victor left for work, the day was basically hers. They still maintained their lunchtime phone call, but the rest of the day she could do what she wanted. It was much like her life had been before she moved in. Abby read books, wrote, shopped for groceries, and volunteered when she could. Victor's only requirement was she be home when he got there after work, but he always gave fair warning of when that would be.

Lately, Abby had been doing a lot of volunteer work. She had found some fundraising activities close to home that were interesting but also met his safety requirements. They were taking up more and more of her day, though, and Victor was starting to notice. He had discussed it with her several times before, and now he was commenting on it again over breakfast.

"Your schedule is getting busy, little one. Are you sure you can handle it?"

She looked up from her oatmeal and gave him a reassuring nod. "The ALS one is going to finish up tomorrow."

He frowned. "You still have a lot of other projects on your plate, and you seem to be stressed out. I don't like it."

Now he had her attention. "I'm still getting all of my chores done."

"You are, but I am more concerned about your health than the chores. Make sure you take time to relax."

She sighed, as she had heard the threat in his voice. "Okay. I'll do my yoga workout later on this afternoon. That always helps."

He gave her a kiss on the forehead. "Good. I'll see you tonight."

Once he was gone, Abby went about her day. She had two volunteer events in the morning and also had to pick up some dry cleaning. Then she had the lunchtime call with Victor, another volunteer gig in the afternoon, and a ride out to a vendor to pick up some raffle items. When she got home she would have to squeeze in the yoga workout before cooking dinner. It was busy, but she was confident she could get it all done.

She didn't. It was one of those days where nothing went as planned. Both morning volunteer events ran over, and Abby didn't have the heart to sneak out early. That meant she had to skip the dry cleaners. Then in the afternoon, she was guilted into doing more work for the ALS foundation. She knew Victor would not be pleased, but at least it was data entry that could be done at home. Abby would discuss it with him over dinner. She also needed to tell him about the barrage of phone messages coming in from her in-laws. She hadn't listened to them per his instruction, but the worry of what they might say caused her even more stress.

When Abby finally got home, it was late afternoon. She changed her clothes, popped the yoga DVD in, and halfheartedly did the moves. By the time she reached the Shavasana pose, she was so tired she fell asleep. Victor's text woke her up. He was letting her know he was on his way home.

Abby rushed to get up and put away her yoga mat. Then she got dressed, brushed her teeth, and ran down to the lobby to get the mail. When she returned, she hurried into the kitchen to start dinner. A quick perusal of the fridge showed her there wasn't time to make any of the pre-packaged meal kits from Home Chef. They were starting to stack up, and she noticed one had already expired.

Abby opened the freezer and pulled out one of the ready-made meals Mrs. Sokolov had left for them. She popped it in the microwave to defrost. Then she threw it in the oven and started to make the salad. She was still chopping vegetables when she heard the key in the lock.

Victor walked in, and as usual, the sight of him lifted her heart. Abby went to greet him and take his lunch cooler. He pulled her into his arms for a deep kiss and noted the lines of strain on her face. Her hair was also messy, but she still looked lovely.

Victor went to change and saw the mail neatly stacked on the dresser. That was good, but then he realized the dry cleaning was not hanging in the closet.

When he joined her in the kitchen, Abby was just plating the salad. He went to the fridge to get the dressing and noticed the Home Chef boxes. One of them was expired. He looked at his girlfriend thoughtfully.

Over dinner, they discussed their days. Abby quickly told him about the in-law calls. He took her phone, listened to the messages, and then deleted them. He told her, "I will take care of this. You will need to give me their address."

"Okay. My address book is in the desk drawer. But what did they want?"

He shook his head. "I told you they were my problem now. I don't want you worrying about it, understood?"

"Yes, but—"

"No buts, Abby. We are done discussing this."

She sighed and stared down at her plate. She hated when he shut her out like this. Now she didn't want to bring up the ALS project, but she knew she had to get his permission. She waited until he seemed more affable and then broached the subject.

His scowl was immediate. "Absolutely not."

"Why?"

"I don't have to give you a reason."

"But my other project is done tomorrow. I should have plenty of time, plus I can do it from home." She could hear the whine in her own voice and hated him for it.

Victor looked at her skeptically. "Really? If you have plenty of time, why is it we keep eating Mrs. Sokolov's meals while the Home Chef boxes are expiring in our refrigerator?"

She didn't say anything.

He went on. "And where is our dry cleaning? I believe you were going to pick it up today, but I don't see it hanging in the closet."

Abby sighed. The man missed nothing.

Victor stood and took his plate to the sink. Then he leaned down and clasped her face in both his hands. "I don't give a rat's ass about the chores, baby, but I do care about you. If you don't slow down, you're going to make yourself sick." He left the room to go handle the Shea issue, and Abby was left to stare at her plate.

Victor did some searching online and found the number for Adult Protective Services down in the Tampa area. He then dialed and reported the elderly couple were living in an unsafe environment. By law, APS had to go out and investigate within twenty-four hours. At the least, they would get the water turned back on, which was why the Sheas had called. Victor was hoping APS would do more than that, though, and would get them some badly needed care. The social worker assured him they would call back after their visit. He would know then if he needed to do anything more.

Abby was curled up on the couch when he came back out. Victor sat next to her and wrapped his arm around her shoulders. He explained the Shea issue had been handled, but she knew better than to ask for details. They settled down to watch the news, and Abby kept stifling her yawns. Victor noticed and finally put her to bed at nine. She was so tired, she didn't even protest.

The next morning, they were up at their usual time. Abby worried Victor would do something about her busy schedule, but he never brought it up. Even when they discussed their agendas for the day, he didn't bat an eye. She went to take her shower in relief. She knew she needed to slow down, and once she finished these commitments, she promised herself she would cut back.

Abby got out of the shower and went to get dressed. Victor always lay her clothes out on the chair by the bathroom door. There was a silk teddy laying on the armrest. She pulled it on, and the navy material clung to her body. The front was cut tight and low, so the fullness of her breasts was on display. The back rode up almost like a thong, and her firm ass cheeks were peeking out from the bottom. The fabric was soft and comfortable, and Abby felt sexy as she looked in the mirror.

Then she realized there was nothing else on the chair.

She went in search of Victor. He was slugging down the last of his coffee and packing his briefcase. He looked at her and smiled as he took in the view. Then he opened his arms wide and pulled her in for a bear hug. His left hand quickly found a breast while his right hand roamed further south. Reluctantly he pulled away.

As he was leaving, Abby remembered she needed clothes. "Victor, you forgot to put out my clothes for today."

He looked down at her and fingered the silky material. "What are you talking about, silly? You're wearing some lovely clothes."

She teased. "I suppose I could wear this in public. But then I might get arrested."

His face suddenly got serious. "Sounds like you have a problem because this is all you're allowed to wear today." There was steel in his voice.

Abby looked up at him in confusion. Then she realized what he meant. "But I have to deliver gifts to the fundraiser today. They're in my car."

There was no sympathy in his voice. "I told you to slow down. Now you will be forced to do as I say."

Victor walked toward the door, and Abby followed him. Without those gifts, the fundraiser would be a disaster. She pleaded with him. "Please, Victor. Just let me drop the stuff off. Then I promise I'll come home and wear nothing but this all day long."

Now he was pissed. He grabbed her by the arms and leaned her up against the door. "I have tried to be patient, Abby, but now I am done! You will stay here. You will also call each and every one of those damn volunteer groups and quit them for good." His hands were still holding her arms up against the door as he leaned in to kiss her. When he was done, he sucked on her lower lip and then bit down on it. As she gasped, he continued, "When I call at lunchtime, I expect you to have canceled all of your obligations, do you understand?"

She nodded.

"Good. Tonight when I get home we will also be refreshing your memory on obedience." He gave her a teasing smack on the ass and left for work.

Abby pounded her fists on the door in frustration. She tried to stay mad at him, but she knew he had given her plenty of warning. She really had no one to blame for this but herself. Instead of wallowing, she decided to concentrate on the fundraiser dilemma instead. One option was to just throw on some clothes and go. Abby knew she could never do that, though, as her need to obey was getting stronger by the day. Another option was to call Vince and see if he could deliver the gifts. That had potential, but then she realized Vince would see how she was dressed. She flushed in embarrassment at the thought.

Abby realized she needed a woman's help with her problem, and so turned to her friends. She texted them one by one to see if anyone was off. She got lucky when Lindsay responded. She had worked a double-shift at the hospital the night before and was home. Abby quickly called and begged her to make the delivery. Lindsay agreed and would be over in less than an hour. In the meantime, Abby got busy and started calling the volunteer organizations to quit. She was met with astonished disbelief on each call, and the clinic woman tried everything in her power to get Abby to stay.

By the time Lindsay showed up, Abby was exhausted from all the confrontational calls. She opened the door and then realized she had forgotten to warn her friend about the teddy. Lindsay took it in and then started laughing.

"Oh my god, Abs! Are you trying to hit on me, or is Victor coming home for a nooner?"

Abby laughed in spite of herself. She wouldn't put it past the bastard. It would be his way of assuring she obeyed orders. But she simply said, "Sorry. I forgot to warn you. Victor and I are in the middle of something."

She gave her friend the spare set of keys to her car along with the address to the ALS headquarters. Then she thanked Lindsay profusely, shut the door, and sank down on the couch in relief. She had two hours before Victor's phone call, and she thought about what to do. Before she knew it, Abby was sound asleep on the couch.

The ringing phone woke her up. Victor immediately honed in on the sleep in her voice. "Did I wake you?"

She yawned and sat up. "You did. Sorry. Guess I needed a nap."

He nodded in satisfaction. "Mmm hmm. And how did you make out with your phone calls?"

She explained she had quit all of her volunteer jobs. She also told him about Lindsay and the hard time the clinic woman had given her.

Victor was pleased. "Ah. Glad to hear you figured a way out of your problem. And I know all about that bitch from the clinic. She had the nerve to call me here to see if I could persuade you to stay. How she knew we were a couple is beyond me."

Abby laughed. "I used you as a reference, remember? They were very picky about who they accepted to volunteer. Glad to know she is going to miss me, though."

"Maybe when things settle down I'll let you pick one to go back to. No more than that, though. You clearly cannot handle it."

Abby apologized. "I know. I'm sorry I didn't slow down when you asked me to. Sometimes I get caught up in things and forget to take it easy. I do the same with my writing."

He was pleased by the apology. "Glad to hear you say it, little one, but you are still going to be punished."

"Yes, doctor," she said in a sultry voice. "Would you like me in any particular position when you get home from work?"

Victor was hard instantly. It always amazed him the effect she could have with just a look or a few simple words. He decided to make her squirm. "Why, yes. I think I would like you kneeling at the front door. Make sure your hair is up, and take the black belt from my closet. I want to see you holding it in your lap when I arrive."

She nervously agreed, and their conversation moved on to more mundane topics.

Abby spent the rest of the day putzing around the house. She watered the plants, organized her work area, cleaned out the fridge, and prepared one of the Home Chef meals. She covered it with Saran wrap to pop in the microwave later. She knew dinner would be the last thing on Victor's mind when he got home, and she wiggled in anticipation of what was to come.

Abby was now somewhat fearful of all his punishments, and a belt was an entity she hadn't encountered before. But she knew she trusted the man, and she was at least grateful he hadn't asked for a cane. In truth, she was more excited to learn what he had in store for her than afraid.

She was just sitting down to enjoy a cup of tea when her phone rang. She looked at the number but didn't recognize it. Abby hesitated. It could be one of the volunteer coordinators calling. Then she decided even the clinic woman wouldn't have the nerve, and she picked up the line.

Yuri was on the other end.

Abby glared at the phone. She didn't know why he made her so uncomfortable.

"Heh, Yuri," she said. "How are you?"

He could hear the reserve in her voice. "I'm good, thanks. Sorry to bother you. Kate gave me your number. I've been trying to reach Victor, but he hasn't picked up."

"Oh. He's doing surgeries today, so he's probably away from his phone. He should be done by four if you want to try him again after that."

Yuri chose not to tell her he'd been calling his friend for three months now. It was unlike Victor to hold onto anger this long, and he was starting to miss the man. He was also curious how they were getting on with their relationship.

"Okay. And how are you doing? Have you adjusted to living with Victor?"

Abby smiled. "Yes. It was a lot easier than I thought it would be. We get along well together."

"Mmm hmm. And how are you adjusting to his control issues?"

She quickly replied, "Fine," but there was a hint of discomfort in her voice.

"There's no need to be embarrassed, Abby. I'm a psychiatrist. Plus, I am well aware of Victor's tastes when it comes to sex. I just want to be sure you can handle it. Tell me, has he used any tools on you yet?"

Abby was stunned. It was an inappropriate question and none of his business. She tersely replied, "I really don't want to talk about that."

Yuri tutted at her. "It's okay. I know you're new to all of this, and I assure you I am only looking out for your well-being. Sex with a Dom can be a scary thing. Please know you can always call me if you need to talk to someone. There is nothing you would say that would shock me."

Abby was embarrassed and angry. The whole submissive thing was a sore topic for her, and it was like he was subtly trying to break them up.

Her tone was abrupt. "I need to hang up now. I have to get dinner ready."

"Please don't be angry. I am your friend in all of this. I hope you keep my number. And there's no need to tell Victor I called. I'll catch up with him later."

They hung up, and Abby stared at the phone. She had no idea what that had been about, but the entire conversation left a sour taste in her mouth.

At five o'clock sharp Victor walked through the front door. He was home earlier than usual, and she wondered if the thought of punishment had rushed him home. She was waiting exactly as he had asked, and he set the briefcase down and grinned. Victor had carried the image of her in that sexy teddy with him all day long. Now seeing the belt in her lap and the flush on her cheeks sent his libido into overdrive.

He squatted down and stroked her cheek. Then he took the belt from her hands and wrapped it around her neck. He looped the end through the buckle but did not cinch the tongue into a hole. Instead, he stood up and pulled on the belt. It tightened around her neck like a leash, and she looked up at him in shock. He started to walk and had her follow on all fours behind as he pulled on the belt. Victor led her to the side of a chair and told her to stay on all fours. He patted her on the head as he left the room, and she felt like a friggin' dog. It was humiliating and infuriating all at the same time.

Victor went and poured himself a glass of water. Then he poured more water in a bowl and set the bowl on the floor in front of her. Abby glared at him as he sat down in the chair. He continued to stroke her body like he was petting a dog, and she silently fumed. Then he set the tumbler on her back and told her not to move. "Don't spill my drink, pet."

She sat there on all fours and tried to be still. Victor turned on the news and was watching it and ignoring her. As far as punishments went, this one was rather boring. If he wanted her to be a dog, then she would give him what he wanted. Abby wiggled her ass like she was wagging a tail, and the drink immediately slipped off her back and spilled on the wooden floor. She looked at the spill and then up at her boyfriend with a smirk. Maybe now she would get some action!

Victor was trying hard not to laugh. He knew Abby was as horny as he was, but he wanted her to squirm a bit more. He shook his finger at her in disapproval.

"Naughty girl. Now you have to clean it up."

She looked at him hesitantly but then started to crawl on all fours to the kitchen to get a towel. He pulled on the belt and stopped her.

"No, my pet. That is not how a dog cleans up a spill." He stroked her face with his hand and then pushed one finger into her mouth to touch her tongue. "Dogs much prefer to use their tongues."

Her eyes flew to his face in disbelief. Was he serious?

He continued to stare at her expectantly, and she hesitated before slowly lowering her head to the ground. It was beyond mortifying, but Abby stuck her tongue out and began to lap up the spilled water.

Victor closed his eyes in satisfaction before quietly getting up from the chair to stand behind her. Then he gently pulled her into a standing position. He held her tightly against his body.

"Have you learned to obey me yet, Abby? Or do I need to continue to train you like a dog?" His hand slid down between her thighs, and he could feel how wet she was.

Abby moaned and pushed her ass against his pelvis. She could feel his erection and wanted it inside her. She cocked her head up at him. "I will obey. You don't have to train me like a dog anymore." Then she whispered, "But I think you should fuck me like one."

His pupils dilated in response. Damn, but he loved this woman! Victor unzipped his pants and pulled his dick out. He sat down in the chair and had her straddle his lap while facing him. He undid the belt and pulled it off her neck. Then he folded it in half and had her hold it while he tore her teddy open at the crotch. Victor inserted his finger in her vagina and fucked her with it until she was close to a climax. Then he lifted her with both hands and pulled her hips down over his cock. It was buried deep inside of her, and she moaned as she started to ride him in earnest.

Victor let her lead but was rocking his hips to thrust in deeper. He knew it wouldn't be much longer, and he grabbed the belt from her hands. As she started to cum, he slapped her ass hard with the folded belt. Each time she came down on his penis she felt the sting of the belt on her ass, and her orgasm seemed to go on forever. When Victor's own orgasm hit, he let go of the belt, grasped her hips, and pulled her down hard on his dick. He held her there until he exploded inside of her, and the feel of his hot cum carried her orgasm even further.

They finished in a sticky, sweaty mess and clung to each other. His dick was still buried deep inside. Once their breathing slowed down, Victor finally pulled out.

"Fuck," was all he said.

Abby nodded and teased, "I think that's what we just did."

They grinned at each other and then went to have dinner. While they were eating, she told him about Yuri's phone call.

He scowled. "How did he get your number?"

"Kate gave it to him." She noticed his facial expression and decided not to tell him the details of their conversation. Instead, she simply said, "He was trying to get ahold of you. When you didn't pick up, he tried me instead."

Victor nodded. He hadn't talked to his friend since Abby had moved in, but he didn't tell her that. Instead, he murmured, "I'll have to call him," and steered the conversation on to something else. He wasn't sure how he wanted to handle Yuri. In truth, he hadn't missed the man at all.

Chapter Thirty-Seven

The next day Abby was at home happily working on a sewing project. She hadn't had time to do crafts in ages, and she reveled in the creative process and let her mind wander. She was jolted back to reality when the phone rang.

It was her agent calling. "How's my favorite writer doing?" It was a line of crap Ginny gave all her clients, but in Abby's case she meant it.

"I'm good. But before you ask, no, I have not started on my next book!"

They both laughed.

"That's okay. You're going to need time for what I have to tell you. I just landed you a tour. The publisher thinks they can expand your books in the European market. They want to send you on a three-week tour across Great Britain. You'll get to see Ireland, Scotland, and a good deal of England. Can you believe it?"

Abby was stunned. Book tours were becoming a thing of the past in the writing world. She knew her sales had steadily gone up, but this was still an unexpected surprise.

"How did you manage to pull that off?"

"I didn't. They actually called me. A feminist organization is running conventions across Great Britain, and they want products that appeal to their demographic. The publisher thinks your books fit the bill. They are willing to pay all of your travel expenses, and they will have a travel agent arrange your transportation and lodging. You basically just have to show up and promote the book. They'll even have someone there selling copies, and you'll be talking to the women and signing the covers."

Ginny went on to explain more of the details. The tour would begin in October, and Abby would attend twelve conventions in all.

After they hung up, she paced the condo in excitement. She had been to France once in her early twenties, but she had never been anywhere else in Europe. This was a trip of a lifetime, and she couldn't wait to tell Victor.

He arrived home later than usual. He had seen patients in his office, and he'd had to admit several to the hospital. That always slowed things down. Abby met him at the door, and the sight of her lifted Victor's spirits. He pulled her in for a hug.

"As always, you look beautiful."

She grinned at him. "As always, you look handsome. Now go change. Dinner will be ready in ten minutes."

He chuckled as he walked toward the bedroom. She was turning into quite the bossy little domestic goddess.

As soon as he sat down to eat, Victor could tell Abby was excited about something. Her eyes were sparkling, and she was squirming in her seat. She looked like a kid waiting to open presents. He took a bite of his lasagna and gave her an amused look. "Are you going to tell me what you're so excited about, or are you going to make me guess?"

She grinned. "Well, Dr. Turov, your girlfriend has just been invited on a fabulous book tour in Europe!" She clapped her hands together in excitement.

Victor got very still. "What do you mean?"

Abby explained and eagerly gave him the details. He started bombarding her with questions, and she assumed he was happy for her. Then she noticed the expression on his face. It was grim, and a muscle in his jaw was working overtime. She paused mid-sentence.

"Wait…do you have a problem with this?"

"How could you think that I wouldn't?"

She gaped at him. "Because it's not Cancun. Or Mexico. It's Europe. Plus, I'm not going to party with my friends. I'm going for my writing career."

Victor was getting angry. "And that makes it better? There are terrorist attacks in Europe. And you know how easily you get lost. Who will be with you? What do we know about who is organizing this? What happens if you need help over there? They may speak English, but even I am easier to understand than a Scotsmen. I cannot possibly allow you to do this. It's dangerous and not worth the risk, especially for something as silly as your books."

She stared at him in disbelief. That last part had hurt. She fought back the tears.

"I know I don't save lives like you do, Victor, but people like my books. And I love writing them. It's part of who I am." She got up and rushed out of the room and into the bedroom.

Victor sighed and rubbed his neck in frustration. He looked at the bedroom doorway with regret. He hadn't meant to insult her, but he was damned if he was going to let her go wander around Europe on her own. The woman got lost leaving their condo building! She was also way too sweet and trusting of people. He pushed his chair back and followed her into the bedroom.

Abby was sitting on the chair by the door. Her legs were drawn up against her body, and she had her arms wrapped around them with her chin resting on her knees. She was crying softly, but when she saw him come in the door, her tears turned to anger.

"You can't interfere with my career, Victor!"

He stood and looked down at her. Then he quietly asked, "Are you under contract to do this?"

She looked confused. "I don't know. I don't think so. Does it matter?"

"Of course it matters. Go get your contract, baby."

She got up off the chair and went to get the contract off her computer. When she came back, she wordlessly handed it to him.

Victor took the document and started to read. He found the marketing clause on the second page and swore softly. She was under contract to attend public relations events per the publisher's discretion. He looked at her as he read off the clause, and there was anger in his voice.

"How could you not know what's in your contract?"

She shrugged her shoulders. "They're all basically the same. And they've never asked me to do anything like this before. It's a rare opportunity."

"Fuck, but you're going to have to go." Then he glared at her. "But there is no way you're going alone. And from now on I will be reviewing all new contracts. Really, Abby, don't you have a legal counselor or agent to help you with these things?"

She glared at him. "I have an agent, Victor. And like I said before, this is a rare occurrence. I've been writing for years and it's never been a problem. It wouldn't be now except for you being such a damn control freak."

His eyes narrowed. "I suggest you lose that attitude, little one, unless you want me to get out the cane and lose it for you."

She gasped and then shut her mouth and gave him a weak nod.

Victor was back to reading the contract and muttering to himself. "I can't get away for that long, so we're going to have to find someone else to go with you."

"The publisher can barely afford to send me. There's no way they will pay for someone else too."

"I will pay. It is worth it to keep you safe. Now we just have to figure out who is available to take three weeks off."

They discussed their friends one by one and finally landed on Abby's brother, Henry. He was currently unemployed. Victor didn't like it, as the man obviously had a drinking problem, but he couldn't come up with a better alternative. Abby gave him Henry's phone number, and he motioned for her to give him some privacy while he made the call. She stormed out of the bedroom in irritation. Then she paced in the living room for ten minutes before Victor finally came out.

He was smiling. Henry had agreed to go, but it had taken some convincing. Not only was Victor paying his travel expenses, but he also had to pay off some of Henry's bills. It reaffirmed Victor's opinion that the man was an asshole, but he didn't tell Abby that. Instead, he told her to contact her agent and get Henry added to the travel itinerary. Abby agreed to do it the next morning, and the two finally went in and finished their meal.

Over the next few weeks, they prepared for Abby's trip. Victor thought of all the little things she never would have, such as setting up her phone for international calls, getting an adapter for her blow dryer, and making sure she had coverage with her health insurance. He even found the phone number and address of the American embassies in Ireland and Great Britain and had reviewed all of the hotels she would be staying in for safety.

Abby appreciated his help, even though she found some of it to be overkill. They were getting along well together and also banging like rabbits every chance they got. She knew she would miss Victor, but part of her was secretly glad for the three-week break. His reaction and interference in the book tour had really opened her eyes. He had crossed a boundary she wasn't even aware she had, and Abby knew she needed some distance to think about their relationship.

As for Victor, he felt no such misgivings. He was very happy with the way things were going aside from the damn trip. The thought of it worked his stomach into knots, and he knew he would worry the entire time she was gone. He had to keep telling himself it would be over soon enough, and she would never be allowed to go on a trip like this again.

On the day of her departure, Victor drove to the airport. It was a Saturday afternoon, and they swung by her brother's place first to pick up Henry. He was surprisingly ready to go. His bags were by the door, he had shaved, and his eyes were clear and sober. Abby took it as a good sign, but Victor was more skeptical.

When they got to the short-term parking, Victor pulled Henry aside for a private chat. "Make sure nothing happens to her. I'm counting on you to keep her safe."

Henry gave him an amused look. "Dude. She's my sister. Don't worry about it."

"Just make sure you don't get drunk and forget about her. I mean it. I will hurt you if something happens to Abby!"

Henry was completely taken aback. He didn't have time for a rebuttal, though, as it was their turn in line. Once they were checked in, Victor walked them to the security line. He pulled Abby in for a final hug, pressed his forehead against hers, and whispered, "I am going to miss you so much. Please be careful. And don't forget our rules."

She smiled up at him. "I promise to be safe, and I will follow all the rules. We're going to talk every day, and those three weeks will go by in no time."

They kissed each other deeply, and then Victor let her go.

Now that she was truly leaving, Abby was surprised at the force of her feelings. She was really going to miss him, but she knew the break would do her good. Whenever she was around Victor, all reasonable thought flew right out the window. She followed Henry through the short security line and gave her boyfriend one last longing look before disappearing into the airport.

The flight was long. Abby never did well with time changes, and she wanted to crash as soon as they hit the hotel. But first, she needed to send Victor a text. It was in the middle of the night back home, but he responded immediately. Abby sighed. The man had obviously stayed up to make sure she got in okay. She knew how much the trip was stressing him out, and the thought made her happy but ticked off all at the same time. She fell asleep quickly, but she was vaguely aware his warm body was not lying next to hers. The thought left her feeling bereft. It reminded her of when Nate had died, and she quickly pushed the thought out of her mind.

The first stop on the tour was the next day. Abby was jet-lagged but excited to see Dublin. It looked like a fun city, and the venue was an old and interesting looking building. By noon the place was packed, and she lost track of how many people she had met. She had expected women, but quite a few men were also coming up to talk to her about her books.

As for Henry, he was true to his word and was sticking close to the booth. He watched his little sister interact with people and couldn't help but feel proud of her. He suspected some of the men were there just to flirt, but that was nothing new. In high school it had been the same way, only back then she had been young and naïve. Now she was an adult. Henry was confident his sister could take care of herself, but he also understood why Victor had sent him along for the ride. She had a terrible sense of direction, and, if this venue was any indicator, it would be easy to get lost on the tour. That didn't mean Henry approved of Victor's decision. He didn't like the guy, but he knew better than to say anything to Abby.

The weeks passed quickly. The tour kept them busy, and what little leisure time they had was spent sightseeing. They got to know their fellow tour travelers well, and they would often spend their free time with these folks at dinner or on an excursion. Abby dutifully followed the rules and got Victor's permission before going on each one. She also stuck to her two-drink limit and called him daily during his lunch hour. Those calls soon became the highlight of her day, as she was missing Victor terribly. The feeling was mutual.

Henry was well aware of the calls and check-ins Abby made to Victor, and they irritated the fuck out of him. She sometimes sounded like a child talking to a parent. One day he actually overheard her asking if it would be okay to go to dinner with the old ladies from the candle-making booth. At that point, he couldn't hold his tongue any longer, and he lashed out at her.

"Abs, what the hell are you doing?"

She looked at him in confusion. "What do you mean?"

"Why are you asking this guy permission to do things?"

Abby sighed. "It's no big deal. I just do it to put him at ease. He worries."

Henry looked at her in disbelief. "Worries about what? We're having dinner with a bunch of old ladies. Who cares? And what business is it of his anyway?"

"He's just being protective, Henry. He's a surgeon, so he's used to being in charge of everything."

"Well if you ask me, he's a controlling dick! You should have heard what he said to me at the airport. And you know Mom and Dad would never have approved. They raised us to be confident and independent people. If Mom were alive, she would be pitching a fit right now. You know how she was."

Abby nodded. Her mom had been a strong woman, and she never would have understood this relationship with Victor. But Abby was not like her mom. She said as much to Henry. "Look, I know you don't get it, and Mom probably wouldn't have either, but I love Victor. Our relationship works for us, and we're having fun. That doesn't mean I'm going to run off and marry the guy, so quit worrying. And he did pay for you to come on this trip, so cut him some slack!"

Henry thought about what she said and nodded. "Well, it is your life. And I can't complain about this trip, because it's been nice. Just promise me if he gets out of hand and you need help, you'll call me or John. He may be big, but if we team up we can take him!" He was trying for humor, and it worked.

Abby laughed. "You've got yourself a deal. Now let's get ready for dinner."

Meanwhile, back in the States, Victor had just finished up a surgery. He was dictating his notes on the procedure when a call came in from Yuri.

Victor hesitated. He hadn't spoken to his friend in months, and he wasn't sure he wanted to now. But Abby was out of town for one more week, and he was missing her terribly. Perhaps a distraction would do him some good.

"Kopyev, how are you?"

Yuri was relieved. "Finally. I was beginning to wonder if you were ever going to forgive me. I'm doing good. How about you?"

"Good. Good. Just typing up some surgery notes."

"Ah. You're busy as ever, my friend. And how are things with Abby?"

Victor filled him in on her trip.

"Good for her. That must make you proud."

"It makes me more angry than proud. I am counting down the days until she comes home."

Yuri smiled. "I can imagine. This is way outside your comfort zone, isn't it?"

"Yes," was the clipped reply.

"I'm surprised you let her go. That shows tremendous growth on your part."

Victor grunted. "I had no choice. She was under contract with her publisher. You can bet that will never happen again."

Yuri laughed. "So much for the growth. But at least the time apart will do you both some good."

Victor was getting angry. "Now why would you say that? We don't need any time apart. We are doing just fine."

"Relax. I didn't mean to insinuate anything. Every couple can use time away from each other. That's all."

"Well, that may be true, but all it's done for me is make me miss her even more. I love her, Yuri."

The psychiatrist was stunned. "Wow. You've never said that before. Then this is more serious than I thought." When Victor didn't say anything, he continued. "How far have you taken it sexually? Is she able to give you what you need?"

"I really don't see how that's any of your business."

Yuri was surprised and disappointed. Victor hadn't had any problems sharing the details of his sex life in the past. It was another indicator of just how different his relationship with Abby was. Yuri was dying to know what she was like in bed, if nothing more than to fuel his fantasies. He was smart enough not to push it, though, as Victor knew him well. If he figured out why Yuri was so interested, it could ruin their friendship. As much as he enjoyed his fantasies, he didn't want to lose Victor as a friend. So instead he suggested they go to dinner.

Victor turned him down. "Not this week. I've got too much going on. Let's shoot for a week or two in the future, okay?" Yuri agreed and hung up, and afterward Victor thought about their conversation. He really wasn't that busy, and he wasn't sure why he'd said no, but he soon forgot about it as he got back to work.

***

The book tour flew by in a blur, and before Abby knew it she was heading home to Cleveland. It had been a lot of fun, and she had sold a lot of books, but she was exhausted and needed to see Victor. Her conversation with Henry had gotten her thinking about the rules, and she wanted to discuss changing some of them. Abby was okay with a lot of his demands, but she would be damned if she would allow him to interfere in her career again. She was finally ready to make a stand.

As she came down the escalator, she saw Victor standing by the baggage claim. Their eyes met, and she felt her heart flutter. God, she had missed him! As soon as she reached the bottom, Abby launched herself at him and nearly knocked them both over in her happiness. Victor laughed as he picked her up and spun her around. Then he crushed her against his chest and breathed in her scent. God, he had missed her!

The two spoke animatedly as they waited for the bags, grabbed the car, and drove to Henry's house. They had all but forgotten about him sitting in the back seat, and he shook his head in disgust. He was happy to be home and couldn't get away from them fast enough.

Henry was surprised when Victor handed him an envelope just before getting back into the car. He opened it as soon as they were gone and found ten crisp one hundred dollar bills inside. There was also a short note that said, "Thank you for keeping her safe!" Henry laughed. The Russian fucker had actually paid him a bonus. It almost made up for Victor being such a dick. Almost.

Meanwhile, the couple was happily on their way home and still talking non-stop. Victor could tell Abby was exhausted, and he had every intention of putting her to bed as soon as they walked in the door. But she was having none of that. She had bought him all kinds of quirky gifts in Europe and insisted he open them. Then she curled up on his lap and started kissing him, and before he knew it they were both naked and melding their bodies into one.

Afterward, Abby fell asleep. It was still early, so Victor pulled out a medical journal to read. In truth, he spent more time watching his sleeping beauty than doing any actual reading. She was finally home and safe, and he realized he was about as content as a man could be in life. He savored the moment before he, too, fell asleep.

Chapter Thirty-Eight

The next day was Sunday, but Abby was too tired to go to church. She slept in and spent the morning putzing around the house. Her fatigue was more than just a case of jet lag. The book tour had worn her out, and she commented on it to Victor.

"I'm so glad it's over. It was fun, but it was also exhausting."

He looked up from his laptop and smiled. "Traveling always takes it out of you. That's why so many people need a vacation after their vacation." He started clicking on his mouse as he continued talking. "The good news is you'll never have to do a book tour again. I did some hunting online, and there are plenty of contracts that eliminate the marketing part. Hell, you might not even need an agent with your next book. This stuff is pretty self-explanatory. Come take a look."

Abby stared at him as she slowly walked over. The man had actually researched book contracts! Part of her was touched he cared enough to look, but the other part of her was annoyed. This was her life he was messing with, and now it was affecting other people, like Ginny, her agent. She had hoped to put off the rules conversation, but it would appear she needed to do it now. Abby's stomach was doing flip flops, but she took a deep breath and broached the topic.

"Victor, I want to talk about some of our rules." She sat down next to him at the kitchen table.

He looked at her determined face and closed his laptop. Then he turned so he was facing her. "Okay. What about them?"

Abby nervously pressed her lips together as she looked at her boyfriend. She picked up a dish towel from the table and started twisting it. Her voice was hesitant. "I'm really having a problem with you getting involved in my career. I was thinking maybe we could keep that out of your control in the future."

She risked a glance at him, but his expression was benign.

With more confidence, she added, "If I want to go on a book tour, then I should be able to go. And I shouldn't have to take a babysitter with me. I'm thirty years old and perfectly capable of taking care of myself!"

Victor sat quietly as if thinking about what she said. Then he reached over and placed his hand on top of hers. "Anything else?" he quietly asked.

She thought about it. "I don't know. Maybe? Some of your rules are a bit ridiculous. Surely you can see how over-protective you are being?"

Victor gave a bitter laugh. "Is there really such a thing as being too protective of someone you love?" When she didn't answer, he continued, "And what if I tell you no, Abby? Then what?"

She gave him a sad look and chose her words carefully. "Then I'm not sure I can keep living like this."

Victor blew out the breath he hadn't known he was holding. He ran his hand through his hair and asked, "What brought this on? I thought you were adjusting well to our relationship."

"I was. I mean, for the most part. But the book tour got me thinking about my career. And then Henry pointed out how our parents raised us to be independent. I feel like I'm letting them down."

Victor scowled. Henry, that drunken piece of shit!

"You have to live your life for yourself, little one, and not for other people. I thought you were happy."

"I am! I love you and I love living with you." She tried to find the words. "I just need more freedom is all."

Victor sighed. She had no idea what she was asking of him. He looked over and could tell she was on the verge of tears. He pulled her into his arms and cradled her against his chest.

"I don't want to lose you, but letting go of control is a big deal for me. Maybe we can go see a counselor to talk some of this out."

Abby snuggled in and sighed. "I would be too embarrassed to discuss all this with a counselor. If anyone knew I let you spank me, I would be so humiliated!"

Victor cupped her chin so she was looking at him. "Why are you ashamed? I keep telling you what we do is normal for a lot of people. And counselors have very open minds. But if it makes you feel better, we could talk to Yuri. He is well aware of our lifestyle, and I promise he won't judge."

Abby pushed away from his embrace with a surprising force. "Yuri? God no!"

She started to walk away, but Victor snaked his arm around her waist and pulled her back in. Her adamant refusal had surprised him.

"Why not Yuri? He's an excellent therapist and a good friend."

She didn't respond. Instead, she just shook her head no.

Victor stared at her. "Did something happen between you and Yuri?"

She shook her head no again, but he could see the uncertainty in her eyes.

"You either tell me now, Abby, or I will spank it out of you."

She hesitated. "He just gives me the creeps. Some of the things he says..."

Victor's eyes narrowed, but he tried to act nonchalant. "What kind of things?"

"I don't know. He's always asking about our sex life. And the last time I talked to him he asked what 'tools' you used on me. What kind of a question is that?"

Victor inhaled sharply. "Why am I just hearing about this now? How can I trust you when you don't tell me these things?"

"How could I tell you? He's your best friend, and you've known him your whole life. You've only known me a year. This might all be in my head anyway."

But Victor knew Yuri and knew it wasn't. He had no one to blame for this but himself. He knew what his friend was capable of, but he had assumed Yuri would leave Abby alone. He had been wrong. Victor thought about how to handle the situation, then simply said, "You mean more to me than Yuri ever will. How could you not know that?"

She shrugged her shoulders. She was suddenly very tired, so the two agreed to shelve the issue for later. They ended up binge-watching shows on the couch, and Abby went to bed early. After he tucked her in, Victor went back out to the living room and poured himself a drink. He thought about their conversation.

Victor was terrified of losing Abby, and he considered loosening up on the rules. But the thought of doing that brought on even more fears. His need to control her was strong! Since he couldn't solve that problem, he turned his attention to the Yuri issue instead. Victor needed to know if his friend had crossed a line, but Yuri was smart and would clue in if he made obvious inquiries. He decided to call his friend and invite him over for a casual dinner. That way he could observe the two of them together without it being obvious.

Yuri picked up on the second ring. The two chatted for a few minutes about work before the conversation moved on to Abby.

"I can imagine you are relieved your little submissive is back home and safe?"

"Oh, yes. I was very happy to see her. She had a good trip but was worn out from all the traveling."

"Mmm hmm. I bet you had quite a reunion in the bedroom, which wore her out even more."

Victor frowned. "Of course. But I didn't call to discuss my sex life. I wanted to invite you over to our place for dinner. I feel I have been neglecting you. I also want you to get to know Abby better."

Yuri was surprised and thrilled by the invitation, and he immediately accepted. They agreed he would come over the next night and hung up shortly after.

Victor told Abby about the dinner in the morning. Her first thought was that he had arranged a counseling session, and she was pissed. "I told you I don't want to discuss our issues with him!"

Victor grinned. She had her hell-cat face on with the flashing eyes he found so sexy. "Calm down. I just invited him over for dinner. We had made tentative plans to get together while you were out of town, but it never happened. I figured we might as well do it now and get it over with. I will order the food in so you don't have to worry about cooking."

Abby looked at him suspiciously. She didn't care for Yuri, but he was Victor's best friend, and a dinner was harmless enough. She nodded her assent, even though she knew she had no choice.

Victor gave her a quick hug before leaving for work. He promised to be home promptly at five.

He was true to his word. He rolled in at 4:57 carrying two large bags of food. It smelled delicious, and Abby figured if nothing else she would eat a decent meal.

Victor went to change while Abby popped the food in the oven to keep it warm. When he came back out, he told her, "I put some clothes on the chair for you to wear tonight. Go change, and I don't want to hear any complaints about what I chose or left out."

Abby nodded. She was so used to him picking out her clothes that she didn't think much about it. Then she saw the outfit. It was a short, soft, semi-sheer dress in pale pink. Abby loved the dress, but he had not laid out a bra to wear underneath. There was a pair of nude silk panties and high heels, but a bra was noticeably absent.

Abby was not happy. She put on the outfit and looked at herself in the mirror. The dress was skimming over her breasts, and you could just make out the outline of her nipples underneath. She walked back out to the kitchen and glared at Victor, but he just ignored her as he poured himself a drink.

When the doorbell rang he pulled her in for a kiss. All he said was, "Remember to trust me, little one." She looked at him in confusion as he went to open the door.

Yuri had brought several bottles of wine. He handed them to Abby as he gave her a quick hug, and he immediately noticed she wasn't wearing a bra. He resisted the urge to peek down her dress and instead asked what was for dinner.

Victor took over the conversation and led Yuri into the living room. Once they were seated, he asked Abby to pour his friend a drink. When she brought the vodka, he then asked her to bring out some appetizers. After that, he reminded her to fold some sheets that were still in the dryer. He had her do it out in the living room so she could take part in the conversation. He and Yuri watched her fold as they continued to chat.

Abby was puzzled by the sudden barrage of orders, but she went along with it. When they were ready for dinner, Victor had her set the table so he was at the head with Yuri on his left and Abby on his right. They had a lively conversation during the meal. Yuri asked about the book tour, and she gave the highlights of the trip. Then the men started reminiscing about their medical school days, and they had Abby laughing at all of their mishaps.

Victor kept the drinks flowing freely during dinner. He was pouring wine into Abby's glass as well, and she was surprised. She wasn't drunk, but she was over her two-drink limit. Something was up, but she knew better than to ask what it was. If they attempted a counseling session, she vowed to clam up.

When dinner was over the men headed back out to the living room. Yuri sat on the couch, and Victor chose a straight-back chair directly across from him. They both watched Abby clearing the dishes, and then Victor ordered her to brew a pot of coffee. His tone had become much more autocratic, but she was just tipsy enough not to notice.

Yuri had, though, and quietly commented on it. "I must say, I am impressed with your skill. She has become quite submissive."

"I know. She will do anything I ask her to."

Yuri nodded as he continued to watch Abby in the kitchen. She had bent over to pick something up off the floor, and the short dress inched up higher on her thighs. "You are one lucky man!"

Victor just grunted and sipped his drink.

Abby now had her back to them as she washed the dishes in the sink, but occasionally she would turn and reach up to put something in the cupboard. When she did, her profile was on display along with her perky breasts. Yuri was watching and unconsciously reached down to rearrange his pants. When he looked back at Victor, his friend was watching him carefully.

"Do you like what you see?"

Yuri was startled. He hesitated as if debating what to say, but then he softly replied, "Yes, very much."

Victor's eyes darkened, but he gave a short laugh. "You always were a boob man."

They continued to stare at each other, but Victor's posture was relaxed. He was leaning back with one knee crossed over the other, and he had a neutral expression on his face.

Yuri took it as a good sign and cautiously steered the conversation back to their school days. "Remember what else we used to do back then, my friend? At the club?"

Victor laughed. "Sure. That was a long time ago. I was a lot younger and a lot hornier than I am now!"

Yuri grinned. "Oh, I don't know. You're still young. Plus, you have a smoking hot girlfriend now. That has to stoke your fires."

"I can't argue with that. If nothing else she will keep me young."

Yuri hesitated again. "And do you remember how much I used to like to watch when we were younger?"

"If I'm not mistaken, you still frequent the clubs now to watch," came the dry reply.

"Sure. Sure. But there's not a woman in the club that could hold a candle to Abby."

Victor sat up straighter and looked at his friend. "What are you trying to say? Do you want to watch me and Abby?"

"God, yes!" was the emphatic reply.

Victor's eyes narrowed.

Just then Abby walked back into the room and handed them both a cup of coffee. Victor took a sip of his and set it on a table. He motioned for her to sit on his lap and turned her so she was directly facing Yuri. He wrapped his arms around her waist and nuzzled her neck while the men continued to talk. Then Victor's hands wandered up to the buttons at the front of her dress. He slowly started undoing them.

Abby reached up to stop him. "What are you doing?"

Victor nibbled on her ear and whispered, "Relax, little one. You know you can trust me."

His left hand reached inside the dress and started fondling her breasts. She was mostly covered by the fabric and Victor's hand, but some of her flesh could still be seen, and Abby felt completely demeaned.

Yuri was staring with a rapt expression. He eagerly leaned forward when Victor's other hand reached up under Abby's skirt and started massaging her between the legs.

Abby was completely humiliated. She tried to pull out of Victor's hold and gasped, "I don't like this!"

"Shhh, baby." He tightened his arms around her and continued to stroke her sensitive areas. "I need you to trust me."

She continued to squirm in his arms, so he explained. "Yuri is a voyeur. He enjoys watching other people be intimate."

Abby looked over at Yuri and was horrified to see he had put his hand down his pants to masturbate. "Oh, my God!" she whispered.

"Don't look at him. Look at me." Victor had her stand up and turn around. Then he had her straddle his legs with her back to Yuri. He unbuttoned the rest of her dress and pushed it down off her shoulders so it pooled around her waist. All Yuri could see was her long blond hair running down her bare back, and the occasional swell of the side of her breast when she moved. It was enough, and he continued to masturbate while Victor resumed fondling her.

Abby was screaming a protest inside her head, but somehow she couldn't get the words out. What's more, her body was starting to respond to Victor's attention. She was kissing him back, and her hands were running along his back and biceps and into his hair.

Victor knew he needed to end this soon. He suspected his friend was about to betray himself, though, so he continued to push Abby toward her breaking point.

Sure enough, Yuri breathlessly called out to him in Russian seconds later. *"I can't thank you enough for this. She is so damn beautiful, and she will do anything you ask of her. Would you be willing to give her to me for the night? I would really like to fuck her."*

Victor froze. He had never shared a girlfriend with Yuri in the past, but this is what he suspected was in his friend's heart. Now that he knew, he was angry and saddened all at the same time.

He leaned away from Abby a bit and looked over at Yuri. He pretended to consider it. *"Give me a moment to talk to her,"* he replied in Russian. Then he pulled Abby's dress back up and fastened the buttons. He helped her stand and smoothed her skirt down over her legs. Victor quietly took her hand and led her to the bedroom. She gave Yuri one last look on the way and saw the pure lust in his eyes. His hand was still down his pants, and Abby shuddered in disgust.

Once in the bedroom Victor shut the door and leaned his forehead against hers. Then he pulled away and told her to go take a bath. She was staring up at him with a look of shock on her face. He repeated the order to take a bath more firmly and added, "I know that was way outside your comfort zone, and I am proud of you for obeying. You know I will always protect you. Now go."

Victor shut the door behind him and went back to the living room. Yuri was standing and waiting, and his erection was obvious in his pants. He started walking down the hallway toward the bedroom, but Victor stopped him. "She said no."

The words excited Yuri. "So what. Punish her and order her to do it. She will listen to you!"

Victor scowled at him. "I thought you wanted me to be 'normal,' Yuri. I have never shared a girlfriend in the past, even the more submissive ones. Why would you think I would start now, especially after telling you how much I love her?"

Yuri sputtered. "I don't know. Because she's different. You said it yourself. And she is willing to follow your orders."

Victor shook his head and looked stunned. "I guess now I know she is. But that doesn't mean I'm going to treat her like that." He looked at Yuri. "You're more fucked up than I am. At least I own who I am. You talk to me about my control issues like they're a bad thing. But then you're more than willing to use them for your own perverted needs. Get the fuck out of my house! And stay the hell away from my girlfriend!"

Yuri stared at him in dismay. Deep down he knew he had crossed a line and had lost his friend for good.

After he left, Victor stood in the kitchen and drank some water. He ran his hand through his hair and looked worriedly at the bedroom door. He finished the water and put the glass in the sink. Then he took a deep breath and headed into the bedroom.

Abby was sitting on the chair with her arms wrapped protectively around her legs. She looked at him but didn't say anything.

Victor tried to lighten the mood. "I guess you weren't as obedient as I thought. What happened to taking a bath?"

Her eyes flashed. "Why? Were you going to invite Yuri in to watch me?" She stood up and glared at him. She could feel the emotions bubbling up and tried to contain them. "Do you even know how fucked up that was?" She started crying and couldn't stop.

Victor tried to go to her, but she kept backing up. Now she was screaming at him, and he just let her vent until she ran out of steam. She ended up with her back against the wall and finally sank down on the floor. Victor cautiously sat down next to her. When she didn't resist, he pulled her into his lap and held her while she continued to cry.

"I'm sorry, baby. I had to see how far he would go to know if I could trust him or not. If I had told you my plans, he would have figured it out. He's an expert at reading body language."

She was hiccupping. "But you let him see me naked."

Victor smiled. "He didn't get to see a thing. I kept you covered by your dress and my body. All he saw was your bare back, and he's seen that before."

Abby was starting to calm down as he rocked her in his arms. "So you knew he would do this? Because of his voyeurism?"

Victor nodded. "Yes, little one. When we were in med school Yuri and I used to go to sex clubs together."

She looked at him. "What's a sex club?"

Victor explained it, and she was horrified. "So, you went and had sex with random women?"

He nodded. "I did. I was in my twenties and horny as hell. Medical school didn't allow time for dating, and this was a way for me to get laid and blow off steam. It's also where I learned how to be a Dominant and do all those things to you. I went to have sex, and Yuri went to watch other people having sex."

Abby was trying to wrap her brain around the concept. "So you didn't mind if he watched you?"

Victor shrugged. "I didn't care who was watching me. I was too busy getting laid. He watched everyone, not just me."

The wheels were still turning in Abby's head. "Is that even legal? And what about diseases? What if you got someone pregnant?"

"Yes, it's legal. And sex clubs are great at providing condoms, but I always brought my own. Plus, I tested myself constantly."

"I guess I'm thankful you were tested before we started fooling around," she said in disgust.

"Of course. You should know I quit going to sex clubs back in Russia. Yuri still goes. He's the one that introduced me to all of my submissive girlfriends here in the States. He would meet them at the club, tell them about me, and then arrange for us to meet. If we hit it off, then we started dating."

"Wait. There are sex clubs here? I thought that was a Russian thing."

Victor laughed. "There's a sex club in downtown Cleveland. They're in most big cities. I keep telling you sexual deviance is not as rare as you think."

She looked at him in fear. "Is this something you still want to do? Will you want me to go to a club?"

He stood up. "God, no. In fact, I forbid it! If I ever find out you were at a club, you will be severely punished."

She nodded as he pulled her up to stand next to him. "Like I would even consider something like that!"

He smiled. "Good. Now, what about that bath?"

"Why are you so concerned about me taking a bath?"

"Because I know you're big on symbolism. I figured you would feel dirty after what occurred tonight and would want to take a bath."

She thought about it and had to agree. They filled the tub with water and climbed in together.

Victor held her and massaged her neck and shoulders. Abby leaned back and closed her eyes. She was far from over this, though, and finally asked, "What did Yuri ask you in Russian?"

Victor hesitated. He wanted to be honest but wasn't sure she could handle it. "He was asking me to take it further so he could see more of your body."

She sighed. "Did you let him gawk at your other girlfriends?"

"No. I've never been good at sharing, little one. The only time he watched me was at the club, and that was with random women when we were young."

She tried to turn to look at him. "Then why did he think you would let him look at me?"

"I don't know. I think it's because you're different. You're sweet and gentle and beautiful. That's a heady combination for any man."

She sighed. "Victor, we really need to see a counselor. I'm not sure I can handle all of this. Every time I get comfortable with you, something else happens, and then I'm on edge again. It's not a good way to live."

"I know. I'll ask around at work and see who comes recommended."

"You won't mention the submissive thing, right?"

"Not at work. But it will definitely come up in therapy."

"I suppose it has to."

Eventually, they got out of the tub, dried off, and crawled into bed. Victor pulled her into his arms, but he could tell she was pulling back emotionally.

"You know, Abby, you could have said no earlier. Anytime you are uncomfortable with something if you say no, we will stop immediately. Ultimately you have the final say."

She thought about it. "Yes, but I have trouble saying no to you!"

Victor smiled. "That's because you're my submissive, little one, and a damn good one. Deep down you want to satisfy me. But you've stopped me before, and I am trusting you to stop me again if things go too far."

When she didn't say anything he continued, "If we keep working at it and take baby steps, I think we can come to a place where we are both happy."

"I hope so."

He tried to kiss her, and she pulled away.

"Do you mind if we have normal sex tonight? No toys or tying my hands up. Just normal sex."

"Of course. You want me to make love to you instead of fuck you."

"Well, yes. Can you do that?"

He had done it before, and Victor showed her that he could do it again. Their lovemaking was tender, sweet, and passionate, and she fell asleep shortly after. He watched her for a while before he too drifted off to sleep.

Chapter Thirty-Nine

They went to see a counselor on Friday morning. Mr. Newell had come highly recommended by several doctors at the clinic. They all swore this guy was the reason they were still happily married. That was enough recommendation for Victor, but Abby wasn't too sure. For one thing, the counselor was a man, and she knew that would make her uncomfortable. Add to that her general inability to open up to people, and it was no surprise she sat in the office with her arms crossed and her stomach in knots.

Victor was nervous too. He was afraid of losing Abby and equally afraid of giving up control. He had faith in the counseling profession, though, and was hopeful it would help them.

They sat in an office that was modernly decorated in blacks, whites, and grays. There were green plants tucked into the corners, and a soft water display was flowing on the back wall. The furniture was modern but comfortable, and Victor had his arm around Abby's shoulders.

Mr. Newell arrived right on time, and his appearance immediately put them at ease. He had one of those open, compassionate faces that encouraged confidences. He also carried himself with a quiet dignity. He shook both of their hands and settled into a chair across from them.

After explaining his counseling style and reviewing the strict confidentiality policy, Mr. Newell asked them a few easy questions to break the ice. Then he got down to business.

"So what brought you in today?"

Victor responded. "Abby and I have been dating for almost a year now and are very much in love. We're in a Dominant/submissive relationship, and we need help working through some of the finer points of our arrangement."

There was a brief flash of shock on the counselor's face, but he recovered quickly. Victor ignored it and went on to discuss how new Abby was to the lifestyle. He explained she was having trouble adjusting to some of his rules.

Mr. Newell asked some tentative questions about what happened if the rules weren't followed. Victor readily answered and told him the various ways he punished her. The counselor was trying hard to keep a neutral face, but when Victor told him about the caning, a look of pure disgust flashed across his face.

It was gone in an instant, but Abby had noticed. She flushed scarlet and stared at the floor. She was holding Victor's hand in a death grip and wanted nothing more than to flee the room.

The counselor attempted to get her to talk. "We can discuss the rules in a minute. What I need to know is, are they the real problem, or is it the lifestyle you take issue with? BDSM is an extreme way to live, and it is not for everyone."

Abby cringed as she heard the acronym again. She started to speak, but Victor beat her to it. "She wouldn't have made it a year if she had an issue. And what we do is hardly extreme."

Mr. Newell looked at Victor. "I am talking to Abby now. I need to hear what she has to say."

She looked nervously between the two of them and worked to find her voice. "I'm okay with it."

Mr. Newell nodded and gently asked her, "And are you fully consenting in this relationship?"

Victor was furious, but Abby quickly answered, "Yes, I am."

"Good. And was this something you were naturally drawn to, or are you doing this for Dr. Turov?"

Victor responded. "She had no idea about the lifestyle before she met me."

Mr. Newell turned to him and quietly said, "I was talking to Abby. You are obviously used to being in control, Dr. Turov, but in here you are not the Dominant. In here everyone is equal."

Victor shook his head. "You clearly don't understand this lifestyle if you believe that is true. I am Abby's Dominant no matter where we are or who we are with."

The men stared at each other.

Mr. Newell sighed. "That is not how my counseling sessions usually work. But let's shelve it for now. Why don't we back it up a bit and get some background on both of you? What was your childhood like? Your parents? Did they use corporal punishment?"

Victor and Abby both answered and explained they had wonderful childhoods and great parents. Neither had been spanked as kids. Then Victor pointed out it really didn't matter. There was a slight edge to his voice, and Mr. Newell honed in on it.

"I am simply trying to determine what has drawn you to the lifestyle."

Victor laughed. "That's like asking why someone likes peas instead of carrots. But if you really need an answer, I am drawn to it because of the control. I love having control over things—my job, my life, and most definitely Abby."

Mr. Newell was writing things down. "Why? What is it about control that you like?"

Victor shrugged. "I worry about things. The more I control something, the less I worry, and the better I feel."

"Excellent. And how bad does the worry get?"

"It can get to be annoying. But it doesn't take over my life. I just spent three weeks worrying about Abby while she was on a book tour, but I survived it."

Mr. Newell looked up with excitement. "Survived is a strong word. Would you say your worry is a sign of an anxiety problem?"

Victor snorted. "I do not have OCD, if that's what you're getting at. Let me ask you this. Do you have a spouse or child that you love?"

Mr. Newell looked confused. "Yes, I have an adult daughter. But we're not here to talk about me."

Victor ignored him. "And do you worry about your daughter?

"Of course."

"And wouldn't it be great if you could control some of what she does to lessen that worry?"

"Yes, but that is not how life works. My daughter has to live her own life, just like Abby has to live hers."

Victor smiled. "I agree. But if your daughter was willing to indulge your control issues, by following some rules for instance, then what harm is there in that?"

Mr. Newell gave him a pointed look. "In your lifestyle, Dr. Turov, the harm comes with the punishments."

Victor shook his head. "That's not true. Abby can stop me whenever it gets to be too much. She has all the power in our relationship. Plus,

I never take it too far. I am very cautious when I punish her."

Mr. Newell was writing furiously.

Victor continued. "I'm not here to change who I am, because I don't have a problem with it. I am here to work on my relationship with Abby."

Mr. Newell nodded as he continued to write. Then he turned to Abby and asked if that was why she was there.

"I just told you that was why!" said an indignant Victor.

Abby placed a calming hand on her boyfriend's arm before she spoke. "Yes. I'm having trouble adjusting to some of the rules."

Mr. Newell gently asked her, "And what brought this on?"

Abby didn't hesitate. "Part of it had to do with my book tour and Victor not wanting me to go. But mostly it was because of the whole Yuri incident."

"Okay, good. Tell me about the Yuri incident."

Abby looked away in embarrassment.

Victor sat quietly with his arms crossed and stared at the counselor. Finally, after a very long silence, he explained, "Abby is shy, and this is way outside her comfort zone. She is too embarrassed to tell you."

The counselor looked at Abby. "It's okay to be embarrassed. What you are doing is not mainstream behavior, and it can be difficult to talk about. But I promise, once you get it out in the open, you will feel so much better."

Victor grinned. "I tell my shy girl that all the time, but she is not so easily convinced. If you like, I can spank it out of her." He had purposefully said that to get a rise out of the prick. He wasn't an expert like Yuri, but the counselor's body language and choice of words was saying a lot. The man wasn't open to them or their lifestyle.

Sure enough, Mr. Newell pitched a fit. "I cannot condone such barbaric behavior in my office! I really must insist we keep this environment safe and on equal footing for everyone."

That's all Victor needed to hear. He stood up and took Abby's hand. "So what you're saying is you don't think BDSM is safe. You clearly do not have an open mind about our relationship, Mr. Newell, and are therefore not the counselor for us. Thank you for your time." He led her out of the room.

Abby wordlessly followed along. When they were back in the truck they looked at each other, and she laughed. "You did that on purpose, didn't you?"

"Yep. That guy was looking at me like I was some kind of monster. What an asshole!"

She shook her head in amusement. "I told you this wasn't normal."

Victor got serious immediately. "Over one-third of Americans have tried our lifestyle, baby, and quite a few of them are in it for the long haul. Don't let that prick make you feel like you're doing something wrong."

She looked at him thoughtfully. "I don't think we're doing anything wrong. I just don't know if I can keep doing it. I feel like I'm losing myself piece by piece. First, it was the volunteer work, then my house, and now my writing. I'm afraid someday there's going to be nothing left, and you're going to have me locked in a closet or something."

Victor hugged her. "First of all, I would never lock you in a closet. And secondly, things are overwhelming now because we're still new at all of this. It takes most couples years to adapt to each other. I'm sure it was the same when you married Mr. Shea. But if you give us time, I promise it will all work out. And I will search harder to find a counselor who understands our type of relationship. You just have to be patient."

She sighed. "Okay."

Victor drove back to their condo and dropped her off. He had to get to the clinic for some surgeries, but he gave her a kiss before he left and tried to lighten the mood. "What are you going to do with the rest of your day?"

"I think I'm going to take it easy and do some reading."

"Good. You could use the break. Maybe take a nap too. Tonight we need to reconnect between the sheets."

She rolled her eyes in mock shock. "Like we don't 'connect' all the time!"

Victor grinned. "Yes, but after a counseling session I hear it's quite good."

She smiled as she watched him leave the condo, but he had noticed a furtive look on her face when she locked the door behind him. He dismissed it as a reaction to the session and concentrated on the drive to work.

Once he was gone, Abby fixed herself a cup of ginger tea before sitting down at her desk. What she hadn't told Victor was her plan to do some reading on BDSM. She suspected he wouldn't like it, and as she typed in the acronym on the computer, she realized she probably wouldn't either. But Abby was done hiding behind her self-imposed ignorance.

She needed to know exactly how far their relationship could go.

An hour later she pushed away from the laptop in stunned silence. There had been a copious amount of information on the internet including facts, photos, and even videos showing BDSM in crystal clear detail. The visual stuff had been the worse. It opened a Pandora's box inside Abby's head, and there was no way she could undo what she had just seen.

There had been choking, knives, and breasts bound up so tightly in ropes they were purple. She had seen collars, painful-looking piercings, and balls shoved in mouths. There had even been crazy things attached to sensitive parts of the body, and women locked in cages and coffins. And what the hell was that shrink wrap shit?! It all looked painful, humiliating, and about as far from normalcy as sex could get. What's more, Abby recognized herself in some of the photos. The deep red welts on many a backside brought to mind the caning she had received from Victor. The realization that she was one of them was like a slap in the face.

Abby tried to calm down. She loved Victor, and she trusted him to stop if she asked him to. But she couldn't get those images out of her head. She didn't want him to do any of that to her, and they added fuel to the doubts she already had about their relationship. She relived each and every uncertainty in glaring detail, and she lingered on the whole Yuri issue. Victor could have handled that so much better than he did. She was a private person, and she would never allow him to do that to her again!

As the afternoon wore on, the doubt inside her grew into a panic that couldn't be stopped. Abby started throwing things into a suitcase without even thinking. Her gut told her she had to get out of there, and she called Rachel and Joel to see if they would come get her. There was no way she could drive in the state she was in.

Meanwhile, Victor was finishing up a surgery. It was a routine operation, and he had time to think about the counseling session while he worked. He was still pissed off at the narrow-minded therapist. The man had made things so much worse, and Victor knew he needed to find a new shrink in a hurry. He could sense Abby was at her breaking point. The furtive look she had given him earlier was making him uneasy. Victor couldn't shake the sense of foreboding that surrounded him. He ended up having a resident take over his procedures and headed home early.

The condo was quiet when he arrived, but there were two suitcases and Abby's laptop bag lined up by the front door. His heart sank. Victor anxiously called out her name and rushed through the condo. He found her lying on the floor in the walk-in closet crying.

"Oh no, little one. What are you doing in here?"

Abby mumbled, "Seeing if I could live in one."

Victor laughed in spite of himself. Then he lay down on the floor next to her and reached out to hold her hand. They both stared at the ceiling in silence.

Finally, Victor whispered, "Are you leaving me?"

"Yes," she sniffled. And then she was sobbing.

Victor rolled onto his side and pulled her into his arms. "Why? What happened?"

She looked at him and tried to find the words. Instead, she just cried harder.

"You have to talk to me, Abby. Tell me what's wrong." He spoke gently, but there was a hint of panic in his voice.

She worked to steady her breath. "I did some research online," she whispered.

"Oh no. Why would you do that?"

"Everyone kept bringing up BDSM. I needed to see for myself how far it could go."

Victor was angry. "I keep telling you we will only go where you allow me to take you. I would never do anything you didn't want to do."

When she didn't say anything, he continued, "Things are always so much worse in your head, Abby. Once you get past that, you usually like what I do to you."

"I didn't like the cane," she said petulantly, "Or Yuri watching us."

Victor chose his words carefully. "I stopped the cane as soon as you asked. And I will never do anything with you in front of another person again. I am learning as we go what you can and cannot handle. I think a counselor will help us to sort all of this out."

"You told Mr. Newell you weren't there to change, Victor. But that's all I'm doing. I have altered my life so much to accommodate you, and I don't think I can bend any more than I already have. It's too much. I'm worn out, and I just want my old life back!"

Victor felt her words deep in his core. He had feared this all along. He knew he was a lot for any woman to take on, but he had hoped Abby's love for him would push through any doubts she had.

He sat up in a sitting position and pulled her up with him. Then he wiped the tears from her face. In a resigned voice, he asked, "Where will you be staying?"

"At Rachel and Joel's."

He nodded. "Can I still see you?"

"I don't know. That might just make it worse. When I'm around you, I forget about everything else."

He put his arm around her. His mind was racing trying to find a way to keep some connection. "Do you still love me, Abby?" his voice was shaking.

She peered up at him. "Yes. Of course, I do!"

He nodded. "Good. I still love you too. In fact, you are the best thing that has ever happened to me. That's why I don't think we should end this permanently. Why don't you take some time to think about things, and I'll look for a more suitable counselor?"

She hesitated. "I don't know, Victor."

"Please, Abby." There were tears in his eyes, and she felt her heart breaking even more.

Just then the doorbell sounded. They slowly got up, and both were wiping their eyes dry. When they opened the door, Rachel looked worriedly between the two of them. Joel raised his eyebrows and then quietly grabbed the bags and took them down to the car. When he came back up, he took Abby's keys. He would drive her car, and Rachel would drive Abby back to their place.

Just before she left, Abby ran back to Victor and gave him one more hug. She was sobbing again, and he held her tightly. He whispered in her ear, "Please try to follow the rules, little one, even if I'm not there. They will keep you safe."

She nodded and then rushed out of the door without a backward glance. As soon as she was gone, Victor sank down on the couch and held his head in his hands. He had lost her, and it felt like his life was completely torn apart. He cried like he had never cried before.

Chapter Forty

The ride to Rachel and Joel's house was silent. Rachel had tried several times to get Abby to talk, but that had been met with stifled sobs. Her feelings were just too raw to vocalize. Instead, she stared out the window and tried to keep it together.

When they got to the house, Abby told her friends she needed to be alone and would talk when she was ready. Then she escaped to the spare bedroom and curled up in the fetal position on the bed. It was the same room she had stayed in when Nate died, and she realized she felt just as lost now as she had then. Abby pulled a quilt over her shivering body and let the grief wash over her. She eventually cried herself to sleep.

A week went by, and Abby was still not talking. It was driving Rachel crazy. She watched her friend going through the motions and trying to put on a happy face, but her suffering was obvious to everyone. All Abby did was walk Charlie, clean up around the house, and sleep. She was barely eating, her laptop never made it out of the bag, and some days she didn't even bother to shower.

They knew Victor wasn't doing any better, but he at least had work to keep him distracted. He was calling Joel daily to get updates on Abby, and the pain in his voice was evident. Joel tried to reassure him, but he gave the same report every day, and they were all starting to worry about Abby's depression. As if the calls were not enough, Victor was also bombarding Joel with texts throughout the day.

Is she eating?
No.
Why not? Cook her something simple and make her eat.
We can't force her to eat, Victor.
Is she drinking coffee?
Yes. A lot.

Jesus. That will raise her heart rate. Have Rachel check her fucking pulse.
Will do.
Is she writing?
No.
Going out with friends?
No.
What the fuck is she doing, then?

This went on and on, and to Joel's credit, he took it well. He answered every question Victor threw at him and tried to do what the doctor suggested. But Abby was lost in her own world, and she barely acknowledged them or the food they kept putting in front of her.

Victor had also attempted to text her once. He had a patient come in that had raved about her books, and he sent her a quick message to let her know. She sent him back a smiley face but nothing else. He took it as a sign she didn't want to hear from him, and his heart broke even more.

Victor hadn't given up, though. He felt horrible for making her so miserable and knew he had to make some changes. After vainly searching on his own, he finally broke down and called the last person he wanted to for a counseling referral.

Yuri was thrilled when he got the call. He eagerly answered the phone. "How are you, my friend?"

"We are no longer friends."

That startled Yuri. "Then why are you calling?"

"I need a referral to a counselor familiar with BDSM and open to it. Do you know anyone?"

There was silence on the other end of the line. Then hesitantly Yuri said, "Yes. You're talking to one now."

"Not you, asshole. I need someone Abby will be comfortable with, and someone I don't hate."

Yuri cringed. That had hurt, but he knew he deserved it. "Are the two of you okay?"

There was another long silence followed by an abrupt, "We broke up."

Yuri could hear the anguish in his friend's voice. "Oh, Victor, I am sorry. I know how much she means to you." Then to change the subject, "I know a man locally, but Abby might be more comfortable with a woman. There's a really good one down in Canton. She's in the lifestyle and is a Femdom."

"That sounds good. What's her office address and phone number?"

Yuri searched for the information. While he was scrolling, he apologized. "I need you to know how sorry I am for getting out of hand at your place. I'm hoping someday you can forgive me, and we can still be friends."

Victor snorted but didn't say anything. Yuri gave him the contact information.

"Please think about it, Victor."

"What's there to think about? You wanted to fuck her, you prick!"

"Can you blame me?" Then he tried for humor, "So I guess she's available now, eh?"

Victor abruptly hung up.

***

Another two weeks went by, and Rachel was done waiting for Abby to snap out of it. She called Lindsay over on Saturday night for drinks, and her plan was to do an intervention on both her friends. Rachel realized wine wasn't the smartest choice for Lindsay, but she knew they would need it to get Abby to talk. She wisely only put out two bottles.

Abby curled up in a chair and half-listened to Rachel talking about work. Lindsay was keeping up the other end of the conversation, so all she had to do was sit back and pretend. Their voices were soothing to her nerves, and the wine she was drinking was going down easily. After her second glass, and having barely eaten for three weeks, Abby was feeling a pleasant buzz. It was the first non-painful feeling she'd had since breaking up with Victor. She considered drinking a third glass, but her innate need to follow his rules brought her up short. The man still had control over her even after the breakup!

Rachel could tell Abby was tipsy because she was starting to slur her words. She poured Lindsay another glass of wine and then turned her full attention back to Abby. It was time to start the first intervention.

"Abs, we're worried about you."

Abby shrugged. "I know. I'm worried about me too."

"What happened? You might feel better if you talked about it."

"I wouldn't even know where to start. And I don't think you would understand. Plus, it really doesn't matter. Victor can't change, and I've changed as far as I'm willing to."

Lindsay piped in, "Do you still love him?"

Her eyes filled up with tears. "I do. I miss him so much." She swiped the back of her hand across her face.

"He misses you too," said Rachel. "He calls Joel every day to see how you're doing."

"He does?" The thought sent a surge of joy straight to her heart. "Then why isn't he calling me?"

"I think he's afraid you don't want to talk to him."

"Oh." The tears were rolling down her cheeks now, and she quit trying to hide them.

"Why don't you tell us what happened?" said Rachel. "We promise not to judge, and we may be able to see it from an angle you haven't considered."

Abby took a sip of water and wiped her face with a tissue. She would love to tell them about her relationship with Victor, if for no other reason than to get it off her chest. But she knew it would freak them out. Then again, at this point who cared?

"Okay. But don't say I didn't warn you. And you can't breathe a word of this to anyone." She fiddled with the hem of her sweater. "Victor isn't your normal kind of boyfriend. He's very protective and very controlling."

She looked up, but neither said anything, so she continued. "He has all these rules he expects me to follow."

Rachel and Lindsay gave each other a quick glance.

"What kind of rules?" asked Rachel.

Abby gave a nervous laugh. "All different kinds." She went on to tell them some of the more salient ones. She could tell they were shocked and knew her next statement would send them over the edge. "When I don't follow the rules, or obey him, then he punishes me." She bit her lip and looked at them.

Rachel stood up quickly and was looking furious. "Wait. Are you saying he hits you?!"

Abby nodded. "It's not like you think, though. He usually just spanks me or paddles me, and it's kind of fun, and then we have amazing sex after. But if I really screw up, he hits me hard enough for it to hurt for days."

She looked at her friends. They were looking back at her in complete shock. Lindsay was the first to speak. "So this is like S&M stuff? Does he tie you up and shit too?"

Abby grinned. "Oh, yeah. That I don't mind. Sex with him is always mind-blowing."

Rachel sat back down and was shaking her head. "I can't believe you would agree to something like this. Why would you ever consent?"

"Because it's with Victor. And I love him. Plus, I could stop him whenever it got to be too much. He always stopped when I asked."

Lindsay was thinking about it. "Actually, I don't think it sounds that bad. I've seen how sweet and protective he is with you. And with the rules you would always know exactly where you stood with him and what was expected, right?"

Rachel gave Lindsay a disgusted look. "Yes, but he *hits* her!"

"But she just said she can stop him, which shows a huge amount of trust. I think it sounds kind of hot," said Lindsay.

Abby cupped her chin and looked at Lindsay in amazement. Her friend actually got it. The thought made her feel a little better.

"He would never hurt me like you're thinking, Rach. He just needs control."

Rachel gave her a pointed look. "If that's the case, then why did you break up with him?"

Abby sighed and could feel the pain again. "Because I was afraid he would eventually control everything about me, and then there would be nothing left. Plus, I did some research online, and there's some super crazy stuff out there he might try in the future. That scared the crap out of me."

Lindsay was still thinking. "I don't know, Abs. It sounds like there's wiggle room. Can't you negotiate what he can and cannot control? And what crazy stuff he's allowed to do? I mean, to me it seems negotiable. Or isn't he that open?"

Rachel interrupted before Abby could speak. "Why would you want her to go back to that? My god, Linds, she needs to get over him and get on with a normal life."

And there was that normal word again. Abby felt the judgment deep down in her belly.

Rachel now turned her attention to Lindsay and asked, "Speaking of normal, isn't it time you and Kent quit dicking around and decide what to do with your relationship? You've been stuck in this limbo for so long, and your drinking is getting worse and worse. We are worried about you too."

Lindsay purposefully drained what little wine was left in the glass and poured herself another. "I know I'm drinking a lot, Rach, but I'm not dependent on it. I also know I need to figure out what to do about Kent. But it's not that easy. We've been together a long time. And, like Abby, I can't make these quick and decisive choices. We are neither of us as strong as you, so give us the time we need to work it out for ourselves!"

Abby raised her eyebrows in surprise. She looked over at Rachel worriedly, but her friend seemed to be taking it well. Abby tried to lighten the mood, "Just don't go on a bender and do something illegal, Linds. I mean, I'm willing to bail you out of jail and all, but still!"

They both started laughing. Rachel tried to keep a stern face, but then she was laughing too. "What the hell am I going to do with you crazy bitches?" she asked.

Now they were howling with laughter, and Joel came in from outside to see what all the fuss was about. Rachel saw him and gave a reassuring thumbs-up. She made a mental note to talk to him later. Abby clearly wanted to hear from Victor, so she would have Joel pass that message along. She was totally opposed to their relationship, but she also hated seeing her friend suffer.

Abby didn't get out of bed until noon the next morning. They had stayed up late and watched movies and done the girl talk thing. It had been a good time, and she smiled as she trudged out to the kitchen to pour herself a cup of coffee.

She stared at her mug in consternation. It was the one rule of Victor's she had no problem breaking. Since they had split, she had little to no appetite, but she could get fluids down easily. That meant she was living on coffee, juice, and glasses of milk. The text came in while she was stirring cinnamon into her coffee.

How are you?

It was from Victor, and Abby felt a rush of joy.

Miserable. You?

The same. Found a new counselor. She reminds me of Mrs. Turner.

That made Abby grin.

Are you sure Nurse Ratchet is a good choice?

So far so good. Seen her twice. Think she can help. Let me know when you're ready.

Abby felt her heart sink. She couldn't bear to be judged again.

Okay. Not yet.

Miss you, little one.

Miss you too.

She beamed when she put the phone down. It was the first day Abby felt like doing anything besides sleep. She wasn't sure if it was talking to the girls last night or hearing from Victor, but she felt a little better. Who the hell was she kidding? It was hearing from Victor.

Abby hooked Charlie to the leash and took him for a walk. It was a glorious late autumn day. The wind was blowing, the sun was out, and the air had that crisp feel to it she loved so much. She could smell fires burning in some of the neighboring yards, and the scent made her nostalgic for her childhood. On the way back she noticed how much yard work needed to be done at Rachel and Joel's house. They had a lot of leaves in the yard, and they still needed to cut back some shrubs for winter. Abby decided she was going to do some of the work. It would be the perfect way to thank them for letting her stay.

She went inside to change and found her friends in the family room. Lindsay had decided to spend the entire weekend there, and she was regaling them with a story about Kent's dingy underwear. Abby stopped to listen, and she laughed with the rest of them at the vivid description. Then Abby explained she was going to do some yard work and headed to her room to change. The three looked at each other with hopeful grins.

Rachel and Joel ended up helping Abby in the yard, and they worked on it all afternoon. They tackled the landscaping, while she raked leaves. Charlie was running back and forth between her leaf piles and his parents and was barking up a storm. Abby giggled and kept dumping piles over his head. He would wiggle his way out and then lunge at the leaves as if to attack them.

It was cold out, but the sun and exertion were making Abby sweat. She kept taking breaks in the shade to cool down. Her face was flushed, and she felt her head pounding in her skull. Abby blamed it on the wine she drank last night. She had noticed she was also a lot weaker than usual, and she blamed that on the lack of food over the past few weeks. She knew she needed to do better, and she vowed to eat a healthy dinner that night.

There was only a bit of raking left to go, and then they could haul it all to the curb. Abby dug in to finish the last area, but then she felt her hands begin to shake. It got so bad she couldn't hold onto the rake anymore, and she let it drop to the ground. Then she bent down and put her hands on her thighs to steady herself. She was feeling light-headed and nauseous, and her breathing was getting erratic. A brief thought flitted across her brain that Victor would blame it on the coffee, and then everything went dark. Abby crumpled unconscious to the ground, and her lips made a soft sound as her head hit the hard earth.

Rachel and Joel had not noticed. They had their backs to her and were cutting down a stubborn holly bush with some electric trimmers. Charlie's barks finally got their attention, and Rachel was the first to see the still form on the ground. She shoved Joel out of the way as she ran to Abby's side. After checking the pulse, and finding it through the roof, she screamed at Joel to call 911. Then her nurse practitioner skills kicked in, and she worked on her friend and tried to bring her back to consciousness.

Abby was finally conscious when they loaded her into the ambulance. She was nauseous as hell, and it felt like her heart was going to jump right out of her chest, but she didn't want to go to the hospital. Rachel ignored her protests and was at her side barking out orders to the paramedics. That made Abby smile. She tried to reassure her friend, but a paramedic had slipped an oxygen mask over her face, and all she could do was hold Rachel's hand.

Meanwhile, Lindsay and Joel had hopped in a car and were following behind the ambulance. They were taking her to St John's hospital, and Lindsay was driving. Joel pulled out his phone and called Victor.

Chapter Forty-One

It was chaotic at the hospital. The ER was packed, and the staff kicked Rachel out immediately as they started hooking Abby up to machines. She was forced to go sit out in the waiting room with Joel and Lindsay.

Rachel was not one to sit around and do nothing, though, and she quickly put in a call to Dr. Babkin. She was Abby's primary and an internist at St Johns. She also had a good working relationship with Rachel, and as luck would have it was at the hospital that day. Dr. Babkin agreed to come down to the ER right away.

While they were waiting, Victor came flying into the waiting room. He had a look of pure panic on his face. He stopped at the desk but then saw them sitting in a corner and strode over.

"What the hell happened?"

Joel started to explain, but Rachel cut him off. "What are you doing here?"

Joel explained, "I called him."

"Why? They broke up. He's the last person she needs to see right now."

Lindsay cut in. "Come on, Rach. Give the guy a break. And you know how much she is missing him. He has as much right to be here as any of us."

They all started arguing at once. Victor realized he would get nowhere with the group, and he headed back to the front desk. He had no practice rights at this hospital, but he was hoping he could finagle his way in to see Abby.

Just then Dr. Babkin came out. She saw Rachel and walked over to talk to the group. Victor joined them and introduced himself.

"Why does your name sound familiar?" Dr. Babkin asked as she shook his hand.

He explained he worked at the clinic and was Abby's cardiologist. "If you look in her chart, you will see consultation notes from my office."

Rachel cut him off. "He is also Abby's ex-boyfriend, Dr. B, and I don't think she will want to see him."

Everyone started arguing again. Dr. Babkin took it all in before motioning them to follow her down the hall. She had them sit in a room and went to grab the ER resident and Abby's chart. When they were all in, she shut the door.

Dr. Babkin introduced them to the resident, Dr. Jessie. Then she explained.

"Normally we can't talk to non-family members, but Abby has given her consent to speak to all of you," she pointedly included Victor with her eyes.

Dr. Jessie then took over and explained they were still running tests, but everything was coming back normal. Abby's heart rate had been high but was now back down below ninety-nine. She was dehydrated, and they were giving her a liter of fluid. In the resident's opinion, Abby was safe to go home once the final tests came in.

"She's young and otherwise healthy. I think she'll be fine, especially if she's going home with a nurse practitioner to keep an eye on her."

Victor gave the resident a scathing look. "There is no way in hell she is going home! She has a history of this occurring with no known etiology, and she was unconscious for how long? It is not safe to discharge her under such conditions. You need to run more tests and keep her overnight at the very least." He had stopped looking at the resident and was directing his comments to Dr. Babkin.

The resident was furious. "You have no rights here, Dr. Turov, and it would appear we follow a different protocol than the almighty clinic."

Victor glared back at the woman. "It would appear you do. Actually, it's good you are discharging Abby. That way I can admit her to my hospital and get her the care she needs."

Dr. Babkin put a calming hand on the resident and looked thoughtfully at Victor.

Meanwhile, Rachel was yelling he could not just drag Abby to the clinic. Then they were all talking at once again. Their voices were getting louder and louder, and Dr. Babkin was getting fed up.

She finally stood and yelled, "Enough!" as she slammed her hand on the table. When they were quiet, she spoke. "I am going to talk to my patient, and then I will let you know what I decide." She walked out of the room, and Dr. Jessie followed. The four of them were left staring at each other.

Dr. Babkin thumbed through the test results. The tachycardia made no sense, and she tended to agree with Dr. Turov that they needed to dig deeper. She liked Abby and loved reading her books. She also knew what the poor girl had gone through when her husband died. Her gut told her this wasn't serious, but she needed to check with her patient to be sure.

Abby looked tiny in the bed with all the wires and tubes connecting her to the monitor. She was staring at the wall with unfocused eyes, but she smiled when she saw the doctor.

"How are you feeling?" asked Dr. Babkin.

"Embarrassed."

"How so?"

"I just passed out while doing some yard work, and now everyone is treating me like I had a heart attack or something." She was trying for casual, but there was fear in her voice.

Dr. Babkin smiled. "I don't think you're in danger of a heart attack, but we do need to figure out why your heart keeps acting up. Dr. Turov agrees with me on this."

At the sound of his name, Abby blushed, and the doctor noticed her heart rate went up on the monitor.

"He's quite handsome. And Rachel tells me the two of you just broke up?"

Abby nodded.

"And how are you handling that?"

Tears swam in her eyes. "Not good. I feel like I buried another husband, only he's still here. Somehow that makes it worse."

Dr. Babkin nodded. "Break-ups can be tough. Have you been eating?"

"Not well."

"How about liquids? Are you drinking anything?"

Abby nodded. "Milk. And Coffee. Sometimes juice."

Dr. Babkin sighed. "How much coffee?"

Abby hung her head. "A lot. Maybe six cups a day."

"How about sleep? Are you sleeping?"

"Well, I try. I spend a lot of time in bed, but I'm not really sleeping well."

"Hmm. Probably from all that coffee. What about writing?"

"No. I'm not really in the creative mood right now."

Dr. Babkin gave Abby a kind smile. "It sounds like you're depressed." She thumbed through the chart again. "I think your body is just off balance from the lack of food and sleep. I want to admit you overnight, run a few more tests, and keep an eye on your heart. I'm going to order something to help you sleep, and we need to start getting nutrients back in your body."

Abby nodded.

"I'm also going to put in an order for no visitors. I'll make sure they all know you're doing fine, but I think you need a break from people."

Abby gave her a grateful smile. "You know Rachel will give you a hard time."

Dr. Babkin laughed. "I am well aware. I suspect your ex may as well, but you let me deal with them. If you find your depression continues, we can explore the possibility of counseling or meds in the future. But for now, let's start with the basics."

She left Abby and went to the station to order more tests. She signed the admission papers to have her transferred to the telemetry unit, and then she went back to talk to the group. They were still sitting in the conference room and were quietly talking to each other. The anger had left the room, and it was obvious they were all just worried about Abby.

Dr. Babkin didn't beat around the bush. She explained her suspicion Abby was just dehydrated and unbalanced, and she told them about admitting her to the telemetry unit. Victor nodded his approval. Then she explained she had ordered a sedative to help Abby sleep, and she did not want her to have any visitors that night.

As soon as Dr. Babkin left, Rachel started yelling at Victor. "This is all your fault, you know. She wouldn't be in here if it wasn't for you!"

Victor had a pained expression on his face. He was in complete agreement with her, but he didn't say anything.

Joel did, though, and pointed out Victor looked just as bad as Abby did.

Rachel stopped long enough to notice he was right. Victor looked like shit. He had dark circles under his eyes, his face was haggard, and it looked like he had dropped some weight. It was enough to stop her yelling, and the two just stared at each other across the room.

Victor was the first to break the stare. "Call me if you hear anything," he said to Joel, and then he was gone.

Chapter Forty-Two

It was just past seven p.m. when Victor got back to their condo. He tried to eat, but his appetite was shot. Instead, he poured himself a glass of water and paced in the living room. He was so worried about Abby, and not being able to see her was driving him crazy. The entire situation was making him feel damn helpless, and he worked to calm his mind with the techniques the new counselor had taught him.

After thirty minutes of mindless pacing, though, he gave up. The love of his life was lying in a hospital bed, possibly with heart issues, and he was sitting here like an idiot. It was time to take control. Victor went to put on some scrubs and threw a stethoscope around his neck for good measure. He knew most hospitals had too many doctors coming and going, and the nurses could not keep track of all of them. He was hoping that would be the case at St Johns, and he would be able to waltz into Abby's room without anyone stopping him.

His plan worked. Not only did the nursing staff greet him, but they offered up Abby's chart on the computer for his perusal. He sat down and read over all of the test results before heading into her room. Dr. Babkin had noted in the chart he might show up, and she had signed off on it. That made him smile. He wasn't sure if it was because they were both doctors, both Russian, or if Abby had said something to the woman. Regardless, he was grateful.

It was dark inside the room, but there was a muted light on the back wall. His baby was lying fast asleep on the bed, and the sight of her immediately eased the pressure in his chest. He gazed down, and he could tell just from her face she had lost weight. Her complexion was also pale, and his gut hurt as he realized he had done this to her.

Victor looked at the monitor and noted everything was in the normal range. Once he had assured himself the equipment was hooked up properly, he settled down in the chair next to the bed. It was just as small and uncomfortable as the ones at the clinic. He adjusted himself as best he could and then took her hand to hold it. After three weeks of worry and spinning out of control, Victor finally felt at peace. This is where he needed to be, and she was the one he needed to be with. He fell asleep quickly.

At some point, a nurse came in to check on Abby, and she threw a blanket over Victor out of kindness. Neither one had woken up, but shortly after Abby began to stir. She was lying on her side, and she could feel someone holding her hand. There was a lovely warmth seeping into her arm from that grip, and with a start, she realized it must be Victor's hand. Her eyes flew open, and she stared at him.

He was sitting upright in a chair, but his head was lolling to one side as he slept. There was a soft glow of light surrounding his head, and it made him look sweet and vulnerable all at the same time. Abby felt her heart flutter, and once again she was reminded of how much she loved the man. She involuntarily squeezed his hand, and that jolted him awake within seconds. Brown eyes stared at green ones, and they both got lost in the depths of each other's emotions.

Victor was the first to speak. He sat up straight but did not let go of her hand. The blanket fell from his lap as he asked, "How are you feeling?"

"I'm okay," she answered. She had noted the dark smudges under his eyes. "How are you?"

He yawned and stretched. "Better now."

They continued to stare at each other. Finally, Abby motioned at the hospital room and said, "I don't really do that well without you, Victor."

"So I noticed," came the dry reply. Then he added, "I have been downright miserable without you. The only thing that kept me going was the reports Joel sent me." Then he gave her a disapproving look. "You have been drinking a lot of coffee, little one."

The man was bringing up rules now? She rolled her eyes and then stuck her tongue out at him. It made them both laugh, and just like that the tension was broken.

Abby pulled on his hand to get him into bed. "I'm cold."

He kissed her forehead as he crawled in, and then he gently lifted her into his lap. As he held her, she relaxed into his chest and could feel his warmth seeping into her bones. "God, I missed this," she sighed.

Victor pulled the blanket over both of them and held her. "We have to figure out a way to make this work. I am incapable of living without you, and it would appear you need me just as much."

She nodded. "You know I followed all of your rules except the eating and coffee ones. I found I couldn't bring myself to disobey you. Even with the break up you still had control over me."

Victor grinned as he buried his nose in her hair to draw in her scent. "We have a strong connection. That's why I'm sure we can work this out. The counselor I'm seeing is really good. She pointed out to me we don't have to be all-or-nothing with my rules and your life. We just have to compromise so it works for us."

Abby sighed and snuggled in deeper. "I don't know if I can go back to a counselor, Victor. That was so humiliating the first time!"

He gently rocked her body. "I could kill that asshole for making you feel this way. I don't want you ever to be ashamed of our relationship. The new counselor is a Femdom. She's been married over twenty years, and she won't judge us because she's in a similar relationship."

Abby looked up at him in confusion. "What's a Femdom?"

Victor grinned. "That's a woman like me, baby. She demands control over her husband like I do over you."

"Wait, are you saying she spanks her husband?"

"Well, we haven't really discussed what she does in her relationship, but I would imagine so. That's pretty much the basic move of all D/s relationships."

Abby was intrigued. "And they've been doing this for twenty years?"

"Yep. They have a strong relationship, and her goal is to help us have one that is equally strong."

"Oh." Abby had a lot to think about. Part of her worry over the whole BDSM thing was that it couldn't possibly last. Now that she knew others had been in it for the long haul, she saw their relationship in a whole new light. Then she slyly said to Victor, "I knew there were some powerful women out there."

He laughed. "Sure there are. Just not in this room." Victor wanted her to think through things, but he also wanted her to be comfortable. He had her lie down flat on her back. Then he lay on his side at the edge of the bed with his arm across her body. When they were settled in, he asked, "Does this mean you'll consider going to see her?"

Abby gave him a sleepy look. "Yes. I like that she's a woman. I also like the idea of spelling things out. It will make me less nervous, and then you can't pull any of that crazy shit on me." Her voice was trailing off. The sedative in her system was pulling her back down, and Abby soon fell back asleep.

Victor continued to hold her as he thought about what she said. He wasn't sure what she had meant by 'that crazy shit', but he was sure it would come up in counseling. He wasn't going to worry about it. Victor had had a small taste of what life would be like without Abby, and he vowed to never go down that road again. This was his second chance, and he wasn't going to blow it.

When the nurse came in for another check, she found them curled up in the bed together. This was against hospital policy, but the nurse was a romantic at heart, and they looked so peaceful. She ended up leaving them be.

Chapter Forty-Three

Abby was released from the hospital the very next day. Much to Victor's chagrin, she had opted to go home with Rachel and Joel instead of him. She explained she needed to keep some distance before their counseling session. He understood but wasn't happy. To make up for it they resumed their daily phone call. Each night he also drove out to Bay Village to spend time with her.

Victor brought dinner on those nightly visits. Part of that was to make sure Abby ate a healthy meal, but the other part was to appease Rachel.

Rachel had been openly hostile at the hospital, but she had toned it down since then. She hadn't told Joel about Victor being a Dom. She had promised Abby she would keep that information to herself, but the thought was stewing in her brain. She couldn't understand why any woman would put up with such rough treatment, and she vowed to keep a sharp eye on her friend for signs of abuse.

On Friday afternoon Victor picked Abby up and drove them to the counseling session. She wasn't as nervous as she thought she would be, and that was because of Victor. Being around him again was making her serene and happy. She also knew she couldn't live without him, and that was motivating her to try.

The office wasn't nearly as nice as the last one. It was in an old building next to some railroad tracks. The walls were painted a cheerful yellow, but the furniture was old and shabby. The couch creaked when they sat in it, but they were still able to sit side by side and lean into each other.

Abby wasn't sure what she expected from a dominatrix, but the counselor looked like a softer version of Mrs. Turner. She was in her late fifties, and she wore her gray hair up in a tidy bun. Her clothes were fashionable, and her eyes were bright. She greeted Abby warmly and introduced herself as Lily. Abby liked her immediately.

They started by discussing confidentiality. Lily explained her counseling style and assured Abby she was not only open to BDSM but had also been in the lifestyle for several decades. Then she discussed what Victor had been working on in previous sessions. Lily finished by asking Abby where she would like to start.

Abby thought about it. "I guess I'm worried our relationship won't last over the long run. I don't really believe I'm a sub, and at some point, I'm afraid I'll run again because I can't live with Victor's rules."

Lily gave a reassuring smile. "There are thousands of people in a D/s relationship, and each and everyone is different. Instead of trying to put a label on it, why don't you just call it 'my relationship with Victor' and do what works for the both of you. That can be our goal in counseling: to figure out what's going to work."

"I'm still going to need rules and control," said Victor.

"Of course, Dr. Turov, but all relationships require some amount of give and take, even a D/s one. First, we need to know what Abby can't tolerate. Then we can discuss ways for you to adapt so it's no longer an issue. That doesn't mean you give up control. It just means you handle things differently than you do now." She turned to Abby. "What areas of the relationship are you struggling with?"

Abby didn't hesitate. "I don't want Victor interfering in my career."

"Okay, that's a good place to start. In what ways does he interfere?"

Victor explained. "I did not allow her to go on a European book tour alone. As it stands now, she's not permitted to go on a book tour ever again."

"He also doesn't let me work when we're together," added Abby.

Lily was writing things down. Then she looked at Victor. "Would you be willing to allow a book tour in America? One that isn't too long?"

He shook his head. "No. Frankly, I don't want her traveling anywhere by herself. She gets lost too easily and doesn't pay attention to her surroundings."

"I'm not that bad!" countered Abby.

Lily smiled. "What if you arrange her book contracts so she can only travel at certain times of the year? Then you can block off that time from work and go with her."

Victor grunted. "I can do that."

Lily turned to Abby, "Does that work for you?"

"Sure. But book tours are rare, and I doubt I'll get offered another one. I'm much more worried about my writing time."

"Okay. Why don't the two of you negotiate times when writing is permitted and block them off on the calendar?"

Victor scowled. "That's not the problem. Once she starts writing, she has a hard time stopping when I ask her to."

Lily shrugged. "Then you punish her."

Now Victor was grinning. "That I can do!"

Abby rolled her eyes but nodded. She was trying to hide the smile on her face.

"Great," said Lily. "We're making progress. What else is a problem?"

Abby knew what else she wanted, but she hesitated. She tried to move away from Victor a little, but he put his arm around her and pulled her back in.

"Spit it out, little one."

She responded, "I want to be able to drink coffee again."

He was ticked. "Absolutely not! You just got out of the hospital for that very reason."

Abby's eyes flashed. "You don't know that!"

Victor explained her recent stay at St Johns and his belief coffee had contributed.

Lily nodded. "Can you allow her one cup a day and test her? You should be able to determine if the caffeine is to blame, right?"

Abby smiled triumphantly. "That's what I've been saying all along!"

Victor scowled. "It's not that simple. My girlfriend has an addiction to coffee. She won't be able to stop at just one cup."

"Well that's easy enough," murmured Lily. "If she drinks more than one cup, then you punish her. I'm sure you can come up with some creative ways to nip that behavior."

He thought about it. "Oh, yes. I can think of a few things right now." Then he gave Abby a severe look. "But if I find you keep going over your limit, or there's a connection to your heart rate, then we go back to the old rule of no coffee ever. Understood?"

She solemnly nodded.

Lily laughed as she moved them along. "What other rules are bothering you?"

"None," said Abby. "The rest I'm fine with."

Victor sat up straighter in surprise, and he and the counselor looked at each other.

"So you're okay with Victor controlling you?" asked Lily.

"Sure. It makes my life easier. I don't have to worry about things, and I stay organized. Plus, I don't know, it makes me feel safe."

Victor smiled and kissed the top of her head. "It makes me feel the same way."

Lily was beaming now. "You two are doing great. Let's move on to the incident that broke you up in the first place. I think we need to hash that out."

Abby's heart sank. She didn't want to talk about Yuri, and she could feel her body tensing just thinking about it.

Lily went on, "Dr. Turov has already told me what occurred. What I need to know is how you are feeling about it right now?"

Abby stared at her lap. "I didn't like it, but I'm over it."

Lilly frowned. "You say that, but your body language is telling me something different. You're all tensed up, your hands are in fists, and you're not looking at anyone."

Abby unclenched her hands and tried to relax.

Lily continued. "I think you're angry, and, based on what occurred, you have every right to be. Try telling Victor how his behavior made you feel."

"I don't want to," whispered Abby.

Lily smiled gently. "Expressing your feelings is going to be an important part of your relationship, and something I'm going to have you work on. For now, just say one thing to Victor about the Yuri incident, no matter how small."

Abby bit her lip and then looked at her boyfriend. "That was humiliating. Don't ever do it again," she whispered.

He reached for her hand. "I promise I won't."

Lily nodded. "That's a good start. Let's put that on the 'no' list. Every D/s relationship should have a list of what each of you is unwilling or unable to do. Involving other people in intimate acts can start the list. Now then, what else should we add? Perhaps we should look at punishments to see if there is anything Abby doesn't consent to."

Victor frowned. "I'm not sure that's necessary. I don't plan to take it very far with her, and I like the element of surprise."

Lily chuckled. "Who doesn't? But you know there are a myriad of ways you can still surprise her."

He reluctantly agreed.

"Communication is critical in any relationship, Dr. Turov, but especially one that involves punishment. You need to be more forthcoming with Abby about what you plan to do to her beforehand. Since she is new to the lifestyle, this will go a long way to ease her fears."

Victor nodded.

"Good. What punishment tools are you using now or plan to use in the future?"

Victor ran down the list, and Abby listened in amazement.

When he finished, Lily looked surprised. "No whip?" she asked.

He shook his head. "I've never been able to control one well enough."

The counselor nodded. "They can be tricky."

Abby rolled her eyes at the both of them.

Then Lily turned to Abby and asked, "Is there anything Victor just mentioned you want to put on the 'no' list?"

"I don't think so. I don't even know what half of that was."

Now Victor was grinning like the Cheshire cat.

Abby continued, "I just don't want him to try any of that crazy stuff on me."

"Such as?"

Abby squirmed uncomfortably. "Well, I don't really know what you call it all. But the piercings, the ball in the mouth thingy, the wrapped boobs—oh, god, and that shrink wrap shit."

"Somebody has been doing research on the internet," explained Victor.

Lily nodded. "What you keep forgetting, Abby, is you are actually the one in control. You can say no to anything he proposes." She turned to Victor, "Do you have a safe word?"

"Not really. All she has to do is say 'stop' and I will."

When the counselor looked surprised, Victor shrugged. "We don't really role-play. We don't need it."

Lily turned to Abby, "Are you comfortable saying stop?"

She nodded.

"Good. And do you trust he will stop if you ask him to?"

Now it was Abby's turn to look surprised. "Of course he would!"

Both Lily and Victor smiled in relief, and the counselor said, "I really don't think the two of you will have any problems." She went to write down more notes, and Abby grinned at Victor.

He looked back at her thoughtfully. "I think we need to add a new rule, little one. No more researching BDSM on the internet. You think too much, and your imagination is always so much worse than the reality. Take for instance—what did you call it?—the 'ball in the mouth thingy'. That's just a gag. I've gagged you before, and you didn't mind. The ball gag is a lot more comfortable than what I've already used on you."

Abby gave a shudder. "But it looks so ugly!"

Lily finished writing and looked up. "Is there anything else we should put on the 'no' list? I can add the ball gag."

They looked at Abby, and she sighed. "I guess we can leave it off if you really want to try it."

Victor grinned. "Seems I found a new punishment."

Abby glared at him.

Then Victor turned to Lily. "Put the piercings, breast bondage, and latex on there." He turned to his girlfriend. "That's the shrink wrap shit." Then he continued, "I'm a doctor, so I'm not into any dangerous stuff. No edging, knives, or breath work. I also don't like cages, medical instruments, or fisting. And it goes without saying, but let's put it on there, that there will be no animals, children, or human waste ever involved."

Abby was getting pale. "I have no idea what most of that is."

Victor gave her a serious look. "Good. We're going to keep it that way."

Lily was writing furiously. "There's still plenty of fun stuff you can try. Are you okay with suspension, plugs, a Sybian, or a chastity belt?"

Abby interrupted. "There's a chastity belt for real?" She was intrigued.

Victor ignored her. "I wouldn't mind suspension, but I don't really have the equipment for that. As for the others—I don't know, maybe? Mostly I like to just wing it. Sometimes I punish Abby by depriving her of things. It all depends on what she's done."

Lily nodded. She had pulled up a photo of a chastity belt on her iPad and handed it to Abby.

Victor pushed the iPad away and scowled at both women. "Did I not just forbid any research on the internet?"

Lily chuckled and patted Abby's hand. "I suspect, my dear, you may be seeing one of those in your future."

Abby faked despair, but the thought had her excited.

It was time to wrap it up, so Lily gave them both individual homework assignments. Victor was to continue working on his coping mechanisms, and Abby was to work on expressing emotions. The counselor suggested she write them out since that was a medium Abby was comfortable with. They scheduled another session, but Lily explained they probably wouldn't have to come back much after that.

"I think you two will settle down nicely now that we've spelled things out. You may have to come back and renegotiate in the future, but I don't see any serious relationship issues here."

Victor and Abby looked at each other in relief.

As they were gathering their things to leave, Lily continued. "Most D/s relationships end because the Dom can't do it anymore. It takes a lot of energy and responsibility to keep the control going over the long run. But you two have a connection that extends beyond the physical. I think you could easily have a traditional relationship if you wanted." She laughed. "I don't really see that happening, though. Dr. Turov has an innate need for control, and that's not likely to change."

"Lucky me," muttered Abby, and then all three of them laughed.

Lily walked them to the door but cautioned them. "A D/s relationship naturally gets more benign the longer it goes. You will have less sex and do less scenes the longer you are together and the older you get. That's normal. But the beauty of D/s is the bond it forms along the way. You will be more honest and intimate with each other, and that's a gift, so let it happen and cherish it." She gave them each a hug before they left the office.

They walked to the truck in silence. Once they were both in, Victor leaned over and pressed his forehead against Abby's. Then he pulled away to look at her.

"Are you coming home now?" There was pain in his voice, and he looked so vulnerable that Abby's heart contracted.

"Of course I am!"

Epilogue
One year later

Abby was in her office in the back corner of the condo. They had converted the space six months ago upon Lily's suggestion. Victor liked his living environment neat and tidy, but Abby needed more of what she called "creative chaos" when working. It had caused quite a few punishments in the past. Now she had her own private space and was allowed to leave items laying out in the room. Victor's only stipulation was she kept everything in neat piles. He also insisted she keep the door open at all times. That way he could easily glance in and see if she was obeying him.

Right now she wasn't. She had the music cranking and was joyfully working on a scrapbooking project. There were bits of paper, tape, and photos strewn everywhere, and Abby knew her man would not be happy. He wasn't due home for another hour, though, which gave her plenty of time to finish and clean up.

The scrapbook was of her life with Victor, and it was full of photos and memorabilia. The current page layout was of an Outer Banks trip they had taken over the summer. They had rented a house on the ocean and gone down with the same friends who had accompanied them to Hocking Hills.

Even Yuri had gone. At some point, Abby had gotten over the whole voyeur incident and had forgiven both men. She had encouraged Victor to do the same, and now the two Russians were talking again. Victor still went into protection mode anytime the psychiatrist was around, and Abby was never allowed to be alone with Yuri, but the arrangement was working for everyone.

As for the rest of their friends, they had long since figured out what type of relationship Victor and Abby were in, but no one ever said anything. Rachel still struggled with the whole punishment concept, and she frequently looked Abby over for bruises. When Rachel saw one, she always asked if her friend was okay or needed a place to stay. Abby would laugh when that occurred and wave the worry away. Abby trusted Victor completely, and she had gotten quite used to their D/s lifestyle.

The more comfortable she had become, the more creative Victor had gotten with his punishments. Now she found herself looking forward to them in spite of the pain endured. His control still annoyed her on occasion, and when that happened they always talked it out. The only time Abby ever truly balked was when Victor punished her in public. She found it so humiliating, and she knew she would never accept what they had as being normal. But she had long since realized "normal" was overrated.

Abby continued to tape photos into the scrapbook. She picked up one of Victor with his arms around her at the beach, and somehow it reminded her of Nate. She smiled wistfully as she thought about her late husband. He had been the love of her life and had given her six wonderful years of marriage. She knew she would always love Nate, and she missed him terribly, but she also knew Victor was her future.

While Nate had been her first true love, Abby realized Victor was her soulmate. They had a connection that extended beyond anything she had experienced before, and she cherished it. If anything ever happened to her Dom, she didn't know what she would do. But life had taught her not to worry about the future, and so Abby chose to focus on the present instead.

At the moment her "present" was leaning against the doorway watching her. Victor had come home early to surprise her, and, based on the mess in the room, had been successful. He noted the intense look of concentration on Abby's face as she worked and shook his head. She was oblivious to everything else around her.

Victor reached down and turned off the music. Abby looked up with a start and then smiled when she saw him standing there. "Oh! You're home. I didn't hear your text." Then she looked down at the mess, realized how bad it was, and promptly hung her head in chagrin. She was staring down at the floor, and he had to stop himself from laughing.

"Look at me, little one." When she did, Victor gestured with his arm at the mess in the room. He forced his face into a severe expression, even though his eyes were twinkling.

She was too distraught to notice his eyes. "I'm sorry, Victor. I usually keep it much neater than this. I was going to clean it up before you got home, but somehow I lost track of time."

He didn't bother to tell her he was home early. Instead, he said, "I don't want to hear your excuses, Abby. I made this rule to keep you organized, but it doesn't seem to be working, now does it?"

She sighed. "I guess not."

Victor shook his head. "What am I going to do with you?"

She peeked up at him with a shy smile, but his look was still severe, so she hung her head back down and waited. She was already anticipating what was to come.

He stifled a chuckle and forced his voice to sound stern. "Perhaps a reminder is in order. Come with me."

Victor took her hand and led her out of the room. He guided her down the hallway to the couch. It was the location of most of her punishments, and she felt quite at home on the soft leather.

"Stay put!"

Abby watched as he headed toward the bedroom. When he returned, he was carrying some ribbon and a blindfold. He set them down and then ordered her to put her hands out with the wrists together and the palms facing up. Once she complied, he quickly bound her wrists with the ribbon.

"Keep your hands up with your elbows at your side." She nodded, and then he slipped a blindfold over her eyes.

Abby always got a little scared when Victor used a blindfold. She hated not being able to see what was coming, and she had once admitted this to him. He had laughed at the time and shook his head. Then he pointed out that when he didn't use a blindfold, she almost always shut her eyes, and therefore he was certain she could manage her fear.

Now Abby was straining to hear what Victor was doing, and she speculated on what was to come. Maybe he would strike her on the palms with something. Or maybe he was going to have her hold a punishment tool until he was ready to use it on her body. The thought had her squirming in her seat, and her mind kept running with all the fearful possibilities.

Victor was watching her from the kitchen and noting her facial expressions. He rolled his eyes in exasperation, as the woman's mind was her own worst enemy. He slowly walked over until he stood in front of her.

"Be still!" he ordered.

Abby tried, she really did, but she was skittish by nature. When she felt him place something on her palms, she lurched on the couch and almost toppled over. Victor had to grip her shoulders and prop her upright all the while trying not to laugh.

Abby felt the object. It was small and square, and both hands curled around it in wonder. She had no idea what it was.

Victor took a deep breath. "I love you, baby, and I want to protect you. I also want to keep you on track and organized, which is why I think you need more discipline in your life. I'm hoping this item will help."

He gently pulled off the blindfold and smiled down at her. She blinked a few times and then looked down at her hands. She was holding a ring box. Abby looked stunned for a second. Then she smiled up at him.

"Is that what I think it is?"

He grinned as he noted her smile. "Yes, little one. I think it's time we make this official. I can't imagine my life without you, and I want to take care of you for the rest of our lives. Will you have me?" His voice was full of emotion.

Abby didn't hesitate. "Of course I will!" She was crying tears of joy as he pulled her up and into his arms.

Victor slipped the ring on her finger and looked down with pride. Her wrists were still bound with the ribbon, and seeing his mark of possession on her hand sent his libido into overdrive. He gave her a sexy grin before picking her up and throwing her over his shoulder. Then he slapped her ass hard before hauling her off to the bedroom.

Abby squealed in delight and let him. He was, after all, her Dom, and now it looked like he would be for life. She couldn't have been happier.

The End

About the author

Gibby is no stranger to the perils of romance. Single until the age of 37, she dated many an interesting (dare we say crazy) guy until meeting the love of her life, Jim. The two are now married and live in the Cleveland, Ohio area. They are joined by their very spoiled dog, Scoob. Gibby believes there is no true norm when it comes to relationships, and they all take hard work and dedication. When she isn't writing, she can usually be found hiking in the park or attending the theatre. Check out her blog at www.gibbycampbell.com.

More Black Velvet Seductions titles

Their Lady Gloriana by Starla Kaye
Cowboys in Charge by Starla Kaye
Her Cowboy's Way by Starla Kaye
Punished by Richard Savage, Nadia Nautalia & Starla Kaye
Accidental Affair by Leslie McKelvey
Right Place, Right Time by Leslie McKelvey
Her Sister's Keeper by Leslie McKelvey
Playing for Keeps by Glenda Horsfall
Playing By His Rules by Glenda Horsfall
The Stir of Echo by Susan Gabriel
Rally Fever by Crea Jones
Behind The Clouds by Jan Selbourne
Trusting Love Again by Starla Kaye
Runaway Heart by Leslie McKelvey
The Otherling by Heather M. Walker
First Submission - Anthology
These Eyes So Green by Deborah Kelsey
Dark Awakening by Karlene Cameron
The Reclaiming of Charlotte Moss by Heather M. Walker
Ryann's Revenge by Rai Karr & Breanna Hayse
The Postman's Daughter by Sally Anne Palmer
Final Kill by Leslie McKelvey
Killer Secrets by Zia Westfield
Crossover, Texas by Freia Hooper-Bradford
The King's Blade by L.J. Dare
Uniform Desire - Anthology
Safe by Keren Hughes
Finishing the Game by M.K. Smith
Out of the Shadows by Gabriella Hewitt
A Woman's Secret by C.L. Koch

Her Lover's Face by Patricia Elliott
Love Times Infinity by K.L. Ramsey
Naval Maneuvers by Dee S. Knight
Love's Patient Journey by K.L. Ramsey
Perilous Love by Jan Selbourne
Patrick by Callie Carmen
Love's Design by K.L. Ramsey
The Brute and I by Suzanne Smith
Love's Promise by K.L. Ramsey
Home by Keren Hughes
Worth the Wait by K.L. Ramsey
Only A Good Man Will Do by Dee S. Knight
Secret Santa by Keren Hughes
The Christmas Wedding by K.L. Ramsey
Killer Lies by Zia Westfield
A Merman's Choice by Alice Renaud
Theirs to Keep by K.L. Ramsey
Line of Fire by K.L. Ramsey
Theirs to Love by K.L. Ramsey
All She Ever Needed by Lora Logan
Nicolas by Callie Carmen
Torn Devotion by K.L. Ramsey
The Story of JESS & AVER by K.A. Neeson
Theirs to Have by K.L. Ramsey
Fighting for Justice by K.L. Ramsey

Our back catalog is being released on Kindle Unlimited
You can find us on:
Twitter: BVSBooks
Facebook: Black Velvet Seductions
See our bookshelf on Amazon now! Search "BVS Black Velvet
Seductions Publishing Company"

Black Velvet Seductions